T0353084

THE WAR NURSES

ALSO BY ANTHEA HODGSON

The Drifter
The Cowgirl

THE WAR NURSES

ANTHEA HODGSON

MICHAEL JOSEPH
an imprint of
PENGUIN BOOKS

MICHAEL JOSEPH

UK | USA | Canada | Ireland | Australia
India | New Zealand | South Africa | China

Michael Joseph is part of the Penguin Random House group of companies
whose addresses can be found at global.penguinrandomhouse.com

Penguin
Random House
Australia

First published by Michael Joseph in 2023

Copyright © Anthea Hodgson 2023

The moral right of the author has been asserted.

All rights reserved. No part of this publication may be reproduced, published, performed in
public or communicated to the public in any form or by any means without prior written
permission from Penguin Random House Australia Pty Ltd or its authorised licensees.

Cover images: nurse © Mark Owen/Trevillion Images; planes © MasPix/Alamy Stock Photo;
textured linen background © Oleg Golovnev/Shutterstock.com; smoke © Everett Collection/
Shutterstock.com; plant shadows © StonePictures/Shutterstock.com
Photograph of Minnie Hodgson (p. 392) from Australian War Memorial (ref P02783.009)
Cover design by Laura Thomas
Typeset in 11/18 pt Sabon by Midland Typesetters, Australia

Printed and bound in Australia by Griffin Press

A catalogue record for this
book is available from the
National Library of Australia

ISBN 978 0 14377 910 0

penguin.com.au

MIX
Paper | Supporting
responsible forestry
FSC® C018684

We at Penguin Random House Australia acknowledge that Aboriginal and Torres
Strait Islander peoples are the Traditional Custodians and the first storytellers of the lands
on which we live and work. We honour Aboriginal and Torres Strait Islander peoples'
continuous connection to Country, waters, skies and communities. We celebrate
Aboriginal and Torres Strait Islander stories, traditions and living cultures;
and we pay our respects to Elders past and present.

For Minnie Hodgson,
For all the nurses of the Vyner Brooke,
And especially for the girls on the beach

PROLOGUE

17 October 1945

Maisie Shipley put down her copy of *The Daily News* and gazed out her kitchen window, momentarily taken an ocean away, to the jungles of Sumatra, and to a beach on a small tropical island. Outside the house yard the wheat crop was drying in the warm spring winds, while all around the house, the garden had burst into life, filling the air with perfume and the buzzing of bees. The irises had arranged themselves beside the rambling sweet peas, already passing full bloom and tumbling back down the trellis; the Geraldton wax by the water tank was festooned in tiny pink flowers; and the sweet-scented jasmine clung to the verandah in heavy garlands.

HOLLYWOOD WANTS FLOWERS TO
WELCOME POW NURSES.
Hollywood Repatriation Hospital is appealing to the public for wildflowers and garden flowers for a very special occasion . . .

Maisie went to the laundry and gathered up some buckets and old jam tins. She filled them with water and started cutting the Geraldton wax first, its small pink and white flowers sitting up proudly. She carefully snipped the jasmine, then took the irises off at the base.

She settled them all in the buckets and tins, then headed back for the sweet peas and daisies, cutting and arranging until her garden was bare and the back of her ute was full.

So, they needed flowers, did they? Maisie Shipley had *plenty*.

Early that morning, she'd placed the newspaper in front of her husband Bill as he tried to fish a wild oat seed out of his work sock.

'Hollywood Hospital is in Perth,' he said.

'Yes, Bill.'

'I've got the shearers here tomorrow. I can't drive you down, you know.'

'I know *that*,' Maisie sniffed. 'I'll drive myself.'

'But you've never driven in the *city* before, dear.'

'No. That's true, I haven't.'

'You can't wait a while? See if I can take you next week?' He found the seed and dropped it into his empty teacup.

'The nurses are arriving tomorrow. I shan't let them down, Bill. I shall make sure they know we care. The Hodgson girl was matron at Kondinin, you know.'

Bill nodded. 'I knew her father. We were in the rifle club together.'

'Well, then. It's decided. I shall take the ute and be back late tonight. I'll be here in time to feed the shearers tomorrow.'

Bill glanced at her as he reached for another piece of toast. 'You'll be all right, dear?'

'Of *course* I'll be all right. Those nurses survived a *war*, Bill – starvation, disease and beatings and God knows what else. I can drive myself to *Perth* and back. Don't you worry about that.'

Once Bill had left for work and the breakfast things were packed away, Maisie checked her hair was neat and tidy and that she had a spare handkerchief. She'd taken out her floral spring dress for the occasion. She'd made adjustments to its waistline over the years to accommodate her change of life, but her lipstick hadn't changed. It was still a bright orange–red shade, even though her hair was now almost entirely steely grey. She took a smart navy cardigan in case the temperature dropped after sunset, and made sure her comb was in her handbag for her arrival at the hospital.

She paused for a moment, assessing herself in the mirror, trying to see if she was the sort of woman who drove to Perth on her own. She decided she was. She listened to the familiar sound of Bill whistling in the sheepyards, then climbed into the ute and began the long drive to the city.

CHAPTER 1

MARGOT
Sydney
1 February 1941

'Bloody boats, hate 'em,' a voice behind Margot McNee grumbled. 'Give me a long road droving cattle any day. Or a month on horseback. Anything's better than this.'

Margot dropped her suitcase onto a bunk and glanced around the cabin of the *Queen Mary*. The woman who'd just spoken was tall with broad shoulders and bronzed skin. Her uniform was haphazardly ironed. She followed Margot into the cabin and inspected a neatly made bunk. Her face was frank, her hair cut into a forgotten bob, her nose long, her mouth short. Her masculine features softened into a grin as she held out her hand.

'Beth Scanlon, Sandy Creek Station, Queensland,' she said.

'Margot McNee, Leederville, Western Australia. And I quite like boats, so far.'

'If it gets choppy you'll soon change your mind.'

'I'm not even sure if I *get* seasick,' Margot said.

'Maybe not, but *I* do, and *I'll* be tossing up all over our cabin. I bet you won't like *that*.' Beth's accent was flat and slow, like the long plains outside Townsville.

5

Margot shook her head. 'That *does* sound pretty grim.'

From her bag, Beth retrieved a photo of a horse surrounded by shining black cattle and a blue heeler leaping across an open gate. She placed it next to her bed. 'So, we're roommates, then.'

'Yes, and I hear they're moving a camp bed in, so there'll be more of us soon.'

'No problem for me. I'm used to bunking down.'

'I'm sure we'll all be used to it by the end of the war.'

'Knock knock!' A tiny woman with blonde hair popped her head through the doorway. 'Are you Beth and Margot?' Her eyes were bright blue and she wore a confident kiss of pink lipstick which gave her the very pleasant appearance of an actress playing a nurse about to embark on a voyage.

'Yes.' Margot shook her hand. 'Margot McNee.'

'Lola Llewellyn. From right here in Sydney. I just waved goodbye to my father as I came on board. I'm going to miss him so much.'

'What about your mother?' Margot asked.

'She couldn't make it.' Lola swung her bag into the corner, and Beth held out her hand.

'Beth Scanlon, from Queensland.'

'Well,' Lola said, 'now that we've covered all that, perhaps I should go and track down my camp bed?'

'I think we should share the camp bed,' Beth said. 'I mean, it doesn't seem fair you should have to make do for the whole trip – it'll probably take weeks.'

'I agree. Let's do three nights each,' Margot added.

'Oh, don't worry, I'm the smallest and I'll be fine.' Lola dropped her suitcase on the floor. 'As long as I'm in good company, with a chat and a song, I'm as happy as a clam.' She pushed open a small door beside her. 'Oh, look. We've got a bathroom.'

'Let's go find the purser anyway,' Margot said. 'I think he's on the first level sorting out the sleeping arrangements.' She held the door for Lola, who sailed through with a flair Margot had never been able to muster.

'Thank you, I'd appreciate your help,' she admitted.

Beth paused before joining them. 'You're not *really* going to sing, are you?'

The *Queen Mary* had been a cruise ship before her nautical glamour had been dulled by a thick coat of grey camouflage paint. Renamed *HTQX*, her luxurious cabins had been stripped of excess furnishings and artworks and filled to the brim with standee bunks for the troops. Her walls were still rich with rare timbers, her carpets still plush, but she was no longer an ocean liner: she was a troop carrier going to war.

She had been joined in Sydney Harbour by several other ships as they patiently awaited deployment in service to the Allies. The decks had filled as troops had been ferried aboard for days, bands had played cheerful tunes and families had gathered to farewell loved ones, piling thick layers of luck around them ahead of their journey.

'Where do you think we're going?' Lola asked as they stood on the crowded deck, watching the activity below. 'My family were trying to guess, but apparently it's top secret.'

'Oh, yes, it's top secret all right,' Beth said, 'except that they've forgotten to hide the labels on the supplies.'

'What? Where?'

Beth pointed. 'Over there on the dock, behind the group of men with the trolleys . . .'

Lola squinted. 'Elbow Force – Singapore,' she read. 'Singapore! Oh, Singapore! I was wondering about Ceylon – it's such a romantic name – but Singapore. What luck!' She nudged Margot. 'I've often thought I could fall in love in Singapore.'

'I like the sound of the place,' Margot said, 'but there are all sorts of rumours. They could be trying to confuse the enemy, you know – our real destination is still a secret.'

'Well, I'm willing to go wherever they send us, but I must say, I hope it's close to Australia,' Beth declared. 'Either way, we'll do some good for our boys while we're gone, eh? And it'll make coming home all the sweeter.'

'I'll miss home,' Margot said. 'I thought I'd never leave Australia. And yet here I am.'

A small nurse with a short dark bob and blue eyes approached and leaned on the balustrade. 'Meet Agatha,' she said.

'Hello, Agatha,' Margot replied.

'Not *me* – I'm Minnie,' the nurse said and grinned. She held up a small pot plant. 'This is Agatha Aspidistra. Cast iron plant. She's planted in Australian soil. Whenever I feel a bit seasick, I'll just take a great whiff of Agatha's pot and I'll instantly feel better.'

Margot liked the nurse's open face straightaway. 'Has Agatha been taking a stroll about the deck?' she asked.

'Yes, but only because we've got an internal cabin and she's desperate for some sunlight. Do you girls have space for one more? She doesn't talk much. I do, of course, but that's because when there's not a lot going on at home, you have to keep yourself entertained.'

Margot and Beth considered her. A happy chatterbox might be a good fit.

'Let me see. I think we could wedge Agatha on our shelf if we put a couple of books next to her, and drag another camp bed into our room for you,' Margot told her.

'Oh, thanks so much. We're both very grateful.' Minnie grinned. 'I'm not much of a gardener as a rule. I could probably kill a pinecone. But I gave Agatha an undertaking she'd be all right.'

'We're happy to have you both,' Beth said. 'I like a chat.'

Margot inspected the plant's thick leaves. 'She looks all right so far. Don't worry, Agatha, you'll be living it up on a Singaporean verandah before you know it.'

'How does she feel about cigarette butts?' Beth said.

'Not good, Beth. You're not a smoker, are you?'

'Only when I drink,' Beth assured her.

'Are you an adventurous type too?' Minnie asked Margot. 'You look rather sensible. But I've seen all sorts. Sometimes you meet a girl who's just waiting for the chance to put down her knitting, and away she goes.'

Margot laughed. 'No, I'm one of those timid brown-haired types. I can't knit, but I probably should. I'm a bit of a wallflower, actually.'

'Well, I'm not one of those,' Minnie said. 'I'm from the wheatbelt in Western Australia. We all muck in to get things done. No time to be shy.' Minnie took Margot's hand and gripped it firmly. Her eyes were pale blue like a summer sky. 'Pleased to meet you, Margot,' she said, 'have you been away from home before?'

'Yes, for nursing. But I've never left the country.'

Minnie's face was almost boyish as she smiled back at the distant shore across the water. 'This will be quite an adventure for us all.'

'I think we'll be busy with onboard training,' Lola said. 'I've heard the other girls talking about orientation to familiarise us with the ship, and lectures on the sorts of wounds we can expect to see overseas.'

'Well,' declared Beth, 'no time like the present. Let's get your things moved into our cabin, Minnie.'

A few days later, Margot was woken by the sound of shouting. She peered through the gap left by the peeling paint on their porthole to see a flotilla of boats circling the ship.

'What on earth?'

'Bloody cheek,' grumbled Beth. 'Sounds like the Japs have already found us . . .'

Lola joined Margot at the porthole. 'We're surrounded by boats,' she said. 'Everyone's come to see us off.' She grabbed her notebook and began to scribble. 'Come on, girls. Get into uniform as quick as you can. I want to toss a message in a bottle into the harbour. Perhaps it'll wash up at Maroubra!'

Her enthusiasm was contagious and within minutes the nurses along with hundreds of soldiers were on deck. The harbour was filled with boats and people holding placards with messages, waving handkerchiefs to catch their loved ones' eyes before they sailed away.

The Governor-General, Lord Gowrie, dressed in all his finery, was delivering a farewell speech to the assembled crowds. The girls chattered on the deck of the ship, unable to hear him clearly, before a brass band struck up 'Auld Lang Syne'. Lola's voice rang out clearly among the deep voices of the men.

At the end of the song, Margot noticed Lola's bright blue eyes were shining, and felt her own tears spring sharply. Someone offered her a handkerchief, and when she looked around, Minnie gave her a wink. They stood for a long while, watching the brass band and the teary crowds on the dock. Were they really going to Singapore? What would it hold for them? Who among them would make it home? And how could she, Margot McNee, with her timid heart, ever really help anyone at all?

The band then launched into 'Now Is the Hour', a traditional New Zealand farewell song. Margot searched for her family on the dock even though she knew they weren't there. Perth was too far away.

The first time Margot had heard 'Now Is the Hour' she'd been in the cool room of her father's butcher's shop with Ben, a young farmer from New Zealand. She was sixteen at the time and Ben had stayed in the McNees' back room for a month while looking for a shearing team heading to the Nullarbor. He had dark sandy hair and eyes so brown they were almost black. Margot's father had given Ben work butchering sheep, and he'd taken to it easily, working methodically with the cool carcasses, stripping meat from bones with his strong hands. But eventually, word came that there was a team, that he could meet them in Esperance. He was leaving.

Margot didn't know how to say goodbye. He was nothing to her, really, and she was nothing to him. She was just a shy girl who helped behind the counter, who was quick with change and who knew how the old ladies liked their bacon. Ben was older, maybe twenty, and wanted adventure. When Margot, blushing furiously, had stood beside him, marvelling at his height, blurting 'Goodbye! Good luck!' he had taken her hand and said, 'There's a song, you know, in New Zealand – it's about goodbyes. Would you like me to sing it for you?'

She'd been so embarrassed, so moved, so *overwhelmed* as he'd leaned on the bench and sung the words to her, she thought she'd die. But of course she hadn't, and he left the next day.

And then her father hired Neville. And that was that.

The flotilla of boats filled with smiling families waving at the servicemen and women lifted Margot's spirits. Sydney Harbour was alive with voices and music as the great ships pulled out from Bradleys Head, past the Hornby Lighthouse, rolling gently into the embrace of the deep dark ocean, heading south.

'Better give them all an extra wave,' said a soldier standing beside her. He had a cigarette perched in the corner of his mouth.

'Why?' Margot asked. 'Do you have someone in the crowd?'

'Nah, but the rumour is Hitler is offering medals and a \$250 000 bounty for any submarine crew who can blow us out of the water. He hates the *Queen Mary* because she's too good at her job.'

'But don't we have protection? I hear there are gunners sleeping up on the verandah grill deck. And I was assured they had plenty of very large guns on the sun deck – including some rocket launchers.'

'Guns aren't much use against submarines.' He gave his cigarette a burial at sea. 'Still. She's the fastest liner in the world – she goes up to twenty-nine knots – and that might help against the planes when we get a bit closer to the fighting.'

'Oh, marvellous,' Margot said faintly. She waved at the crowd again, helpless, trying to catch someone's eye. Wondering if they could see the fear, stuck like a splinter in her heart.

'I wonder what we'll find in Singapore,' Margot mused as she brushed her hair the next morning.

'Gunshot wounds, I expect, and severed limbs.' Beth stretched out in her bunk and slowly sat up.

'I suppose I was wondering more about the city, where we'll live, who we'll meet—'

'Handsome soldiers, I hope,' Lola piped up.

'Oh, calm down,' Beth said. 'We're only here because we're too old or too ugly for the soldiers to fall in love with. It keeps things simple.'

'We are not!'

'Of course we are. A bunch of career nurses. Plain Janes. Even the youngest of us are pushing thirty. We were recruited because no one will be *distracted* by us.'

'Well, I never. I just thought we were the best nurses for the job,' Lola said.

'We are,' said Margot.

'Anyway, it doesn't worry me why they let me go to war,' Beth said. 'I'm only here for one thing.'

'To save lives?'

'To shoot a Jap.'

'I beg your pardon?'

'You heard me.'

'Beth, I don't think they'll give us service revolvers.'

'Someone will. Plenty of them about.' Beth sniffed. 'I'm going to find a man who'll give me a gun, and I'm going to shoot any of those bastards who come near me.'

'I don't think that's allowed.'

'Of *course* it is, it's *war*, Lola. That's the whole point. I won't be told to sit by my patient's bedside waiting to be attacked. I'm here for revenge.'

'You've lost someone,' Margot said.

'I have.'

'Was he a family member?'

'He was a friend.' Beth sniffed again dismissively, ending further speculation.

'Come on,' Minnie said. 'We've got a lecture on eye infections in the ballroom in twenty minutes – you won't want to miss it.'

*

Later that night as they lay in their beds, Margot could feel the light swell of the ocean beneath them and the hum of the massive engines pushing them further from home. During a 'welcome aboard' briefing, one of the officers had assured the nurses that the *Queen Mary* was twice as big as the *Titanic*. He had meant to be comforting. He'd failed. In the darkness, Margot drifted, homesick; the scent of the sea so different from the roses which grew outside her bedroom window in Tate Street, the churning ocean so cold and vast, pouring into the gap she'd left behind. She imagined her father turning off the wireless and heading outside for a final cigarette before bed; her mother whispering her prayers and tying a snood around her greying hair so that it would be tidy when she woke. Perhaps they would kiss each other goodnight and mention her before they fell asleep. Perhaps they would send another quick prayer to God, just in case.

When Margot finally slept, she dreamed of Neville, feeling her guilt, packed tightly into her suitcase, like stained clothes or a forgotten sandwich.

'Margie, when will you marry me?'

'I am *fond* of you, Neville, I'm very fond of you—'

'There. You see? We're *fond* of *each other*. Your father says we should—'

'I'm not ready to marry anyone just yet . . .'

'We could have children – they could help me in the shop. I'd be a good husband, you'll see. I can take on the business when your father retires. He can't keep going forever, you know . . .'

'I know that, Neville—'

'You should be happy I'm taking you off the shelf.'

She woke with a start. She could hear the steady breath of her roommates, and feel the floor swell beneath her. She was right to leave home. It wouldn't do, to stay in the house behind the butcher's shop while Neville fashioned ground pork and beef into trays of rissoles, watching to see if she'd arrived home from work at King Edward Memorial Hospital. Her fear of being trapped in marriage had outstripped her fear of leaving, and one brave morning she'd caught the tram into town with another nurse to sign up.

Neville, with his thick fingers, his pale blond hair and his prized strings of pork sausages, was behind her now. Margot McNee's future lay beyond the sea.

There was a shout in the corridor and some laughter, followed by the stamping of feet on the stairs.

'Let's go up on deck,' Margot suggested. 'See if the sailors can give us any advice about life on the waves.'

'Don't tell me you're looking for a shipboard romance, Margot?' Minnie asked.

'Don't be silly. I'm twenty-seven. I'm too old for all that.'

'Well, I've left a very nice man back in the wheatbelt. I might go back to him after the war, if he'll have me,' Minnie said.

'Why wouldn't he have you?' Margot asked.

'Oh, I don't know, he's a farmer. We've been seeing each other a bit at local dances mostly, but it's not official.'

'Hmph. "Not official" means he has an eye elsewhere, if you ask me,' Beth said.

'You don't know that,' Minnie said. 'Stan's a bit shy, that's all. And he has his mother to think of.'

'Oh dear, there's a mother on the scene? He'll always be hers. Mark my words.'

'I think we may well become engaged when I get home – so it shows what you know.'

'Believe it when I see it.'

'Do you get invited to many weddings, Beth?' Margot asked.

'Not many, more than enough,' Beth said. 'They bloody love a wedding in Queensland. Any excuse for a beer.'

They passed through Piccadilly Circus, the main hall of the ship, climbed to the top of the stairs and stood on the deck of the *Queen Mary*. Other nurses were there, and a few soldiers, laughing and smoking in the sunshine.

'Why did you sign up if you and Stan have reached an understanding?' Margot asked Minnie.

'I thought I might see the world a bit.' Minnie looked away, taking in the vast ocean as it crashed beneath them. 'I've never really been away from home before. I suppose I wanted to do my bit – have an adventure before I settle down. Stan's very busy with the farm – he's very practical. And he doesn't like crowds. I think he likes me because I can chat to anyone.'

'I don't suppose farmers take many trips as a rule,' Margot said. 'How did your parents cope with you heading off to war?'

'Oh, Dad doesn't ever really say too much – pat on the back, that sort of thing. I think it was hard for them. My brother drowned when we were young. I'm not sure my family has ever recovered.'

'Oh dear,' Lola said. 'How tragic.'

'Yes. I get back to see my parents as often as I can, but, it's difficult.'

'They'll be waiting for you to come home,' Lola replied.

'Yes. Watching the door.' Minnie gripped the guard rail and gazed out to sea, and Margot fell silent.

'Well. Let's count the lifeboats to make sure we can get you home,' Beth announced. 'Just in case something – and it *won't* – goes really bloody wrong.'

'There are twenty-four boats,' Margot told her. 'It was one of the first things I asked. And I'm beginning to suspect you slept through the safety briefing the first morning?'

Beth grinned. 'So, how many to a boat?'

'One hundred and forty-five.'

'That sounds about right,' Minnie agreed, gazing out at the decks heaving with humanity. 'I think that will sort itself out perfectly.'

'That's why the rule is no one on deck without a life vest,' Margot said. 'I saw a couple of men using theirs as pillows, and they had their boots confiscated by the officers. Very annoying.'

'They probably enjoyed having cool feet for a change,' Beth said. 'Good on 'em, I say.'

'Beth, there are *rules*,' Margot told her.

'Yeah, but not all of them count. Some rules are made to be broken.'

'Do *not* play those damn bagpipes inside!' Beth shouted in the grand ballroom of the *Queen Mary* that night. 'They're too bloody loud!'

'Eh?' A Scotsman by the name of Jock McTaggart, who'd been talking to Margot earlier about some McNees he'd known in Kilmarnock, turned to her. 'What's that ye say?' he shouted back. 'Ye want a wee dance?' He grabbed Beth's hand. 'Well, I think I can accommodate ye, then!'

He was a large man with red hair and a face that looked as if it wasn't accustomed to smiling. It was a face that belonged in the back pew of a cold Methodist church nodding along in general disapproval. But a smile had crept across his cheeks at the sound of the pipes, and the bone-ringing joy of it couldn't be contained.

'Come away then, lass! Get those knees up!' He pulled Beth into his arms and executed a graceless polka around the room, joined by Lola, who'd snatched the hand of the nearest man and had followed suit. Before long, the noise of the pipes drowned out all conversation and had pulled the crowd onto the floor, dancing a jig, a reel, taking quick nips of whiskey from flasks and tall drinks of lemonade splashed with tinned pineapple juice.

Margot marvelled at Minnie, as she disappeared into the crowd to grab a young soldier she'd met earlier in the day, relaying, with perfect recall, the man's parentage, place of birth and hobbies. Minnie was alight with the possibility of humanity, swept away by people, by their stories and their quirks, delighting in their tales and taking their memories as her own.

Margot joined in the dance and the four women were swept into the arms of smiling soldiers, whirling through the hot crush of bodies.

'Oh my goodness,' Minnie called out after the piper paused for a rest and a drink. 'I need a good sit down. Can you sing us a tune, Lola?'

'Well, I must say, I don't need to be asked twice,' Lola grinned.

'Yes, a song. Something about giving Hitler what for!' Beth called out.

Lola climbed onto the makeshift stage with a microphone in hand. '"We'll Meet Again!"'

'Did it yesterday!' came a shout.

'Do it again!'

'"Berkeley Square!"'

Margot saw Lola smile. It was her favourite. She often sang the song about two lovers meeting in spring while putting her uniform on for the day or queueing in the mess for lunch.

The song could have been written just for her. Soft, sentimental and romantic. There was no doubt in Margot's mind Lola was the girl in Berkeley Square, ready to fall in love, hearing magical birds, and living happily ever after.

Lola's voice carried, clear as a bell, over the silent gathering, as the *Queen Mary* moved slowly through the black night, following the other Allied ships into war.

As she sailed from Sydney to Melbourne and then on to Hobart, the *Queen Mary* carried over ten thousand passengers. The nurses were assured that she could carry up to fifteen thousand, although they couldn't see how they could possibly fit another body on board. She crossed the Great Australian Bight, paused in Fremantle to take on supplies and disembark some soldiers who were unfit for duty, then, finally, joined the convoy of waiting ships as they set off west, travelling slowly towards the sunset.

'There you are,' Lola said. 'It's the Middle East for us. We'll be in Egypt before you know it.'

'Nah, we're too wide for the Suez Canal,' Beth replied from her bunk.

'How would *you* know?' Lola asked. 'You're a jillaroo.'

'Barry. He's always smoking up on the back deck. He used to work on ships. He says *Mary* has the biggest rudder of any ship and huge engines. He also says she's the quickest.'

'Does he now?' Lola said. 'And the fattest?'

'Yep. Well, not *the* fattest. Just *too* fat. At least for the Suez.' Beth gave a satisfied nod, locking her fingers together and placing her hands behind her head.

Margot watched Lola consider responding. She rolled her eyes and performed the sign of the cross instead, asking the Lord to give her strength.

The fat *Queen Mary* sailed on, moving slowly through the ocean towards Africa.

Every morning, the sun seemed warmer and the sky a deeper blue. Most of the ship's large public spaces – the smoking rooms and bars – had been converted into hospital wards, surgeries or dormitories. The first-class ballroom had become a fifty-bed surgical unit where the girls reported for duty, caring for upset stomachs, blisters and sunburn, or listening to lectures on gangrene and other diseases. Eventually, humidity began to gather in the corners of their cabins, and they spent more time on deck, searching for sea breezes.

It was a warm morning in the surgical unit when the *Queen Mary*'s massive engines, rumbling quietly through the water, roared to life, shaking the ocean around them.

'Quick!' Margot called to the girls. 'Up on deck!'

The nurses dashed up the stairs to watch as the huge vessel split the ocean, pushing it aside with such force the waves peeled from the bow in a great tide.

'We're turning!'

'We're leaving the convoy!'

'We're going to Singapore after all!'

The *Queen Mary* pulled away from the other ships with a blast of her great horn. She was free, and as soldiers and nurses stood cheering and waving at their comrades from the deck, she performed a massive circle of farewell in the Indian Ocean. The mighty ships all tooted and honked at each other like sea monsters, and the soldiers cheered and *cooeed*, as the *Queen Mary* headed north-west. The adventure was just beginning, the tales and jokes they told each other were already nothing, the stories of their lives would soon be written in the jungles of Malaya and the streets of Singapore.

One afternoon Margot and Minnie found a spot on the lower deck where they could hide in the shade and observe the men in their life vests smoking on their break. Lighting up on deck at night was banned in case they were spotted by the enemy.

'Oh, sorry.' Minnie noticed a solider sitting nearby. 'I didn't see you there.'

The soldier straightened and stood up slowly. He smiled, tired. 'It's all right. I'm supposed to be sleeping in the first-class swimming pool, but there are a hundred and ten other blokes there, and at least half of them have thrown up.'

'Oh dear,' Margot said. 'Have you tried the second-class pool?'

'No, but a hundred and twenty-four other men have. It's a bit crowded as well.'

'I can't believe you get any sleep at all.'

He nodded ruefully. 'I don't. We've been sleeping in shifts, and it's my eight-hour shift, but I think I'd rather wait until Singapore to sleep.'

'I can see why,' Minnie said. 'We've got four in our room and I thought that was bad.'

'That's luxury, let me assure you,' the soldier said.

'I do feel for you. We've been training in the first-class smoking lounge all morning, but only because it's a hospital ward now.'

'I'll be glad to reach dry land again,' he said and gave them a nod. 'Good luck, girls, I hope you have a good war.'

Days later, Margot woke to find they were moving slowly past islands covered with thick green jungle. The conversation the night before had been about the South China Sea and the Singapore Strait, so she imagined this was it. They were finally nearing their destination and she felt the passengers around her surge with anticipation as she listened to the excited voices in the corridors.

As they prepared to dock, Singapore Harbour was crowded with ships of all sizes, from naval vessels to small junks, moving up and down the archipelago. The jungles behind the city tumbled down to the water's edge, allowing grand white buildings with terracotta tiled roofs to peer out, waiting breathlessly for breezes to carry the scent of orchids through their shuttered windows.

'Let's go up on deck and have a proper look,' Lola said, pulling at Margot's hand. They dashed up the stairs to secure a good spot near the guard rail, beside another nurse called Mavis, a stout woman with long chestnut hair. Mavis was from Broken Hill, and had all the self-sufficiency of someone from the bush. The girls stood watching the people moving with purpose on the dock, overseeing the loading of boats and passengers, heading home, or perhaps arriving on the island for the first time.

The crowd seemed to be a mix of Chinese, Indian and Malay, along with Europeans in large hats, marching down to the wharf with their children in tow, pulling heavy trunks and cases. They were probably getting out while they still could. The air was heavy with a strange, sweet scent of flowers and rotting leaves, of diesel fuel, and the spicy aroma of cooking meat.

Margot smoothed the front of her starched uniform as the ship pulled into dock, wondering in which direction the hospital lay. All around her, the gathered nurses vied for a view of the gangplank. She could hear them murmuring to each other as the life of Singapore spilled, squealing, shouting and ringing, onto the dock.

'Oh look, I think that man's selling piglets!' Lola exclaimed.

'And look at this fellow over here,' Minnie added. 'I've no idea how he can carry so many flowers on a bicycle!'

'What do you think they drink here? I'd kill for a beer,' Beth said.

'Hush,' Lola muttered. 'I think that's the governor's wife.' She pursed her lips as an elegant woman in a pale linen dress and large colourful hat approached. The nurses fell into a line and stood up straight. Margot wished she'd had time to brush her hair, and she assumed Lola felt the same way, because she was patting her curls into place with such startled enthusiasm it was almost as if she was checking her head was still there.

'Good morning.' The woman approached Beth and shook her hand.

'G'day, Madam,' Beth replied.

A British major, dripping with sweat, stepped forward. 'This is the honourable Lady Daisy Thomas, wife of the governor of the Straits Settlements.'

'Very pleased to meet you, Daisy,' Beth said.

Lola gazed at Beth in horror. 'Your *Ladyship*,' she breathed, dropping into a deep curtsey.

'And how was your voyage?' Lady Thomas inquired.

'Too bloody long!' Beth declared. Lola gasped. 'Sorry. Your Majesty,' she amended. 'It was, however, *quite long*.' She bowed to let the governor's wife know she regarded their exchange as at an end.

Lady Thomas moved along the row. 'And where are you from?' she asked Margot.

'I'm from Perth in Western Australia,' Margot said. 'It gets pretty hot there, but I think you have it worse here.'

'Oh, yes, you'll find the humidity tiring at first. One does get accustomed to it, after a while. And we have a marvellous swimming pool. Do you Australian girls swim?'

'Yes, we have wonderful beaches in Australia. We enjoy the out-doors as a rule.'

'Oh, yes,' Minnie piped up. 'We swim in the country as well! We have a lake in my town where we swim in summer. It flows all the way down to the Swan River in Perth.'

'I didn't know that. Although I've heard of the Swan. Such a pretty name for a river.'

'Yes. Although swans can be utter swine – my dad was attacked by one when he was just a lad . . .'

'Oh dear, I hope he survived?'

'He did, but the swan didn't. Grandpa shot it.' Minnie shrugged. 'Sorry, but it's true. Fed the dog for a couple of days apparently, so he must have been a good size . . .'

Lady Thomas turned to Lola. 'And do you swim?'

'Not with any great success,' Lola admitted. 'I do like to sing, though . . .'

'How marvellous. We shall have to find you a party at which to perform,' Lady Thomas said.

'She'll knock your socks right off!' Minnie promised.

Lola nodded sincerely while Beth rolled her eyes and gave one last little curtsey for good measure.

The skies hung in a low blanket of cloud, and the clanking of metal chains against the wharf rang out over the chatter and the bellowing of horns. What would Neville make of it all?

'What do you want to go to the bloody war for, when you can stay here?' he'd asked.

Margot recalled the weight of Neville's proposal, like a shawl around her shoulders, comforting and warm. He was a good man, and she knew there were plenty who weren't. She could marry him and help run the butcher's shop. She knew the accounts, and the customers were her friends. It would be easy to marry Neville and have children. At night she would darn his socks and complain about the aphids eating her roses. It would be a good life, a life to which she was well suited. Just thinking about it, her fragile heart felt safe again. Perhaps she *could* go home. Just turn and walk back to her cabin and wait for the ship to take her back to Australia, to Neville, and her roses.

'Come on, Margot.' Minnie was dragging her suitcase down the ship's gangplank towards the crowded dock. 'You waiting for a cabin boy?' She glanced about at the rush of nurses in uniform flowing past her like a tide. 'The cruise is over; time to get to work.'

'Hurry up, McNee!' shouted Mavis, grinning with excitement.

'I'm coming,' Margot said, grasping the handle of her suitcase in her warm, damp hand.

They were finally in Singapore. Margot felt her scalp prickle in the heat. She was stepping into a new country, a country on the edge of war. Neville had been right. She wasn't the adventurous sort. He'd often joked that she'd have taken up a career as a librarian if the excitement hadn't threatened to prove too much, and he was probably right.

The Japanese were fighting in French Indochina and who knew when they'd arrive here. They were set on removing European rule in Asia, and soon they were bound to advance on Singapore, 'the Gibraltar of the East'. Churchill was convinced they'd never take the city, but some of the soldiers on the ship weren't so sure. Margot flinched as a couple of aircraft flew low overhead and a cheer went up.

Minnie squinted at the sky. 'One of ours, I hope,' she said.

Margot's heart began pounding again. 'Yes. I hope so too.'

Minnie cast another long glance at the sky as the plane disappeared, just to make sure.

'Come on, you lot. Matron says there's a couple of trucks waiting to take us up to St Patrick's,' Lola called. The nurses hurried across the dock to the green trucks which waited there.

'It's back to school for us, girls,' said Mona, a short woman with glorious red hair. They began piling their bags onto the back of the truck, then clambered into the tray, perching precariously as the vehicle rumbled to life.

'Hold on tight, ladies,' the driver called out of the window, and he was greeted with a cheer. The truck bumped along the potholed road, heading up through the narrow, jumbled streets teeming with people lugging bags of rice, suitcases, tin buckets filled with fleshy red fruits, and rolls of bright fabrics. Children jostled to watch the soldiers marching by and the band of happy nurses heading to their new home.

Some of the expatriate population had moved out as soon as the war had begun, but many had stayed on, hoping that Churchill would be proved right. Margot thought they were optimistic; southeast Asia was under pressure, the troops were gathering and as her mother would so often say, where there's smoke there's fire.

St Patrick's School was to be the army hospital base, although Margot wasn't sure how long they would last there. She craned her neck to find the two matrons chatting in the front of the truck. Matron Drummond sat stoutly on her suitcase, her glasses lightly fogged in the humidity, while the glamorous Matron Paschke, with her dark hair and bright red lipstick, smiled and waved at the children they passed.

Margot leaned out of the truck to breathe in the tropical air, carrying with it the scent of spice, flowers, stagnant water and diesel. A jeep filled with sunburned soldiers came rumbling down towards the wharf. When the nurses' truck rounded the muddy corner, Margot heard the distinct cry, 'Welcome to the land of stinks and drinks!'

CHAPTER 2

MINNIE
Singapore
February 1941

St Patrick's had been abandoned. Its long buildings were three storeys high and capped with steep terracotta tiled roofs. Its lawns were overgrown, but Minnie could see an effort had been made to mow them, to keep the wildlife at bay, and to bring the school to military order.

'Girls, your accommodation block is to the rear. I'm told there are some single rooms and some of you will be sharing. I hope that I can trust you all to make your own arrangements.' Matron Paschke grinned and started handing out suitcases from the back of the truck. Minnie took hers and quickly found Margot.

'Fancy a roommate?' she said. 'I thought perhaps Beth and Lola could join us as well if there are any dorms for four.'

'I feel like a nursing student again,' Margot said. 'I'm sure they'll be happy to share.'

'What's that?' Beth said as she unloaded three large suitcases. 'Sharing?'

'Yes, the four of us.'

'Sounds good.' She winked at Minnie. 'As long as you stop snoring every night we'll get along fine.'

'I do *not* snore!'

Beth laughed and wandered off.

The room, when they found it, had a view of the gardens.

'Very exotic,' Lola said. 'I never dreamed I'd live in the jungle.'

'It's Singapore, it's a city,' said Hazel, a friendly nurse with short dark hair, as she passed their room, dragging her suitcase.

'Well, tell *them* that.' Lola pointed out of the window to a couple of monkeys playing on the edge of the grass. 'Looks like *jungle* to me.'

They unpacked quickly, arranging their belongings on their small metal beds, placing hairbrushes and cosmetics on tiny bedside tables, and hanging their dresses and uniforms in the narrow wooden wardrobes. They'd already noticed their mess hall was next door, an attap-thatched hut, with a dining hall at one end and a recreation hall at the other.

Minnie fell back into one of two easy chairs in the corner of the room for a moment and watched Lola unpack. 'You have such pretty dresses, Lola,' she said. 'You must cut a very glamorous figure around Sydney.'

'I do like to wear bright colours. Mum says it's vain, but I like to think Jesus forgives me cerise as long as my neckline heads to heaven.'

'Yes, and not your hemline!' Minnie added.

Lola almost blushed. 'Exactly.'

'Do you have a boyfriend, Lola?' Minnie asked her.

'I did. But we ended things some time ago.'

'Was he your romantic hero?'

'Well, yes. He worked in a bank. Had all sorts of plans about becoming a bank manager of his own branch. A nice central branch, you know, like Paddington.'

'Did he join up?'

'I don't know. He may have. We're not in touch anymore.'

'His loss,' Beth declared, lying on her bed with her feet hanging over the end.

'Attention, nurses.' Matron Drummond appeared in the doorway. 'We are meeting in the mess hall in one hour to discuss facilities, duties and shifts. There will be some adjustments to be made, so I am expecting you all to muck in until we've organised ourselves into a suitable routine.' She moved away to the next room and repeated the message.

'Matron seems nice,' Lola said. 'Where's she from?'

'New South Wales originally, I think,' Minnie said. 'But she's been working in Adelaide lately. I had a chat with her on the ship. She's quite reserved, but she's a good sort of person. We've agreed to meet for a cup of tea as often as our duties allow.'

'She reminds me of my grandma,' Lola mused.

'Hang on, she's only thirty-five!'

'Oh well. She seems sensible, a no-nonsense type,' Lola said. 'I like her. I wonder if she ever wanted children.'

'I don't imagine she has time,' Beth said. 'We're not *all* built to have children, you know.'

'Well, "matron" means mother,' Lola replied stoutly. 'So maybe she already *is*.'

Minnie smiled as she took her sensible cotton blouses from her suitcase and hung them in the narrow wardrobe. The process reminded her of boarding school. It was just like the start of term, with all the girls getting to know each other. Some were rule breakers, prone to bad language and over-sleeping; others were more political, keen to know what was going on and eager to follow the rules; and some were dreamers, unable to finish their homework without thinking of boys, or films, or trips to New York.

Minnie wasn't really any of those. She was Oliver's sister, the tomboy who followed her twin brother around everywhere he went. If he was chasing sheep, or fencing, so was she. When he fixed the old motorbike, she'd be holding the wrench. She laughed at the same silly things, and the sound of their laughter was almost exactly the same. When he met a nice girl at a school dance, she'd cast an approving eye. If his hair grew too long, she'd be the one to nag him to have it cut. Oliver told her boarding school wasn't so bad. That pretending not to be shy ended up being almost the same thing. He taught her to swim in the lake at Yealering, striking out and daring her to catch him. It was Oliver who taught her to wink. She could be anything at all, as long as she was with Oliver. And when he died, she became almost nothing, as if she was not really even there at all.

Over the ensuing weeks, the women's routines held them together as a nursing service in waiting. February in Singapore seemed wet and hot to the nurses, until March arrived and they found it rained even more. The nurses wilted in their woollen uniforms, and made trips to the markets to order cotton uniforms from the tailors. April came, with no news of war, just the constant rumours, the rapt attention to the radio, the repeated conversations overheard in the Raffles Hotel and gossip from the officers' mess. The nurses tended to minor ailments and wrote letters home. There appeared to be no relief from the humidity, but they were determined to enjoy their free time, going on picnics, exploring the city and shopping for beautiful silks in the markets.

'So when did you first notice the rash?' Minnie asked the young corporal.

'About a week ago. I thought it would go away, you know? Just the heat.'

'And it's been itchy, by the look of it.' Minnie stifled a yawn. It was late afternoon and the sticky heat was exhausting.

'Yeah. Hard to sleep now.' The corporal grinned at Minnie. 'What do you reckon? Will I survive?'

'I think you'll pull through. It'll be irritated for a while, though.' She handed him an antifungal lotion. 'You can apply this yourself,' she said.

'You going to the dance at the mess on Friday?' he asked.

'Perhaps. I don't mind dances, as a rule.'

'Good, I thought I might ask you to dance – you know – to thank you for saving my life.'

Minnie grinned. She had never been a great beauty, but the ratio of nurses to men was well and truly in her favour. The enlisted men were limited, socially. They weren't officers, so were denied access to the clubs of Singapore, like the Raffles Hotel. The British regarded them as not quite the thing, with their broad accents, and even broader humour. They happily mixed with the locals, with the Chinese laundrymen and restaurant owners, though. The British expat community would never be seen mixing with friends of the staff. The nurses, on the other hand, were socially blessed. They were officers, and they were women, invited to dances, private homes, clubs, golf, the swimming club. They found themselves sought after in a way they'd never been at home. Well, apart from Lola. She was always bound to be a heartbreaker.

'I *haven't* saved your life; I've treated a slightly nasty rash,' Minnie told the young corporal. 'There's a difference.'

'Maybe,' he allowed, 'but there's not *much* of a difference, is there?'

She laughed. 'Yes, there is. Now, you may be able to do me a favour, if you'd like to . . .'

'What can I do, Sister?'

'Keep that Dhobie's itch dry and use the medicine I just gave you.'

The corporal furrowed his brow. 'All right, although we're pretty busy, you know. So it's hardly my fault if I don't have time.'

'If you can remain rash-free, I'll let Sister Llewellyn know you're after a dance partner. She's a keen dancer too.'

'Is she the singer?'

'Yes. Lola's her name,' Minnie said as she washed her hands. 'Marvellous voice. She's quite a talent. She's from Sydney, but we can't hold that against her, can we?' She smiled. 'She told me her grandmother was a wonderful singer in London years ago and that once she even sang for Queen Victoria.'

'Perhaps she could sing us a tune?' the corporal asked.

'I'm certain she'd be delighted. Now. Thanks for the chat – you can go back on duty.'

The corporal straightened his uniform while Minnie filled out the paperwork. Rashes were the most common medical complaint she dealt with. As much as she didn't want to see anyone get hurt, she did wonder if she'd head home with exciting war stories about the time she lanced a boil, or the time she told a particularly recalcitrant soldier to keep his rash dry.

'So, I see you've had a go at your uniform too?' the corporal said, looking at Minnie's bare arms.

'Yes, I didn't want to ruin it – it cost me over fifty quid – but the sleeves are too hot in this weather, so I gave in and cut them off last night. We've ordered some new cotton blouses from a local tailor, but we don't have them yet. We can't be fainting all over our patients.'

'You could faint over me, if you like,' he grinned.

Minnie allowed herself another smile. She glanced at his record. 'Corporal Tanner, I am old enough to be your *much* older sister, but thank you for making the effort.' She stood up. 'I *may* see you at the mess – for that dance.'

Corporal Tanner grinned even more broadly.

'And if you don't stand on my toes, I'll introduce you to Sister Llewellyn. If anyone can convince her to jump in with the band, I'm sure it will be you.'

The corporal saluted. 'Deal, Sister. And thanks for the cream.' He disappeared down the corridor and took a quick left towards the verandah, greeting every duty nurse along the way.

Minnie smiled. It felt as if her first few months had been filled with seminars on beriberi and malaria and commonplace conditions, but the gossip around the hospital base was that conflict couldn't be avoided. Japan and China had been at war since 1937, and they'd been fighting long before that, with skirmishes occurring over decades. Japan had invaded Manchuria, had taken Shanghai and Nanjing, and China was fighting back with support from the USSR and America.

Minnie sighed. She wasn't sure how long they would be in Singapore, but troops were moving across Malaya and tensions were rising. She glanced out of the window and saw storm clouds gathering.

She decided to write a letter home, to let her parents know she was okay. They'd be worried about her. *I'll be watching the door*, her mother had said as she'd left for Perth. *You come home safe and sound. And I mean it, I want you back home where you belong.* She remembered her mother's hands refolding her tea towel into a small rectangle and the anxiety in her fingers as she pressed it into the kitchen table. *Are you sure you don't want to come to the train?* her father had asked. *No. There's no need for that. You just come home, soon. That's all.* Her mother had unfolded that tea towel, smoothed it flat on the old pine table, then gathered it into her hands again. Minnie had handed her father her suitcase, hugged her mother's defeated shape, and left her there, her knuckles white, as if she could wring the tea towel's throat.

The sun had blasted the verandah where her brother Oliver's boots sat waiting by the back door. Minnie had wondered if they should bury them with him, but her mother hadn't been able to bear the thought that he'd never come home to fill them again. So the boots had stayed, gathering dust, the sun warming the leather every afternoon.

Minnie checked through the overnight charts and looked at her watch. It would be time for evening rounds with the doctor on duty soon. She took the water jug and filled some glasses while the men slept or read old copies of the *Australian Women's Weekly*. Then she sat down to write.

> *Dear Mum and Dad,*
>
> *We have been in Singapore for a while now, and I think we are finally accustomed to the heat. It's so humid we are drenched in sweat all the time, but we're lucky enough to have the Singapore Swimming Club nearby, and me and the girls often go for a dip on our days off. You'll remember I mentioned Beth, Margot and Lola? We are all good friends now – having been together for so long, and working side by side during the day. Matron Drummond and Matron Paschke keep us on our toes, even though they are very different women. Matron Drummond is gentler by nature, a little stern,*

but kindly. She is a plain woman, but sensible, while Matron Paschke is very glamorous. She has beautiful dark hair and wears bright lipstick. She is quick to laugh and likes to know the latest gossip – she's such fun!

We shop at the local markets on our days off, and we're often invited to events with the British ladies, who are pleased to have a few more women in their group to balance things up a bit with all the officers in town. I've even learned to play golf!

I'm hoping for a day off next week – there's a nice cool place in the hills we might visit, but of course it all depends on the fighting, and what's safe. Please don't worry about me. We really are very safe here now – the worst thing I have to worry about is bad cooking in the nurses' mess. Keep watching the door – I'll be home soon.

Your loving daughter,

Minnie xx

'Just how many beds are we supposed to make up?' Lola complained, dropping another pile of sheets into Minnie's waiting hands as the sun rose over Singapore. 'My back'll give out if we do any more – we've been here for ages and we've barely had a decent patient yet.' She tossed a pillow to Hatty, a short blonde nurse with twinkling blue eyes. Hatty McArthur was from Adelaide, where she'd moved as a student nurse. The bright lights had obviously seeped into her skin, because she never went home to her parents in Quorn, but stayed on working in Adelaide until the call to service saw her board the *Queen Mary*.

'Don't worry,' Beth told her, darkly. 'I expect there'll be plenty of patients soon enough.'

'All this rain,' Minnie added. 'The mosquitoes will have a field day and we'll be swamped with malaria, just you wait.'

'I wonder if there'll be more Australian soldiers arriving?' Lola said.

'Oh, I'd say they'll send any they can spare from Europe and the Middle East,' Beth said.

'Why?'

'Tensions are on the rise here,' Beth said. 'You know, after the Nanjing Massacre, and all that.'

'What's that?' Lola asked, slapping a pillow into shape.

'Lola, really?' Beth said. 'The Japanese have been fighting with China for years. In 1937 they took the capital, Nanjing, and killed hundreds of thousands of people. Raped women and murdered entire families. The US and the USSR blockaded oil supplies as a punishment. The Japanese aren't happy.' Beth completed a perfect hospital corner.

'I had no idea.'

'Don't you listen to the news? Read the paper?'

'No. Dad thinks I might find it upsetting. *Now* I can see why.'

'I just read the wedding notices, you know, in the hatches, matches and dispatches . . .' Minnie admitted.

'Well, I read the paper cover to cover,' Beth said. 'I like to know what's going on in the world. Just because I'm from God's own country doesn't mean I don't feel sorry for the rest of you bastards.'

'Thank you, Beth. Very kind, I'm sure.' Minnie smiled.

'Yes, we appreciate your concern,' Lola added.

Beth grinned magnanimously. 'You're very welcome.'

'Why would they send more soldiers here? There's nothing happening.'

'You wait. Singapore is an important port to the Poms. The Japs will want to see if they can take it from them while they're busy with Hitler.'

'Why?'

'Why do men do anything? Power, money, oil, rubber . . .' Beth patted the pillow on the freshly made bed. 'You'll see.'

'I bet we win the war in Europe and go home by June,' Hatty predicted. 'The Japs will back down once Hitler's done and dusted.'

'Easier said than done,' Minnie said, folding a pile of towels.

'I reckon a lot of people are going to croak between now and then,' Beth said.

'What about us,' Minnie asked her. 'Do you like our chances?'

'I like *mine*,' Beth said. 'My dad always said you couldn't kill me with an axe.'

Matron Drummond paused in her inspection of the ward, a jug of water in her hand. 'Enough talk, girls. We're here to serve our country. We don't need to worry about the duration of the conflict – we need to be prepared to provide the best care possible for our soldiers.'

'Yes, Matron.' The girls filed back into the supply room to continue their inventory, the warm wet air pressing the sweat into their backs.

'You going to the dance on Saturday?' Lola murmured as they made their way across to their accommodation later that day, the steady patter of tropical rain battering the tiled roofs and pouring into the lush garden beds.

'I don't know,' Minnie said. 'I suppose I will, but I feel as if I'm always out at dances these days. I'd rather be in bed with a good book. I'm exhausted.'

'Well, I can't wait,' Lola said. 'The army band is playing and lots of the boys will be there.'

'Seems a bit much to be dancing and drinking when the Japs are coming,' Hatty said. 'Listening to the girls talk today, it feels as if they're breathing down our necks.'

'All the more reason to sing and dance while we can, then,' Lola said. 'If I'm about to get bombed, then I may as well go out singing.'

'Oh, you'll be singing all right,' Hatty told her. 'A million Japs will come over the hill and you'll burst into a chorus of "Roll Out the Barrel"!'

'Hatty, stop it. We can't think about that, or we'll go mad.'

'I'm just saying,' Hatty said. 'You can be as positive as you like. Won't change a thing.'

'Soldiers, Harriet,' Lola snapped. 'We'll be surrounded by Australian soldiers. They'd never let anything happen to us.'

'I can only hope you're right,' Hatty said, unsmiling. 'Of course, they may be *away fighting* when we're attacked.'

'Let Lola have some fun,' Minnie said. 'She may even surprise you and survive the evening.'

As Minnie entered her room, she glanced at the small teak table on which she'd placed a picture of her family in their Sunday best. It had been taken by a newspaper photographer at the Perth Royal Show. Her mother was in her hat and gloves, wearing a neat frock she'd reserved for the occasion, and her father was in his best trousers and hat. Oliver's hand was firmly in Minnie's. Her mother's arm was on her back, guiding her.

She was an old-fashioned sort of woman. She wasn't fancy in any way, but she was kind. Minnie sometimes wondered if she was a disappointment to her parents. She wasn't as clever as her brother, and as a child she'd been shy. It was Oliver she followed, with his charm and friendly curiosity about other people. Oliver who winked at her when she asked an old lady about her brooch.

After Oliver died, her mother visited the cemetery every day. Local farmers and their wives would pull up alongside the family car and join her there, talking and praying for his dear soul. The Lord was working in mysterious ways, and he wasn't to be questioned. But Minnie had questions. Prayers for them all were sent to God, who was always watching, especially now he had Oliver in his care.

Minnie picked up the picture and allowed herself a moment with her brother. At seven years old, he was already taller than her. He was smiling at the camera and she could still feel the bounce in his step as her hand held his, ready for adventure. She missed his smile. She was often told hers was the same.

She took off her shoes and ran her fingers through her hair, trying to pull it back into shape despite the humidity. Then she lowered herself onto her bed and reached for an old copy of the *Australian Women's Weekly*. It had been doing the rounds and she'd read it a dozen times already, but it wouldn't hurt to read it again.

Before long Mona was back from her shift. 'Oh, it's so stinking hot,' she moaned. 'I hate this humid weather.' She flopped down onto her bed. 'I'm exhausted and I'm not even very busy. Goodness!' She rolled over and considered Minnie. 'Hey, Margot and I are going to the swimming club if we can find a ride. Would you like to come along?'

Minnie looked up. 'I'd love to. Let me find my costume.' Minnie rummaged through her belongings and threw her bathing suit and a towel into her bag, looking forward to a change of scenery and the relief of sinking into the cool water.

In a few minutes they'd all piled into the back of an army jeep which lurched off under the shady corridor of trees. The warm air, heavy with the scent of orchids and papaya, kissed Minnie's face. 'It's so humid,' she heard Margot say. 'I can't wait to get into the water.'

Minnie smiled as they rumbled along. After just a few months, life in Singapore had become almost routine for the nurses. *Just be thankful we have breathing space*, Matron Drummond would tell them at morning briefing. *We'll be busy soon enough. We need to remain vigilant with our protocols. We'll save more men if we remain calm, if we hold firm to our procedures. Rules will keep us safe. Do not forget that.*

But late that night, with the whine of Brewster Buffaloes in the distance, Minnie listened carefully to Singapore, trying to hear if the Japanese were pushing closer, wondering exactly when the heavy skies would open. She tried to sleep; closed her eyes and recalled the rumble of the jeep that afternoon, tracing her journey through the bustling streets where bright children shrieked and played with sticks in the wet drains and chickens in cages squawked and shook their feathers, impatiently awaiting their fate.

'Minnie! Minnie!'

Minnie had finally fallen asleep and woke with a start at Lola's voice. Her book dropped to the floor. 'What's going on? Are we under attack?'

Lola was wearing a smart dress, bright lipstick and a worried expression. 'Minnie, I need your help . . .'

'What's wrong? Has there been an accident?'

'No, but there might be. It's Beth. She's gambling at the cookhouse and getting in pretty deep. We need to get her out of there, but I can't get her to leave without making a scene.'

'How much does she owe?'

'She'd emptied her purse when I left her. Probably more now. She's drunk.'

'It's Beth. How drunk?'

'I've seen men pass out from less.'

'Wow. Queenslanders, eh?'

'Can you come? She won't listen to us, but she'll listen to you. Margot's on shift in the malaria ward and said you'd help.'

'Okay,' Minnie sighed. She pulled her dressing gown around her. 'Just the cooks?' It wouldn't do to get caught by one of the officers, or by Matron, sneaking out after midnight.

'Just the cooks,' Lola said.

They slipped out of the nurses' quarters and down the hill. A temporary kitchen had been set up in the gymnasium of St Patrick's and Minnie peered around in the gloom to make sure no one could see them.

'Where have you been?' she asked Lola.

'Raffles. We met a couple of Australian officers there who invited us back for a drink. They headed home ages ago, but Beth isn't ready to call it a night.'

Minnie sighed again, bracing herself. 'I've pulled my dad out of the pub a couple of times. Let's talk some sense to her.'

She stepped through the dark doorway and saw a couple of standard lamps lighting a wooden table around which Beth and two cooks, still in their white uniforms, sat. There were also two officers in their dress uniforms, jackets undone and glasses of whiskey in their hands.

'Good evening,' Minnie said.

At the sound of her voice, the two officers shot to their feet. 'Good evening,' they said in unison.

'Don't stand on our account, we're just here to . . .' she hesitated.

'To take Sister Scanlon home,' Lola finished the sentence.

'Bullshit!' declared Beth. 'I'm on a roll here!'

'Beth,' Minnie said quietly, 'you've got ward duty in the morning and Matron Drummond will have kittens if you're ill.'

'I'll take the day off!'

'Well, then . . .' Minnie noticed that the officers were staring at her with interest. She looked down and saw that her dressing gown had come adrift and her nightgown was peeping out at them. She pulled the gown closed, her face blazing with embarrassment. 'Perhaps the gentlemen will allow you to settle your debts and come along—'

'No! No! Miss must play!' One of the cooks tapped the table with his knuckles as he spoke.

'Miss must *come home* now, I'm sorry to say,' Minnie told him.

The cook stood and glowered and Minnie tried not to shrink back. She gave the assembled men the benefit of her darkest glare. 'I'm certain you wouldn't want Sister Scanlon to be punished for fraternising with the officers after hours.'

'She owes me money,' the cook said.

'Oh, for goodness' sake, I'll pay you. How much?'

The cook said something in Chinese.

'I'm sorry, how much did you say?' she asked.

'Week's wage!' the cook declared, writing a figure on a small yellow pad.

'Really? I find that hard to believe . . .' She glanced at Beth.

'They cheat,' Beth grumbled.

'Well,' Minnie said, gesturing to her night attire, 'as you can see, I have no money on me . . .' The cooks gave her an appraising glance. 'So, I will return in the morning with whatever is owed – even though it may take me a little time to collect.'

'Pay now!' the cooks said in unison.

'*I'll* pay.' The voice was deep and amused. It came from a man who had been sitting in the gloom on a large chesterfield lounge, which had no doubt been requisitioned from a private club somewhere. He stood, and Minnie was surprised at how tall he was, six foot two at least. She gazed up at him, noting his uniform and dark eyes.

'How kind of you to offer,' she said. 'Are you a friend of Beth's?'

'I hardly know her, but she cleaned me out a couple of nights ago. I've been watching the game with interest.' He leaned forward and Minnie felt his warmth. He took the yellow pad and assessed the tally. 'I'm not convinced they're *not* cheating, you know,' he murmured.

There were howls of outrage. 'No cheating!'

'All right, all right.' The man reached into his shirt pocket and produced a wad of cash. He counted out the bills with a casual air then tossed them onto the table. 'There you go, gentlemen. Now, Sister Scanlon is heading home. Thank you for your hospitality.' He grinned at Minnie. 'They provided the scotch.'

'I'll bet they did,' she said. 'I'm sure it pays off in the end.' Minnie glanced down at her dressing gown again, wishing her knees weren't part of the conversation. 'I'm sorry to say Beth won't be able to pay you back for months.'

'I suspect we don't have months. Maybe I'll take it out of her hide.'

Minnie smiled. 'I'd like to see you try. She's from north Queensland. Station country. I suspect she'd take it out of yours.'

The man laughed. 'What's your name?'

Minnie pulled her dressing gown more tightly around her waist. 'Minnie, Western Australia.'

'Harry, Brighton.' He smiled. 'I like your dressing gown.'

'I feel at a disadvantage,' she said, taking Beth's arm.

'On the contrary. Late at night with more than a few drinks under my belt, I meet a terrifying woman in a floral dressing gown and I'm utterly disarmed. You have me at your disposal.'

'Oh good, because I suspect Beth is going to get pretty heavy on the way back to quarters.'

'Oi!' Beth said.

'You want me to take her to the nurses' quarters?' Harry said. 'That's just *asking* for trouble – I could be court-martialled.'

'Well, no, I'm hoping you can deposit her at the nurses' station without anyone being the wiser.'

Harry gave Beth an assessing glance. 'Seems like she's worth it,' he observed.

'Yes, Beth is a good egg, despite the drinking, gambling and swearing. She's a fine nurse. I'd hate to see her have a black mark against her name.'

'I, however, am a different matter,' Harry mused.

Minnie shrugged. 'I don't know you.'

'Well, despite the drinking, gambling and swearing, *I'm* a good egg too.'

'I'll take your word for it,' Minnie said and grinned.

Beth had run out of outrage, money and luck. She spat on the ground, and Minnie winced, wondering if it was a precursor to something worse.

'She seems to have had rather a lot to drink,' Harry said.

'I'm from *Queensland*,' Beth explained.

Minnie looked around. There was no one nearby. A searchlight swept the sky, bouncing off the low clouds, making ghosts in the darkness. A bird called from the gardens a few streets away.

'Are you as *Queensland* as your friend?' Harry asked Minnie.

'No, although I can be rather independently minded when the mood takes me.'

Harry hauled Beth a little higher. 'Is that right?'

'I ran away from boarding school when I was a girl.'

'Did they catch you?'

'No, they did not – I suspect they were pleased I was gone!'

'Well, I must say, I'm impressed,' Harry said.

'Me too!' added Beth.

The night was warm, but showers had drifted across the school grounds and made puddles on the pathways. Minnie had time to glimpse the low sky above them, hanging heavily after midnight, tired from the weight of the rain and the worries of the people of Singapore. They walked as quickly as they could, Lola trotting ahead as if to show them the way, Minnie and Harry following with Beth's tall form between them.

'Now, Beth,' Minnie said once they'd reached the nurses' station, 'we're about to cross the verandah. Do you think you can tiptoe?'

Beth rallied and raised a foot, pointed her toe in mid-air and placed it gently down on the ground. She repeated the action with her other foot, and kept it going, performing a wonderful tiptoe on the spot. Harry gave Minnie the nod and they began to move forward again.

'Stairs,' Minnie whispered, and Beth's knees went higher. The floorboards creaked, and they paused, glancing around.

'Where's my bed?' Beth mumbled.

'Not long now, we've just got to get past the wards and we'll be—'

'That'll do,' Beth declared. 'I need sleep. Goodnight.' She lurched away from them and barrelled through the doors towards the main ward.

Most of the patients were recovering from only minor illness and surgeries, spending little time on the ward, so there was a selection of empty beds. Beth fell into one with the confidence of a woman who trusted gravity implicitly. One foot hung off the side of the bed. Minnie sighed and poked it back in, pulling a sheet over the pile of Beth.

'Do you think she'll be all right?' Harry whispered.

'She's had plenty of practice,' Minnie said. 'She'll wake up again in six hours and sneak back to the nurses' quarters.'

'What about your matron? Does she sleep?'

'Nobody knows. We believe so, because she's occasionally sighted in her dressing gown, like a medical ship in the night. I'll just check the coast is clear.' Minnie crept to the corridor and glanced left and right, then beckoned for Harry to follow.

'Minnie.' It was Margot, still in uniform. 'Thanks so much for fetching her, I bet she was a handful.'

'She took a bit of frogmarching, but Harry here was very helpful. If he can execute a clean getaway, I'll be very grateful.'

Margot grinned at Harry. 'Thank you so much,' she said. 'I'm sure Beth will learn the folly of her ways one day, but it was kind of you to see her home safely.'

'It was my pleasure,' Harry said. 'I've spent a lot of time lately in the company of men. This made for a pleasant change.'

They walked back through the dark, disused classroom corridors, until the long verandah came into view. Margot glanced about in case Harry was spotted. 'It's not far if we cut through here,' she said. 'You can get out without being seen. In case Matron Drummond is about.'

Minnie escorted him to the door. 'Thanks, Harry,' she said. 'I almost feel bad tossing you out, but it's for your own good.'

'That's all right,' he said and smiled. 'This is what I get for doing the right thing by Queensland.'

'Just get out!' Minnie made a shooing motion.

Harry moved towards the door, then reached for her hand. 'Beth's lucky to have a friend like you,' he whispered, and was gone.

'Well, I think we both deserve a cup of tea,' Margot announced shortly afterwards.

'Make mine strong,' Minnie said, linking her arm through Margot's as they made their way back to the nurses' station. 'I'm a woman who needs her rest, Margot. No more adventures.'

Margot laughed. 'I rather suspect our Beth is used to adventures.'

'You know, I was terrified we'd get caught by Matron Drummond.' Margot admitted. Minnie giggled.

'It was just like boarding school,' she agreed. 'Sneaking around without the housemistress knowing.' She took the cup of tea Margot handed her.

Margot grinned. 'Did I hear you once ran away from school?'

'Yes, I did.'

'Surely not over the quality of the food?'

'No, I was a terrible student. I couldn't sit still. I had endless meetings with the headmistress. And one day she gave me a good dressing down. She wrote 'unsatisfactory' on my report. I was horrified.'

'So you left?'

'It seemed the right thing to do,' Minnie said. 'I packed my school bag and left.'

'What did your parents say?'

'Well, they didn't know until I turned up on the farm.'

'The school hadn't contacted them?'

'No. Perhaps they were hoping I'd just show up.'

'How on earth did you travel so far? How old were you?'

'I was fourteen. And I found my way, traded my hat for a ride on a train, sat in the back of a couple of trucks. I met some interesting characters. I walked quite a way.'

'You must have hated school.'

'It wasn't for me. I wanted to be a nurse and I couldn't see why I had to be at school at all. My parents were horrified when I walked up the front drive. They let me stay home for a while, then they sent me to another boarding school. I finished my schooling later and went into nursing training.'

'I think you were very brave,' Margot told her. 'I wish I was as brave as you.'

'I wasn't brave,' Minnie said, gazing into her tea. 'I just found my way home again.'

In a few short months, Beth had developed a reputation as something of a medical marvel. No matter how much she drank the night before an early shift, she always managed to clamber out of bed, usually with considerable complaint, and face her patients with all the care and professionalism befitting an Australian Army nurse. Perhaps even more.

There were, however, a few things Beth Scanlon did *not* enjoy. These included boats, singing and early mornings. The fact that Minnie quite liked an early start to the day proved to be a source of constant disappointment. When Minnie's alarm clock rang at six o'clock one Monday, Beth groaned and rolled over. 'Shut the bloody thing off before I stick it up your backside!'

'Sorry, Beth.' Minnie flicked it off and glanced about. Margot and Lola were still on the wards. 'When's your shift?'

'Six-thirty,' Beth grumbled.

'I'm on just after you, then. Would you like to swap?'

'Nah, I'm awake now.'

Minnie watched as Beth stumbled to her small wardrobe and began to take out her uniform.

Outside, the city was slowly waking, the staccato buzz of motorbikes echoing along the narrow lanes. Roosters, ruffled by the damp air and weak sunshine, crowed at shadows. The air was cool for a change, and puddles decorated the roads and laneways, splashing out rich brown mud as bicycles rattled through.

Beth pinned back her hair, added a slick of lipstick, brushed her teeth in the basin and patted herself down.

'Are you a bit under the weather, Beth?' Minnie asked. 'You were out rather late last night with Hatty and Mona.'

'Bugger off, Minnie,' Beth grumbled, rubbing her face.

Minnie grinned. 'Your secret's safe with me. Those girls certainly like a good time. I don't think any man is safe while they're around.'

'Last night they had champagne with a bloke who reckons he's a prince.'

'A *prince*?'

'That's right, the Sultan of Jahore. Who knows? Singapore's that kind of place. He loves the Poms so Aussie girls are a good second best. I think he gave them a lift to Raffles in his Rolls-Royce. I thought it best to head home.' She nodded in the mirror. 'Early start.'

'Well, I hope they made it back to barracks or there'll be hell to pay. Now, I'd better dash or Matron will have my guts for garters.'

'Hang on, I'll come with you.'

Minnie and Beth made it to the ward just before six-thirty.

'Almost late, Sister Scanlon.' Matron glanced at her watch. 'Another late night, I presume?'

'Yes, Matron.'

'At least you have friends to keep you punctual.'

'Yes, Matron.'

'We've had a dozen cases of malaria overnight. Bound to happen in the tropics, but it means we'll have to be careful with our quinine stocks.'

'Maybe we'll be able to get some more supplies from the Poms – we're looking after their men too,' Beth said.

'I'll have a word to the doctors. I suspect most deals are done late at night in the officers' mess.'

Beth rolled her eyes. 'Boys' clubs. Always the way. You should just let me join them with a golf club in my hand.'

'I don't think they play golf with women, Beth.'

'Oh, not to *play* – I'd belt one of them over the head with it until they give me more pills!'

'Sister Scanlon. Time to look after the malaria ward. Unarmed.'

'Yes, Matron.'

Minnie took some fresh towels to the ward, along with a jug of water for the men who were starting to wake. The ceiling fans were spinning quickly, trying to cool them as they slept, drenched in sweat, or shaking with cold. She noticed a young private she'd been speaking to the day before. He'd suffered a minor injury to his hand and had developed an infection, and a dose of malaria to boot.

'Hey, Sister, I survived the night,' he said with a grin.

'Good morning. I'm surprised. I bet Sister Llewellyn you'd be long gone.'

'I'm tougher than you give me credit for. How much did you bet?'

'A bar of chocolate.'

'That's your bad luck. Shouldn't bet against a Victorian.'

Minnie poured him a glass of water. He looked slightly jaundiced although he was generally pale. Possible anaemia, she thought. He opened his mouth as she placed a thermometer under his tongue.

'You miss the bush?' he managed before she frowned at him to keep him still.

'I'm used to the heat, but it's drier at home. I miss the distance. The silence. I miss my family.'

'You sound homesick.'

'I suppose I am, a bit,' Minnie said. 'It's worth it, though. I needed to *do* something. Home will still be there when the war is over.'

'Too right.' Beth was handing out medication. 'We had to do *something*.'

'Why?'

Beth watched the young soldier swallow his pills and made a quick note on his chart. 'I lost a friend to the war,' she said. 'He was shot down over Germany. He was a natural with a rifle. He could take a roo before I'd even seen it. One day he came onto the verandah in his big boots with his hat in his hands and told me he was heading to the war. "What do you want to do that for?" I said. "Stay here and get some bloody work done. They'll be all right without you." But no, he had to go. "What if I don't go and the Germans come for us all? We can't have that. I'll be right. No one'll be able to catch me. And I'll be back before you know it." We shook hands. And I never saw him again.'

'I'm sorry, Sister.'

'Yeah. Well.'

'Is that why you're here?'

Beth glanced about the ward, where Matron Drummond was overseeing a leg dressing change and a Chinese orderly was sweeping beneath the beds. 'These girls are here to help the war effort, to save our men,' she said quietly. 'I'm here for that too. But what drove me to come was that time my friend Blue shook my hand.'

'You're here for your friend?'

'I'm here for revenge.'

Minnie watched Beth closely, noticing the shadow that had always been there, the passing grief that caught in the corners of her eyes. She wondered about Blue and if he knew what Beth had lost when he left for war.

CHAPTER 3

MARGOT
Singapore
May 1941

Even though the Raffles Hotel had been built over a hundred years before, it was still the jewel in Singapore's crown. At night, it shone like a wedding cake, its windows glowing with lamps, the sound of laughter drifting across the verandahs where the British officers liked to gather to drink gin and Singapore Slings. Margot adjusted her uniform and glanced back at Minnie and Beth, the latter of whom was smoking a cigarette she'd cadged from a British soldier on Beach Road. Hatty and Mona had dashed up the steps ahead of them and disappeared inside to find a cold drink. Margot could already hear Mona's huge laugh bellowing through the crowd.

'What time is Lola singing?' Minnie asked. 'I'd hate her to think we'd missed it.'

'I don't think she's on for half an hour.' Margot checked her watch and paused for Beth to finish smoking.

Music from a grand piano floated through the windows of the hotel, the ivory notes lifting the damp air and allowing it to gently fall to earth again, forever changed. Margot sighed. The Raffles Hotel. Did she ever dream she would be visiting such a place in such a city? She checked her uniform again; it was immaculate, her red cape rather dashing, her hair neat and tidy. She climbed the steps to the verandah as a group of revellers wandered outside with their drinks to chat in the warm evening.

'Follow my lead.' An arm had placed itself through the crook of her elbow. She looked up in surprise to see a tall and rather handsome man with dark hair glance briefly down at her, then take the stairs with an energy that pulled her along.

'I beg your pardon,' Beth said, behind them. 'He a friend of yours, Margot?'

'Yeah, is he from the butcher's shop?' added Minnie.

'Yes,' the man said over his shoulder. 'I was a regular at the shop – best lamb chops in the world.' He grinned and added, 'And the prettiest butcher's daughter!'

'I don't know you!' Margot responded. 'What on earth are you doing?'

'I have a friend inside. I'm relying on your personal charm to get me in,' the stranger murmured, glancing up the steps at the doormen.

'I don't *have* any personal charm,' Margot said.

'None at all?'

'No, that's *me*,' Beth interjected. '*I* don't have any personal charm. Margot knows how to grease the wheels all right, but she's a bit of a goody two-shoes.'

Margot turned to Beth. 'Enlisted men are not *allowed* in Raffles. It's a rule.'

Beth laughed. 'And who made that rule? The king?' She rolled her eyes. 'Bunch of snobs, that's who. Margot, you've got to get this nice man in. Do it for egalitarianism. Do it for Australia.' She flicked her cigarette butt carelessly aside.

Margot laughed and took in the man who was now grinning broadly, his blue eyes twinkling. 'What am I supposed to tell them?' she muttered as they approached the door.

'I have faith in you,' the man told her. 'You'll think of something.'

'Oh, all right,' Margot laughed. 'I'll give it a go. What's your name?'

'Gull. But feel free to make something up.'

Margot paused on the top step. 'I suspect you're not the right sort of person for this place,' she grinned.

'I'm *exactly* the right sort of person – I'm here to rescue a pig.'

'A pig?' Beth said. 'Why? Is the pig in trouble with the law?'

'Yes, and aren't you a little embarrassed?' Margot added as they got closer to the door.

'To ask a woman for help?' His blue eyes were filled with promise.

'No, that Raffles will allow a *pig* into their esteemed establishment – and they *still* won't have *you*!'

The hotel was alive with music and laughter. Once they got past the doormen, Gull had warmly shaken Margot's hand before vanishing into the crowd. Margot watched him until she could no longer make him out, still able to feel the warmth of his hand.

The band knew their crowd and were playing Glenn Miller's 'String of Pearls' and the floor had filled with dancers. Red, white and blue streamers hung around the stage and across the windows, while the waiters carried cocktails high on silver trays, garnished with pineapple, melon and mint. When the band changed tunes, Lola appeared before them, beaming.

'Girls, I did a quick run through of a couple of tunes with the band. It was marvellous!' She swayed to the music and pulled Minnie into a hug.

'When are you on?' Margot asked.

'I think after ten,' Lola said. 'Look at all these glamorous people. Can you believe it? I'm going to sing at the Raffles Hotel!'

'We're very excited to hear you,' Margot said. 'You'll be wonderful.'

Lola graced her with a kiss and launched into song. 'Come fly with me, let's fly, let's fly away . . .' She did a neat turn Margot felt she'd seen at the pictures once, and sailed off through the crowd.

'She'll be singing all day tomorrow,' Beth said. 'It's like living with bloody Vera Lynn.'

'Vera wouldn't empty a bedpan no matter how much you paid her,' Minnie pointed out.

'Yeah, and Lola would, and *then* she'd make up a song about it,' Margot added. 'So we're way ahead.'

'Ladies.' It was Harry, the soldier who'd helped rescue Beth. He looked very fine in his dress uniform. 'I do hope I find you well?'

'Yes, very well, as it happens,' Beth said. 'I hope you weren't too put out by our little stroll the other night?'

'Not at all. I was vastly entertained.'

Minnie reached forward and shook his hand. 'Dance with me,' she said. 'I'm too exhausted to stay here for long – at least make it worth my while.'

'Minnie, it would be my pleasure,' he assured her. 'It's nice to finally see you dressed!'

Margot watched Minnie, smiling into her glass. This was a lot fancier than the Perth dances she'd been to, that was for sure. Mostly they just set Mr Spencer up at the piano with a few plates of sandwiches and cakes for later. This was fully catered, with staff bringing piles of food from the kitchen and drinks being served at the bar. And not just beer for the men, but cocktails for the women as well.

She stood for a while, idly watching the crowd, the men dashing in their uniforms, the ladies shining in silks and jewels. Despite her best efforts, she always felt she was the big sister, observing the girls, making sure they were safe. She'd always been that way. The girl who sat at the front in class; the young nurse with the neatest uniform. She liked the protocols of medicine, the way science, combined with great attention and discipline, could save lives. Hospital rules gave structure to her life, gave her a career, and gave her treasured colleagues. But she couldn't help but sigh as a beautiful couple sailed past her, in each other's arms.

Beth came to stand beside her. 'Lola's having a good time.'

'She's been looking forward to this all week. I think she'll dance every dance and fall in a heap tomorrow.'

'She may as well, there's plenty of men to go round. I believe Captain Blair was *very* pleased to see Minnie.'

'Do you think so?' Margot asked.

'I've been to enough country dances to know what's what,' Beth told her confidently.

Later, the hotel patrons were lucky enough to be entertained by Lola, who held them in thrall. Her voice rose like the warm flame of a candle, flickering with the lights of home. Margot stood at the back of the room and let Lola's voice wash over her. She imagined she was sitting at home with some darning on her knee, listening to the wireless. Perhaps the 7.30 from Perth Station would come through and she'd lean in a little to hear the words. Her Singapore Sling was still chilled in her hand, the condensation pleasantly cool.

Beth drained her beer and headed back to the bar for another. Margot grinned. Matron Paschke would have something to say if Beth got drunk at Raffles!

Someone waved at her and Margot turned to see a flurry of arms cartwheeling across the doorway to the side bar. There were muffled shouts until the door was pulled closed with a bang and the crowd began to applaud Lola, unaware of the commotion next door. Margot glanced around as Lola launched into 'They Can't Take That Away from Me', and moved to the door, opened it a fraction, but withdrew quickly as a head crashed against the timber. The door shook. Quickly, and without nearly enough thought, Margot took a deep breath and opened it fully.

'What on earth is going on here?' she asked the room. No one could hear her over the shouting and fisticuffs. In front of her were three bloodied soldiers, a large angry man in a cook's apron, a couple of anxious waiters, what appeared to be an oversupply of whiskey and one rather alarmed pig, which was racing around under the barstools, squealing in despair.

'Stop it! This instant!' Margot shouted. The men froze. The large man had his fist hovering inches from another man's face. That man seemed to have taken a couple of blows already, and was sporting a split lip and an expression which suggested he was happy to see her.

'Margot,' Gull said. 'It's you!'

'Gull? You're still here? I thought you . . .' she began, but the man in the British Army uniform swung at Gull again and she yelled as Gull ducked the blow.

'How dare you!' Margot dashed into the fray, only to step on the escaping pig, causing distress in both quarters.

'Stop that pig!' someone shouted, and Margot instinctively grasped at the animal as it bounced, squealing, into her knees. She grabbed its leg. The pig shook itself free; she grabbed at its porky middle, but it squirmed away, squealing and snorting in outrage.

'Oh!' Margot called, 'I don't think I—'

'Hold on to him!'

'I haven't got him at all!'

The pig stamped all four trotters and dashed off in the opposite direction, scampering under the chairs and tables. Margot crouched down to get a better view of the pig's hind quarters disappearing under a long table at the end of the room, covered in platters of tropical fruit, samosas and cheese straws.

'Piggy! Piggy! There's the fellow!' Some of the British officers had been observing the chase through the bottom of their whiskey glasses, and apparently their money was on the pig for an escape.

A brigadier stood to lead the table in song. 'Tom Tom, the piper's son! Stole a pig, and away he run!' The men raised their glasses in his honour.

A lady in a long pale grey silk gown gracefully descended to the floor and peered underneath the linen. 'He's there,' she stage-whispered.

Margot dropped to her knees and had a quick look. The pig was frozen under the table, his pale pink snout twitching in fear. On the other side of the table, Margot saw the tablecloth lift, and a very handsome face appeared to assess the situation.

'There you are, Mr Pinky,' Gull whispered. 'Let's see if we can get you into a nice basket.' He glanced across at Margot and winked. Margot fell back in surprise. 'Hey, there, don't back out on me now,' Gull said. 'You chased him under the table – you owe it to me to get him out!'

'I'm not sure I chased him under the table at all, Mr . . .'

'Gull, just call me Gull. I'd shake your hand, but I think Mr Pinky here would make a run for it.'

'What do you want *me* to do?'

'Could you crawl under the table a bit? If you can get him to rush at me, I think I can tackle him enough to take him into custody.'

Margot hitched her skirt and crawled forward. Mr Pinky regarded her with dark shining eyes, his snout twitching.

'Mr Pinky,' she murmured. 'Time to go home.' She clapped her hands lightly and the pig shot out from his spot under a wooden chair and past her. He then scrambled under the fabric for a moment and dashed out from under the table with a squeal of triumph.

They chased the animal down a well-lit corridor until a door opened and soon found themselves running through the steam and heat of the kitchens, chefs looking up from their tasks in disbelief. The pig, taking full advantage of the confusion of the room, skirted under the benches and into the pantry.

'I think we've got him,' Gull said, breathing hard, creeping behind the dessert chef as he sliced mango for a tart.

'Be careful,' Margot breathed. 'I bet he's still got some tricks up his trotters!' She'd picked up a towel from a trolley in the corridor and she slowly handed it to Gull.

'Get out of my kitchen!' a white-aproned chef demanded, brandishing a huge carving knife.

'We're *trying* . . .' Margot began.

Gull leaped into the pantry and in a flash both man and pig were united in a dash, a roll, and a final squeal. Gull stood, bleeding, grinning and triumphant, his quarry wrapped tightly in the towel like an angry baby, grunting at the assembled kitchen staff. Margot slumped back against some shelves.

'Thank goodness,' she breathed.

'Out!' The angry chef pointed to the door.

'We do beg your pardon,' Gull told him as the door shut behind them. They trotted quickly to the hotel verandah.

'Well,' Margot said. 'What on earth was all that about?'

'Hold him.' Gull pushed the pig into Margot's arms and she clutched Mr Pinky to her chest. 'I'll find a car.' He cast about the street outside Raffles. Footsteps sounded. 'Quick.' He pushed her towards the space under the stairs and she scrambled with the pig to get further under, Gull scooting in behind them both.

'What's going . . .' she began, but Gull pressed two fingers against her lips. There was someone on the top step.

'Where is the gentleman, sir?' a voice asked.

'He was here a moment ago. Not an officer, no bloody right to be here at all. There are *rules*, you know.'

'I'm *well* aware of the rules, sir.'

Margot held her breath, Mr Pinky closed his eyes quietly, and Gull froze, his arms around them both. She could feel him breathing heavily, his chest rising and falling in the shadows. Despite finding herself apparently on the run, Margot McNee felt safe.

'We need a car,' Gull whispered. Margot shifted around to find his face was a little too close.

'Hang on,' Margot whispered. 'How did I get dragged into this?' She moved slightly so she could see him more clearly. 'You *have* your pig, you have your freedom. Now you may continue your evening, while I continue mine.' She clambered out from under the stairs with as much dignity as she could muster.

Gull grinned. 'You can't leave now. Mr Pinky trusts you. He'll be upset.'

'He'll get over it.'

'*And* you're a nurse.' He gestured at his face. 'I'm fairly sure I'm injured. Haven't you sworn some sort of oath to save me?'

'I believe I *already* have.'

'Well, yes, but I could do with *more* saving, if you have the time.'

'Why doesn't the pig trust you?'

'Because I'm going to give him to a Chinese restaurant.'

'As a main course?'

'The Chinese do wondrous things with pigs. I'm taking him to Fatty's. He'll be very much appreciated.'

'I'm leaving,' Margot said. 'And I've a good mind to take this pig with me.'

'You can't. He's mine.'

'As you say, he seems to like me,' Margot told him. 'And *I* won't *eat* him.'

'You're not a *vegetarian*, are you?'

'No, I'm a butcher's daughter.'

'So you know *just* how delicious he'll be—'

'Hush.' Margot covered the pig's large hairy ears. 'You'll upset him.'

'He only speaks Chinese.'

'How do you know?'

'I won him off a Chinese cook.'

There was a burst of laughter from the dining room as the doors swung open and a jazz standard Margot had heard Lola sing many times on her rounds floated out on the warm night air. She hesitated for a moment. 'I'd better be going,' she said.

'Look, if you can drive, I'd really appreciate a lift back to the barracks.'

'Why on earth would you need a lift?'

'Well, I've got a pig to look after and I'm feeling a bit woozy – probably the blood loss, although the mild concussion may have something to do with it. I really don't think you should be sending me off into the night like this.'

'All right,' Margot said, 'where's your car?'

'Just up the street a bit,' Gull assured her. 'Try to look casual.'

As they made their way up the street, the pig snuggled into Margot's arms, glancing surreptitiously around.

'Here it is,' Gull announced as they reached a jeep. 'I'll just have to . . .' He began to look in the glovebox. 'Find this . . .' He pulled out a screwdriver. 'And do this . . .' He leaned over the dash, fiddled around with something, and the jeep rumbled to life.

'You don't have the key?'

'No. But I'm in the army so I'm sure no one will mind.'

'This isn't *your* jeep?' Margot was appalled.

'No, it's the army's. And I'm in the army.'

'But you'll be court-martialled.' Margot paled. '*I'll* be court-martialled!'

'For returning a jeep to base?' Gull asked, dropping into the passenger seat. 'For saving an enlisted man's life?'

'Well, I'm saving a *pig's* life, at best,' Margot protested.

'Well, yes,' he said, 'although, I'm starting to feel lightheaded.'

'That's fine. You won't die for *ages*.'

'Oh, really?'

'Oh, yes, you nurse for a few years and you can tell at a glance. My friend Beth can assess who's going to make it just by the look in their eye.' Margot cast another sideways glance at his handsome face, hair still dark, face paler, lips losing colour, eyes still smiling. 'You'll pull through,' she told him. 'You seem like the type.'

Singapore at night was filled with secrets. From the ladies of Lavender Road to the markets along the river and the spices from the street vendors which hung warmly on the breeze, Margot could feel the mysterious east coasting on the air of the city, like a story being told all around her. To the north was the Indian quarter where silks and spices were traded by the descendants of the workers brought to build the city years before. As she drove, she passed by churches built by the British, mosques by the Malays and temples owned by the Chinese; all Singaporeans, all waiting anxiously to see what the next chapter held.

Eventually, even Mr Pinky seemed curious about the great city, and he crept up onto Margot's lap and peeped over the door at the passing city, his ears waving lightly like little flags in the low streetlights.

'Have you been to Singapore before?' Margot asked. Sometimes it helped to know a patient was still with you.

'Once. On my way to India. We stopped here for a while and I changed ships.' Gull's eyes were blinking more slowly now. Perhaps shock was setting in.

'You've been to India?'

'Yeah, and by land through to Arabia, Egypt and parts of Africa.'

'You do like to travel.'

'I *love* to travel,' he said. 'I love people. So different, always the same.'

'How did you come into the company of a Chinese pig?'

'I was gambling with some kitchen staff – doing quite well for a change, actually. We ran out of cash, so the cook put up the pig. It seems he changed his mind when I came to collect him.'

'Why did you want a pig?'

Mr Pinky's trotters did a jig on Margot's skirt. She winced.

'I won him for a friend. Fatty.'

'Who's Fatty?'

'He's the son of the best Chinese restaurateur in Singapore. We enlisted men can't go to the clubs – the Poms don't want to know us, too uncouth. So we make our own fun and we go to the local restaurants. Fatty's been kind to us, so I thought I could thank him for his hospitality.' It was Gull's turn to wince. 'Turn left here, and stop for a bit.'

Margot pulled into the side of the road and a couple of bicycle riders rang their bells as they shot past. She turned to watch Gull as he sat up a little and tucked his shirt in. The blood was still flowing down his cheek but he didn't seem to care.

'Do we want to get our stories straight?' she asked him.

'Our stories?' Gull smiled as Margot pulled back out onto the street. 'I assumed you were going to dump my body next to the gate.'

'I'm prepared to agree with whatever lie you want to tell. Unless you've killed a man. I have to draw the line somewhere.'

'Well, I haven't yet,' Gull said. 'I've just had an interesting night.' He pressed his side and winced. 'Not all of it bad, I have to say.'

'Thank you,' Margot agreed, absently. 'I think Mr Pinky is having an interesting night too.'

'Yes, I wonder if we should choose another name, though.'

Margot gripped the wheel and tried to speed up as much as she dared.

'I mean, it may be easier to kill him and eat him if he's called something more . . . threatening.'

'Like Adolf?' Margot said.

'Perfect.'

Adolf snorted dismissively.

'Get down, Adolf, we're here.' Margot pushed him into the footwell and tossed the towel back over him. Adolf grunted in surprise, snorted at her feet, then fell silent as they pulled up at the gates and entered the base unchallenged.

'Don't forget Adolf,' Gull said as he eased himself from his seat outside the hospital.

'I won't, but I'm more worried about you at the moment,' Margot said. He'd lost more blood and his face was pale. She moved around the vehicle to help him. He put his hand on her shoulder and pulled himself to his feet. 'Now, slowly does it.'

They crossed the verandah and opened the door. Mavis was there to greet them.

'Hello, what's been going on here?' she asked. 'Fight?'

'Yes, he copped a trotter to the face,' Margot said.

'Dr Lawrence is on duty – it's been fairly quiet – mostly rashes and upset stomachs. He'll probably be quite happy to see an actual wound. We can take it from here,' Mavis told Margot. 'You go home. You're back on duty early tomorrow.'

'I could help?'

'Margot, he'll be fine.'

Margot was slightly annoyed to see Gull grin. 'Thank you for saving my life, Sister,' he said as he was escorted inside. 'I can't think of a better partner in crime.'

Margot smiled back at him. 'I'll see you tomorrow – if you survive the night.'

'Margot, you're here.' Gull Flannery had slept through until late morning. 'How's Adolf?' His eye was swollen and he had a couple of stitches which were protected by a plaster.

'He's fine,' Margot said. 'Better than you at the moment. I asked some orderlies to look after him.'

'Send him my regards, will you?' Gull touched his eye and winced. 'I'd hate to think he was missing me too much.'

'You do know you're not allowed to give him to Fatty now, don't you?'

'But he has a terrible name now,' Gull said. 'Can't you even *try* to imagine him with little jackboots?'

'No,' Margot said. 'We're friends, it's too late for that.'

'Damn it. Are you friends with all pigs now? Because I feel as if I should take you to dinner, to thank you for your help last night. It would be sad if pork is totally off the menu.'

'I haven't decided,' Margot told him. 'And you should get some more sleep. You look terrible.'

'Ouch. That hurts more than my face.' He grinned.

Margot's chest flooded with warmth, which bloomed on her cheeks like roses. 'I was happy to help, Gull. I'm glad you're all right.'

He reached out and shook her hand, holding it for a few long moments. His face was tired, his blue eyes darker than she remembered; the bruise blooming from his eye socket down his cheek looked painful. She reached up and smoothed his hair back from his brow, where his stitches had been carefully bound. It was a kind face. Beneath the damage were laughter lines and perhaps a little sadness.

'Me too,' he said.

At the end of her shift, Margot did a final check on the ward. She plumped a couple of pillows and gathered some plates onto the trolleys the orderlies would soon take away to the kitchens.

'How long have you been stationed here?' Gull asked, sitting up in bed.

'Four months now,' Margot said. 'It was quiet at first. I think I've played more golf here than I ever thought I'd play in my entire life! It's busier all the time now. Regular nursing, really; skin problems, illness, the occasional injury.'

'I'm impressed. It takes guts to do what you do.'

'Play golf?'

He scoffed. 'Sign up for battle medicine. You know when the fighting begins you'll be swamped with horrific injuries. You'll lose a lot of patients. I think you're all very brave.'

'And you? Is the army your career?'

'I don't think so. Too many rules for my liking. But I like the men – brave bastards the lot of them. But no, I don't think I'll stay in the army beyond the war.'

'When did you join up?'

'Early last year. I was thinking of heading home, actually. I was just back from an extended trip through South America. I made it as far as the port at Fremantle. I was going to visit my family for the first time in a couple of years.'

'And did you?'

'No. I had a drink at a pub near the docks. It was a warm afternoon and I thought I might have a couple of beers to celebrate my return to Australia.'

'And what happened?'

'I joined up instead. I met a bloke at the pub and we got talking. He was from South Australia, and he was joining up. It seemed like a great adventure at the time. I love to travel. It's why my nickname is Gull – short for Gulliver from *Gulliver's Travels*.'

'Your family must have been keen to see you.'

'Yeah, they were looking forward to it. I feel bad about leaving again without seeing them, but it felt important.' He paused. 'Anyway, I let fate decide. I tossed a coin. Heads won, and here I am.'

'You tossed a coin to decide if you should go to war?'

'I thought it as good a way as any.' He grinned at her. 'It's all fate, really, isn't it? Whether we stay safe or embrace life. We could have been sent anywhere. And here we are. Where we're supposed to be.'

Margot regarded him for a long moment, sorry that his family was worried about him, but pleased he was in her ward, that he was going to be all right.

'Well, you get some rest and I'll find you a cup of tea.' She picked up his chart. He was on painkillers. When she glanced up he was watching her closely. His voice softened.

'Think I'll live?' he murmured, rolling a penny in his fingers. 'Heads or tails. I just want to see if my luck's still in.'

'Okay, but I should tell you I have terrible luck, so it's not really an indication.'

'I'm a lucky man. I just got beaten up and I still have all my teeth.' He grinned again. 'And I even came out of the evening with a pig!'

Margot rolled her eyes. 'What are we really tossing for?'

'Just to see if we'll be friends.' He flicked the copper coin high in the air. She looked up to watch its arc. He caught it and slapped it onto the back of his hand.

'Now, let's be clear,' he said. 'If it's heads, we'll be friends?'

Margot blushed. She was far too old to blush. 'Yes, heads means we'll be friends.'

He removed his hand without looking down. 'Heads,' he said.

'You didn't check.'

He smiled and her heart spun like a sixpence in flight.

'I don't need to,' he said.

CHAPTER 4

MINNIE
Singapore
1941

Minnie put down the letter. Then she picked it up again, folded it carefully into a small square and placed it in the pages of her diary. She put her diary in the top drawer of her cupboard and sat on her bed, watching the chest of drawers, wondering what to do. There was nothing to do. It had been done. She opened the drawer again, closed it, and left the room.

Dear Minnie,

I hope that you are doing well in Singapore. Everyone in town was very interested to hear that was where you ended up – they must be glad to have a nurse like you who knows her business so well.

We've had a lot of rain this week and the new crops are looking quite good. Lambing has gone well too. Good numbers, plenty of feed and just enough cloud at night to keep the little blighters warm.

I know you know I'm not much of a letter writer, but I must write you this letter before someone from the district gets wind of the news and tells you yourself. I've proposed

to Rose Carpenter and we're to be married in February, after
harvest. She's a nice girl and she'll be useful on the farm,
I'm sure. Mum is very fond of her – they spend a lot of time
cooking together in the kitchen.

   I was sorry to end things with you a year ago, but I imagine
now you can see that we are not right for each other. I hope
that you'll be happy for us and that we will be friends when you
come home to the wheatbelt. I wish you all the best, Minnie.
   From Stan

Minnie liked writing letters. She'd been a faithful correspondent during her years away at school, and the habit had stuck with her as a nursing student. Her mother was also a good correspondent, her letters were frequent and newsy enough, sometimes repetitive, rarely amusing, but plainly written and always full of love. If her mother had time, she'd always include a story about the dog, as if the stories about Oliver had been transplanted. Instead she would write about how Gilbert's paws were with the grass seeds coming up, whether his ears were being stung by horse flies, if he'd annoyed Dad by racing for the trough instead of chasing sheep on a hot summer's day. If her mother was busy, or feeling low, she wouldn't mention him at all. Occasionally Minnie would ask after him, in case it prompted her mother to expand.

   There was no mention of Gilbert today; no letter from her mother at all. Minnie patted her hair to make sure it was neat and headed to the ward for her shift.

'The reading matter here is terrible – just the *Women's Weekly* – and they're making the war seem like a garden party.' Minnie's patient was a shearer from Victoria. He'd been admitted with a foot infection from wearing in new boots in the humidity. The infection appeared to be healing well, but he was bored with the business of sitting still in the muggy ward.

'Did you get the copy from July?' Minnie asked him. 'That's a favourite. I think there's a picture of Cary Grant there somewhere.'

'I'm more of a James Stewart man, myself. Do you like the pictures, Sister Hodgson?'

'I'm not really one for the pictures. Sister Llewellyn, however, loves them; musicals in particular. I'd be surprised if you're not treated to a show sometime this week.'

The sound of British planes growled low overhead and they both glanced up as if they could glimpse them through the dull red tiles. 'Looks like we might be busy soon,' she said.

'We'll be right. The bloody mosquitoes will get us long before the Japs do.'

'We're already searching out more quinine. Malaria is running rife in the jungle.' Minnie sighed. It was true, she was certain they'd lose more men to disease than enemy fire.

The girls worked steadily in shifts as more troops gathered on the peninsula. There had been no enemy attack yet, but the gossip among the men and nurses was constant, and Minnie felt a calamity couldn't be far away.

The air was forever heavy in their lungs, the breezes pallid, and the sweat gathered at their necks and rolled slowly down their backs. Minnie's legs constantly ached. She yearned to sit for a while with a cup of tea on the verandah. She yearned for roast lamb even though the local fish curries were tasty enough. She'd certainly eaten more coconuts than she'd ever seen in her entire life. She'd be happy if she never saw another sago pudding. But the rattle of linen trolleys and hum of conversation kept her company as she neared the end of her shift.

At the end of every day, Matron Drummond turned out the lights, and the nurses worked with lamps, the hospital windows blacked out with blankets as the buildings crouched in the darkness in case of attack. Just before midnight another ill soldier arrived on a stretcher from Jahore.

The man's arm was clearly infected. Minnie leaned in for a closer look at the red swollen skin and the oozing wound, stretching from the elbow down the forearm. The young Tasmanian's voice was so soft it was hard to hear him.

'What do you think, Sister? Will I keep it?'

'Yes, I'm certain you will,' she told him. 'But I'm sorry to say it's going to be sore for a while. We can hopefully fix it up quickly with sulphonamides.'

'It bloody hurts.'

She stood up. 'I can see that. I'll get the doctor to come round as soon as possible, and we'll start medication and get a decent dressing on it.' She took his temperature and checked his blood pressure, then headed down the corridor to the nurses' station.

'Have you seen Lola?' Beth asked her. 'She's late for her shift and Matron Paschke is about to go on the warpath.'

'No, is she at Raffles? She said she might go with Mona.'

'No idea. But I'm going to have to take her shift if she isn't back soon and then *I'll* be on the warpath.'

'You're a good friend, Beth.'

'I'm a sucker, that's what I am. She's going to cop it if I end up on the ward for her.'

'Who's in trouble with Beth?' It was Lola, dashing down the corridor, straightening her collar.

'Just in time,' Beth said. 'I'm off to bed. See you back here for changeover.'

'Thanks, Beth.'

'Hope he was worth it,' Minnie said.

'He was.'

'You're not fraternising, are you, Lola? You know what Matron will say.'

'Oh, I was just having tea with a young man from Maroubra. We catch up now and then if he's about. He's working for a colonel who's based here.'

'Is there a romance in the making?' Minnie asked.

'No.' Lola grinned. 'But sometimes I like to give Beth something to think about.' She paused. 'And you? Any sign of that nice Harry person?'

'No, not for a while. I heard he's stationed up at Kluang.'

'I bet he turns up at a dance soon. He seemed quite taken with you.'

'He's a friend, that's all. I'm far too busy to worry about men.'

If it was quiet, Minnie sometimes used her shift to compose letters in her mind.

Dear Mum and Dad,

It's been a long time since I've heard your voices, but don't worry, I can still hear them clearly even over here in beautiful Singapore. Matron Drummond is a stern but kindly woman who runs a tight ship, but she also likes to catch up with her girls over a cup of tea. It feels like home. We have a couple of huge teapots (you know our makeshift hospital is an abandoned school) and we sit around drinking lovely strong tea with a selection of biscuits and cakes from the local shops. Singaporeans certainly know how to eat! It's lucky I'm working most days, or I'm not sure I'd do anything else!

We certainly found ourselves in the army this week. It
was decided we should all know how to march, I'm not sure
why, but the order was given, and those of us not on shift
were dispatched to the flat roof of the nurses' quarters to
march about for a few hours. We are fine nurses but terrible
at walking in time. Left right! Not too hard to achieve? Well.
Too hard for us. How we giggled! At one point Mavis said
if the drill sergeant didn't call out halt we were in danger of
marching right off the roof!

That's all from me in Singapore, please give Gilbert a pat
for me, and if you see Stan at the Co-op, pass on my very best
wishes.

Your loving daughter,
Minnie xx

Minnie liked to check on all the wards each night before she
finished her shift. She made her way quietly between the beds, hoping that everyone would be comfortably asleep. As she walked down
the corridor, Margot fell into step beside her.

'Final check?' she asked.

'Yes, just for peace of mind.' Minnie yawned.

A young soldier was sitting up in bed, watching them make their
way towards him.

'How are you feeling?' Margot asked. 'Is your throat comfortable?'

He nodded and spoke in a whisper. 'It's fine. Matron Paschke
got me some painkillers a few hours ago.' He smiled. 'I wanted to
thank you.'

'We didn't do much,' Minnie told him. 'It was only a tonsil
removal.'

'Yeah, fancy coming all the way here for something so boring,' he said. 'Still, it's nice to know we have such great care available. I hope we give you nothing more serious to worry about in the future.'

'Oh, it takes a lot to worry us,' Margot assured him.

They made their way out of the ward and onto the verandah, where Singapore lay before them in darkness.

'Do you think the fighting will reach us, Margot?' Minnie said.

'Yes, I do. I can't see Japan backing down. I think something terrible will happen and we'll be at war in the Pacific before we know it.'

'But it seems as if it's all passing us by,' Minnie murmured. 'I can't say I'm sorry, although I would like to feel as if I've helped.'

'You already have,' Margot said. 'And don't worry, you'll be in the right place when the war comes to us.'

'I must say,' Minnie smiled. 'If I'm to face the Japanese Army, there's no one I'd rather serve beside.'

Margot rested a hand for a moment on Minnie's back.

'And you? Ready for the Japanese to attack? Or are you too taken with Gull to care?' Minnie asked.

'I'm ready,' Margot said. 'We could be here for ages, then perhaps another front further afield. Who knows?'

'And what about Mr Gull?' Minnie persisted.

'Oh, that's nothing. He's trouble. I'm not about to lose any sleep over him.'

'So you think you'll stay a nurse, then?'

'I think so. I can't imagine a life not helping others.'

'I really couldn't see you as a butcher's wife, anyway.'

'Me neither. You can tell when someone feels something for you, can't you? Neville would have spent forty years looking over his newspaper at me, wondering if I truly loved him.'

Minnie sat down on the top step, and Margot joined her. 'Anyway, what about you? What happened with that nice chap you write to? The one with the mother?'

Minnie glanced around. 'He wrote to me last week.'

'Well, that's a good sign.'

Minnie sighed. 'He wanted to let me know he was marrying a nice girl from Kulin.'

'Oh.'

'Yes.' Minnie took out her watch and began to polish it on her skirt.

'Are you okay?' Margot asked.

'I'm . . . not sure,' Minnie said. 'I'm sad, of course, but perhaps it's for the best. I think *I'm* Neville, gazing over the newspaper. *Now* I put the newspaper down and get on with my life.' She smiled. 'I suppose I'd rather not go home for a while, either. Perhaps I'll earn a medal first, to cheer me up a bit.'

'You were obviously too good for him,' Margot said.

Minnie laughed, her eyes shining with tears.

'I bet you go home, smothered in medals, and on the ship you meet a mysterious man . . .' Margot put her arm around Minnie's shoulder. 'And he'll say something like, "Minnie, you are *everything* I've been looking for in a nurse. I have terrible haemorrhoids and only you can save me!"' Minnie giggled, so Margot continued. 'Or a nice young man says, "Minnie, I have an old and slightly dotty aunt who is about to drop off the perch and leave me her millions . . . What would you say to keeping her comfortable in her final days and dancing the nights away with me at the Ascot Ballroom?"'

'Well, *he* sounds rather nice. And *no piles*, you say?' Minnie said.

'None whatsoever.'

'And he likes to dance?'

'Very much,' Margot said, grinning.

Minnie sighed. 'Then count me in! And while we're discussing the weaker sex, Gull was asking about you when he thought I wasn't paying attention.'

'Really?' Margot said.

'He's rather handsome now his face is healing. I think he'd like to see you – outside of the hospital.'

'Don't be silly, I'm sure he's just being polite. We have joint custody of a pig.'

'Yes, Margot.'

'Don't say *yes Margot* like that.'

'No, Margot.'

'Minnie.'

'Yes, Margot?'

'Stop it.'

'Yes, Margot.'

CHAPTER 5

MARGOT
Singapore
1941

It was late on a Friday night when Gull found Margot on the ward. He'd been discharged the day before and his injuries had begun to heal. She felt his eyes on her before she saw him.

'Gull,' she said. 'You look well.'

'So do you.'

'What are you doing here?'

'Looking for you,' he said. 'I thought we could visit Adolf, explain to him his role in the circle of life.'

She put her hands on her hips. 'I do hope you're joking. Adolf deserves a chance.'

'He's already had it. How many pigs get cradled in the arms of a beautiful woman?'

'Good grief, I think your injuries have affected your brain.'

Gull laughed. 'But not my eyes.' He came a little closer. 'I was hoping we could visit Adolf and maybe I could lure you to the officers' mess later.'

'Sorry, I'm on duty for the next hour. You'll find it quite boring.'

'I'm sure I won't. I'm developing quite an interest in medicine, actually. I've sat through a lot of talks on malaria in the past month.' He smiled at her. 'Perhaps I can even be useful. Is there a job I could do for you?'

'Can you make tea? I was just about to bring one to Rodney. He's third from the end, takes it black.'

'I'll do my best,' Gull said and disappeared.

Margot busied herself with her malaria patients, some of whom were muttering in their sleep, sweating and turning restlessly. She readjusted the fans they had stolen from the kitchens to keep them cool. It wasn't long before Beth arrived.

'Why is the light on in the nurses' station?' she asked.

'Gull's in there trying to make tea.'

'How long's he been gone? Because there's no one in there now.'

'What? I thought it was taking a while, but you know, he's a man. We can't expect miracles.'

'You can say that again. I've been working in the VD clinic all week.' Beth picked up a pillow that had fallen on the ground. 'I've seen some *things*, let me tell you.'

'Oh, yes, I was there last week. I can't even *tell* you how many times I washed my hands. The whole place was rife with Dhobie's itch.'

'Well, they had more than a fungal infection today,' Beth said darkly. 'I had to tell a number of soldiers their penises were about to fall off.'

'Good Lord, why?'

'For my own amusement, mostly,' Beth said.

'They'll be back down Lavender Road before next Friday,' Margot said.

'Probably there already.'

'What did I miss?' It was Gull.

'A dose of the clap, hopefully,' Beth replied.

'Well, you know they tell us to avoid two things here in Singapore – women and mosquitoes.' Gull held out a bottle of scotch. 'We take the advice more as a suggestion.'

'Hang about, where's the tea?' Margot said. 'We're not allowed whiskey on the wards. There are rules. I gave you sole responsibility for the tea and you come back with whiskey?'

'I'll have a whiskey!' Rodney called out from his bed.

Gull poured a generous slug into a teacup. 'Hope you feel better soon, mate.' He turned to Margot and offered her the bottle. 'Easier than tea. When do you get off shift?'

'About now,' Beth said over her shoulder. 'She's not *on* shift any-more. She's just hanging about getting in my way.'

Margot hesitated. 'Are you sure, Beth? I could stay on and help out until midnight.'

'Don't be silly. Mr Seagull here is waiting with a perfectly accept-able bottle of scotch. And I'm giving him the benefit of the doubt and assuming he's disease-free.' She took the clipboard Margot was holding. 'You go and have a drink on the verandah. I wouldn't be taking guests into the nurses' quarters.'

'I'm not drinking alcohol *anywhere* in the hospital. If Matron finds us, there'll be hell to pay.'

'Actually, I was hoping you'd come check on Adolf's welfare,' Gull said. 'He's found a new group of friends and I hope you'll approve. And I hear there's a two-up game running down at the officers' mess. Which is *not* the hospital.' He took a few steps towards the door and gestured for her to join him. 'Come on, I'll provide the drinks, you bring the luck.'

Gull and Margot made their way across the grounds of St Patrick's, leaping the monsoon drain which ran through the lawn. The clouds were still heavy and the air was warm. Gull must have sensed her looking up at him and he smiled, handing her the bottle.

'No thanks, I'm not one for hard liquor.'

'Your mother will never know, and things may get rough down at the mess,' he warned her. 'We've got a real job beating the Chinese cooks. Gambling is in their blood.'

She sighed and took a small sip. It burned her throat and she coughed. 'I'm not sure why I'm here at all. I've never won so much as a chook raffle in my life.'

'Well,' Gull said, laughing, 'if that's true, then you're well and truly due a change.' He took a swallow of scotch as they approached a small hut, slivers of light peeping around the blinds. 'We're here. Now I warn you, you may hear some language unbecoming.'

'So will you, if anything's happened to that pig.'

Gull knocked on the door.

'Wait,' Margot whispered.

'What?'

'Are we *allowed* to be here? I mean, I'm a woman and you're not an officer.'

'No, probably not, but we come bearing money.'

'But we could get in trouble.'

'We won't. It's late and the Japanese are unlikely to pull up at the gate without us noticing they're on the island, and no one's fussy about cards.'

The door opened to reveal a room thick with smoke and a group of men concentrating on the floor in front of them. A gramophone was playing Count Basie and the bentwood chairs and wicker furniture had been pushed back as if the men had wanted to dance, although the shouting suggested they were more focused on the game. A colonel was sweating over poker with a Chinese cook in the corner, eyeing him carefully as he placed a queen of hearts on the table.

'Heads.' There was a shout and the circle of men turned to each other to exact their payments.

'Gentlemen,' Gull said, 'we have Sister McNee here, so keep yourselves tidy.'

'Bugger off! We're busy!' There was laughter.

'Please don't mind me, I've seen a few of you in the VD clinic,' Margot said, 'so I feel as if we're old friends.' There was a howl of protest. She held up her hand magnanimously. 'Don't worry, gents, I'm as silent as the grave.'

'Make space, boys, there's a lady present.'

Gull turned to her. 'Do you know how to play two-up?'

'No,' she said. 'As I say, I barely even bother with raffle tickets.'

'Would you like me to sort out your bets?'

'Certainly.' She handed him a little less than she could afford to lose.

'All right, lady and gents, put your money down. Frankie, come in, spinner!'

A tall thin man stepped into the ring with two pennies on the kip. He tossed them high in the air and everyone followed their arc.

'Ewan! Toss again.'

'That means one of each, no result. Frankie'll toss again.'

'What are we on?'

'Tails.'

'Come in, spinner!' The coins flew.

'Heads!'

There was a cheer and Gull collected his winnings, flicking Margot a grin as he pocketed some and held out the rest. They went again. Another cheer, and dispute over the toss. Margot had a turn with the kip, and then another when she was declared good luck by a major who'd won big. With the ceiling fans whirring slowly overhead, she listened to the sound of the men's voices over the music and felt exhilarated. She moved outside and sat in the warm light of the verandah and finished her drink.

She thought of Beth, working away back in the hospital, and felt the tug of responsibility. A hushed curtain of rain swept across the yard and over the guard house, before reaching the officers' mess, trickling down the attap thatching and splattering on the damp earth. She took another sip of whiskey.

After a short time, Gull came outside and sat with her in the gloom, his shoulder warm next to hers. She offered him her glass.

'Did we win?' she asked.

'Yep.' He placed some Singapore dollars in her hand, closing her fingers around the money. 'There's someone here who'd like to see you.' Gull took her by the hand and led her to the back of the officers' mess where there was a verandah and a small garden surrounded by a brick wall. Adolf the pig was snuffling in the grass, his trotters deep in mud. She heard him grunt contentedly, pushing his nose against the root of a tree.

'Adolf!' He looked up at the sound of her voice and his large ears trembled. She turned to Gull. 'You saved him.'

Gull smiled. 'Well, he was our sidekick, escaping the Raffles Hotel in the middle of the night, and I didn't want to disappoint you.'

Margot blushed. 'I'm pleased. What's he going to do now?'

'He's our mascot,' Gull said, proudly. 'We may have to rename him at some point. Perhaps "Churchill" would be more fitting.'

'Thank you, Gull,' Margot said. 'I'm sure he'll be a brave mascot for you all.'

He kissed her.

She really didn't see it coming. She'd drunk so much she'd have battled to see anything coming, but he pulled her gently to him, his warm lips slow across her mouth. She gasped in surprise and softened as he found her, breathing him in. Her hand crept up to his cheek.

'I'd better take you home,' he murmured into her hair. 'Matron is probably waiting up, with a feeling in her waters.'

'I think I may have a feeling in mine.'

He laughed. 'Come on, McNee!'

She leaned against him a little as they crossed back through the grounds. The air was cooler now the rain had passed, the lawns were soft under foot, and the searchlights flickered across the ghostly clouds from the harbour. They walked in silence for a while.

'You won't go falling in love with me now, will you, just because we kissed?' Margot said.

'Of course not, I'll kiss anybody. I kissed Colonel Wells earlier and he only got stationed here on Tuesday.' He gave her hand a squeeze. 'I was probably just swept away by the moment.'

Beth was sitting on the steps when they arrived at St Patrick's. 'There you are,' she said. 'I was hoping you were back, safe and sound.'

'Gull escorted me,' Margot said and felt his warm hand squeeze hers again.

'She's quite a gambler,' Gull said, and despite the darkness of the midnight sky, Margot was certain she saw Beth smile.

'Is she now?' she said.

'Margot! Wake up!' Margot was dozing one warm afternoon prior to her nightshift. She'd been dreaming of home, and as she left the jacarandas of West Leederville far behind, she realised Minnie was sitting on her bed.

'Minnie?' She sat up.

'The Japs have bombed Pearl Harbor! It happened. This morning.' Minnie was holding a large mug of tea. She took a small sip.

'Pearl Harbor? Is that Hawaii?'

'Yes. So the Americans are in the war now. They won't take that lying down. Gull turned up at the hospital and he wants to talk to you.'

'Oh. Perhaps he's had news.' Margot swung her legs over the side of the bed and thought for a moment. 'How bad was the attack?' She began to pull on her dress.

'Hard to tell at this stage, but they hit a lot of ships in the harbour, at least five battleships, over a hundred planes. The death toll is enormous.'

Margot's fingers flew over her buttons and she reached for her comb. War had arrived, silently, across the Pacific. There was no turning back. She thought of Gull waiting for her and felt the fear to which she was so accustomed sting her heart like a wasp.

'Why did the Japs bomb the US?' she asked, slipping into her shoes and tying the laces.

'It's like Beth says, the Americans have been embargoing oil but the Japs need it and they're on their way here. They want to stop America interfering when they come here to get it. There's a rumour they might attack Malaya any time now.'

Margot checked her reflection and patted her hair into place. 'So it's here,' she said. 'And Gull is leaving.'

'Yes. It's here.' Minnie handed Margot a mug. 'Have this while you wake up, and hurry, he's waiting for you on the verandah.' Minnie smiled sadly and headed back to the wards.

Margot stared into her tea. It had become easy to pretend it would never happen, that they would go on with their routines,

and their golf, and their nights at Raffles until, somewhere in
Europe, a victory would be won, which would mean an end to
the conflict for the whole world. Her tea was shaking, as if a tiny
bomb had been dropped at the edge and was sending shockwaves
through its ocean.

When the tears came, Margot was ashamed to feel so afraid.

'Gull!' He was standing in the gardens of St Patrick's, waiting for
her. She ran down the steps. 'I don't have long,' she told him. 'I'm on
duty soon.'

'You've heard, then?' His face was grim, but his eyes were worried. He seemed to recognise the fear she thought she kept hidden.

'Yes. It's terrible.' She wanted to reach for his hand. 'What will
happen now?'

Gull looked away for a moment. 'I've been posted. The Japanese
have invaded Kota Bharu in the north. We have troops there, but
we'll need more.'

'You're heading directly for the fighting?'

'It's *all* fighting now, Margot. The Poms thought they'd be
attacked via the port. All their defences are facing the wrong way.
The Japs are coming from the north – and we've got to stop them.'

'I wish you weren't going,' Margot whispered.

'We've all got to do our bit.'

'But you shouldn't even be here,' Margot said. 'You were supposed to be home, with your family. You only tossed a coin. It's
not fair.'

'It's completely fair,' he told her. 'I've got the same chance as
everyone, and so do you.' He took her hands in his and her whole
body coursed with hope. 'I'm exactly where I should be,' he murmured. 'How else would I have met you?'

'Now, I don't want to get sentimental,' Margot responded. 'But you do know how to *duck*, don't you? I mean, you seem to get in a few fights, so I assume you've had practice?'

'I know how to duck, don't worry. And I know how to shoot, as well.' He pulled her close. 'I'll be fine, Margot. I'll be back as soon as I can.' He kissed both of her cheeks. 'I'd ask you to keep an eye on Churchill, but I suspect you'll be too busy.'

'I'll do my best. When do you leave?'

'Tonight.'

Despite her best efforts, tears filled her eyes again and Margot turned and dashed up the hospital steps. 'Good luck!' she called out.

'Margot!'

'What?'

Gull sighed. It was as if there was something he wanted to say but couldn't. As he slowly climbed the stairs, she was anxious to get away in case she betrayed herself again.

He reached her. Took her face gently in his hands and kissed her mouth, softly and slowly, and with enormous care placed his lucky penny in the palm of her hand.

'Just in case,' he whispered.

CHAPTER 6

MARGOT
Tampoi Hill, Jahore, Malaya
December 1941

Finally, after months of nursing and waiting in Singapore, the girls received new orders. They were moving out.

'Tampoi Hill? Where's Tampoi?' Margot asked as she sat on the end of her bed.

'It's just north of here, on the Malay mainland, at Jahore Bahru. Someone said we've just bought it from the Sultan of Jahore for twenty-five thousand pounds,' Minnie told her.

'Why did we do that?' Lola asked.

'It's close to some key locations. Airfields, railways, RAF bases. And it's not too far from Singapore.'

'Matron says we're to take over an old lunatic asylum,' Minnie said, fossicking in her cupboard for a fresh blouse. 'I'm told it's huge, even though the wards aren't complete for incoming wounded. We'll be living in a property on site.' She had already started packing, having heard rumours the nurses were to be moved to another hospital the day before. With her blouse located, she slid her trunk out from under her bed and began to fold her uniforms.

'Is it safe there?' Margot said. 'It seems closer to the fighting, not further away.'

'Oh, it's pretty safe,' Beth said. 'The Japs will fly right over the top of us on their way to bomb Singapore. Better to be at Tampoi than there, I say.'

'I wonder if I should take Agatha?' Minnie murmured.

'Bring her along. It seems a shame to leave her now,' Lola said. 'And they're taking eight hundred tons of equipment, so Agatha should be allowed.'

'Yes, bring her along,' Beth said. 'She's like an old friend now. We can use her as a Christmas tree in a couple of weeks.'

'There you go, Agatha, even *Beth* wants you to come, and you know she's *very* difficult to get along with!'

'How long do we have?' Margot asked, pushing a picture of her parents into her case.

'About an hour, I think, then we head out and wait for the trucks.'

'I'll miss this place,' Beth said. 'I hope we're back soon, once the bloody Japs are on their way.'

It wasn't long before Margot was loading her travelling box into the back of an army truck with the other girls. They had been based at St Patrick's for almost a year, and it felt like home.

'Well, you're ready to go, ladies. Good luck to you all. Don't forget your helmets!' The major gave them a brief nod, banged the side of the truck and took his leave, his departure punctuated by the roar of a Brewster Buffalo flying overhead.

The convoy drove through the heat to the north of Singapore, crossed over the Jahore Causeway and travelled into Jahore Bahru for almost an hour before they came to Tampoi Hill. It had been a mental facility, recently abandoned for their arrival, expanding out in two long wings, partially surrounded by jungle. They drove up to the hospital and paused.

'Look at the size of this thing. The corridors must go on for miles.'

'We'll need bikes to get around . . .'

The corporal who had driven them turned and gestured to an accommodation block. It had been built for jungle conditions, with large verandahs and wide corridors separating the rooms. The roofing was attap thatching, with shutters on the windows ready for monsoon winds to blow.

'You'll be in here, ladies,' the corporal said. 'There's plenty of troops around, so you'll be safe.' He smiled. 'In fact, you have the only telephone in your quarters, so you'll be our alarm system for bombing raids from the Japs.'

'Really?' Margot asked. 'What do we have to do? Call the king? Shoot the buggers out of the sky?'

'I'd give it a go,' Beth growled.

'No, if you get the call, you just ring the bell.' He gestured to a huge metal bell hanging from the verandah. 'Anyone not on duty runs to the jungle – they'll be aiming for buildings – anyone on duty up the hill will hit the deck, hide under beds, or in doorways.' He looked almost apologetic. 'Sorry to say, the attacks are likely to become more frequent. The Japanese are making their way down the peninsula now, and we're caught like rats in a trap. We can only hope the Poms send troops down after them.'

There was silence except for the sound of a distant bomber passing over from Singapore. Futile. Margot tied her hair back with the scarf she'd been wearing around her neck and glanced at the modest rooms they'd be sharing, noting the narrow beds and old chests of drawers. The thick walls felt cool to the touch but Margot knew the heat of the day would soon crawl inside and leave the air sticky until it rained again.

'Well,' she said, 'best we start unpacking. If they're as close as all that, we'll be treating patients almost immediately.'

Lola trotted down the dimly lit hall. 'Here's my room,' she announced. 'It's got a view of the jungle, so I can watch out for the enemy.'

'And sneak boys in . . .'

'No fraternising with the men, you know the rules.' Matron Drummond, a thin line of sweat beading along her upper lip, appeared at the doorway to Lola's room. 'And you'll be sharing with Sister Scanlon, so there'll be none of that.'

Beth groaned. 'Lola, are you going to sing *every* bloody night?'

'It's the only way I can get to sleep,' she said. 'You'll just have to live with it.'

'Can I smother her with a pillow if it gets too much?' Beth asked the matron.

'If you must,' Matron Drummond replied. 'But wait until she's due a day off, so I've got time to fill the roster.'

'Canteen's just across the way,' the corporal said. 'The Poms are in charge of feeding us, and I've got to warn you, it's pretty grim.'

'Not tinned herrings again?' Minnie asked.

'Yep, it's mostly goldfish. And the occasional horse thrown in for a change.'

'Eugh! Couldn't they make a curry? I think the local cooks could show them how.'

'Perhaps it might be a good time to write home to your families,' Matron Drummond said. 'They'll be worried if they read in the papers about the Japanese advance. Give them a little comfort that we are safe and well. We'll be busy over the next couple of days and you may not get the chance. And don't forget, Christmas is coming.'

*

Before long, the Japanese invasion of Malaya was all anyone was talking about. The attack on Pearl Harbor had seen America enter the war with a vengeance. Their remaining planes had taken to the sky, and their ships battled with the Japanese for control of the Pacific. Oil reserves were vital for fuel and rubber for manufacturing, while local metals were needed for the instruments of war. To control Malaya and the Dutch East Indies was to control vast resources. The day after the Pearl Harbor attack, the first bombs were dropped on Singapore.

The girls took to using bicycles to get around the hospital, the long corridors stretching seemingly for miles. They found sledgehammers and attacked the bars on the windows, knocking them out so their patients wouldn't feel imprisoned. They organised the wards, they wrote letters home, they entertained themselves leaping out from empty rooms, scaring each other in frenzies of shrieks and laughter. They turned the lights out at nightfall, listening to the sound of the planes overhead, the bell ringing to tell them to run for the jungle again.

One morning a leading aircraftman arrived at the hospital with such horrific injuries, Margot nearly fainted. She had treated plenty of patients in Perth, but this was different, the man's wounds so awful she couldn't tell where one ended and the next began. She recoiled, then gritted her teeth. His body was peppered with bomb fragments, his eyes had been destroyed in the attack, his face was a bloodied mess and his hands had been completely blown off. She physically shook, rattling the surgical tray before placing it down in surgery for the doctor to commence work on the patient. They worked on him for a long time, he was awash with blood, the surgical team awash with sweat. And when he finally woke while Margot was tending his sutures, he spoke. 'You should have let me die,' he said.

Margot didn't sleep a wink that night. There was too much pain and fear all around her.

Over the ensuing days, it haunted her, but then it drove her on. She'd fall asleep with nursing directives on her lap, looking for new methods, new rules to keep them all safe. She walked the corridors of the asylum, already filling with the wounded from battles at the front. The Allies had no tanks to defend themselves from land attack, and even if they did, the jungle would have thwarted the heavy machinery. The Japanese were sweeping south towards them on bicycles, followed by small tanks which could pick their way through the jungle tracks.

'They've sent us plenty of quinine this time, but not enough Plasmoquine,' Beth said as they unpacked medical supplies.

'I'm just grateful to see a good supply of morphia, although we'll be relying on aspirin before too long. There never seems to be enough.' Margot sighed. She reached into the box to discover a dozen bottles of Scott's Emulsion, methylated spirits, some bandages. 'At least we have some basics, but not much for infection.'

'I unpacked the sulphonamide tablets earlier,' Beth said. 'There's enough to keep us going, but we won't be short of customers.' It was stiflingly hot in the storeroom, and Beth dragged her arm across her brow. 'Look, we have tinea cream. That won't go far. A bit of vitamin B1 and some iodine. Guess it could be worse.'

'Perhaps they'll send more tomorrow,' Margot said. 'Or some of our patients might be sent south. A lot of them won't be fit for service anymore; they'd be better to ship them home and save the beds.'

'It's a bloody tragedy is what it is,' Beth said. 'But I'm sure the men will cheer up when I tell them we've got plenty of cod liver oil.'

*

The heat at Tampoi was exhausting; relentless humidity followed by rain, bringing scant relief at the end of each day. Storms would often gather close to the moist jungle late at night and Margot would feel the warm air on her skin before the brief respite of another squall. She changed bloody dressings and dispensed pain medication and sulphonamide, watching carefully as sutures pulled the torn skin on men's bodies together in the operating theatre.

Malaria began to stalk the troops as mosquitoes from the sodden jungle clustered; soft grey battalions attacking before machine guns had even had the chance. The order came to carry gas masks, tin hats and emergency kits at all times. If Tampoi was captured they were to head for the coast in small groups. The decision was made to remove the Red Cross from medical vehicles when it was discovered the enemy was using them as targets. The hospital's capacity was increased from six hundred to twelve hundred beds.

The nurses rotated between the fractures ward and surgery. Margot emptied bedpans, bathed wounds and bound broken bones. She spent hours in surgery, the lights and the hessian over the windows smothering them all, drenching them in sweat as they worked. The men she saw sometimes broke her heart, because she knew they were going to die in the tropics, far from home. She wheeled beds filled with the injured and the dying down the long corridors, hoping for a cool breeze to comfort them, or for a break in their fever when malaria or infection took hold of their bodies. She held their hands as they murmured in the night, and held cups of tea to their quivering lips. She worked silently through the long dark hours, praying for Gull, waiting for the roosters to crow in the morning, and for the day to begin again.

*

After two weeks of long days and nights on the wards, Margot felt as if she'd hardly unpacked her trunk and Christmas was fast approaching.

'Have you heard who's serving the patients their Christmas dinner?' Lola asked as they queued for breakfast at the British mess one morning.

'Us?'

'No, the officers. They've got some chickens and they've managed to get some ham as well. I'm heading up to decorate the wards with bunting. You coming?' Lola was helping herself to scrambled eggs and a couple of pieces of papaya.

'Of course.' Margot nibbled on a bread roll and sipped her tea as they made their way back to their table, where Beth was waiting, her helmet under her chair, just in case. 'I'll see if anyone can drive the ambulance up – or we can walk – it's only a mile.'

'Yeah, but it's a mile in a steaming bloody jungle,' Beth said. 'We'll be drenched before we even get there.'

'Ladies don't sweat,' Lola said.

'Well, *I'm* from Queensland and *I* sweat like a bastard,' Beth replied.

'Beth, you would make a nun blush,' Lola said.

'I don't even regard *that* as a challenge. And anyway, Hatty and Mona would make more nuns blush than I ever could.'

The exploits of Hatty and Mona when they were stationed in Singapore had kept the nursing service entertained for months. They were always up for a good time, readily accepting invitations to lunch, dinner, dancing, cocktails and picnics. Hatty and her partner in crime, Mona, were always up for an adventure, preferably with a handsome man.

'Stop it,' Margot giggled, 'and anyway, they're not that bad. I think they've left Major Weldon alone.'

'Only because he sweats even more than I do.'

'Beth!'

'I'm not insulting the man, I just find his condition extremely relatable, that's all.'

'Nurses, I'm sure your personal hygiene is a topic for another day.' Matron Drummond appeared at the head of the table, her glasses perched on the tip of her nose, the edges threatening to fog. 'Let's concentrate on giving our patients the best Christmas we can, under the circumstances.'

'We'll keep them alive, and they can be grateful for that,' Lola said.

'And *I* won't sweat on them, and they can be grateful for *that*,' Beth added. 'Sorry, Matron.'

Matron Drummond sighed. 'That's all right, Beth, but I'd appreciate it if you'd take the bunting and the newspapers up with you. I've got Mona and Hatty ready to make decorations as best they can, and the amahs are chasing the chickens around the yard as we speak.'

'Yes, Matron.' The girls collected the boxes of treats that had arrived a week earlier from Singapore: Anzac biscuits, which had gone soft in the heat; melted Violet Crumbles; old copies of the *Australian Women's Weekly*; fruitcake and tins of jam; anything that would cheer the troops.

They had taken to parking the ambulances a safe distance from the hospital. They used jeeps and trucks to move staff and patients, always aware of the endless flights of bombers overhead, bearing down on Singapore, dropping their loads, returning to safety to do it again.

When Margot woke on Christmas Day 1941, she allowed herself a few minutes to think of home. She lay perfectly still, imagining her mum waking early, putting the kettle on and starting the oven for the turkey. Her father would have been up late the night before, stuffing the bird, and drinking beer with the Chiappinis, the Italian butchers who made continental sausages in Subiaco. He was often home so late from his visits that Margot would hear him on the front steps after midnight. *They had to head off to midnight mass*, he'd explain. *The Italians love a midnight mass for Christmas. I said to 'em, I like me own bed at midnight!* Margot's mother would tut-tut and shuffle off. *You'll be tired in the morning. I'll see to the turkey.*

And the sun when it rose over the hills was hot. Pure and clean, not a sweating sun like a steamed pudding, hiding behind the clouds as it did in Singapore. No, it was always a big roasting sun, baking Perth like a Christmas ham, while everyone dressed for church in their Sunday best, and set the table with the bright red tablecloth ready for lunch when they got home, footsore in their best shoes . . .

When Margot eventually got up and wandered out of the room, she could see Christmas was well and truly underway.

'Hurry up, Margot.' Beth was sitting impatiently, her carefully folded newspaper crown on her head, bright red lipstick slashed inexpertly across her mouth. 'All the beer will be gone if you don't get a wriggle on.'

'Calm down, we're still early and Lola is going to kill us if we leave without her.'

'Then she'd better get a wriggle on too. More putting her sandals on, less singing "Silent Night", if you ask me . . .'

'Oh, Beth, let her sing, it's Christmas, for heaven's sake.'

'I've already let her have a good go at most of them. She's done "We Three Kings" at least half a dozen times. Grimmest bloody carol of them all.' Beth glanced in the mirror and straightened her paper hat. 'I suspect it's not even Jesus's favourite, and it's *his* birthday.'

'Well, I shall be singing a few carols today, so you'd better join in.' Margot grabbed her paper Christmas hat. 'And what's more, I'm driving, so everyone in the jeep!'

When they got to the officers' mess they found some of the British soldiers were having trouble gaining access to the party.

'Cool-bear?'

'Nup!'

'Cullbeer?'

'No!' The corporal laughed. 'What's the penalty for not being born Australian, boys?'

'Beer!' The British soldier was handed a pint glass and ordered to skol.

'What's the password, ladies?' the corporal then demanded.

'Coolabah?'

'You're in.' He waved them through and went back to torturing Englishmen.

The doctors served a fine Christmas lunch, helped by festive supplies from the Salvation Army. The party was brimming with food and good humour, and as Margot drank a cocktail with a couple of soldiers with shrapnel wounds, the war seemed a little further away.

'To a happy new year,' she said, grinning. 'I hope you get home soon.' She readjusted her newspaper crown as she collected plates and sent up a tiny Christmas prayer that they would all be okay; that the soldiers would be safe and that they would make it home.

After lunch, she wandered outside, hopeful that the rains would wash some of the heat from the jungle. When Minnie and Beth came outside to find her, Minnie was eating a lump of melted chocolate on a saucer with a teaspoon.

'What's that?'

'Violet Crumble,' she said, taking another gooey nibble. 'Died in service; the heat and humidity have taken their toll.'

Beth took a swig of beer. 'Have you heard from Gull?' she asked Margot.

'He's near Port Swettenham. He's sent messages down with service vehicles. Someone probably owes him somewhere along the line, but he assures me he's safe.'

'You'll miss him.'

'I hardly know him, Beth. We've only met a handful of times.'

'Even so. My uncle fell in love quickly too, with a beautiful girl from Rockhampton. Clapped eyes on her at a cattle sale, of all places. Love at first sight.'

'And did they live happily ever after?'

'Nah, he died of a stroke.'

'Oh.'

'Poor bastard.'

Minnie ate another teaspoon of chocolate and honeycomb. 'Beth, are all Queenslanders like you?'

Beth stood a little straighter and shot her a grin. 'I like to think so.'

CHAPTER 7

MINNIE
Jahore, Malaya
January 1942

Minnie woke in the cool of the morning to the sound of birdcalls from the surrounding jungle. There had been no bombers yet, but she knew they wouldn't be far away. She was getting used to their thin whine, held high on the air before they crossed the horizon and scorched the sky above. She barely noticed them anymore while she was on duty in the wards, but when she did, she'd tell herself that they were all going to be safe, that they would make it home.

After the initial attack on Kota Bharu in early December the Japanese bombing raids intensified. The Allies were only able to delay their assault upon the rest of Malaya, pushed back, day after day, south towards Singapore. They were running out of aircraft, one of the injured soldiers had told her one afternoon. 'We can't win,' he'd said, 'we can barely even slow them down.'

Those are our *planes*, Minnie would tell herself as she took a soldier's pulse, or dressed an infected wound. *That one is ours and he will end the war in Malaya. That one is an Australian and he'll turn for home soon and be safely back in Singapore before afternoon tea. That one flew too high and too fast for them to catch him.*

She'd hear the whine of a distant plane from beyond the jungle, the climbing growl and the swoop of its wings above her, before rushing on to Singapore as if it were falling over the edge of the world. And every morning, she lay still for a few long moments, knowing it wasn't time for stories anymore, it was time for work. *Those are our planes*, she would tell herself. *They'll stay safe.*

She climbed out of bed and hurried up the hill on her bike to the hospital.

'Oh, there you are, Minnie. I put the kettle on and I'll just make us a quick cup before rounds, if you like. I think we have time.' Matron Drummond was a plain woman in her mid-thirties, although she seemed older, with her unfussy hair pulled back from her face and kind eyes peeping out from steel-rimmed glasses.

'I'd love one. Do we have any milk?'

'We do.' They settled at a small table. 'Now, have you written to your mother? She'll be worried about you.' Matron Drummond touched the pot, checking its temperature.

'There's nothing for her to worry about, Matron, we're miles from any danger.'

'Mothers are strange creatures, there's nothing they won't worry about, and nothing they won't do for their children.' Satisfied the tea was ready, she poured into floral cups. Minnie wondered where she'd found them.

'I'd rather not upset her, Matron. I'd only add to her worry.'

'Why do you say that?' Matron Drummond took a sip, nodding as if she and the tea had just been introduced.

'We lost my brother Oliver years ago – he drowned. I think my mother's worried she'll lose me too. I don't want to frighten her.'

'Oh dear. You've lost a brother. What happened?'

'He was in the Swan River. Well, he was in a rowing boat, he was cox in the school team. He reached for an oar and fell in.'

'How dreadful. I'm so sorry, I didn't know. Was he older than you?'

'We were twins. We did everything together. I don't know when I won't look for him coming home at the end of the day. I was glad to move out of home, just so I didn't have to wait for him anymore.'

'Your poor mother. I'll bet she's still waiting. I know she'll be comforted to hear from you. She must be so worried, knowing the pain of losing a child.'

'She's waiting for me to come home.' Minnie smiled. 'I'll do my best not to disappoint her.'

Matron Drummond offered her a biscuit. 'You'll be back soon with tales to tell.'

'What's this? Gossip without me?' Matron Paschke paused in the doorway, carrying a tray of instruments. 'Matron Drummond. Is that shortbread I see?'

'It most certainly is,' Matron Drummond said with a smile.

Matron Paschke placed her tray on the desk and took a biscuit. 'I was about to take these back to surgery, but a quick spot of morning tea won't kill me. I hear Lola is making quite an impression on a couple of our patients.'

'She's a ray of sunshine,' Minnie said. 'I can see how they're taken with her.'

'I'm hoping one or two of the men might take a shine to her,' Matron Paschke said. 'Such a sweet girl. I heard there was one soldier she met a while ago—'

'I disapprove of gossip as a rule,' Matron Drummond interrupted, 'but when it comes from another matron, I'm prepared to put up with it.' She picked up her teacup to listen.

*

When Minnie entered the ward later that day, Lola was laughing with a patient who, despite a rather impressive head injury, looked thoroughly charmed to be lying in a hospital bed.

'Morning, Sister Llewelyn,' she said.

'Good morning, Sister Hodgson,' Lola replied. She excused herself and joined Minnie. 'Beth keeps telling me to keep my pants on, that we're here because we're old and plain, but I do like a chat when I have time. And you never know where love may find you.'

Minnie laughed. 'It's probably true. The orderlies certainly think so. But what an opportunity. I feel sorry for those pretty young lasses at home, too dangerous to be let loose on the troops.'

Lola paused in the tepid morning air and gazed at her in admiration. 'You know, I don't think I realised until now that you are in possession of a pioneering spirit!'

Minnie put her arm around her shoulder and gave her a quick squeeze. 'You know, Lola, neither did I!'

The infection in Baz Hardy's leg was typical in the tropics and it was getting worse by the day.

'Ah, nurse, do you have any more sulphonamides? I feel like I ate the last lot up and it didn't even give the bugs a tickle.'

'Oh dear, how are you feeling, Baz?' Minnie leaned over and examined the soldier's wound, which was inflamed and oozing.

Baz looked apologetic. 'It's a bit itchy.' His leg was a worse colour than it had been the day before. It had taken on a tight red shine while other areas were starting to darken.

'We'll find a way to get the infection under control. In the meantime, I'll get you some water so you stay hydrated, and some morphia for the "itching".'

There was a sigh. 'Thanks, I appreciate it.'

Minnie found Dr Lawrence tending to a young red-headed man with a nasty eye wound. She waited while he finished examining the patient.

'Dr Lawrence? I think you should look at Baz Hardy's leg as soon as possible. It's heavily infected.'

'Lead the way, Sister. We gave him sulphonamide? And he's been on it for how long?'

'A week,' Minnie said. 'I have his chart here.'

The doctor took it from her and checked on Baz. 'Looks like your leg's giving you a few problems, Baz.'

'It's so painful, is there anything I can take? I'd rather cut the damn thing off than live with the pain.' Baz's face was pale, bathed in sweat. Minnie's heart sank and she hoped it didn't show. *Careful what you wish for, Baz*, she thought.

'Let me have a look. I'll sort out some morphia to make you more comfortable, and we'll have another go at the treatment. I'm sure it'll work this time.'

Dr Lawrence glanced at the leg again and Minnie could tell he was already wondering how much he'd have to amputate if it came to it. Once gangrene set in, time was short. He gave Baz morphia and some more sulphonamide, and handed Margot a packet of powder. 'Place this on the wound, I think it should do the trick,' Dr Lawrence said. 'But it may take a few days before he feels any better.'

'He was worried about losing the leg earlier,' Minnie said.

'I think he'll keep it. Always better to have two.' He paused. 'Do you have time for a cup of tea on the verandah? I'm meeting with a group of nurses shortly.'

Minnie glanced at her watch. 'Yes, I'm a couple of hours past my break. I'll let Lola know too.'

Dr Lawrence nodded and headed out to the warm shade of the wide verandah. By the time Minnie and Lola joined him, there was a group of over twenty nurses waiting to hear what he had to say.

'Sister Hodgson, thank you for joining us. I wanted to tell you all something rather important.' He sat in a cane chair next to a large pot of tea. 'I think it's imperative that you all understand the gravity of the situation in which we find ourselves.'

Minnie pulled up a seat. 'Yes, Doctor,' she said. 'I think it's only fair. What is it?'

'Yes, what's going on? Are we to be evacuated?' Lola asked.

Dr Lawrence leaned forward. 'We've had word that on Christmas Day in Hong Kong, the Japs took a hospital – a front-line hospital at St Stephen's College.' He took a deep breath. 'I'm afraid that, when the doctors surrendered the hospital to the Japanese Army, they murdered them.'

'Oh!'

'No!'

'It was an outrage. They cut their tongues out, cut their ears off, then killed them.' He paused. 'And there's more.'

Minnie's heart skipped a beat. 'Go on.'

'They bayoneted patients in their beds, they murdered nurses. We believe over one hundred were killed.' He glanced up and down the verandah. 'I'm sorry to say, they . . . forced themselves on the nurses as well. Many of the victims were mutilated. A nurse was raped on the bodies of her nursing sisters. She survived to tell the tale.'

'Good God.'

'Savages . . .' breathed Lola.

'I'd rather *die* than be raped,' Hatty said. 'I'd rather lie down and *die*.'

'Yes,' Dr Lawrence said. 'The Japs *do not play cricket*. We need to evacuate all of you as soon as we can. I've spoken to Drummond and Paschke.'

'We're not going anywhere. We're needed here. We have work to do,' Minnie said.

'That's what those other doctors and nurses said. And I respect your bravery, but I'm telling you these terrible things so that you know we *must* be practical. Moves are afoot to get some hospital ships out. We've lost the war here.'

'We can't just leave because we're frightened, Doctor,' Beth said. 'Our soldiers don't leave because they're afraid – and neither will we. Just give me a bloody gun.'

'Now, now, we need you, there's no denying that. But listen to me.' Dr Lawrence took another deep breath. 'How do you think the troops will cope if our nurses here are raped and murdered? What will *that* do for morale? If the order comes to evacuate Singapore – as it *must* and *soon – do it!* Don't wait for the surrender. *Go!*'

The wounded had begun arriving steadily, like rain, week in, week out, in the six weeks since the Japanese invasion. In the humidity, their wounds were susceptible to infection. They were prescribed sulphonamides and rest, and watched closely, the doctors and nurses trying to save what limbs and lives they could. Some couldn't be saved and the nurses braced themselves for more to come. When it did, it was malaria that overtook the wards.

'Another ambulance,' Lola announced late one afternoon, looking out of the window of the nurses' station. 'Make that another *three.*' The nurses rushed outside, orderlies with stretchers already moving quickly to the ambulance doors. Minnie and Margot stood silently, waiting for the new patients, preparing for whatever they might find. At first they'd made grim predictions about the sorts of injuries each ambulance would produce, but they'd been horribly right and horribly wrong so many times they'd given up trying to predict what they'd be faced with. They waited in silence, only wondering if they could help their patients survive.

The doors to the ambulance opened and the orderlies began to bring the men out into the meagre evening light. The first man they saw had a bad head injury. Minnie reached out for the man's hand.

'Oh,' whispered Margot, so softly that Minnie wouldn't have noticed at all, except that she knew Margot's voice so well now. She turned to see her friend lose all colour, her eyes fixed on his face.

'Gull,' she said. 'It's you.'

His head was bound with a field bandage, his face grey. He'd suffered bullet wounds to his left leg; it was hard to assess at a glance, but his shirt was vermillion red and his hand was badly injured and so dark with blood the girls had to lean in to count his fingers.

'Get them inside, quickly,' Matron Paschke said. 'These two straight through to surgery please. We'll have time to attend to the injuries in the next ambulance – just a break from what we can tell so far. He can wait an hour or so.'

'You want to take him?' Minnie said.

Margot nodded and took his hand from Minnie. 'I'll take him,' she breathed.

The surgery was filled with doctors drenched in sweat. As Minnie and Margot stood at the doorway another gurney was pushed past them with a heavily bandaged and unconscious patient, his limbs moving under the sheet.

'I don't think I can go in,' Margot whispered.

Minnie took her hand, squeezing it hard. 'Nonsense, of course you can. You don't know what's going to happen to him, but you'll never forgive yourself if you don't do every single thing you can to keep him alive.'

Margot wiped tears from her eyes and Minnie did the same.

'Time to scrub up, and see what's what,' Minnie said.

'Ah, there you are, Sister McNee,' one of the senior doctors said. 'Hurry along, this chap doesn't have all day.'

They prepared for surgery and returned, Margot watching anxiously as Gull lay quietly.

'We've knocked him out,' Dr Lawrence said. 'There seems to be quite a lot of damage, but some of it is probably just a patch up and a couple of stitches. I'm going to fix his head first – he's only got one, and I suspect he'd like to keep it.'

Minnie blanched as she took a razor and did her best to shave Gull's skull.

'Good God,' someone muttered, and she realised that the large bloody scab she had imagined she was about to wash away was actually a piece of shrapnel.

'Hold on,' Dr Lawrence said. 'It's got to come out, hopefully it's not too deep. That's the thing with heads – they bleed like a bastard.'

Margot moved the surgical tray a little so that the arterial forceps and gauze were close at hand. 'There's so much blood,' she whispered to Minnie. 'How can there be so much blood?'

'He'll be okay,' Minnie said. 'I promise.'

Margot smiled weakly, without glancing her way, and Minnie knew she didn't believe her, but she picked up the kidney dish and held it steady while the doctor gently eased the piece of metal from Gull's head. It dropped into the dish with a heavy clang.

'Got it,' Dr Lawrence said. 'Now, just put pressure on the wound, I'm going to suture this quickly, he's losing too much blood for my liking. Do we have any blood in stock?'

'I'm afraid not. We're waiting on new supplies, but the malaria . . .' a junior doctor began apologetically.

'I have plenty,' Margot said.

'Blood type?'

'A positive.'

'No good, not a match, I'm afraid.'

More precious blood seeped from Gull's wound.

Minnie spoke up. 'Take mine. Good old O positive. Common as muck, that's me.'

The surgeon smiled. 'Someone take Sister Hodgson aside and see what she's made of.'

Minnie grinned and gave Margot a wink. 'You stay here while they sort out the easy stuff,' she said. 'He'll be fine, I'll give him the best I've got!'

Minnie sat in the ward to donate, wishing the blood would flow more quickly so that it could go to Gull, but in the heat she'd become dehydrated, and her blood flowed languidly while she anxiously watched the surgery door. Finally, Matron Drummond took her donation and disappeared, and it was some time later that the door opened and Margot came out, her uniform drenched in sweat and her face as white as Gull's had been. She sagged onto the chair next to Minnie, and sat perfectly still. Minnie smiled at her expectantly. She reached out and gently touched her friend's arm.

'I hope Gull's all right, Margot. Could you tell him to try to stay alive? He mustn't stop being lucky on my account,' she said.

Margot turned to Minnie, with her bandaged arm, her face alight with hope. 'Thank you,' she whispered and burst into floods of tears.

'Damn mosquitoes,' Matron Drummond said. 'We're not able to empty all of the water sources and we've had men dropping for weeks.'

'I just wish we had more mosquito netting and insect repellent,' Minnie said. 'We'll probably lose more men to disease than battle.'

'We'll see what we can get from supplies. The British have been here for years and must have something up their sleeves.'

'I hope the mosquitoes are biting the Japanese as well,' Minnie said. 'We'll be out of here, soon, back to Singapore. Bet they've shot all the mosquitoes there by now.'

'Bloody hope so,' Beth declared.

'How's Margot?' Matron Drummond asked. 'Is she worried about her young man?'

'Yes, I think so. But Dr Lawrence did a wonderful job, and Gull's looking better today.'

Matron Drummond glanced through the doorway to the ward where Margot was just leaving Gull's side. 'Has he regained consciousness?' she asked.

'Not yet,' Minnie said. 'He will, though. There may be infection there, but I'm sure he will.'

Margot left the ward and joined the other nurses. 'He's still asleep,' she said. 'But he promised me he'd be all right. Before he left. And I intend to hold him to it.'

'If there are no complications, I'd imagine they'll evacuate him as soon as they can,' Matron Drummond said. 'I don't think he'll be fit for duty for quite a long time.'

'I hope you're getting some rest,' Minnie said to Margot. 'When are you back on shift?'

'Tomorrow morning, but I'll stay here with him until midnight – there'll still be time to get some sleep before I start work. As long as I know Gull is all right, I can cope.'

'Well,' Minnie said, 'I'll get the orderlies to bring you a cup of tea. You spend as much time as you like.'

'Thanks, Minnie. I'll try to stay out of the way.' She glanced longingly back at Gull, who lay silent and still.

'Always happy to have you on my ward, Margot.'

The Japanese invasion was unstoppable. Soldiers arrived with stories of the Japanese Army's relentless progress. The island of Penang had been abandoned on 17 December, with the arms and supplies left to the Japanese invaders. The entire northern region of the Malay Peninsula was taken by the first week of January; the 11th Indian Division fought bravely for Kampar, but lost the battle; the British retreated to fight for Slim River, but the battle was lost and the victorious Japanese Army was only sixty-four miles from Kuala Lumpur. They occupied the city unopposed on 11 January. Then they took Malacca, and headed south again, to Jahore.

'There's no stopping them now,' Beth declared. 'We're done for here. Pack your bags.'

'Perhaps the English will send help,' Lola said. 'They won't lose Singapore.'

'Don't bet on it,' Minnie told her. 'The Poms are flat tack fighting in Europe – we're on our own.'

Gull's improvement was slow, his hand developed an infection, and he suffered headaches which persisted for days. Margot spent every moment she wasn't on duty by his side, watching over his sleep.

It wasn't long before they were ordered to abandon the hospital at Tampoi Hill, and Gull and the patients were loaded onto trucks to be evacuated south to Singapore, and back to St Patrick's School. The trap was closing around them. The nurses gathered their things together and sat with their patients, watching the skies warily for any signs of planes coming over the grey horizon.

'We're not going to make it,' Margot whispered to Minnie as they perched, knee to knee, on their travel cases.

'Yes we will,' Minnie whispered back. '*All* of us. Especially Beth. Couldn't kill her with an axe!'

On 31 January the Japanese were on the doorstep of Singapore. The Allies were in retreat, marching across the Jahore–Singapore Causeway. And then, in the early hours of the morning, the last of the Gordon Highlanders marched across the bridge, accompanied by a couple of pipers. Engineers had set two charges, and when the massive blasts cut the bridge in half, a gaping hole separated Singapore from the mainland. The trap had closed around them, the British were to lose Singapore, the Gibraltar of the East, and all they could hope to do was slow the Japanese Army down.

A couple of days later the nurses were called to a meeting right before the evening shift. 'Nurses. Thank you for your attention.' Major Black was a tall man, which had the advantage of providing everyone in the St Patrick's ward with a good view of his face as he spoke. The ceiling fans whirred and the humid night air pressed heavily through the open windows as the nurses stood silently.

'The Japanese invasion of Singapore is imminent. We've heard on the radio that our hospital at Tampoi has been taken, so we've moved back to St Patrick's without a moment to spare. It is now imperative that we all store water. Most water on the island comes from beyond the Jahore Strait and we believe the Japs will be cutting the supply as soon as they are able – they're already bombing our facilities. We have a million people moving towards the port. Sewerage across most of Singapore is already compromised, and I don't need to tell you we can expect further illness and infection to follow. Collect fresh water however you can, use whatever you can find. Fill the baths, fill pots and pans, fill the sinks. We won't last long without it, and we fully expect the Japs to take it away within days.'

There was a rumble of conversation and Major Black raised his hand for silence.

'In related matters, it is important that we consider our withdrawal. I will be looking for nurses to volunteer over the next couple of days to begin the medical evacuation.'

Silence.

'It is vital that we get you all out safely. Now, I know none of you are keen to leave, but leave you must.'

Matron Drummond stepped forward. 'Nurses, I think Major Black has made his point. Now it's time to get back on the wards please. There's still plenty to be done here.'

'I'll go and tell Gull,' Margot said, moving quickly.

The nurses scattered. Minnie went back to loading instruments onto the surgical trolleys. The rows of beds had been carefully organised, so that the most seriously injured were first, behind them was the row for the next most serious, and so on. She found a box of intravenous drips.

'Lola,' she called. 'Were you looking for the drips earlier?'

Lola took them from her with a smile. 'Thanks, Minnie. I've nearly got this row finished. Just pyjamas and towels to go on each bed. She blew a few stray hairs from her brow, sticky in the heat. 'I must say, I'm getting sick of the smell of burning rubber.'

Minnie nodded. 'Me too. But better the stink than the Japs get the rubber plantations. We can't make it too easy for them.'

Mona came past with a trolley loaded with jugs of water and teapots. 'Drinks for the fridge, water for tea for the next couple of days,' she said.

Eventually the trolleys were ready. Minnie did one last count, just as the familiar whine of the air raid siren sounded yet again.

'Hats, girls! Men, if you can get under your bed, do it now!' She reached for her helmet, strapped it on and ran to the nearest row of patients. She reached Sergeant Thomas as he was leaning over, casting around for his pan.

'Here you go,' she said. 'Keep it on until we get the all clear.'

'Sister, my bedpan needs emptying.' It was Fred, a once tall, cheerful man and a favourite of the nurses, who'd lost his legs the week before.

Minnie dashed to the open window and sloshed the contents out. 'Here,' she said, putting a towel inside it as she ran back. 'Now put the damn thing on your head.'

'Yes, nurse,' he said and grinned. 'It's not all glamour, is it?' he added, his bedpan sitting at a jaunty angle over his left eye.

'Stop talking, Fred, and hang on to your hat!' Minnie dragged another bedpan from under the bed next to him and placed it over the face of a patient who'd been unconscious all morning.

'Everyone, stay down!' Hazel yelled.

The planes roared overhead, shaking the windows like leaves, making the ground tremble with the thud of bombs as they hit the grounds of the hospital again and again. Minnie crouched next to the row of beds, trying to count them, so that she could guess when the attack would end. More than five. More than ten. Still they came, the bombs dropping from the sky, trying to find them. She pulled her helmet a little tighter, as if it would make any difference.

Finally, the noise of the attack petered out and some of the nurses began to stir. Beth and Minnie nodded to each other and struggled to their feet.

Then came a different sound. The booming of cannons.

'Artillery fire,' Matron Paschke said. 'Brace yourselves, everyone. Stay put and keep low.' The sound of bombs smothered the hospital and the walls shook. Small clods of plaster dropped from the ceiling and dust choked the air.

'Matron, we need to get out!' a voice called.

'Stay put. Don't let them know we're worried. If they see us running outside, we'll be target practice,' Matron Paschke called back.

Boom. Boom. Boom. The pounding on the walls became deafening. Minnie's teeth rattled no matter how hard she clamped them together. The tremors came closer. Louder. Until finally a blast smashed into the corner of the ward, and the wall shuddered into fragile bricks, giving way in slow motion.

'I think the bloody wall is going to come down!' It was Mona, staring wide-eyed at the hole.

'It'll hold!' another voice called out hopefully. It wobbled again, and the nurses' and orderlies' heads shot up to watch it tremble, bricks pushed inwards. Beth and Mona were closest. They dashed to the bed in the corner and dragged it away, the patient still lying helplessly on top, gazing wide-eyed at the hole in the wall. The room filled with dust and Lola started coughing loudly.

'Bloody Japs!' she yelled. She shoved a bedpan back at a pale-faced patient. 'Keep it on, for God's sake!'

There was a pause in the shelling, and then it started again. Minnie glanced around for Margot and saw her curled in the doorway, her eyes clamped shut and her arms visibly shaking. She wanted to call out to her, but she worried anything she'd call out would make it worse, and that Margot's determination to hide her panic was all that was holding her together. To her left she could hear Lola, humming tunelessly to herself, having stepped away for the moment into one of her picture shows.

Dear Oliver, Minnie thought. *I'm still being brave.* She rubbed her sweating palms on her skirt, gritted her teeth and thought of her mother, watching the door.

'Sorry! We're not in for visitors today!' Mona called out, and Minnie heard giggles. Her heart fluttering, she crawled across to the window and peered outside. 'Looks like the tennis courts are gone, along with the marquees,' she reported quietly. 'And the kitchen is flattened. I hope the amahs and orderlies got out.'

'All right, nurses, on your feet,' Matron Drummond said. 'Let's clear this mess up so we're ready for next time. Mona, Lola, Hatty, can you do a quick check on our patients, please? Let me know immediately if anyone needs medical assistance.' Matron Drummond stood slowly and began to dust off her knees. Even the sight of the matron on her feet again gave the nurses confidence. They were back to work.

'Yes, Matron.'

Minnie headed to the bed at the end of the ward, where Fred lay quietly. 'Are you all right, Fred?'

His hand came up slowly and removed his bedpan. He was smiling. 'I hope we get to keep these after the war. I feel as if this bedpan and I are becoming old friends.'

'Just let me know if the orderlies are doing a good job washing them out. I imagine you'll be the first to notice if standards start to slip!'

Minnie began to help the other soldiers back into their beds. The guns and bombs were close, but Matron Drummond was there with a calmness beneath the thunder of battle that made Minnie feel ready for almost anything. *Concentrate on what is before you*, she told herself. *Don't worry about what you can't control.*

But the attacks grew worse. The Japanese Army bombarded Singapore with artillery shells and peppered the homes with machine-gun fire. Houses lay open to the monsoon rains, bodies still trapped inside. The dead lay in the streets with no one to collect them. The roads ran with sewage after the rains came and the air was thick with smoke, burning rubber and the smell of diesel.

St Patrick's filled with wounded soldiers, injured as the Japanese squeezed them into their trap. They ran out of beds, and the men were forced to lie on stretchers, then the floor, in garages, tents and dugouts. The nurses piled their travelling trunks around their patients, pulling tarps over the temporary walls to keep them under-cover and hidden, safe from the rains that came each day, but not safe from the mosquitoes and the endless howls of the Nells as they ploughed the skies above. Minnie slept with a towel wrapped around her head; it was unbearably hot, but it muffled the sound, and dulled the glow from the burning rubber plants and oil refiner-ies as they threw black smoke like plumes of funeral feathers into the air.

At night, in the darkness of their dormitory, Lola prayed, while Minnie, Margot and Beth sat by in silent vigil, mending their uni-forms, rolling bandages, talking in low voices about their homes and those to whom they would return one day. As the attacks tumbled down upon them in a firestorm they waited for blessed silence, which never came.

The army started preparations for the loss of Singapore, for evacuation. The nurses dragged white sheets and some red fabric Matron Drummond had bought in a market to form a huge red cross on the lawn outside St Patrick's, hoping that it might afford them some mercy. It didn't seem likely. 'These bastards don't care about the Red Cross,' Beth had growled. 'They're savages!' And as if they had heard her, the Japanese flew low overhead, machine gunning around the hospital, forcing the patients to reach for their helmets and duck for cover again.

'Can't you dig a bit faster?' Minnie asked. 'Just give me the shovel and I'll give it a go.'

'You won't be any better,' Beth grunted.

'Nonsense, I've dug a few post holes in my time.'

Minnie glanced around at the grounds of St Patrick's, at the fine buildings and the playing fields, now covered in jeeps and tents, and then back into the hole where the earth was dark. Orderlies were digging beside them, making a huge trench, deep enough, but not so deep they couldn't dig down again like pirates, one day.

Beth sighed and climbed out of the hole, her face red with exertion and wet with sweat. 'Do your best then, we've got at least ten more of these to bury before we go.'

Minnie glanced up to count their trunks, filled with their favourite clothes, photos, letters, jewellery and knitting. They had twelve left. There was no room for trunks on the small ships that would take them to safety, only knapsacks. They could escape, but they had to travel light, and they had little room for sentiment.

Minnie scraped another shovelful of earth onto the pile. The humid air was thick, filled with the scent of oil and ashes. She wiped her face with her handkerchief and kept going. It was a slim hope they'd return for their belongings, but it was the best hope they had; there were a few ships ready to take them through the firestorm of Singapore Harbour and home, but who knew what would happen to those they left behind?

'We'll be back,' Minnie assured Lola. 'I'll count out how many steps we are from the fence and we'll either come ourselves, or we'll write a letter, give the coordinates, like a treasure map.'

'It'll be like Christmas,' Lola said. 'All our things arriving from Singapore, perhaps a year later. It'll give us something to look forward to.'

'I'll probably be too fat to wear any of these clothes by the time I see them again,' Beth said, shovelling a large sod of soil. 'I'm going to go home and have a batch of scones and a bottle of beer a day every day until I explode.'

'I'll come visit you and we can have a couple of batches together,' Minnie told her. She dragged her trunk into the hole. It slithered down the side and landed at an angle, so she gently kicked it into position like a small coffin and gave it a pat goodbye.

Beth sat down on the ground with a thump. 'What's the favourite thing you've buried?'

'Letters,' Minnie said. 'Mostly from Mum – a couple have pressed flowers in them from her garden. And a letter Oliver wrote to me years ago, when I was going through a hard time as a junior nurse. I was a poor student, convinced I couldn't complete the training. It's the only letter he ever wrote to me. I can still hear his voice when I read it – as if part of me has forgotten he died. *Be brave – don't forget the girl who gave her headmistress a piece of her mind and found her way home. You'll be all right with these nurses. Just don't forget how brave you are, and know you'll always find your way.*'

Margot sighed loudly and jumped back down into the hole. She opened Minnie's case and began rummaging around in her things.

'What are you doing?' Minnie said.

'I'm looking for that damn letter,' Margot told her as a Hurricane roared overhead. 'You're going to need it.'

The final days in Singapore flew by. It would surely fall, and soon.

'We're here to see Dracula.' A group of soldiers holding their slouch hats stood in the doorway, silhouetted in the tropical light.

Minnie stopped taking the pulse of a soldier just out of surgery. 'He's in Ward C,' she said. 'But if you're hoping to donate blood, I should warn you, he'll probably knock you back.'

'Why? We're all fit.'

'I assume you're just back from duty in the jungle? Malaria. We can't risk it, blood-borne disease, you know.'

'We're fine, and these blokes need our blood.'

'But they don't need a bout of malaria.'

'Bloody mosquitoes.'

'You *can* be some help, if you like.'

'Love to, Sister. What do you need?'

'Well, it's nearly sundown. Can you help us put the blankets up in the windows?'

'Of course.' The sergeant held out his hand. 'Wally. Happy to help.'

'Thanks, Wally, the blankets are in that box over there. If you just hang them over the curtain rail, that would be great.'

Wally took the first few blankets and slung them over the rail, and the ward dimmed a little. 'Must get hot in here,' he said.

'Yeah, stinking hot, and now we can't even cool it down with the night breeze.'

'You girls deserve a medal,' Wally said. 'More than one.'

'I could do without the medals. I just want to see the end of the war. And have a day without the smell of antiseptic and blood.'

'Don't hold your breath.'

'Really?' Margot said. 'Because sometimes I find that actually helps.'

'Nurse!' Fred called out from his bed at the end of the ward. 'I was wondering if I ever told you about my dog, Colin? I've thought of a good story for you, if you've got time?'

'Of course I do, Fred, I'll come and change those dressings while we talk.'

'You're a kind girl,' Fred called back. 'One day they'll make a statue of you lot – and I'll bloody salute!'

CHAPTER 8

MARGOT
Singapore
February 1942

The long hot night was spent nursing Australian, Indian and British soldiers. And Gull. As the fighting in the jungle had grown more desperate, more stretchers were called for, more antiseptic, more bandages. Margot felt as if she ran all night, prepping the wounded for surgery, bringing them precious water, before spending every spare minute with Gull, who lapsed in and out of consciousness.

She paused for a moment to help Lola with a Sikh soldier, cutting his uniform away from his chest wound. His turban was askew and she reached up to remove it.

'Stop, nurse!'

She froze.

Matron Drummond glared at her.

'Matron?'

'Did you not hear the directive? We are *not* to remove turbans or daggers unless the patient is conscious and able to give consent.'

'It doesn't look very comfortable, Matron.'

'Your patient will tell you if he'd like his turban removed when he regains consciousness, Sister McNee. Leave it.'

'Yes, Matron.' She stepped back from the soldier apologetically.

By mid-afternoon the ward had filled with yet more casualties. The Japanese were closer, they were taking ground, they were winning battles, and the injured were streaming into the wards, battered and bleeding. Margot noticed one soldier lying quietly on his stretcher, his face almost pure white. It was his unnatural stillness she noticed the most. Not a twitch, or a wince of pain. She knelt beside him. He was young, with a deeply tanned face and stubble on his chin. Tentatively, she lifted his blanket to check his injuries. She gasped. The stretcher was awash with blood. She dropped the blanket, her breath held tight. He opened his bright blue eyes and gave her a wink.

'Still here,' he whispered.

The bombs fell like doom, then like confetti, as if they didn't matter at all, and the nurses worked on, barely raising their heads to check the roof was still intact. The dead continued to arrive. Strangers, and then, inevitably, some friends they'd made before the fighting took over their lives. One morning they heard Jock McTaggart and his friend, who'd taught Beth and Lola the reel on the *Queen Mary*, were both killed while fighting in the jungle at Jahore. A young officer was shot by machine-gun fire as he tried to defend his troops from the Japanese tanks coming from the north. Another young soldier came in with multiple chest wounds and insisted on having a cigarette before surgery. When he took a puff, smoke curled out of three holes in his chest.

They didn't have time to cry. They didn't dare. They camped in abandoned homes, left empty by families fleeing the Japanese. At night they took to sleeping beneath the houses where it was cooler, and where the sound of the planes and the bombing was more muffled, their hands reaching for each other in the darkness and holding on tightly as if the war could pull them apart before sunrise.

The inevitable evacuation became a constant topic of conversation. *The Japs raped more nurses and forced their officers to watch; the Japs captured some nurses and forced them to walk in front of Japanese troops in case of snipers or booby traps; other medical facilities had received targeted bombing, casualties were huge . . .*

Colonel Wells asked his superiors every day for the nurses to be evacuated, and every day it was delayed.

'I was offered some morphia today,' Lola said, as she poured tea into enamel mugs on the verandah.

'Morphia? Why? What's wrong with you?' Margot asked.

'Nothing at all. It was Smithy from the pharmacy. He quite likes me, and he thought I might like to keep a dose. Just in case.'

Margot sipped her tea. It was practically dishwater, but they were trying to make the pot last so they'd topped it up with boiling water at least three times. 'Whatever for?'

'To kill myself peacefully in case the Japs get here.'

'*What?*' Margot put down her mug.

'He's heard what they do and he wanted to help.'

'Did you take it?' Beth asked.

'No, I'd rather use it on the patients.'

'I'd take it. One glimpse of a Jap coming at me and I'd chew it right down, glass and all,' Hazel declared.

'I heard some officers talking about it last week. They said they'd shoot us before they let us fall into enemy hands,' Minnie said.

'Oh, they *will*, will they?' Lola asked. 'I heard the same thing and I tapped Captain Callishore on the shoulder and said, "Hang on, if the Japs *do* take Singapore, I'm *only* twenty-five. I'll take my chances, please."'

'What did he say to that?'

'Not much.'

'They'll get us all out in time, nurses and patients,' Margot said.

'Is this talk of evacuation?' Matron Drummond and Matron Paschke had arrived with their mugs in hand. 'Our place is beside the men. We didn't join the war to run away when things become difficult.'

'No, Matron, we didn't. But we must follow orders.' Matron Paschke gazed sternly about. 'We are officers of the Australian Army and we have sworn to follow orders, regardless of how we feel about them. If we're ordered onto the ships, then we owe it to our country to follow orders, or we are no better than undisciplined rabble.'

'But if we scamper like frightened rabbits in the face of danger and neglect our medical duty, we are no better than rabble anyway,' Matron Drummond replied.

Margot and Lola sipped their tea. Silence fell.

And more bombs exploded into Orchard Road.

'Nurses,' Matron Paschke said, 'the *Wah Sui* is leaving port today with one hundred and twenty passengers on board. Now, she's only a riverboat, but she's painted with the Red Cross and she's already made a successful run to Java. I have a list of nurses here who will be sailing on her, to accompany their patients. There will be no discussion, this is an order. Those nurses whose names I read out will have one hour to pack.'

'But, Matron, I can't go yet, we have too many wounded coming in every day.' There were tears in Lola's eyes. 'I could go later, I could stay a few more days to help, surely? We need everyone—'

'I'm sorry, nurses. These are our orders.' Matron Paschke began to read the list, and the nurses sat in silence. 'Sisters Heffernan, Terrell, Palmer, Baldwin, Newland, Healy . . .'

Margot froze, hoping she wouldn't hear her name and, at the same time, hoping she would. She'd stopped sleeping, instead listening to the fighter planes coming back from sorties, waiting for a siren to tell her to rush to the wards to watch over the patients in an attack. She yearned to fall asleep in the comfort of her own bed, and to wake to the sound of the train making its way past the pine trees at Cottesloe early in the morning on its way to Fremantle. She couldn't leave. It was her duty to nurse the wounded. The thought of abandoning them and her new friends was worse than her fear, and she clenched her fists tightly, trying to hold on to Singapore with all her might. The names kept coming. Lola gasped and Margot realised Stella Godwin had been called.

'I was hoping Stella could stay on for a few more days,' Lola muttered. 'She'll be very upset.'

Margot glanced around to see that Stella's face was damp with tears. 'Where's Beth?' she whispered.

'She's making herself busy on the ward so they won't be able to send her away.'

Margot smiled. Good old Beth. She watched sadly as a group of girls stood and went to fetch their things, in tears. So far her name had not been called.

'And the final name, Minnie Hodgson.'

'Oh, Minnie.' Gladys, a nurse Minnie had worked beside in surgery that week, was crestfallen. 'You're going home.'

Minnie squeezed her hand. 'Toss you for it,' she said. 'I'm sure you have a nice man to go home to.'

Gladys paused. 'All right,' she said. 'You throw, I'm terrible at coin tosses. Tails you go, heads, I do.'

Minnie pulled out a penny and flicked it with her thumb. It sparkled high in the air before twirling back down to her palm, weighed down by chance. She slapped it onto the back of her hand.

'Heads or tails?' Gladys asked.

Minnie lifted her hand and glanced down. 'Heads. You're leaving on the *Wah Sui*,' she said, 'and good luck to you!' She turned and disappeared through the crowd.

'Minnie,' Gladys called, 'you didn't show me the coin!'

But it was too late: she was gone.

'Excuse me, nurse?' A young corporal stood puffing and sweating in his uniform.

'Yes?' Margot said.

'We hear you girls are on your way home.'

'Some of us are. Gladys here is going, although with all the bombing, who can tell?'

'Well, I've got a couple of letters here from my mates for our families. Would you mind taking them with you? You could post them when you get home.'

Gladys reached out and took them from him. She smiled. 'Of course. I'll be sure to post them as soon as I get ashore at Perth.'

'Thanks so much. Good luck.'

'To you too.'

Matron Paschke held her hands up to get the attention of the nurses as they made tearful farewells. 'Those names who were called. There are ambulances waiting to take you to the ship. Be quick, and good luck!'

'Jesus Christ, that's a blow.' Beth had arrived and was watching the nurses depart. 'How are we going to nurse the rest of the wounded after they've gone? We'll only be getting more patients, not less.'

Matron Paschke spoke to the group again. 'The next group of nurses will follow soon. You may be aware that the Japanese are patrolling the South China Sea, both with ships and planes. They are attacking anyone they see trying to leave the region. Our retreat will be dangerous, but I know we are up to the task.' She took out a clipboard. 'Now. I need as many of you as possible to volunteer to evacuate tomorrow. We intend to break our nursing service into two groups. Fifty-nine of you will board the *Empire Star*, and a further sixty-five will board the *Vyner Brooke*. If no one volunteers, I will pick names and you will be ordered to leave. We don't know when the Japs will take over the city, but we all know what happened to the nurses in Hong Kong. It's time to go, girls, whether we like it or not.'

'Are you putting your name down, Margot?' Lola was watching the nurses moving about the mess, talking about how the evacuation would play out, where the patients were to go, how they would fit, what medical supplies they'd need.

Margot sighed. 'I'll stay on for as long as I can. I'm worried about Gull. His hand is looking dreadful and I'm desperately hoping we can travel on the same ship.'

'I'm sure it's just a temporary setback and there are so few ships left now, I think you've got a good chance. You mustn't worry too much.'

'But I do. I was helping Matron Paschke decide who should go on the *Wah Sui* and his name came up. I can't bear the thought we might be separated.'

'I'm staying on too,' Beth said. 'But I'm getting hold of a pistol and I'm going to shoot those bastards if they come into my hospital. You'll see.'

The *Empire Star* was to sail at dawn. The nurses had collected their things and walked up the gangplank in tears, glancing back towards the blazing fires and the cheery waving hands of their sisters.

'Goodbye! Good luck! See you in Australia! See you when we all get home! Don't get seasick!'

Margot fell into step next to a nursing friend. 'I hope you make it back to Adelaide in time for your brother's baby,' she said. 'I think being a doting aunt will make a lovely change from all these damn bombs.'

'Yes, if we make it.' She glanced around. 'I didn't think it would come to this, Margot. Not Singapore. I thought the rules were *the British always win*. But they haven't. And the Japanese don't abide by the *rules*.' She stepped onto the gangplank. 'It's luck of the draw at this point.' She gave Margot a brief hug. 'It's been wonderful to work with you and I wish you well.'

'And to you too. I'll pray you get through.'

Torrents of Japanese twin-engine bombers flew overhead and more bombs smashed into the sea at the edge of the harbour, sending white plumes of water into the sky. Then the British planes came over the horizon, flying low with guns blazing to chase them away. It wasn't going to work. The nurses wept as they left, waving handkerchiefs and hanging over the edge of the ship as it drew further away.

'Goodbye!' Margot and Minnie stood on the dock as the *Empire Star* began a mighty turn.

'Good luck!' Minnie called out. 'I hope you make it home.'

'I'm sure they will,' Margot said. 'They'll catch a huge tide and be down to Darwin before they know it. They won't even have time for a shipboard romance.'

'I feel as if I deserve a shipboard romance,' Minnie said.

'Then we'll make sure you're carefully positioned next to Captain Blair,' Margot said, giving her an affectionate nudge in the ribs.

The *Empire Star* seemed to tremble, her mighty engines churning the dark water beneath as she pushed out to meet her fate. The ocean was so large, Minnie thought. They'd be able to hide among the islands, to creep along until they were close to home. They'd make it. Despite the warm, heavy air around her, she shivered.

And still more bombs sounded like thunder in the distance.

Minnie took Margot's hand as they gathered their knapsacks together and headed for St Andrew's Church to sleep. Margot had spent her meagre time off tending to Gull again. He was slow to recover, and she watched him anxiously, willing his injuries to heal.

'We'll be all right, Margot,' Minnie assured her friend. 'We'll get out tomorrow. You'll see.'

Margot nodded and gripped Minnie's hand tighter still. The streets were alive with the movement of a million frightened Singaporeans. Abandoned cars huddled together in the crush with nowhere to go, and people called out to each other under a sky heavy with clouds, filled with planes seeking each other out above the chaos.

'I hope those bastards shut up soon,' Beth grumbled from her spot on the back pew. 'I'm tired enough to sleep for a week.'

'We might get some rest on the way home I suppose,' Lola murmured into her knapsack.

'I hope so,' Minnie said. 'I'm exhausted, but every time I close my eyes, I find myself worrying if we have enough medical supplies for the trip.'

'Probably not,' Beth said and sniffed. 'I think most of it will have headed out on the *Wah Sui* and the *Empire Star*. We'll probably have to make do.'

'As long as someone has handed you a pistol at some point, Beth, you can keep us safe while we try to keep the men alive,' Margot said.

'No pistols yet,' Beth said, 'but I've let it be known I'm happy to shoot first and ask questions later.'

'Good Lord,' Lola said. 'In that case, I hope they *don't* give you a gun.'

'I just hope we make it to the ship and don't get bombed in the night,' Margot said.

'They won't bomb us,' Minnie said. 'They're too scared of Beth.'

'But if they *do* bomb us,' Beth said, nodding, 'I'll have a nice big statue in the middle of Townsville of me holding a rifle in one hand and a bedpan in the other.'

'Oh,' Lola said. 'If I get bombed, I'd like a statue of me in my red dress, singing a song to the troops and holding a chrysanthemum.'

'That's terribly specific,' Minnie said. 'Any reason?'

'I love to sing?' Lola replied.

'No, I meant the—'

A massive, bone-shaking explosion rattled the windows of the church and the girls scooted together, huddling on the floor in a heap. Margot reached out and grasped Minnie's hand.

'Dear Lord, I need the lavatory now!' Minnie muttered.

'Oh, for goodness' sake,' Lola huffed.

'Too late for me!' Beth said.

Margot squeezed Minnie's fingers as her blood, warmed by the affectionate giggling around her, began to flow gently through her heart again.

Margot woke before dawn, collected her knapsack and her helmet, smoothed the Red Cross on her sleeve like a talisman, then crept to the door. Glancing back at the sleeping girls, she dashed into the darkness.

'Gull, we're leaving today.' She stroked his hair and he seemed to rouse a little at her touch. 'I'll stay with you as long as I can, then I've got to get back to St Andrew's for embarkation. I've spoken to the orderlies, they'll make sure we end up on the same ship, I promise.'

'Margot . . .' Gull's voice was sleepy, and she hoped it was due to his pain medication. 'Are the Japs here?'

'Nearly, they're knocking at the door.' She squeezed his hand. 'We're leaving today on a hospital ship. We're getting out, Gull.'

Gull smiled. 'Good news. I hope they have room for all the men.'

'Yes, it'll be tight, though.' She leaned closer. 'Who are you looking forward to seeing?'

'My mother, of course, she's a good woman, very no nonsense, and my father – he was happy for me to see some of the world, but I know he's been wanting me home for a while. I didn't think I was ready, but I didn't want to disappoint them. The war was an excuse, really. I'll be glad to shake his hand again and tell him I'm back for good. And I have a young nephew I've never met. I'd like to teach him to play cricket.'

'Well, don't teach him to play cards, or he'll end up driving pigs about strange cities . . .'

'He'll be a lucky man if he does.'

Margot kissed his cheek. 'Good luck, Gull. I'll see you on board.'

'Make sure you do. We've lost enough as it is. I can't lose you too.'

'You won't. I'll be with you, all the way home.'

'Nurses, we have one hour to be on the dock. Gather your things and bring your helmets.' Matron Drummond and Matron Paschke stood side by side.

Margot rolled over and stood, groggily. She'd often thought of the day they would leave, and now she was almost frightened to get onto a ship. 'I think we've left our run too late,' she said to Beth.

'Nah. We'll be right,' Beth said and sniffed. 'They can't kill us all. We've only got to last a few more days and we'll be free of these bastards.'

'I'm glad you're here, Beth. You have a way of giving me confidence.'

'Glad to hear it,' Beth said. 'I know I'm not a particularly fancy sort of woman, but I'd like to think I can still be a comfort to a friend – in my own way.' Beth leaned against Margot for just a moment and then marched outside for a cigarette.

Light was filtering in under the blankets they'd placed in the windows, but it was still early, and a few of the old noises to which they'd grown accustomed remained. A rooster crowed somewhere and a motorbike tooted its horn. The hour passed quickly.

'Here, you want a tin of bully beef or baked beans for the trip?'

'Better give me the beef. Might be the last meat we see for a while.'

'I wish I hadn't buried my copy of *Middlemarch*. It's just the sort of thing for a long trip home . . .' Hatty said.

'Shall I take Agatha Aspidistra?' Minnie asked.

'No, leave her here, she's a local now, and we don't have the space for her anyway,' Margot said.

'I think she'd rather go home with me.'

'Hang on, I'll ask her. Agatha? Do you like this warm weather? And that handsome orchid growing out by the verandah?' Beth threw a crushed set of pants into her knapsack. 'She says she wants to stay. She hates sea voyages as much as I do.'

'She's probably a better swimmer though,' Minnie said and grinned.

'Ha!'

Lola hummed to herself as she packed.

'What's that tune, Lola?' Margot asked.

'"We'll Meet Again", of course.' Lola smiled.

'It's very pretty, I recognise it now. I do love to hear your voice instead of what's going on outside.'

'Me too. When I sing, Margot, I can be anywhere at all. It's the most marvellous gift. If you hear me sing, you know I'm far away.'

'I think it's wonderful,' Margot said. 'Although Beth might disagree.'

Beth rolled her eyes.

'Quickly, nurses. Finish packing, it's time to go. The next ambulances are due here and we mustn't keep them waiting.' Matron Paschke was on the move again.

'Coming,' Lola said. She deposited a kiss on Agatha's outstretched leaf. 'Goodbye, Agatha. I hope Mr Orchid is everything you've dreamed.'

Beth was loaded down with a box of hospital supplies and a couple of knapsacks. She elbowed the door open and held it there for the others to pass through. Margot grabbed a medical bag and her kitbag and dashed past her to the waiting ambulance.

The streets of Singapore were in uproar. The weeks of bombing had taken their toll, spilling sewage onto the roads they passed over, battering the homes, which hung open and destroyed like dolls houses. Fires glowed in the harbour, consuming the remnants of ships and fuel supplies, the drains stank of decaying vegetation and death, as unclaimed bodies rotted in the heat. The families lining the docks formed long chaotic queues. Mothers gripped frightened children, crouching over them as each air raid siren blasted out. And still the bombers from Japan swooped over the fallen city, picking at its bones.

Everyone had heard the South China Sea was thick with enemy ships and bombers, but it was the only passage out of Singapore. Margot looked out in dismay at the harbour. The British and Dutch expats who'd delayed their departure were queuing to board the *Vyner Brooke*, but there wasn't going to be room for everyone, and some families would be left behind, their futures uncertain. Luxury motorcars were dumped in the streets, their doors wide open as children and wives piled out with heavy suitcases, dragging them desperately the final mile to the harbour, hoping for a blessed ship to take them to safety.

As the ambulance wove its way through the chaos, local Singaporean families thronged the streets, trying to escape the city. Children stepped over the dead, then crouched low under their mother's arms as the guns rattled around them. Most had stocked up on supplies, tins of food and bags of rice in the face of uncertainty, while some had brought live chickens. Anyone lucky enough with relatives on the outskirts of the city was moving out. How would the victorious Japanese treat them?

'Miss! Miss!' Two small Chinese children ran next to the ambulance. 'You have a boat?'

'I don't know, we're heading to the harbour, we haven't been told if there's a boat yet.'

'Do you have room for two? We're small! No trouble!'

'But where's your mother? Your father?'

'Our mother sent us to find a boat. Japanese coming!'

The ambulance lurched away, driving over a huge pothole and then a pile of crushed and abandoned leather suitcases. The crowds slowly cleared and the little boy was lost to them, holding his sister's hand, waving at them still, as if to say *come back,* or even just *goodbye.* Margot closed her eyes and said a prayer for them both, and then she added a prayer for Gull as well. She prayed he was all right, and that the porters were moving the wounded to the ship so that she would see him soon.

'Matron!' It was Colonel Wells. 'I see they're finally getting you girls out. Not a minute too soon.' A bomb exploded at the far end of the harbour and the crowd surged, scrambling up the dock like sheep. 'What vessel are you on?'

The matron glanced out into the harbour where the masts of sunken ships were still visible, and where a gaggle of small river-boats were gathering to take whoever climbed on board. The ships were small, and the harbor was smothered in smoke and oil.

'I believe we're about to be ferried out to the *Vyner Brooke*,' she told him.

'The *Vyner Brooke*? Are they mad? You'll never make it on that old bucket – not a hope in hell!' He held up his hand. 'Wait here. I'll go see what's going on.'

'Thank you, Colonel.'

'Matron? Is there something wrong with the ship?' Margot glanced about at the carnage.

'No, there's nothing wrong. Colonel Wells is just making sure it's our best option.'

Margot glanced at a gangplank suspended over the dark water where a tall man was carrying a baby and a suitcase onto a black riverboat. His wife was pushing at his back, urging him to hurry before the gangplank was drawn up.

There was a ripple through the long queue as Colonel Wells made his way back. Another plane scorched the sky above them and the start of his explanation was lost to the wind.

'Oh, thank *Christ*!' A sweating man with a moustache and a pale cream linen suit dropped his suitcase in front of Matron Drummond and Margot. 'I was hoping I'd find Australians. You *are* Australian?'

'We are Australian Army and Navy nurses,' Matron Drummond said.

'Thought so. I know you'll be able to help me.' He gestured around them at the chaos. 'Bit of a jam. I just said to the wife, if we can get to the harbour there'll be some transport ships heading out.' He began to beckon, waving to his wife and children. She'd been crying, but, at his signal, she broke into a weak smile and swept her arm around her two small sons, ushering them closer.

'You'll have room for us . . .' the man said.

'I'm afraid—' Matron Drummond began.

'We'll sleep on the deck—'

'I believe the deck may already be spoken for. I'm afraid I have no say in who—'

'Oh, for pity's sake! We'll sleep in the damn galley; we'll cook and clean. We'll sleep in the bloody engine room.' His voice cracked. 'Please. We've been here two days. Please help us!'

'I'm very sorry, sir, I have no control over who is evacuated. I truly hope there is someone here to help you, but it's not me.' Matron Drummond squeezed his arm lightly, blinking as her glasses fogged in the Singaporean heat.

Colonel Wells returned, and the man and his family moved away, helpless. 'I'm sorry, Matron,' the colonel said. 'The *Vyner Brooke* it is, I'm afraid. Nothing else available.' He shook her hand, his face apologetic. 'Don't worry, I'm sure you'll be fine. You'll get through the China Sea and be in Darwin before you know it.'

'I'm sure we will, Colonel. Thank you.'

He took out a bottle and handed it to the matron. 'Here, take this with you. Just in case.'

'You won't need a nip of brandy here, Colonel?' she asked him.

'No, Sir Thomas has ordered the destruction of all alcohol in Singapore.'

'That seems a bit grim. Is the situation not bad enough already?'

'It's about to get a lot worse. The Japs were drunk when they committed those atrocities after our surrender in Hong Kong. Sir Thomas wants to either reduce the chances they'll repeat the behaviour or take away their excuse when they do.'

Matron Drummond nodded. 'How wise.' She glanced at the bottle in her hand. 'I'm sure we'll find use for it if our morphia runs out. Thank you, Colonel, and good luck.'

'Good luck to you all.' Colonel Wells saluted and disappeared into the crowd.

The *Vyner Brooke* was by no means a big steamship. Requisitioned by the Royal Navy and fitted with guns to protect her as she navigated the waters between Singapore and Australia, she now sat in the middle of the harbour, her dull grey body floating low in the water. Margot surveyed her. She was going to have to do.

'What's your problem?' Beth asked her.

'Oh, nothing, I was just wondering if she's too big – and she'll be easily spotted by the Japanese – or too small, and we won't all fit.'

'As long as she floats,' Beth said. 'We're in no position to be fussy.'

'Nurses,' Matron Paschke called. 'Off we go, into the boats. Make sure you have your knapsacks. We're not coming back.'

CHAPTER 9

MINNIE
Singapore
12–13 February 1942

Singapore was on fire. The sun was setting as the matrons, Minnie, Margot, Beth, Lola, Mavis and a handful of other nurses sat squashed in the tiny boat. They were moving slowly and carefully through the harbour. Minnie glanced overboard and stared into the stained water, slick with oil, diesel and debris. Before long, they reached the *Vyner Brooke* and climbed aboard through a steel door in the ship's side.

'We went to a dinner party on this ship a while back,' Matron Drummond remarked, as she ducked her head under a cable reaching across the doorway.

'That must have been a thousand years ago, Matron,' Lola said.

Matron Drummond handed her the bottle of brandy she'd been clutching. 'It certainly was.'

Minnie turned and watched Singapore burn. It had been a year since they'd arrived in the bustling city, full of anticipation. Churchill's Gibraltar of the East had seemed so bright, so brimming with fabrics and flowers, anointed with steaming rains, teeming with squawking chickens, the aromas of spicy curries, and huge mud crabs cracked open and pulled apart in tiny dimly lit restaurants. Now the ruined city was illuminated against the night sky, the flames almost as high as its crumbling buildings. Everywhere there was the stink of fear.

Here was the fall of a city, the rattling of an empire. The water was black, except where it glowed, reflecting the flames taking over, as Singapore descended into chaos.

'All right, girls, find yourselves a space, and try to keep your things out of the way. We don't want falls or lost items this early on in our voyage.' Matron Drummond swayed for a moment as she collected her sea legs, and surveyed her new domain. Her uniform was starched perfection, giving no quarter to the chaos around her. Minnie glanced down at her own, still in reasonable shape, but wrinkled following the work of loading equipment and luggage onto the trucks and the long wait to board. Still, it would do. They would be able to wash and iron them again at home, soon enough.

Mavis, Beth and Lola made a nest in one of the large lifeboats on board. It was a handy spot to store their things, and it gave a clear view of any dangers. Another group of nurses nestled beside them on deck. They chatted quietly as they stowed their knapsacks and a few spare towels they'd found. Beth had a tobacco pouch, which she was stuffing into her knapsack for another day. Minnie was glad – if she accidentally flicked a match out into the oily water, she was worried they'd all go up in flames.

'Minnie,' Margot called over the crowd. 'Help me find Gull. They brought the patients on an hour ago, but I can't see him.'

Minnie pushed through the milling nurses and crew. 'He'll be down below. I think I saw Fred taken down earlier.' She put her arm around Margot's shoulder and gave it a brief squeeze. 'We'll find him.'

They slowly made their way downstairs, following mothers holding on to sweaty children's hands and old ladies clutching at the rail to keep themselves secure. They entered a large reception area, in which the patients were lying on stretchers. Minnie gazed over the faces of men so injured they'd already passed out from the effort of being moved. Others were chatting comfortably, drinking water from their canteens to stay hydrated.

'Gull!' Margot found him and dashed to his side. Minnie followed and saw him wake, his eyes immediately finding Margot.

'Why hello,' he said, weakly. 'I'm pleased to see you.'

'Me too. I wasn't sure you'd be on board this ship.' She kissed his cheek. 'But I'm so glad you are.'

'Can you stay a moment?' Gull asked hopefully.

'Just a quick moment, Matron Drummond is giving orders like it's her ship!'

'You take your time,' Minnie told them. 'I'll cover for you. I'm sure there's nothing as urgent as looking after our patients.'

Just as she spoke a soldier nearby said, 'Hello, Sister!'

Minnie looked at the patient who'd lost both legs, but was still smiling up at her. 'Fred! I'm so glad you're on board with us. I regard myself as the expert in changing your dressings.'

'I'm grateful for your help. I hope my wife can do half as good a job as you.'

'I'm sure she can, with some practice. Soon you'll be neatly healed and out rounding up the sheep with Colin again.'

Fred's eyes warmed at the thought. 'He's a bloody good dog, Colin.'

Minnie laughed. 'And your wife?'

'She's pretty good too.' He grinned.

Smiling, Minnie headed back upstairs, glancing at Gull and Margot, so wrapped up in each other's company they barely noticed she'd left.

'Help us! Help! Let us aboard!' A pair of canoes had made it to the middle of the harbour. Minnie could make out two Chinese men and two women, along with an old lady and five children. 'Take us with you!' one of the men called out. 'Please! Our home is gone! Don't send us back!' His hand looked burned and his shirt was torn. Minnie could imagine what it must have taken for them to get into the canoes and to paddle so far out into the harbour. The Chinese knew they would be targeted by the conquering Japanese Army, and they knew their chances of survival were slim. She looked back to see the crew watching a small flotilla of rafts and canoes following them, their bodies leaning forward in their tiny vessels, desperate to hear an invitation to survive.

'I'm sorry,' the first officer finally said. 'We just can't carry any more. Your best bet is to wait at the dock for evacuation. The army there is doing its best.' The regret in his voice was heavy.

'We'll never get out! Just one more family!' Even though the man's voice didn't break, Margot could see his face contorting in the light from the fires reflected in the water. He was crying.

'Couldn't we take just a few more?' Matron Drummond asked the first officer.

'I'm afraid not,' he said. 'We're to take injured men, nurses and civilians currently on the list. We're already short on food and water. We have to remain firm.' He shook his head and turned away.

'Oh dear,' Minnie sighed. 'Do you think Australia might send some more ships?'

There was no response, only more shouts that carried over the water, begging for passage far away from the flames of Singapore. Minnie sank down onto her haunches and stared at her feet, her blood running cold. So many people, and she couldn't help them at all. She took a deep breath and thought of Margot and Gull. It filled her with hope.

'Quickly, girls,' Matron Paschke called. 'Everyone to the main saloon. We'll be away soon.'

Finally, in the gloom of the terrible inferno, the *Vyner Brooke* eased slowly out of the harbour, waiting for her chance to run.

Nurses and civilians soon began to organise themselves, finding places to store their belongings and tending to the wounded, many of whom were now settled in bunks below deck.

'Would you nurses like a cabin? I'm sure a few of you can squeeze in together?' an officer asked them.

'No, thank you,' Matron Paschke said. 'The nurses will be on duty for most of the time we're aboard. I'm sure whatever arrangements they have secured already will prove more than adequate.' She motioned to Minnie to join her on her rounds.

'Nurses, we will be meeting in the saloon in half an hour to discuss our duties on board this ship. Our priority until then is our patients and the civilians. I believe there are around one hundred and fifty. I hope I don't need to remind you that Red Cross armbands are to be worn at all times. If the Japanese see them, it *may* protect the ship from attack.'

'Bloody fools,' muttered Mavis.

'Who?' Minnie asked.

'The damn civilians. They've known for months it wasn't safe to be here. *If not years*. And yet, here they are, with their *children* in the face of an enemy attack, begging for a ride. *Desperate*. They should have left under their own steam while the going was good.'

'Don't you think that's a bit harsh?'

'They knew what was coming and they've left their children here to suffer, and might I add, to take places on board the few ships that are going to get out. Thousands won't be able to leave now because these people were too arrogant to leave when they could. Rots my socks.'

'I think that's probably the humidity,' Lola said.

'And bloody fools who think bad things will never happen to them,' added Beth.

A child started to cry, and his mother pulled him into her arms. It had been a long and frightening day.

'Nurses!' Matron Drummond was glaring at them.

'Sorry, Matron.'

She nodded. 'Now, I've spoken with Captain Borton and I'm told we have limited water so there will be no bathing. I need you all to bring your tinned supplies and we will provide dinner for the civilians. It won't be a gourmet meal, but it will be something in everyone's stomach. Can I have volunteers to cook dinner for us all?' A few hands shot up. 'Good, Lola and Rita. You can take charge of the kitchen. See what you can do with some bully beef and baked beans, eh?'

The nurses gave enthusiastic salutes and headed for the kitchen on the lower deck.

'Are we sailing again soon?' Margot asked Beth.

'I think so. I was up on deck and we've come to a bit of a halt. Not sure why.'

Minnie climbed the stairs to the top deck and wandered out again to see Singapore. They were indeed stalled, the engines running. A crew member hurried past her. 'Excuse me,' Minnie said, touching his arm, 'what's going on? Are we lost?'

It was meant as a joke, but the man was sweating, and he didn't laugh. 'Not quite lost,' he said. 'We think we're heading into the mine field laid down to catch the Japs. The *Jarak* usually leads the ships out, but she's busy tonight. The captain is waiting it out for a while. There's enough light to see.' He gestured at the glowing harbour. 'But the smoke is hiding the buoys that will show us the safe way through.'

'So we could drift onto a sea mine?' Minnie whispered.

'Well, we're running the engines, so we shouldn't drift anywhere. We're just going to wait to make sure we're safe.' He smiled at her, but it gave her no confidence.

'I've got to head down to the wards shortly,' she said. 'Promise me we'll find a path out?'

'Promise. The captain's been through the South China Sea before.'

In the distance, two other ships were slowly making their way out of the harbour, their pale lights winking back at Minnie and the sailor.

'Look at that,' he said. 'I bet that's the route. I'd better get back to the bridge. See what the captain thinks.'

'Go,' whispered Minnie. 'And good luck.'

'I don't think we have any left,' he said. 'Might be a good time to start praying.'

Minnie said a little prayer then. She prayed to God to keep them safe, to save those souls left behind in Singapore, and those lying trapped in their ruined bodies below deck, but she knew prayers had been pouring from hearts all day, and that they had floated back down to earth, tangled in humidity and smothered in smoke.

Minnie watched the distant shore for a long time, waiting for the *Vyner Brooke* to find a path through the treacherous waters. Searchlights swept the sky, lighting up like huge beams from a rising sun.

'I can't decide if it's an incredible view, or the worst thing I've ever seen,' she said to herself. She sensed a presence and turned to see a beautiful and heavily pregnant young woman standing beside her.

'I think the latter,' the woman said. 'This is history in the making, isn't it? The British lose Singapore. It'll be in the papers for weeks.'

'Unless the Germans take London,' Minnie said.

'You sound like a farmer's daughter; a natural pessimist.'

'Not usually, you caught me on a bad day.' Minnie held out her hand. 'Minnie Hodgson, Australian nurse.'

'Charlotte Tunbridge-Beckersley. Pregnant wife of a mining executive. From Cambridge originally, but Singapore for the last four years.'

'Nice to meet you. How's baby coping with life at sea?'

'I believe he has his sea legs already. I'm peeing every five minutes, which means I'm permanently in the queue for the facilities. You won't see me much, I'll be gazing longingly at the bathroom doors until we reach Batavia.'

'If I come across an empty toilet, I'll let you know.'

'Much appreciated, I'm sure.'

'So it's a boy?'

'My husband is hoping so. Someone to carry on the family name and all that.'

'You'd like a boy too?'

'I'd rather a little girl, actually. Another female to talk to. But you know how it is – all children are a blessing – as long as it's a healthy baby, I'll be happy.' She stroked her swollen stomach, her floral cotton frock stretched tightly across its girth, like a hill of wildflowers.

'Henny? Henny!' A handsome woman, her long blonde hair in a low bun, was calling out in a European accent. She looked frantically up and down the deck of the ship.

'Can we help you find someone?' Minnie and Lola asked.

'My daughter. Henrietta Van der Feltz. She's a quiet girl. Upset by the loss of her home – I'm sure you can imagine.'

'Of course. Henny? We'll call out to her as we check the wards downstairs.'

'She's afraid of the ocean.'

'Oh, a few of the nurses are no fans of the sea, you should hear Sister Scanlon . . .'

'She saw men in cages, you see. Henny saw them. She's frightened.' The woman stopped. 'It's of no matter. I must know she is safe. If you see her, please send her to me.'

'Certainly.'

Night had fallen when Matron Drummond discovered Minnie sorting cans of food in the galley.

'Minnie, could you find Lola and Beth and see to the patients, please, we'll need the next round of morphia for some of the men soon. Check that they're settled.'

'Yes, Matron.'

Matron Drummond nodded and removed her spectacles to give them a brief polish on her apron. Her cheeks glowed in the heat and her sharp grey eyes cast up and down the deck, looking for nurses and patients, and helping parents who were struggling to find a spot for their children to watch the shoreline of the only home they'd known disappear into smoke.

Finally, the ship started to move again, slowly at first, and then with more confidence, pushing through the dark waters with gathering speed. Minnie glanced at her watch. 8.15 pm. She could hear singing. She turned to see Lola and a handful of nurses singing 'Waltzing Matilda' as the bombs dropped onto the shattered homes of Singapore.

The next morning Minnie woke to a beautiful fresh sky filled with sunshine. The *Vyner Brooke* was making her way through the islands of the China Sea, speeding to safer waters. The captain addressed the nurses, standing on a crate in front of the group to give his report.

'I'm afraid we are not as far from Singapore as I would have liked. We were delayed getting out of the harbour. The Japanese planes will be firing up already and heading out to search for us. I had hoped to be hiding next to one of these small islands by now – harder to spot from the air – but I think we'll be okay. Please keep the food coming for our passengers, two meals a day. We plan to make a dash for Batavia, which will mean travelling through the Bangka Strait.'

'You mean Bomb Alley?' Lola asked, incredulous.

'Well, yes, it has been called that. But we have little choice. Try not to worry too much, you do your job and I'll do mine.' He summoned Matron Drummond to speak. 'Now, Matron has divided the ship into districts. I believe you're all in charge of a different area, and an inspection of your nursing district will be conducted shortly. I'll leave you now so I can keep us safely away from the Japs.'

'Good luck!' Minnie called, and Captain Borton smiled.

'Good luck to us all,' he said.

Matron Drummond spoke. 'I will soon assign your nursing districts. Each one is to be maintained with proper discipline, good hygiene and, importantly, high morale. It's impractical to have drills for the use of the lifeboats, however, we need to discuss evacuation. The *Vyner Brooke* has six lifeboats on the promenade deck. If the order to abandon ship is given, you will hear long blasts from the ship's siren. The crew will take charge of lowering the boats. They hold a total of between one hundred and forty to one hundred and eighty people. Now, we seem to have extra passengers, but I'm told we have around two hundred and twenty-eight on board, which means that many of us will have to use the smaller life rafts. They're just over a yard square, and they have rope handles on the sides. You may fit one person, or perhaps two, back to back. Or you can hold on to the handle and stay in the water.'

'Sounds like fun,' Lola said.

'I don't want to end up in the soup,' Beth muttered. 'Especially not shark soup!'

'We may pray that it doesn't come to that, although I suspect it's rather in the hands of the Japanese,' Matron Drummond said.

'Soup time,' Beth grumbled.

'Please let me know if any of you can swim. In an emergency, you'll be giving up your spot in the boats and you'll be swimming and using the rafts. You can tie the rafts together to form a larger platform – each raft comes with two paddles.'

'Oh, good, so we won't be up the creek without a paddle, then?'

Matron ignored the interruption. 'As I'm sure you've guessed, non-swimmers have priority in the boats. Now.' She reached for a life vest and held it over her head. 'This is your life vest.'

'Just the one?' a voice called from the back, and laughter ran through the group.

'Don't be silly. We have plenty of vests, filled with kapok and cork.' She pulled the vest over her head. 'In the event of an evacuation, you will remove your shoes, hold the vest tightly, tuck your chin in, and jump feet first into the water. It is important to keep your chin tucked, girls, or you may snap your neck on impact.'

Minnie reached out and gave Margot's hand a quick squeeze. Margot squeezed weakly back. *Keep your chin, down, Minnie*, she told herself. *It's all for nothing if you snap your bloody neck.* A sickness rose within her like a tide and refused to abate.

Matron Drummond continued. 'Now, you will not abandon the ship until you have checked below deck to see that all of the passengers are out – and you are given the order by myself or Matron Paschke.'

'What if the ship is already at water level and we just float off?' Margot asked.

'As long as you float off on a raft, clutching a couple of civilians, I'm sure you could be forgiven.' Matron Drummond took a deep breath. 'Now that we've covered the basics, off you go. I'll be conducting an inspection to check that everything is in order. Nurses on lunch duty may then go to the kitchen and begin preparing our lunch. Thank you. That is all.'

'Well,' Beth said, as Matron Drummond departed for her inspection, 'it looks like we may be in for an interesting week.'

'Yeah. I only hope it's not *too* interesting,' Minnie said. 'I think we've had enough excitement already. I'm just here for the bully beef.'

'Me too. I hate the ocean. I'd be bloody seasick if I wasn't scared to death,' Beth grumbled.

'You? Scared to death?' Minnie smiled. 'Nothing scares you, Beth Scanlon, and don't you say it does.'

'I'm not scared of much,' Beth admitted. 'King browns. My Aunt Topsy. And being shot out of this tin can we're floating in.' She smiled back. 'That's about it.'

'Well, I think we'll be okay,' Minnie said. 'At least two of those fears seem unlikely to strike us down.' She headed inside to go below deck.

'Give me a hint!' Beth called after her. 'Which two?'

Minnie was grinning as she turned to answer, and she glimpsed the ocean leaping up into three shining waves, glistening under the sun and the blue sky.

And then she heard it.

The unmistakable sound of a Nell coming over the horizon.

She froze.

'Show them your armband,' she said calmly, and held out her arm, helpless against the swoop of the enemy's plane. She stopped. And as she looked up, she was certain she could see the pilot, that for a moment they looked into each other's eyes, before he dipped a wing, and turned for home.

'That's it,' Beth said. 'They've seen us.' She spat over the side of the ship. 'It won't be long now.'

Mrs Brown was a large British woman in a floral dress which was wilting around her. She was trailed by her daughter, Shelagh, who had a pale complexion and the expression of a disappointed Sunday school teacher. Mrs Brown was married to 'a very important businessman' in Singapore, which meant she was very busy with important social occasions, and liked to apprise others of her status on a regular basis. They arrived on the deck just as the Japanese plane departed over the horizon.

'Shelagh,' Mrs Brown was saying, 'I've had quite enough of waiting for my lunch. Do you think you could get one of the staff to put together a small plate of food? I don't believe it's asking too much.'

'No, mother,' Shelagh said, 'normally I'd say it's not, but I think we're rather short on food. And I suspect the captain has other things to worry about.'

'Oh, he does, does he? Well, I should think so, I *wasn't* suggesting we bother the poor man, Shelagh. I was referring to the *crew*. The nurses are here to help us all. Why *else* are we providing them with passage home?'

Beth balled her hands into fists and glared. Minnie raised both eyebrows and hoped she'd think better of throwing the woman overboard. Just as she thought Beth was about to set the record straight for Mrs Brown, Lola arrived on deck.

'Captain Borton's making a dash for it.' Lola was carrying a bedpan filled with what looked like vomit. 'He's hoping we can make it to the Bangka Strait by morning, to get some distance from where the Japs spotted us.'

'Maybe we should start rowing,' Minnie suggested.

'Just pray,' Lola told her, and held her hand up to judge the wind before she tossed the contents of the pan over the edge of the ship.

'I think if we have to pray, the Lord's a bit slow on the uptake,' Beth said.

'The Lord doesn't help those who are cheeky,' Lola replied.

Mrs Brown glanced about the deck as if checking to see if she approved of anyone else in the vicinity and, finding it lacking, complained to Shelagh that there was no suitable area to sit. 'I might as well go below deck and be terribly sick.'

'Yes, mother.'

'What? You *want* me to be sick? With *my* heart?'

'Of *course* not, mother, I simply meant that if you'd feel more comfortable below deck, we should go – it's not safe up here.'

Mrs Brown snapped her attention to the skies like a frightened bird. 'Indeed,' she said, and turned for the narrow staircase taking them back down into the gloom.

CHAPTER 10

MARGOT
The *Vyner Brooke*
13–14 February 1942

Margot paused on the deck of the *Vyner Brooke* for a moment. She had the strangest feeling that she was delaying the inevitable. Of course she wasn't, the war raged on around her, like a cyclone, all howling wind and devastation. Although the bomb that was going to take her hadn't yet fallen. She was still here. She glimpsed a blue cotton dress beside her and realised she had been joined by a young girl of perhaps twelve with large blue eyes. She gazed out to sea.

'Are you Henny?' Margot asked. The girl nodded. 'Your mother was worried about you yesterday. Did she find you?'

'Yes,' Henny said. 'She's right to worry. We could die tomorrow.'

'We won't die,' Margot lied.

'Why do you say that?'

'I'm trying to imagine I'm lucky. I have a friend who seems to find it helpful.'

'Sounds irritating.'

Margot grinned. 'Probably, in large doses. Why don't you go and comfort your mother? She'd like to keep you close, I'm sure.'

'They put them in pig baskets,' Henny replied to the ocean.

'I beg your pardon? Who?'

'The Japanese. Father and I were trying to get our money out of the bank in town, and I saw the Japanese put the soldiers in the back of trucks in bamboo baskets – the same ones the farmers take their pigs to market in. They were piled up, three high in the trucks.'

'No, I'm sure . . .' Margot's skin crawled.

'They were calling out,' Henny said. 'Dutch and Australian soldiers. Calling out to be saved – and for water. Squashed into bamboo cages for pigs.'

'How awful . . .'

'I heard our house manager tell Father they threw them all into the Java Sea.'

'Oh, my dear.' Margot reached out to the girl, her face frozen, her body trembling. 'You'll be safe with your mother. I'm sure of it.'

'My father has gone into a prison camp. I don't believe I'll see him again.'

Henny was right. Margot knew in that moment she would never see her father in Australia, just as Henny's was also lost to her forever. They would die on this ship, and all she could do was mask her terror until the end, to go down with something like dignity. She had long lain awake at night imagining looking death in the face, and now, standing on the deck of the *Vyner Brooke* with this young girl, she finally knew.

Death was coming for her.

The night was black, the air still warm, and when she'd finished her rounds, Margot crept downstairs to the dank room where Gull lay sleeping. She fanned his face with an old page of a newspaper she'd found in the kitchen. It was in Chinese and she wondered what the news had been that day. Gull was too pale. His body was too still. She didn't like it, but she didn't want to move him when there was so little she could do until they reached Batavia. She sighed.

'It's hard to sleep while it's blowing a gale and someone keeps breathing all over the place,' Gull murmured, his eyes closed.

'How long have you been awake?'

'Forever. It's hot, and I keep hearing Japanese planes, even when they're not there.'

'Planes? What nonsense. The Japanese will never find us,' she told him. 'They've probably given up looking, if they have any sense at all.'

'You think so?' Gull almost smiled.

'Of course I do. Why bother with a bunch of nurses and children? And crippled soldiers? Nothing here for them. They'll have much more interesting targets elsewhere, let me tell you.'

Gull smiled then and reached out for her hand. Margot paused for only a moment before she took his hand in both of hers.

'You're looking much better,' she said. 'Beth said so earlier, and she was right. You know she can always tell if livestock is going to be all right.'

'Really.'

'She says she's just annoyed you're still taking up a bed, when you're so obviously all right . . .'

Gull's pale face lit up. 'Well, please tell her I'm feeling much better. And any time she can spare you to come down and hold my hand, I'll be right here, wasting a perfectly good bed.'

Margot leaned down and gently kissed the back of his hand. It was precious to her, she wanted to hold it in a million places far from the dark belly of the *Vyner Brooke*. She watched his face for another long moment, his lashes settled and closed.

'If you're so well, why haven't you opened your eyes?' she asked.

Gull gave Margot's hands another squeeze. 'Because, Margot McNee, I very much suspect you're a terrible liar.'

When she was certain he was finally asleep, Margot snuck up to the doorway heading out onto the deck. She loitered there for a moment, looking hopefully out to sea, waiting to catch a glimpse of Batavia. It was to no avail. Batavia was still days away.

'Anything to see?' Minnie joined her.

'Just the ocean.'

'I'm not going to sleep tonight.'

'Me neither. I feel as if I haven't slept since December.'

'Do you think that Japanese plane spotted us?'

'Yep. I bet he's reporting back to his mates right now.'

A small group of sailors passed before them in the gloom, their faces hard to recognise in the moonlight.

'What's going on?'

'There's a skirmish to port. Looks like the Japs have found one of our ships.'

'No!' Margot and Minnie dashed with the men to the port side of the *Vyner Brooke* to see searchlights flashing across the water in the distance and to hear the boom of naval guns. The *Vyner Brooke* sat still and silent. There was nothing they could do.

'There's an island to the south, we're going to try to pull in and hide until this is over,' one of the men told them. 'Get below deck.'

The nurses made their way back downstairs.

They reached the small island and nestled in closely to its side, hoping they could disappear. Wishing to stay hidden for another day from the planes they knew were taking off at dawn from Japanese territory to hunt them down. Too soon, they crept out into the dark sea again, before the rising sun brought daylight, heat and the breathless dread of discovery.

'How are we looking today?' Minnie asked. 'Any closer to Batavia?'

'Still half a day behind schedule. Hiding from the planes isn't helping. But let's keep our chins up, eh? We'll be there in a couple of days.'

'Mrs Brown probably won't though,' Beth said grimly.

'Why? Has she fallen ill? Is it her heart?'

'No, her personality. I'm very likely to chuck her overboard before lunch.'

They had eventually anchored overnight behind a small, sandy island, but the *Vyner Brooke* had to run again, before her time ran out. The nurses slept fitfully, squashed together in small airless corners, or tucked away in the tropical night air on deck. Voices murmured to each other in the dark, children called out and grumbled, crew members made circuits around the decks, constantly checking for any sign of another ship, the hint of a Japanese warship, or the sound of a plane coming towards them in the dark. Margot lay beside Minnie, alert. Exhausted. Trapped. Listening to her breathe under the skies owned by the Japanese. And in the morning, the nurses straightened their hair and made their way to their districts once again.

'Nurses.' Matron Paschke was holding on to Winston, a teddy bear she'd just stepped on, much to the horror of his good friend, a little boy named Herbert. She stroked his ears as she spoke. 'It is now my duty to tell you that it is inevitable we shall be bombed by the Japanese. There is nothing we can do about the imminent attack – we can only continue to behave with the level of bravery and professionalism for which we, Australian nurses, are known.'

She placed Winston on the table, as if she didn't want to worry him. 'When the siren sounds in short bursts, you must put on your helmets and life vests and organise your passengers into the safest positions you can find for them, and then take cover. If the worst happens, and we must abandon ship, you will hear a long blast from the horn. You will go to your allotted lifeboat station and assist the crew in loading civilians into the boats. As you already know, two of the lifeboats are for mothers and children who can't swim. If you are a swimmer, you must give up your position in the lifeboat, and rely upon your life vest and your raft. I'm sure both items will be more than adequate. You will await a direct order from myself or Matron Drummond before you abandon ship.'

Margot nodded. There was nowhere to run, nowhere to scream, or cry. Early that morning before sunrise, she'd locked herself in the lavatory so that she could weep. Her tears had been hot and shameful. She'd startled when a fist had pounded on the door.

'There's a queue, you know,' a male voice had called out. She'd quickly rubbed her eyes and dashed out, keeping her gaze level, looking over his shoulder as if he wasn't there.

'Allergies,' she'd murmured. He hadn't responded, but then, he'd been waiting a while.

She stood on the deck now, tears rising again in her eyes, like a tide.

There was a general murmur.

'Bloody hell. Wish I'd practised my overarm now,' Beth said. 'Can't we shoot these bastards out of the sky?'

'Too high,' Hazel said. 'We can stop them getting a good shot at us, but that's about it.'

'Well, I'm not a swimmer,' Mavis said. 'I hope we've got enough boats.'

Matron Drummond spoke. 'May I also remind you all that you must make sure you are wearing your Red Cross armbands so that the enemy can see we are not combatants and are a hospital and civilian ship. We should be allowed to pass peacefully through these waters – we offer no threat to the Emperor and his plans to take Asia. In addition, you must now all pack a small bag of vitals and carry supplies with you. Dressings, morphia and syringes are to be pinned inside your pockets in case we go overboard. We will need to treat survivors as well as our patients, should they make it to shore.'

'Matron, what about patients who are bedbound?' Lola asked.

There was a silence and Margot thought of Gull and Fred, lying below deck.

'Pray that we don't go down,' Matron Drummond replied. 'I will inspect your districts again at eleven am to see that we are prepared for what is ahead.' She strode away, disappearing onto the bridge to talk to the captain.

'Well,' Beth said. 'That's that, then.'

'No, it's not!' Lola said. 'We're close enough to land. We've all got life vests.'

'There's no reason we won't make it,' Minnie said. 'I was a good swimmer back home. I used to swim in the Yealering lake all the time in summer.'

'I'm a very weak swimmer,' Margot admitted. 'But with a vest and a bit of luck I imagine we'll be all right . . .'

'I'll look after you,' Beth said comfortably. 'Because you know what my dad always said about me: couldn't kill me with an axe!'

'Well,' Margot said. 'Let's all go to our districts and make sure everyone knows what to do.'

'Wait!' Minnie said, suddenly. 'Shouldn't we wish each other luck? In case we don't get the chance again?'

Margot glanced at her uneasily. Lola nodded.

'Yes. I would like to formally wish you all lots of luck and all my prayers,' Minnie said. 'It's been an unexpected pleasure getting to know you all.'

'I think we'll bloody get bombed before you finish your speech,' Beth grumbled.

'Let's just shake hands,' Margot said. 'I think a lot can be said with a handshake.'

'Yes, and it's not end of the world stuff, is it?' Beth agreed.

'A good firm handshake is just what we need.'

'Business like, that's what it is.'

'Because we, ladies, are *professionals* – not rabble,' Margot told them.

'Despite any claims made by our marching instructor!' Minnie said.

Margot reached out and shook Minnie's hand. Then she reached for Beth's strong hand and Lola's delicate grip. For the first time that day she smiled. She felt Beth's warm pat on the back and Lola's arm fall easily around her waist.

'Good luck to us all, nurses from Australia! We'll show them what we're made of!'

'What would Matron say?' Beth said and grinned.

'Chin up, girls!' they all replied.

Later, when everything had been prepared, Margot went downstairs to the main ward. Gull was lying on a bunk at the end of the row of beds, asleep.

'Gull, Gull,' she whispered. 'Are you feeling all right?' Gull turned towards her, his face shining red with fever. 'We're going to get bombed. The Japanese have found us and they'll be back soon, we're not sure when.' She gripped his hands, hoping she could make him understand. 'When the ship gets bombed, you must climb these stairs. Make it to the deck. I'll be helping patients and civilians to the lifeboats, but I'll keep an eye out for you.'

'I can climb the stairs,' he said. 'I'll make sure I get as many patients as I can up to the deck in time.'

'There'll be a rush on for the lifeboats, but there probably won't be enough. Can you swim?'

'Well, usually, but I don't think I can swim for long at the moment.'

'We have lots of small rafts – here's a life vest – and make sure someone hands you a raft. You'll be okay if you have a couple of floating devices.' She squeezed his hands again. 'We're not all going to make it, but if we follow the protocols and keep level heads, we should be able to save as many as we lose. Those planes will bring company. Matron Drummond says we can't tell if we'll sink quickly, or if it'll take a while. We're hopeful there're a number of islands about.'

'I understand. I'll try to help as many out as I can.'

Margot's eyes filled with tears. 'Gull. Now would be a perfect time for your good luck to kick in.'

His smile was weak, but he gave her a wink. 'Oh, so now you choose to believe in luck?'

'I'd believe in Father Christmas if he could get us out of this!'

'You'll be fine.' He kissed her cheek. 'Here, I'm giving all my luck to you.'

She kissed him back. 'Save some for yourself,' she said, and with a swift backward glance, she ran up the stairs and into the light. There were protocols and rules for the attack. The rules would keep them safe.

*

The *Vyner Brooke* rolled lower in the water as she made another adjustment in her direction, trying to outpace her hunters. She rocked briefly, crashed through her wake and struggled on, searching for an island that would offer them shelter. All the while the crew sat beside the guns, waiting for the attack.

The nurses moved quickly, talking in low voices, swapping safety pins for hairclips and vials of morphia, tying small bags of bandages, stowing reading glasses carefully. They went back to the families still feeding their children breakfast, then made a quick round of the patients in bed. Margot's heart galloped. The ceiling of the ward was too low. She would be trapped here and die. She took a bedpan to be emptied and glanced at her shoes. Could she swim in them? Of course not. But she'd need them, wouldn't she? In the jungle? She'd seen the infections waiting for soft feet walking on the coral. Would she risk it?

'Hey, Margot?' She glanced up to see Fred, what remained of his legs carefully bound under the sheet. His face was pale, as if the pain was back.

'Yes, Fred?'

'You're looking a bit worried. Something's happening, isn't it?'

'Nothing to worry about, Fred.'

'You don't seem sure.'

Margot smiled at him. 'We *are* at war, you know. You'll have to forgive me if I sound a bit worried sometimes.' She paused. 'We don't want to panic anyone, but we've been spotted by the Japanese and we're expecting an attack.'

Fred smiled. 'Well, I think you should know that this is the best cruise I've been on.' He glanced down at his stumps. 'I was hoping there'd be more shuffleboard, obviously . . .'

'Perhaps we'll play when we reach Batavia.'

Fred held out his hand. It was a farming hand, grown huge with pulling ewes up the race, shearing, wielding crowbars and monkey wrenches, patting Colin at the end of a long day. She wondered how he'd work if he made it home.

'Deal,' he said, and they shook hands as the ship made another turn to the west.

At 11 am there was a shout. 'Japs! Japs!'

Margot ran to the window and stared out to see a bomber flying low over them. She gasped and ran for her station as she heard the rattle of machine-gun fire hit the side of the *Vyner Brooke*.

'They've found us! Get down. On the floor! Now!'

And then came the roar of the plane as it flew past them and raised itself in the air to take in the warm breeze above the ocean, and it flew away.

'Do we have any injuries?'

'Is everyone all right?'

Margot and Beth marched briskly through the rows of camp beds. 'Is everyone all right?'

'We're fine in here, nurse. I think they were just giving us a tickle.'

'They'll be back. We've been spotted and now we're just sitting ducks.'

The enemy aircraft were coming, heavy with bombs. The Japanese pilots were searching for them, following the coordinates their comrades had given them, coming to kill them all. She didn't want to drown, she hoped a bomb would fall right on her head. If she was going to die, let it be done. Her heart shrank in fear, and her blood rushed about her body as if it was trying to escape her. *You are already dead*, it told her.

The *Vyner Brooke*'s engines suddenly roared into life. The captain was heading for the nearest island.

'Keep your hats and your vests *on*!' Matron Paschke called. 'Keep your district calm – everyone remain below deck – we're making for an island. We'll be bombed soon. Make sure you know exactly where to find your lifeboat when that happens.'

Beth and Lola looked at each other. Silence fell. Where were the planes?

'I think I should write to my mum,' Lola whispered. 'Tell her where I am.'

'She doesn't know?' Beth asked.

'I'm not much for writing letters. I'd feel bad now, if I just disappeared and she never knew what had happened to me.'

'You won't disappear,' Beth assured her.

'I didn't know you were such an optimist, Beth,' Lola said. 'You think we're going to make it?'

'No, but when we die, they'll publish our names in the paper.'

'Oh.'

'But they'll be cross about it, because the Japs shouldn't be bombing us, so it'll be a moral victory.'

Margot began to prowl the decks, coming back to her district frequently to check her charges were comfortable.

'Do you think they'll be back?' an English lady with pale blonde hair asked her.

'Yes, I do. We'll need to be brave, but don't worry, we have plenty of lifeboats and rafts to go around. You'll make it to shore, and then I'm sure we'll get to Batavia. It'll just take longer than we'd hoped.'

The woman hugged her daughter close and kissed her soft hair. 'I do hope you're right,' she said.

'You'll see,' Margot assured her.

But the Nells came again, low across the ocean. The *Vyner Brooke* zigzagged, casting from side to side as the bombs fell around her. Captain Borton had spoken to Margot the day they departed Singapore. 'Don't worry too much, we'll get through all right. I've dealt with the Japs before. All you need to do is watch the belly of the plane as it flies overhead. As soon as you see the bomb has been released, the wing dips a little, and you throw the ship into a turn. They won't have time to catch us.'

The ship lurched again and a thin English lady swayed against the wall, pulling two little girls into her skirts. 'We've been hit!' she gasped.

'No,' Margot said and waited for impact, then heard the bomb fall into the ocean with an almighty splash. 'No, we're all right. We're dodging the bombs. We're fine.' She gave the woman a pat on the shoulder. 'Just keep close to the exit in case we need to abandon ship.' She gave the little girls a brave smile, and they stared back at her, wide-eyed.

Margot glanced at her watch; it was 1.30. She wondered if they should find some lunch for the children. It might be a while before they were fed again.

'Planes! Get to your places!' Mavis was calling down the corridor.

'I can't hear . . .' Margot stopped. There it was again, the unmistakable whine of Japanese planes. Her heart lurched.

'There's an island, fifteen miles away – the captain is heading there with all speed.'

It couldn't be as fast as the planes that were descending upon them. Margot flinched at the cracking boom of the ship's cannons, and the rattle of the Lewis guns firing desperately into the sky. She dashed to the window and watched nine planes grouped into three

V formations swooping down towards her. As they gained on the ship one of the Vs formed into a straight line astern, went into a shallow dive and one by one released a bomb. The *Vyner Brooke* swerved again. The bomb missed. The second released, the bomb fell, the *Vyner Brooke* swerved. Another miss. Margot's heart pounded. Another bomb. Another sickening lurch and another almighty splash as it exploded into the ocean beside them. Then came the inevitable scattering of machine-gun fire as the planes flew overhead, their bullets slicing through the deck of the ship, cutting ropes, splintering wood.

'To the bathroom, main deck!' someone called out over the noise of the attack. 'It'll be safer there! Take your passengers!'

'For the love of God, stay under your beds if you are able! It will be over soon! Be brave!'

The nurses gathered as the attack continued, counting the bombs. Seven, eight, nine, ten . . . They peered out of the saloon doors to see the planes coming again in another wave.

'Get back inside!'

They retreated again, the heat of their breath giving them away.

Eleven, twelve. Bombs hit the water around them. The ship lurched from side to side, racing to the island.

Thirteen is coming. Thirteen is an unlucky number, Margot thought. *If we can reach thirteen misses, we'll be all right. Thirteen misses means God will let us live.*

Lola squeezed her hand, sitting in the doorway with a little girl's feet nestled in her lap. Diana, a frail blonde woman who had lived on a rubber plantation with her husband, began to recite the Lord's Prayer.

'Our Father, who art in heaven, hallowed be thy name, thy kingdom come, thy will be done . . .'

And still the bombs fell: nineteen, twenty, twenty-one . . . The ship rocked to and fro in the ocean, crashing into its own wake again, zigzagging desperately, firing back from the three guns on deck. Twenty-two, twenty-three, twenty-four . . . Margot clasped her clammy hands together, her spine aching, her body frozen.

Then the sound of the planes changed. They were coming in a line, lower this time. The *Vyner Brooke* made another turn, trying to shake its fate.

Twenty-eight.

Twenty-nine . . .

CHAPTER 11

MINNIE
The *Vyner Brooke*, Bangka Strait
14 February 1942

The thirtieth bomb hit the *Vyner Brooke*, followed in a shocking flurry by more, hurtling into the deck, falling down the funnel and exploding in the engine room. Another hit between the bridge and stern, the explosion ripping through the lower deck, destroying most of the staterooms where the more elderly passengers had been given quarters.

'The lifeboats! I think we just lost some of the lifeboats!' Lola called out from her vantage point. 'And the gunner's gone!'

'And the radio operator's cabin – Mr and Mrs Hislop are gone!' someone else yelled.

The ship shook, stopped, surged forward as the momentum of the bombs took their course. It listed briefly and then was struck again. Another crash and explosion, another sickening lurch.

And then came the final blow, a near miss to starboard, which opened the ship up to the ocean, its exposed guts allowing the water to roll in, ready to drag her to the bottom of the sea. Minnie ran to help her passengers as the long horn blast sounded. *Abandon ship.*

She saw Lola and Margot hurry to their stations, leading injured passengers to the boats.

'Our boat has gone!' an old lady with a large handbag shrieked. 'What shall we do?'

'Can you swim?' Minnie asked her.

'No!'

'Then wait here and the crew will find you a place in this lifeboat.'

Beth began to marshal the crowd. 'This way for non-swimmers, mothers and children. Hurry! First positions in lifeboats to the wounded, non-swimmers, mothers and children.'

As Minnie darted about finding injured passengers, she caught sight of a nurse from Darwin who'd worked night and day as a theatre nurse before Singapore fell. She was holding a towel to her head but it couldn't quite cover the white gleam of her skull.

'What happened?' Minnie called out.

'I'm hit – split my damn head open!'

'Are you okay?'

'It's painful but I think I'm still in shock. We've got to get off the bloody ship!'

'Come and help me!' Mavis called. 'Bertha's broken both of her legs and we have to get her into the boat!' Mavis was dragging the nurse on a sheet. Her legs were bloodied, her left foot dangling at a shocking angle.

As Minnie dashed to pull her onto the lifeboat, a large man in a pale linen suit started climbing in.

'Excuse me, sir, this boat is for the injured, the old, for mothers and children – you'll have to get out.'

'I can't swim!' He clutched the edges of the boat as if they'd have to cut his hands off to take him.

'We have life rafts and life vests. You'll be fine. This nurse has broken *both* legs and we've got to prioritise.'

'*I'm* injured too!' He raised his shirt. 'Look! I'm bleeding! I've lost a lot of blood!' The gash stretched from his hip to his bellybutton, but it didn't appear to have punctured his stomach cavity, nor the wall of fat and flesh protecting it. There was blood, certainly, but not so much he was about to bleed out. There were many worse cases.

Minnie glanced about at the elderly being helped towards the boats, the children white-faced and weeping, searching for their mothers, some with shrapnel wounds up and down their legs and broken arms. She swore under her breath. There were so many wounded, and this man wasn't even nearly the worst. But to argue with him was going to delay the launch of the boat.

'All right. Stay there,' she snapped, and turned to help two small children scramble in, followed by their mother, her face covered in blood.

'There we are, all ready for a wonderful adventure,' she told them. 'Wait till we tell Daddy!'

Another plane flew low overhead, unworried now that their few guns had gone, stitching machine-gun bullets into the deck and the hull of the ship as if they were sewing it back together. Some old ladies in pale cotton dresses, who'd been gingerly crossing the deck, leaped to one side to avoid the bullets, crying out in pain as they were struck in the shoulders and back. Minnie dashed below deck again. The howling was deafening as the planes rolled overhead, then rose up in the air to turn and attack again, forcing families to scramble for their lives, pushing their children ahead of them up the crowded stairwell into the smoke of the attack.

Amid the rushing and screaming, the struggle of feet and hands and voices, came a loud voice. An order.

'Everybody, *stand still*!' They all halted immediately and gazed about, frozen in panic. Minnie squeezed a little girl's hand and glanced around to see who had spoken. A panic-stricken woman holding a small suitcase spoke up again. 'My husband has *dropped his glasses*!'

There was a long moment of stunned silence followed at first by giggles, then by gales of laughter.

'Good luck to him!' Beth called, one small child under each arm as she marched up the stairs. 'Tell him to buy some new ones!'

'And the big black things falling from the sky are *bombs*!' added Margot. 'Now, hold hands, children, we're going up on deck!'

Matron Drummond was standing by one of the lifeboats. 'Come along now!' she called out. 'We need the injured in first and the non-swimmers. I'll be grouping mothers and children in the boat next. Quickly now, this lifeboat is already hanging further from the ship now and it's getting worse!'

She was right. As the *Vyner Brooke* took on more water, she rolled onto her side, and it was sending the lifeboat dangling on its ropes further from the edge of the ship. It was becoming difficult to get anyone onto it. When it leaned away another couple of inches, it would become impossible.

Hazel was making her way slowly across the deck with an elderly man with a bandaged head.

'Hurry up, nurse!' Matron Drummond said and reached out for the man, holding the boat in place.

Another old gentleman was sitting calmly watching the bustle around the lifeboats, propped up on the deck.

'Sir, it's time to go, can I help you into the lifeboat?' Minnie asked him.

'No thank you, young lady, save my spot for someone who needs it.' He lifted his hands to reveal the bombs had left him almost cut in half by the attack. 'Rule Britannia!' he sang at the top of his voice. 'Britannia rules the waves! England never ever, ever shall be slaves!' And with that, he died, defiant, on the deck of the *Vyner Brooke*.

'*Duck!*'

The Japanese were back again, tearing into the ship and the survivors struggling to the boats. The bullets cut through the ropes to one of the lifeboats, and it fell into the ocean, only half filled with people, and immediately flipped over.

'Girls! Hurry! We're going under!'

Minnie and Margot dashed downstairs again into the main saloon where the wounded lay. Gull was sitting on his stretcher, reaching for a chair to pull himself up. Margot grabbed his elbow and braced herself as she pulled him to his feet, put her arm around his waist and gave him a nod.

Minnie pulled a frail man who'd been suffering severe seasickness to his feet as well. 'It's time to go, Mr Jenkins,' she said. 'Let's get you up the stairs.'

They made their way upstairs while families streamed around them, heading for the lifeboats, calling for each other to hurry over the roar of gunfire and the booming shudder of bombs.

Gull's gaze was at the top of the stairs, as if he was willing himself to climb there.

'Not much further,' Margot said. 'We'll have you in the sea in no time.'

Gull's eyes locked with Margot's, and Minnie could see a future sitting there, comfortably between them. It was palpable, it was hopeful, like a pulse. Minnie felt in that moment on the stairs, as the ship groaned all around her, that she was standing on the edge of their memory, that they had grown old together, and that she was just visiting; that she had already gone.

At last Gull grinned. 'A swim is just what I need,' he said. 'Thanks for fetching me.'

Margot squeezed his hand. 'Of course, I'll never leave you.'

When they made it onto the deck, the chaos enveloped them.

'I say! This is *our* lifeboat! We were here first, and what's more we were promised a position! I don't know who you think you are—'

'Out of the way! I paid good money for my family to travel and I'm not about to be stood aside by someone's hairdresser!'

Minnie glanced as Beth tried to organise families onto the lifeboats that were left. The British and Dutch were insisting they be given preference over everyone else, and were outraged when she boarded them by need.

Gull spoke up. 'Don't put me in a boat, for God's sake, I'll be fine on a raft.'

'Well, put this on,' Minnie said, slipping a life vest over his head, 'and we'll get you to tie a couple of rafts together while we help the other patients.' She put two rafts in front of him. 'Just tie the side ropes and we'll have a decent raft, all right?'

'I'm going back down,' Minnie then told Margot. 'We're lower in the water now. If you get back here before me, you both go over the side. I'll catch up.'

Fred raised a hand and waved Minnie over. 'Fancy seeing you here,' he said. 'I thought you'd be on the beach by now with a gin and tonic.'

'We'll be there soon, Fred. And think of the story you'll have to tell Colin.'

The ship lurched again, sinking, and more water poured in through the shattered windows, already below sea level. Minnie gasped.

'Maybe you'll have one for me, eh?' Fred told her. He gestured weakly at his stumps. 'I'm not swimming ashore now, am I? I can't even get up the stairs.'

'We must try, Fred. We can't give up. Margot's helping patients to boats as well – perhaps if we both lift you, we can get you up to the deck.'

Fred gave her a look of resignation. '*We're* not giving up, Minnie. But *you've* got to go.' He glanced around. 'Don't feel bad. It's war. I can't get up the stairs. I'm certainly not going to swim if I do.'

'But Fred . . .'

He took her hand and squeezed it, hard. 'I'm glad I saw you before I went.'

The water was lapping at her ankles. Fred was right; she couldn't drag him. She saw Lola administering some morphia to an old lady whose arm had been badly wounded. She'd been in bed with malaria and now she was too weak to move.

'This will help you, Mrs Birmingham. For the pain.'

She injected a large dose into the woman's shoulder, and Minnie saw her panic recede in moments.

'Fred, I can give you something.' She pulled out her syringe and a bottle of morphia and drew the clear liquid up.

'Thank you, Minnie,' Fred said. 'You've been a good friend.'

She placed the needle to his shoulder.

'Don't forget to have that G&T for me, will you?'

'I'll toast you from the shore.' She pressed the syringe into his tanned skin, and felt his muscles relax. He would drown in his sleep.

Minnie blinked back hot tears. There was no time to cry, she told herself, no one wanted her sorrow. There was work to be done and more lives to save. She swallowed her grief, wiped her eyes and kissed Fred's hair. Then she began to look around the ward for others in need of her help. There were more patients, unable to move, too injured to make it to the rafts. Minnie and Lola helped as many as they were able.

Up on deck the piles of rafts were sliding into the ocean as the ship tilted into the water.

'Remember to keep your head tucked in and hold on to your life vest as you jump!' Matron Drummond reminded them.

Minnie watched as a nurse leaped from the upper deck, and then fell limp as she hit the water, her head lolling uselessly onto the life vest. 'She's broken her neck,' she whispered to herself.

'I'm not taking my shoes off,' Lola declared.

'You have to – you can't swim with them.'

'I can't bloody swim anyway. I might as well die with my boots on!' She leaped from the deck into the churning waters below.

'Keep your chin down!' Margot yelled after her, and saw her splash, then bob back up, waving at her from the human soup below.

'Oh thank God,' Minnie said. 'Right, is everyone accounted for?'

Matron Drummond was still handing out life vests, then tossing more into the water when she could see they were needed.

'I'm not going! It's too far to jump! I'll drown!' Mrs Shirvington from Dorset said, wringing her hands.

'You'll drown if you stay here,' Matron Drummond told her.

'No! I can't! *I can't!*' She started to sob. Her dark hair was a mess of curls in the humidity and her face was red with heat and emotion.

Matron Drummond responded with a swift push to her back and she flew from the deck of the ship and landed in the sea with a plop. 'Oh, yes you can,' she said. 'Help me, Minnie.' She began dragging coats to the edge of the ship. 'Get these coats down to the boats.' Minnie took some of the garments from Matron Drummond and began throwing them down.

'Take these,' she yelled, 'we'll need them on the island.' The huge dark coats fell heavily into the oily water and were dragged into the boats. 'Matron, it's your turn, into the last boat.'

'We have everyone?' Matron Drummond asked.

'Everyone we can. Some of the boats have been destroyed, but we can make do with the rafts.' Matron Paschke had joined them and surveyed the devastation. The bodies and the deck, slicked with blood and oil, covered in shattered timber, scattered suitcases, broken glass, discarded hats. 'In you go, Matron. I'm coming next.'

Matron Drummond gave her a nod. 'See you on shore.' She tucked her chin in and stepped from the deck of the *Vyner Brooke*, landing in the water with a small splash. Minnie watched as she was dragged onto a raft.

'Wish me luck!' a nurse said to Minnie. 'I can't swim – especially not with this.' She gestured to her torso, where the uniform had been cut open by gunfire. She gripped her life vest tightly, although it seemed to be loosely tied around her waist. She smiled hopefully and leaped into the water.

'I'll throw you down an extra vest, Evelyn!' Minnie called after her.

The ship had sunk so low in the water that a rope ladder had been placed over the side so the last few women could climb down.

Mrs Mills hesitated. 'I can't climb down there!' she declared. 'Everyone will see right up my skirt!'

'I don't think they're looking, Mrs Mills,' Minnie told her. 'Now please take your turn, or I shall have to assist you into the water.' Mrs Mills observed that Matron Drummond had made it onto a raft, and was helping other ladies aboard. She sighed, and began to clamber down the ladder, launching herself into the sea.

Margot and Gull held hands and jumped the small distance into the dark water, bobbing up again in their vests and making their way clumsily to the waiting raft. 'Hurry up, Minnie! Jump!'

'Now, everyone, take up the ropes on the side of the lifeboats, or on the rafts if you can, and we'll all float to safety.' As Matron Paschke spoke, a current curled its cool fingers around the life raft she was in and began to draw it away. 'Keep swimming, stay safe, we'll all meet on the shore very soon, I'm certain.'

Lola had found her way onto a plank of wood with a couple of other nurses, her tin hat still on. They floated from the side of the stricken ship on the same current floating Matron Paschke on its back. 'We're off to see the Wizard!' they sang, 'the wonderful Wizard of Oz!'

The Japanese had finally left them alone, scattered in the oil slick bubbling up from the sinking ship. Minnie glanced around at the mayhem. The sound of the planes was disappearing over the horizon, the voices calling out to each other or screaming from burns and wounds and horror seemed pathetic in the vast ocean. She thought of her brother Oliver, swimming in the lake at home, she thought of her mother, watching the door. She saw her friends in the oil-slicked sea, and she gave them a wave. With a deep breath, she took the final step from the *Vyner Brooke*, surrendering herself to the cool waters of the Bangka Strait.

With her life vest bobbing around her ears, Minnie made her way slowly through the water to Margot and Gull, who put his hand out to pull her aboard their raft.

'Can you see any of the other girls?' Margot asked anxiously.

'Not yet. Some are floating on the other side of the swell. How are you? Are you injured?'

'I don't think so,' Margot said. 'Bit of a bump getting into the water, but nothing to worry about.' She adjusted her grip on the raft. 'And you?'

'I think I'm in shock, actually, the adrenaline is rushing about all over the place. I bet I could have a tooth removed at the moment and not feel a thing. Gull, are you still with us?'

'Oh, yes,' he assured them. 'If I don't respond to you later, assume I've passed out. I've promised Margot I won't die, but I may clock out shortly.'

'Completely understandable,' Minnie told him. 'Margot will get you to shore, I'm certain. She can be quite determined when she wants to be.'

'Very true,' Gull said. 'But if today's the day my luck runs out, there's no better bunch of people to be with than Australian nurses.'

'Thank you for the sentiment,' Margot said. 'We'll certainly do our best to keep you alive.'

'Beth? Lola? Have you seen them?' Minnie asked, glancing about.

'Not yet, but we'll regroup soon,' Margot said. 'I think the currents will bring us all to the same spot.'

A figure bobbed towards the raft, and as Minnie reached out to grab him by the collar, she realised it was Mr Shaw, with his long tufts of white hair, who'd spent over an hour telling her stories about life on the railways in Kent. He was dead, although his injury was hidden under the dark surface of the water. Perhaps he'd snapped his neck jumping from the ship. His eyes stared vacantly back at her, and between his teeth he still held a cigar. She released him and let him drift away. She felt haunted for the first time by Fred's cold ghost, heavy with sorrow and burdened with regret, descending alone to the bottom of the sea. She closed her eyes, trying to keep the horror at bay, thinking of Colin instead, watching over the sheep from the back of the ute while his mate was away.

'Lola! Lola Llewellyn! Beth Scanlon! Are you here?' she called out, over the voices in the ocean.

'Mum! Mummy!'

'Tess?'

'Martin? Are you here!?'

'Mummy, I've got Audrey, she's with me!'

But it was impossible to tell among the flotsam who was answering her call, and who was desperately listening for news of their own.

Finally, Minnie spotted another raft and lowered herself into the water again. Her life vest was almost impossible to swim in, so she untied one of the ribbons and let it rise a little higher, where it dug into her armpits and chafed. It was quieter now, without the engines of the *Vyner Brooke* struggling to get them to safety, without the scream of the Nells, the blasting of the bombs, the rattle of the guns and the wailing of the families as they were torn apart.

Minnie reached the raft and took up the rope. As she cast about for a place to paddle to, she spotted Lola. 'Lola!' she called. 'You're all right!?'

'Hello! Yes, we're all fine here,' Lola said, paddling with a piece of wood towards a group of nurses in a lifeboat about thirty yards away. As the ocean rose and fell, Minnie could see more people in the water, clinging to pieces of timber and small rafts of kapok.

'Have you seen any of the other nurses?' Minnie asked.

'Yeah, a few were here earlier, but I can't see Dolores. She went back to collect her shoes and we got bombed again. Did she make it?'

'I'm sorry. She's gone, Lola.'

Dolores was killed the moment she went below deck.

'Look at them all,' Lola said. 'How can this happen?'

'War,' Minnie said. She started to pull herself onto her raft but left her legs in the water so she could kick. 'That's how.'

'I can't seem to stop crying,' Lola said. 'I don't *think* I'm crying, and then I sob like a baby. So don't be worried if I *look* like I'm crying, all right?'

'Of course not,' Minnie assured her. 'It's the shock, that's all.' She glanced around, her body shuddering, wondering who would even notice another tear anyway.

'Is Margot okay?' Lola asked.

'Yes, they've got a raft up towards the stern,' Minnie said.

'Tell her I'll see her on shore. I'm going to try to catch up with Matron Paschke.'

'Good luck, see you on the beach.'

'There she goes!' someone called out, and Minnie turned back to watch the final slow ripples as the funnel of the *Vyner Brooke* disappeared beneath the waves. The dark ocean circled briefly, then forgot that she had ever been there at all.

Their escape had been blasted away from them, mothers and their children, old men and the war wounded, drowning silently inside the ship's cabins. Minnie glanced at her watch, surprised it was still working. It was 2.25 pm, just fifteen minutes after they had first been bombed. How quickly their lives had been torn away from the hope of escape. How deeply adrift into the nightmare they were now, surrounded by death and fear; what remained of them struggling desperately against the heavy ocean, pulling their bodies towards the air, the light, and the pallid hope of survival.

Minnie wanted to scream out for her mother. Somewhere in her heart she believed her mother could save her still. But she was too far away, making lunch for the shearers, or listening to the ABC news bulletin on the radio at the kitchen table. Minnie's heart felt heavy with fear, and with the knowledge her mother couldn't save her, that she had only herself and her comrades, struggling against the sea. That was all.

She paddled steadily towards Margot's raft. It was gone.

'Margot? Gull?'

Someone called out, 'I think Margot's to the south. I waved to her a minute ago.' Minnie didn't recognise the voice. She circled in the water again, wondering if the sea had turned her around. It was hard to work out which direction she was facing, where the ship had been, where she might find a welcome shore. The ocean pushed her up again and she saw survivors spread out across the water, bobbing like thistles and leaves on a pond.

'Head for the island!' someone shouted.

'Which island?' another called back.

'Over there! A couple of miles over there!'

The sun was still hot. Her face was burning, her hands were sore. She held them out of the water and saw that she'd grazed them on the rope leaving the ship. The Bangka Strait was black with oil and clogged with lumps of flotsam and jetsam from the ship, broken rafts, suitcases slowly filling with water, and corpses from the *Vyner Brooke*, floating away into their silent future.

Minnie started to tremble. She dipped her burned hands into the water and paddled towards the island in the distance. How far was it? A couple of miles? The South China Sea was filled with currents, bumping up against islands and stretching out again, invisible, moving her comrades away from her like toys in a bath. Which current should she catch? Where would it take her? Which one was guided by the hand of God?

Hatty somehow found her, holding on to the rope of her raft.

'Do you think it'll take us long to reach that island?' Minnie asked.

'Hard to say. I've been swimming between boats and it looks like we're being pulled around a bit. I hope we all end up on the same beach but it's hard to tell.'

'I wonder if the Japs control these islands.'

'Probably. Maybe they haven't taken over the smaller ones yet.'

'Which raft were you on?'

'One over there.' Hatty gestured into the mess. 'I was with a couple of crew members but I left them to it. One of them says he's been sunk three times. I reckon he's bad luck.'

'He's still alive, maybe he's *good* luck.'

'Too late now, I probably won't find them again. I must say I'm getting sick of this damn vest, it's rubbing and I'm getting a rash under my arms.'

'Me too, but I'm afraid I'll fall asleep and drown, so I think we're stuck with them.'

Another raft floated close by. A patient and a wounded nurse were sitting on board, and three nurses were holding on to the raft's rope, paddling determinedly. One nurse was praying.

'Hail Mary, mother of God—'

'Shut up, Heather, and grab an oar, wait until we're out of this bloody oil slick, *then* you can pray.'

'Hey! Minnie! Grab that raft, will you? This stretcher isn't working, we'll all be in the drink shortly!' It was Lola, waist deep on a canvas stretcher which was sinking under the weight of the four nurses perched on board.

Minnie dog-paddled to the spare raft, moving her arms carefully to avoid injuring her skin any further. 'Here you go,' she said, and paddled the raft towards them.

'Thanks, Minnie. We'll be faster on this than that soggy old thing.'

The sun was lowering in the sky and as the dark sea rose and fell it was getting harder to see their friends, the crew paddling for shore, the passengers they knew they'd managed to save. Minnie glanced uneasily about. They might spend the night out on the ocean, with the mysterious fish swimming beneath them, with the Japanese patrolling the waters, with the unknown waiting for them on the shore. There was only one thing for it. They had to find an island. *Pray to God, but row towards the shore.*

'Minnie!'

'Hazel!' Minnie looked over her shoulder to see Hazel swimming towards her. Hazel reached out and grabbed the raft.

'Have you seen Matron Paschke? I saw her go into the drink, but now I can't seem to find her.'

'Girls! Are you all right?' It was Matron Paschke's voice calling out over the water.

'Matron! Yes, we were just talking about you, glad you're on a raft!'

'Oh, yes, do you like my new vessel? I'm pleased to have floated for so long and we're all safe and sound. A few injuries, but I'm sure we'll all be on the shore before too long.'

Mrs Brown floated into sight from behind an upturned lifeboat. She was wearing her vest, and her arms were around Evelyn.

'Mrs Brown! I think there's room on Matron's raft,' Minnie called. 'Or there's a raft here, so you can get out of the water.'

'I'm all right, we might need that raft, though. Can we tie two together? Evelyn here is a bit tired.'

Minnie made her way over. She remembered Evelyn's quick smile as she'd jumped from the deck, already wounded. Couldn't swim, and her vest was gone, although it hardly mattered. Her eyes were open as she lay in Mrs Brown's arms.

'I think you can let Evelyn go now, Mrs Brown,' Minnie said gently.

'What? No, I shall *not*. I promised Sister Evelyn I wouldn't let her go and I *shall not*.' Mrs Brown gave Evelyn another comforting squeeze.

'I'm so sorry, but Evelyn is dead, Mrs Brown. It's too late for her.'

'What?' Mrs Brown stroked her hair briefly while she absorbed the news. 'She said to me, *Please don't let me go*. She said, *I can't swim and I'm afraid*. And I promised. I *promised . . .*'

'She must have been greatly comforted,' Minnie said. 'Sometimes, that's all we can do.' She and Hazel gently pulled Evelyn's body from Mrs Brown's embrace, and turned her onto her back, from where Evelyn slowly, silently disappeared beneath the dark surface.

Some distance away, a couple of small children were on a raft, floating with a bedraggled pair of women and an old man, who appeared to be unconscious.

'Where's Winston?' Herbert asked, looking about desperately. Minnie glanced around. Winston the teddy bear was probably long gone, along with Herbert's mother, but she checked anyway, and incredibly saw a brown fluffy ear popping up over the crest of a wave.

'Winston!' she called out and launched herself through the water. The soggy toy was dipping again, soaking up the sea, and disappearing. She reached out and grabbed his paw. 'There you are,' she said to Herbert, and flopped Winston onto the raft with a squelch. Herbert grasped him to his tiny chest. 'Winston! I thought you were lost to the sea!'

Two more nurses floated back into range on a raft. They'd tried to fashion a sail from their uniforms, but it hadn't worked.

'Minnie! Pleased to see you!' a nurse called out, and Minnie recognised Dot and Agnes, two friends from Melbourne who'd been student nurses together years before. 'We've been trying to sail.' Dot was dragging her sodden uniform back on. 'Now I'm not actually sure this is my uniform!'

'It looks fine,' Minnie assured her, as the clammy cotton drill, which had made it over her head and had half-heartedly allowed her arms through the arm holes, refused to go any further, billowing around her bust. 'I'm sure I once saw Rita Hayworth in something similar.' The nurses joined the group bobbing in the sea, and Minnie glimpsed a smile from Agnes, underneath the oil smeared across their faces. 'I should have known you two would try to sail out of here!'

Dot laughed. 'Agnes's idea,' she said. 'But anything is worth a go at this stage, eh?'

They all considered the rafts between them, and began to tie them together.

'All right, we'll take it in turns to be in the water, that way we won't sink the raft, and everyone will have enough space,' Minnie said. 'Are you all swimmers?'

'I'm not much of a swimmer but I can spend quite a bit of time in the water with my vest on.' Dot began to lower herself from the raft.

'Good, with the four of us in the water, the raft will sit a bit higher. If we can just swim and not hold on to it, I think we'll be able to keep everyone safe.'

Minnie lowered herself back into the water, gritting her teeth against the yearning she felt to be on dry land, not bobbing about at the whim of the tides. When she glanced around for the island again, it had grown larger, as if it was reaching out to save her.

CHAPTER 12

MARGOT
Bangka Strait
14 February 1942

Margot swam slowly next to their raft. Gull had drifted off to sleep just after nightfall. She'd been unable to find Minnie, despite calling out for hours. She held on to the raft again, breathing heavily. Her sunburned arms ached in the saltwater. Occasionally people she knew floated past, talking quietly in the darkness, encouraging the mothers holding their children, and the wounded soldiers sitting crumpled in lifeboats, waiting for the tides that would carry them to shore. She glimpsed Matron Paschke, sitting proudly on her raft with a child in her lap, but, even though she'd struck out towards her, the currents had carried her away.

'Margot! Is that you?' It was Lola in her tattered uniform and life vest, floating on a semi-submerged raft.

'Lola, thank God you're all right. I feel like I haven't seen any of the girls in ages. I've lost Minnie.'

'I saw her a few hours ago but our rafts got separated. She's fine. Not long now and we'll all be ashore.'

The great black sea rose again like the arching back of a whale. When the swell had passed, Gull was a couple of yards away. Margot tried to reach for the raft but couldn't.

'Hey!' she called. 'Gull, stay where you are!'

Gull slept on and the sea rose again on its great silent back. He was further away now.

'We'd better swim a bit faster, Margot,' Lola said, 'he's getting away from us.'

Margot struck out a little further but the sea dragged on her hands and legs. Two sailors gave a small shout as they watched Gull float away and began to swim furiously towards the raft. The girls kept their pace steady and their heads down, swimming into the swell of the wave. When Margot paused again to raise her head for air, she saw that there were two waves between them and the raft.

'Gull!' Margot called in alarm. 'Come back!'

Four waves silently rose between them. The distance was too great and the current was dragging them away. Margot stared at the raft in a panic. She couldn't get to it. Gull would roll into the water and drown. And she'd drown too. Her lungs hurt. She stopped swimming and trod water helplessly as the raft crested another low rolling wave, and another, until she could just make out the sight of Gull's body as he drifted away in the South China Sea.

Night fell slowly as Margot and Lola swam, holding on to a plank of wood for hours, floating on their backs, paddling through the water to the distant shore. There was a bonfire on the beach, like a beacon, glowing in the darkening air.

'Lola! Look, we're almost there!'

Lola grunted. 'Doesn't feel like it.'

'No, look, I can see uniforms on the beach. Some of the girls are there already and they're making camp.'

'I hope there's a cup of tea waiting for us.'

'Shh, what's that sound?'

'Is that shouting?'

'I'm not sure . . .'

The night closed around them again, and the girls watched the golden flames from the distant bonfire fade away as they drifted, looking up at God in his black night sky and glancing down uneasily at the darkness beneath them.

They dozed, they paddled, and the currents drew them further away into the night.

As the sun rose again, first in shades of grey and then with a hint of blue, Margot and Lola glimpsed the mangrove swamps along the shore.

'Where's the beach gone?' Margot said, craning her neck.

'Hang on! What's that sound?'

Margot paused and turned slowly. 'A boat, I can hear a motorboat!'

'The bloody Japs are coming to finish us off!'

'Look dead!'

'I *am*! *You* look dead, loll about a bit, won't you?'

'I *am*!' Lola dropped her head back onto her life vest as the sound got louder, moving steadily across the still water.

Margot slowly opened one eye, squinting across the glare of the ocean. 'Hang on,' she whispered. 'I think they're ours! That looks like an Aussie uniform!'

'Oh my Lord, we're saved!'

The small craft pulled up alongside them and two handsome men in RAAF uniforms leaned out of the boat. 'Hello, girls, need a lift?'

'Do we ever!'

'Happy to help. I'm Bruce.'

'Lola.'

Bruce leaned over and dragged her into the boat.

'And I'm Margot.'

'Pleased to meet you. This is Ray.'

Ray was manning the engine and he gave them a nod and quietly moved the boat forward. 'Enemy territory,' he murmured. 'Let's keep it down, eh?'

'Absolutely,' Margot said. 'Have you seen anyone else? Nurses? A soldier on a raft?'

'No, not since we found this boat, but don't lose hope, there are plenty of us making it to the island.'

Ray smiled at her, and she felt relief unfurling in her stomach. Perhaps they would be all right. Perhaps they would find the others. Perhaps they would find Gull.

'There are more . . .' Bruce gestured up ahead and Ray guided the boat to a group gathered on three rafts which had been haphazardly tied together. Hazel was there along with Charlotte, the pregnant Englishwoman, her face burned bright red, and her body almost spent, as she lay panting in the heat of the early morning. Margot gasped. She was clearly in labour.

'Climb in,' Ray said. 'We'll find a place to go to shore.'

'Oh, thank God.' Charlotte's face contorted, as if she was about to cry, but she was too exhausted to make a sound. 'The pain!'

'We're nearly there, Charlotte,' Hazel said. 'Just hold on and we'll make sure you're comfortable and in the shade of a nice tree, with a cool drink of water.'

Margot and Lola pulled her gently into the boat as Hazel and the others pushed from behind.

'We need to find a landing spot,' Bruce said. 'Somewhere safe.'

They motored slowly, scanning the shore, watching for signs of Japanese troops. Eventually they discovered a long jetty. Its greying timbers stretched out into the ocean from one of the tin mines on the island. They pulled up to the end of the jetty, glancing about nervously.

'Oh the pain! My baby!' Charlotte's head lolled into Margot's lap.

'Let's get you up onto dry land, dear,' Lola said, and she crouched in the boat, helping the woman to her feet.

'I'll get her up to the jetty,' Bruce said. He leaped up onto the grey timbers and turned to pull her after him. She shrieked again.

'There, there,' Margot said. 'It'll all be better in a minute when you can lie down. You'll have your baby soon.'

'It's coming!' she hissed. 'My baby's coming!' She moaned and grasped Bruce's arms for leverage.

'Help me get her up, for God's sake!' Ray said, giving her a final push. Margot and Hazel caught her and lay her down. She was right, the baby *was* coming. It was to be born here, on a jetty in the middle of a war.

Charlotte's fragile body pushed and strained, exhausted by the long hours in the sea. Her teeth were chattering, and Margot could make out small snippets of prayer.

'How many months?' she asked.

'Almost eight,' Hazel said. 'But she hasn't felt it move all day.'

Margot glanced at Lola. It was early.

Charlotte pushed and buckled under the pain, wheezing as it took her low across the belly. She shook with the effort and Margot knew they were close. The men watched the jungle for any sign of movement.

Too soon, the tiny baby arrived in the world, at the end of a jetty in the Bangka Strait.

'It's a girl!' Lola cried.

'A girl!' Charlotte's exhausted face lit up, sweating, spent, alive with love.

'Quickly, rub her down with this,' Hazel said, handing Lola her petticoat.

Margot checked the tiny child, looking for her heartbeat. Nothing. She flicked her fingers into her little mouth and gently breathed into her. The baby lay limply in her arms, her pale face and blue lips pursed as if to kiss her mother for the first time.

Charlotte reached out to touch her. 'She's warm,' she said. 'She's *warm*, she's alive . . .'

Margot put her ear to the baby's tiny pale chest. '*You're* warm, Charlotte. She's part of you.'

'She's my baby! She's *mine*!' Her voice raised in panic. 'She *won't* die! Make her breathe! Shake her! Slap her! *Make her breathe!*'

Margot swaddled the child in her petticoat. Her face was pure white and absolutely still. She held her out to her mother. 'Hold her, dear,' she said. 'She's with God now.'

'No!' Charlotte sobbed. She fell back into Hazel's arms and her body clenched around her baby like a seashell, holding on as if she could travel with her, away from this terrible place. Margot knelt beside her, stroking her hair, awash with pointless, bitter tears.

'Charlotte. I'm so sorry. She's beautiful.'

Lola wept openly as she dropped to the ground, holding on to Charlotte. 'I'm so sorry, dear girl. She should still be with you, not out here on this bloody jetty.'

'I'm going to check the shore,' Bruce muttered. 'I'll see if it's safe. We can't tell if the Japs have taken this part of the island yet.' He began to walk briskly down the jetty, glancing this way and that, listening for the sound of gunfire.

'I hate this bloody war,' Lola whispered. 'I hate the bloody Japs,

I hate the sound of bombs. If I hear another bloody shouted order, there's no telling what I might do!'

'Japs! Ray! Start the boat!'

The nurses glanced up to see Bruce running at full tilt back down the jetty, his rifle drawn. 'Jesus Christ!' He jumped into the little boat and Ray gunned the throttle and the dinghy roared away, leaving the nurses lying flat on the jetty as gunfire flew past them.

'What about us?' Margot yelled, but they were gone. The sound of the small engine grew thinner across the still waters of the South China Sea as the little boat disappeared. Margot looked up, squinting against the sun to see they were surrounded by Japanese soldiers, looking sternly down upon them, rifles drawn.

'Looks like we just surrendered,' Lola whispered.

A soldier responded by poking her shoulder with the bayonet at the end of his rifle. Lola flinched and held her hands up. 'We surrender. Australian Army nurses.'

The soldier shouted something in response and she drew back. The women stared up at the soldiers in alarm.

'Australian Army nurses,' Margot repeated. 'Surrender. We surrender.'

'*Koshin! Koshin!*'

'I think he wants us to stand up,' Lola said. 'We have a sick woman here.' She gestured to the child in Charlotte's arms. 'This baby has died, because her mother was bombed, her ship sunk, and she had to swim for hours to get to land.'

The Japanese soldier glanced at the baby, and back to Margot. '*Koshin!*'

'Stand up, everyone, just stand up.'

They struggled to their feet. Charlotte was ashen, holding her baby girl, trying to take in every detail of her face, trying to make her live again with the love pouring from her heart. 'Don't let them take her away,' she whispered. 'Don't let them have my baby girl.'

One of the soldiers glared at Hazel. He took two steps forward and grabbed her shirt, pulling it out from her chest briefly, and glancing down at her breasts.

She gasped. 'Well!' she muttered. 'I wasn't expecting that!'

'I think he wanted to check if you were a boy,' Margot murmured. 'Your hair is rather short, and it's been slicked back with the oil from the ship. I must say, the shirt isn't helping in the feminine stakes either.'

'I don't know if I should feel relieved or insulted!'

'Feel relieved,' Margot advised.

The soldiers made impatient gestures and began to point their bayonets up the jetty towards the shore, and the small group of women fell into step.

They weren't the only survivors who'd made it to shore. As they were slowly herded along the beach, Margot could see other groups moving along the sand with their Japanese captors. Eventually, the soldiers gestured for them to sit, so they fell, exhausted, to the sand, and watched as others were rounded up.

'Looks like they're going to help those people out of the water,' Hazel said.

Small landing vessels, manned by soldiers, were making short trips out into the water and picking nurses and civilians from the waves. One of the rescued included the familiar form of Mrs Brown, whose shrieks of protest upon being manhandled into a boat rang up and down the beach.

'Let me go! *Unhand* me, you devils!'

Her protests were ignored. In fact, Margot was almost amused to note that an extra pair of hands had been employed to drag her into the boat.

'Oh, well. Of course *she* survived,' Lola grumbled, as Mrs Brown, bedraggled and sunburned, took her place among the group of prisoners. The small boat reached the shore and they all climbed out and stood, lost, gazing about as if help were about to arrive any time. Mrs Brown startled and cast around to see that her handbag was still in the boat.

'You there!' she cried. A Japanese soldier turned to her. 'Yes, you! Fetch my bag! It's in the silly boat!'

The solider looked uninterested.

'I beg your pardon, can you *not hear me*? Fetch my bag, it's in the boat!' She pointed, frustrated that he didn't seem to understand her. The other prisoners watched on, waiting to see what would happen. The soldier waded back into the water, collected Mrs Brown's bag and opened it. Inside were handfuls of cash. He carefully shovelled all of the money and some rather smart jewellery into his pocket, and handed Mrs Brown her bag. She was incandescent with outrage.

'Well! *I never!*' She fell back onto the sand with what would have been a thump, could Margot have heard it, and the Japanese soldier went about his day, pulling more people from the water and sending them to join the group.

'Do you think she's getting the picture?' Lola asked. 'She's not in charge here anymore. I think she'd rather have drowned.'

'Can't win 'em all,' Hazel said, and their Japanese escort poked her with his bayonet.

'*Aruku!*'

'Time to go,' Margot sighed. She stood and gently helped Charlotte to her feet. 'I hope they have some fresh water at least.'

CHAPTER 13

MARGOT
Muntok, Bangka Island, Dutch East Indies
15 February 1942

The Japanese soldiers marched them over to another group of civilians, wounded Australian soldiers and nurses.

'Beth!' Margot dashed to Beth's side. She would never have imagined a year ago that she'd have been so pleased to see her large comfortable face. 'I'm so glad to find you here!' They hugged each other breathlessly. 'Who else do we have?'

Beth kept Margot's hand in hers, squeezing it hard. 'We've still got Mavis, Hatty, Kath and Joy,' she said. 'But there are more of us arriving all the time.'

Kath Jenkins was a small woman, known for being a talented cricketer, following in the footsteps of her brother, who'd played for Australia. Margot wasn't surprised she'd survived. She was from Horsham in Victoria, where Margot imagined practical people were built.

Margot glanced around the crowd. 'What about Minnie? Or Gull?'

'Not yet,' Beth said. 'But don't worry, we'll probably find them when we get to wherever they're taking us.'

'Where *are* we, anyway?'

'I think we're on Bangka Island. That's what we've been told.'

'Never heard of it.'

'The Japs have, unfortunately.'

'They're marching us to a town called Muntok – that's all I've heard. I get the sense it's best not to ask questions.'

The soldiers started shouting and gesturing at the bedraggled survivors, still covered in oil and salt from the sea.

'*Koshin!*'

It was time to go. Margot's body ached, the sea salt had settled into her scalp like sand, and her skin stung as it chafed against her damp uniform. Her eyes were gritty with exhaustion, and she blinked again and again as she started to walk.

By the time they reached the abandoned cinema at Muntok, it was late afternoon and the sun was setting over the jungle. Margot glanced around the assembled crowd, looking for familiar faces.

'You! Over there! You sit!' A crumpled group of British colonials were standing by the gates as if they were lost. The soldiers shouting orders at them had a few words of English, but they weren't the words they wanted to hear, and they couldn't quite understand what was happening.

'Mischa! Come to me now! Mischa!' A woman called out for a small pale boy with a torn shirt. He left the tin hat he'd found and dutifully headed towards her. Margot watched the woman's hands tremble as she gathered him close.

A small group of nuns still in their black habits and men in sagging linen suits sat under a teak tree. Along one wall lay wounded soldiers. Many of their bandages had been washed away and they were all badly sunburned. But they had survived. Margot made her way to the wall and walked slowly up and down, helping where she could with a drink of water, or the readjustment of a salt-encrusted bandage, but she couldn't find him. Gull had disappeared. She felt her chest contract, grasping on to hope, trying to hold it tight. Where was he? And where was Minnie? Matron Drummond? Matron Paschke? She went to the doors of the cinema and looked beyond, desperate to see them being led around through the jungle, making their way back to her.

But no one was coming. She turned again to survey the gathered crowd. There were Dutch plantation owners, diplomats, families and soldiers, all milling around, looking hopefully for a friendly face.

'Margot! Lola!'

She turned to see Hatty rushing towards her. 'We heard you made it!' Hatty said. 'You're here!'

'Thank God *you* did too,' Margot replied quietly. 'I lost Minnie. Is she here? Have you seen her?'

Hatty shook her head, glancing through the crowd in case she arrived at the sound of her name.

'Any sign of Drummond or Paschke? And what about Gull?' Margot asked. 'She may be with them.'

'Not yet,' Beth said, 'but there are people coming in all the time.'

'We saw Matron Paschke on a raft with a couple of the other girls and some of the wounded,' Joy said. 'They floated away from us on another tide – I don't know what happened to them after that. I don't think Minnie was on that raft, though.'

'Who's that glaring at us?' Margot asked.

Beth joined them. 'Oh, that *bloody* woman! She's German, a doctor apparently. We had a run-in on the raft.'

'You'll like this one, Margot,' Hatty said. 'She was with us, and of course there were too many people, and we were slowly sinking, so we decided we'd take turns spending time in the water.'

'And everyone was wonderful about it, dropping into the water and holding on to the raft so we could all stay afloat – except *her*. Goldberg is her name, I think. She down right *refused* to get off the raft.' Beth's face darkened at the very thought.

'She kept refusing, saying she was a doctor and a mother – and therefore more important than the rest of us,' Hatty went on.

Beth harrumphed. 'More important, my arse.'

'Anyway, I climbed onto the raft,' Hatty said. 'I was so *furious* with the silly arrogant woman, and I punched her in the back over and over! "Get in the water! Get in the water!" The damn woman yelled at me, but she wouldn't budge. That's until our Queensland friend here got involved.'

Beth may have smiled a little at this point, and Dr Goldberg, who could hear that she was being spoken about, was looking over in obvious irritation.

'Beth got her in a headlock and rolled her into the sea!' Hatty announced. 'It was all I could do not to cheer!'

'Well,' Beth declared. 'Nobody's better than anybody else. If the King of England was on the raft, I'd damn well expect him to take his turn in the water as well. Bloody cheek!'

'Beth, you were wonderful.'

Beth blushed a little. 'It was just a headlock,' she said.

Dr Goldberg moved away in disgust.

'Have we seen any other survivors?' Margot asked.

'No.'

'That's that, then,' Margot said. 'Perhaps we won't see any of the other girls again.'

'Don't think like that, Margot,' Hatty said. 'Where there's life, there's hope.'

There was movement at the door again as more prisoners were marched into the cinema. Margot saw a group of wounded soldiers and a couple of other women she didn't know. She scanned them quickly, looking for Gull and Minnie. He wasn't there. She wasn't there. Her heart sank even further.

She had come to rely on Minnie. How many times had she shot her a quick wink as a patient was throwing up copiously into a bucket, or a doctor was explaining exactly how the nurses should suck eggs. Minnie, with her friendly chatter and interest in stories from newfound friends, had made Margot's world feel a little safer. She rubbed her hands together and pushed down the thought that something had gone wrong. Minnie was a strong swimmer, she'd spent summers in the lake at home. If anyone was going to make it to shore, it was Minnie.

'What are they going to do with us?' Margot asked Hatty.

'No idea. I don't think they expected so many. This cinema isn't going to hold us all for long. We've been here all day, and the numbers keep growing. I'd say we're approaching a thousand prisoners now.'

'They'll probably just kill us,' Beth said.

'Well, they could have done that as soon as they saw us, and just let the locals clean up the mess. I think we're going to be held captive.'

'I hope so,' Lola responded. 'Beats being shot.'

'I just wish I could see more of our girls,' Margot said.

'I saw a bonfire on the beach the night we sank.' Lola glanced around at the crowd. 'I know I saw nursing uniforms before we were swept away again. Has anyone found the girls on the beach yet?'

'No, I saw it too,' Hatty replied, 'but I haven't met any nurses who were there.'

'Maybe there's another collection point for prisoners?'

'I hope so,' Beth said, glaring absent-mindedly at Dr Goldberg.

'It seems to me that's all we have at this point,' Margot sighed.

'*Kyuu! Kyuu!*' A soldier started jabbing a group of smartly dressed people with his bayonet. They looked like Dutch rubber plantation owners, with their pale linen pants and floral dresses. They spoke to each other in low voices, glancing at the doorway.

'Jesus, how many ships did the bastards sink?' Beth muttered.

'Looks like a lot.'

'These people were *leaving*. They're not servicemen, the only Allied soldiers here are the wounded,' Lola murmured.

'They don't care,' Beth said.

'Quiet. Don't say that, you'll get yourself shot,' Margot whispered.

'Now look here, you *cannot* have my watch!' A loud Australian voice rang out. The girls glanced across the rows of cinema seats to see a tall man in a white shirt with an angry expression on his face. 'You've bombed my ship, you've arrested hundreds of civilians and injured personnel and taken us to this bloody cinema. Enough! Now get away from me and leave my *damn* watch *alone*!'

'*Ageru!*' The Japanese officer gestured at the man's wrist again, furiously.

'No! You shall not *bloody* have it!'

The Japanese soldier raised his rifle and looked along its barrel. '*Soto!*' he shouted. '*Soto!*'

The man paled. 'Now look here . . .' he began, but the soldier wasn't interested.

'Out!' He lowered his rifle enough to jab him in the chest. The man stepped back, and the soldier applied his bayonet again, pointing to the door. The man held up his hands and began to walk.

'Have the damn watch,' he said, weakly. 'Take it – it's yours.'

Another jab in the back, another flinch.

Margot watched, horrified, as the man was marched to the edge of the jungle. She saw a couple of small grey sparrows scatter to the trees. Another soldier handed the man a shovel, and she gasped as he began to dig.

'What's going on?' Lola whispered behind her.

'I'm pretty sure he's digging his own grave,' Margot whispered back.

'No! Surely they're just *frightening* him – to let him know who's *boss*.'

Margot watched the man's face wash with tears. 'I think they're going to kill him,' she said slowly.

It took a long time. It took no time at all. The grave wasn't deep, but it collected him neatly enough when he fell.

'Lola!' It was Mona. She had a huge gash down her leg that was oozing blood.

'Mona! Are you all right?' Lola hugged her. 'Your leg looks awful. Are you in pain?'

'I'm all right, you should see Rita. She's been cut up in some mangrove swamps near the lighthouse. She was stuck in there for ages, walking through the mud, swimming around the edges of the island. Some of the insect bites alone look like something tried to chew her legs off.'

'What on earth has happened to your hands?'

Mona's hands were bright red. She glanced down. 'Oh, they're not too bad really, I hurt them sliding down the rope into the sea, so I rubbed my lipstick on them. It was the closest thing to a salve I could find.'

'Thank God that's all it is. I don't think I could cope if all of your skin was gone.'

Mona looked almost apologetic. 'I actually think most of it has.'

Margot looked again towards the doors of the cinema, hoping to see Minnie and Gull. Eventually the doors opened and her anxious wait was rewarded. Gull ambled slowly towards her, his arms around two Australian soldiers, themselves limping with exhaustion.

'Gull!' She ran to him and his face lit up.

'Margot! You're alive!' He kissed her cheek. 'Oh thank God! I thought you'd gone. How many made it to shore? Is Minnie here? And Beth?'

'No sign of Minnie yet,' Margot said. 'I was hoping she might be with you. Beth's here, though, with Lola and some other girls. We're missing a lot though.'

Gull hugged her. 'They'll be all right. I know they will. You mustn't worry.'

'I'll try not to, if you'll tell me what happened to you.'

'I don't really know. I passed out for a while, I heard voices, but they sounded far away and I couldn't seem to call out. I think I was out there for over a day. Eventually I realised the raft was moving with some direction, not just following the swell of the ocean. A couple of Poms had tied their raft rope to mine, and they dragged me in. I'm bloody grateful.'

'So am I!' She smiled at him. 'I hate to admit it, but you still seem pretty lucky.'

'I'm trying to use my powers to end the war as we speak.'

'Try harder!' the soldier holding him grunted.

'Just let me sit down, and I will.' And with that, Gull sank grate-fully to the ground and closed his eyes. Margot plonked herself down beside him, torn between being relieved that he was alive and being terrified she'd lose him again. He was here. But where was Minnie? When would she arrive at the camp? Margot scanned the crowd again, looking for her friend's dark hair. Minnie had been seen during the night and had spoken to nurses who'd made it to shore. She had a raft and a life vest and she was a strong swimmer. There was no reason for her to just disappear. She would return soon enough, with a wink and a smile, and everything would be all right again.

CHAPTER 14

MINNIE
Radji Beach, Bangka Island
14 February 1942

'Minnie! Over here!' An arm reached down and Minnie felt herself being dragged from the sea, swiftly followed by Dot and Agnes.

'Welcome aboard,' Matron Drummond said as the girls were upended into a lifeboat. Matron was gently holding a soldier who'd lost his arm to shrapnel before they'd left Singapore. It looked like the bombing of the *Vyner Brooke* had almost finished the job. He was bleeding from the head and Matron was pressing the fabric of a coat into the wound. 'Can you paddle?' she asked Minnie. A small woman she didn't recognise handed her a paddle.

'I can, or I can get out and swim for a while if you need me to,' Minnie said.

'We were with another raft,' Agnes told them. 'But they sailed away on another current. We can still swim a little, I imagine. After a rest.'

'Let's hope we'll reach the beach soon,' the lady said. 'I'm a little tired of swimming.'

The body of an elderly man drifted past, face down, his necktie floating like a leash behind him. Minnie resisted the urge to pull him aboard.

Japanese planes, swooping back over the ocean, had finished their pass. They roared away towards the horizon, the noise growing softer. But they'd be back. In their absence, the sound of voices from the sea was a blanket. *Help me! Bob! Where's Bob? Fern! Fern! Help! I'll drown!*

The waves seemed bigger, rising, then dipping down to slowly shake the ocean free of the oil, the debris, the bodies. Minnie heaved a sigh of relief. She'd been rescued.

'Push away from the area! In case it catches fire! Move!' a nurse called.

They paddled with everything they had. Those on the smaller life rafts did their best; people in the water kicked their feet, holding on to the small rafts. And the ocean jostled around on itself in surprise, rolling and splashing until the great currents of the Bangka Strait took over once more.

Minnie kept up her steady rate. Stroke stroke, splash splash. The ocean was alive beneath them. 'How many nurses made it out, Matron?' she asked.

Matron Drummond glanced about. 'I think I've seen at least half of the girls,' she said. 'But a couple won't make it.'

'Who? Margot? Have you seen Lola and Beth?'

'Let's discuss that later,' Matron Drummond told her. 'We've got to get these people to shore first. We must set up a nursing station, start treating the injured.'

'Has anybody seen my husband?' a woman in a blue sundress asked. 'We were separated just after the siren sounded.'

'What's his name?'

'Martin. He's, well, he's a tall man with dark hair, but I don't suppose you can tell that at the moment . . .'

The nurses glanced at each other. Nothing.

'Let's hope he's fine,' Minnie said. 'We'll probably catch up with lots of people on the shore.'

'Can I paddle for a while, give you a rest?' A middle-aged man with a handkerchief bandaged over his eye leaned across and took the paddle.

'Certainly, just give it back when you get tired. I'm running on adrenaline – I feel like I could paddle for a year.' It was a lie. Minnie let her arms fall heavily to her lap. How they throbbed with the effort of staying alive. When she glanced around again, she found that they'd drifted further away from the final resting place of the *Vyner Brooke*. The oil slick on the water's surface was dispersing, and the voices were growing less urgent as people found their way onto rafts and determined which direction to swim or paddle. Minnie put her hand into the cool ocean and moved it through the water, as the sea lifted them up on its back and took them closer to Bangka Island.

Eventually, Minnie lowered herself back into the water and they floated towards the island as if it were drawing them in. Her legs ached, but she kicked on, as the shouts and whistles of other survivors were carried on the sea breeze, then drifted away. Seagulls flew overhead, curious, then wheeled away towards the dark green coast. As she looked out across the sea, Minnie was certain she glimpsed another life raft here or there, with another group of bedraggled women or wounded soldiers, being carried away from her. 'Margot!' she called out. 'Margot McNee! Is that you?' There was no response, and Minnie wondered if she'd heard voices at all, or if she was just imagining her friends in the dark ocean. Margot would be on shore by now, she told herself. She'd be terrified, but she'd be all right. The thought gave her comfort.

Finally, the boat neared land, but it dithered there in the shallows, deciding if it was safe to stay.

'Out we get, girls!' Matron Drummond was in the water and pushing at the back of the boat, the water up to her ample bosom.

Minnie's feet finally reached down and touched the sand, just a few yards from the beach. 'Dry land,' she said. 'Safe at last!' Her feet felt numb and weak, and her arms ached.

'Minnie and Dot, pull the lifeboat up onto the beach and we'll get the men out.' Matron Drummond glanced around. 'We'll need to find fresh water as soon as possible. And some shade. We'll probably need some stretchers soon, if we're to transport these men.'

Fifty yards away, a small group of crew and injured soldiers were also making their way to shore. Minnie felt a surge of relief as she heard their voices. They were alive, they had made it. They'd be safe soon. A tall thin man approached, and she recognised Commander Sedgeman from the *Vyner Brooke*. She took a deep breath and helped haul the lifeboat further up the beach, glancing around for signs of danger.

'Glad to see you made it,' he said. His face was speckled with oil and his shirt was torn. He placed his hands on his hips, exhausted but smiling.

'And you,' Matron Drummond replied. 'Any idea how many others are landing here?'

'None, I'm afraid. The rafts are moving about like confetti. It's impossible to tell.'

Matron Drummond nodded. 'All right, girls, let's get our patients lying comfortably. I want you to see if you can shake out the great coats and the blankets a bit – get as much sand out as possible and we'll be able to keep them warm tonight.' She marched up and down the sand as if she was still on the ward in Broken Hill.

'We'll send out a couple of scouting parties,' the commander announced. 'Who's up to heading along the beach? We'll need three teams, one in each direction and one to find firewood in the forest.'

Some hands went up slowly into the air. Minnie glanced around at them all. They were to a man, and woman, exhausted. But they would need water. And food and shelter soon enough. It wasn't long before three groups headed out.

She knelt beside the soldier with one arm. 'Here, there's still a bit of water left. And a group have gone looking for firewood and more fresh water now, so don't be worried about drinking it. These islands are tropical – should be no shortage of water.'

He smiled weakly and took a few sips. 'Thanks,' he said. 'It's a relief to be out of that bloody boat. I'm Kenneth.'

'Pleased to meet you, Kenneth,' Minnie said. 'How's the pain?'

'Not too bad. Considering.' He handed her the bottle.

'We'll find some supplies to help you,' Minnie told him. She glanced up the deserted beach to the dark line of trees. The sun was setting behind the jungle. 'I just hope the scavenger team find us some firewood so we can light a beacon,' she said. 'There must be hundreds of people still in the water – we can't be the only survivors.'

'I saw lots of rafts heading east after the ship went down. God only knows where they'll end up. Maybe the Japs got 'em.'

'Maybe,' Minnie said. 'But still, I bet a lot of them are still floating out there in their vests, and on the rafts. There's still time for them to make it to shore.'

A warm breeze whistled through the trees, and Minnie heard voices calling to them from the west.

'We've found water!'

A weak cheer went up among the nurses and some of the patients.

'How are we going looking for driftwood?' Matron Drummond asked.

'Not bad – finding dry kindling is the challenge – mostly it's pretty green.' Commander Sedgeman was dragging a dead tree behind him.

'But I was a Boy Scout, you know. We'll have a fire going in no time at all.'

He was right. After the fire was lit, the few sailors in the group searched in the jungle again, and they soon had a tall beachside beacon blazing, with a pile of wood nearby to keep it stoked throughout the night. The sight of the flames seemed to lighten everyone's spirits. They hadn't drowned, they were still free, they had water, they had fire.

They gathered in the dark to formulate a plan. Matron Drummond stared up at Commander Sedgeman through the gloom, her eyes moving back constantly to her nurses as they comforted the wounded in the glow of the fire. 'Where do you think we can go from here?' she asked. 'Steal a boat?'

'We've got a boat,' the Commander replied.

'Not big enough to go anywhere, the Japs would shoot us on sight,' a soldier said.

'We're going to need medical supplies,' Minnie said, watching Dot pulling a damp coat over a sleeping soldier.

'And food,' Agnes added. 'We're going to need food in the morning. There are children. They can't go without. Their mothers are already beside themselves.'

Matron Drummond looked at the children asleep, finally, in their mothers' arms. 'This is no place for them, and we have more survivors arriving all the time.'

'We don't have much alternative at the moment,' Commander Sedgeman told her.

'Surrender?'

'Perhaps. Let's see what tomorrow brings.'

'Any chance tomorrow might bring sausages?' a young mother asked.

'Not much,' he told her.

'Hello, there?'

The Commander leaped up from his spot next to the fire and peered into the black night. A woman's voice could be heard again.

'Hello! RAN Nurse Vivian Bullwinkel. I'm here with a couple of friends – we came ashore up towards the lighthouse.'

Minnie ran to her and hugged her. 'Oh, Bully! I'm so happy to see you!'

Vivian looked utterly exhausted. Her pale skin was red and peeling and her chestnut hair was standing stiffly on end, thick with salt. She guided a limping soldier and a woman in a torn dress to a gathering of patients sitting on an oily overcoat, and the two fell gratefully to the sand.

Minnie grinned from ear to ear. 'Any others?' she asked.

'I couldn't say, but I think so. We could occasionally hear voices out on the water. There are more of us about.' Vivian came close to the fire and her tired face seemed to relax a little. 'Although how long before they make it to the island, I couldn't say.'

'We'll take it in turns keeping watch,' Commander Sedgeman said.

Matron Drummond gave Vivian a hug and handed her a bottle of water. 'Drink your fill,' she told her.

Vivian drank gratefully, and passed the water on. 'Who else is here?'

'Around a hundred all up. We have a good number of wounded soldiers, civilians, crew from the ship, twenty-one nurses – Dot and Agnes are just with the stretcher crew now. A couple of sailors. Some wounded.'

As she settled by the fire, Minnie watched the dark stars, so high in the sky they were shining over the wheatbelt back home, crowned by the Southern Cross. So high they were a million years ago, before she had ever been born. She listened to the murmured voices of the nurses, the mothers and the soldiers, and Matron Drummond's comforting rumble, giving orders as if nothing was amiss in her ward at all.

And yet Minnie wanted so badly to hear her father and mother once again, talking in the kitchen, turning the wireless to the ABC news bulletin. She wished she could hear their voices on the breeze, and perhaps she did, until the waves fell softly to the shore and took them away.

'Hello? Australians?' a male voice called out in the dark. 'What a fire! We followed it in from the sea!' A group of wounded soldiers limped up the beach from the south. 'You all from the *Vyner Brooke*?'

'Yes! Welcome to our camp!'

The men fell onto the sand with groans of relief.

'I thought we were done for out there,' one soldier said. He had a head wound and his hair had been shaved. The ragged edges of the surgery were red raw. Minnie fetched more water and cast about for some fabric for bandages. Everything was filthy, of course, covered in salt from the sea. Better to leave the wound for now than to have unsanitary bindings.

'We're glad you made it. I'm still hoping to see a few more faces tonight.'

'You might be lucky, I can hear voices out there, in the dark. It's eerie, but of course they're all ours, aren't they?'

There was silence, while the fire crackled and the sea pushed in and pulled away.

'Help!' A voice called out in the distance. 'Can you help please? Matron Drummond, is that you?'

Matron Drummond marched to the edge of the light and disappeared into the dark. 'Yes, I'm here. Tess Sullivan, is that you?'

'Yes, Matron, and I need some help. A couple of the girls are so badly wounded they can't walk.'

'We have a doctor,' Matron Drummond told her. 'One minute and I'll fetch him. Dr Ho?'

A doctor who had been helping with the wounded looked up from a patient with massive leg wounds. 'Yes?'

'We have some more injured arriving from further up the beach – my nurse tells me they're in need of medical assistance. Could you go with her, please?' It sounded a little like an order.

'No.'

'No?'

'I'm staying here.' He continued inspecting the patient before him.

There was a pause. 'Doctor, we are more than capable of bandaging these injuries; it forms a large part of our work here, as I'm sure you can imagine.'

'I am staying with these patients.'

'There are *other* patients in greater need further up the beach.'

'Matron. I am *busy*. Find someone else.' The doctor moved away to another patient lying on one of the coats Matron Drummond had thrown off the ship.

'Doctor. There *is* no one else.'

He ignored her.

She turned. 'Dot, Minnie, young man, what is your name?'

'Private Carnovale, Matron. Edward.'

'Private Carnovale, would you please accompany my nurses to their comrades and help the injured to get here as quickly as possible?'

'Yes, Matron.'

The camp fell into its own routine. Names were exchanged, water handed around, and then, as they settled again, more groups arrived; British, Dutch, nuns, nurses, a collection of flotsam on the beach, Minnie thought. A loose bundle of people who weren't supposed to survive at all.

During the dark night, the gathering continued to grow, as people joined the vigil like lost children, limping, exhausted, up the beach towards the flames.

'Lieutenant Commander James White, at your service, ladies.'

Minnie looked up from a soldier with a shrapnel wound in his shoulder, to nod at the commander. 'Pleased to meet you. Sister Minnie Hodgson. I'd love a fresh bandage if Matron has one?'

'I'll check now,' he said, and disappeared into the gloom.

When he returned a few minutes later, he had a bandage in his hand. 'It's still wet, I'm afraid, but there's no way around that.' He glanced at the wounded. 'Do you think they'll survive?'

'We can only try,' Minnie told him. It wouldn't do to be honest. 'Which ship are you from?'

'HMS *Shu Kwang*. I think we went down just before you did.' He glanced at the jungle. 'The Japs will probably be back soon to finish the job.'

'Don't say that,' Minnie replied. 'We'll most likely be taken into a camp for the rest of the war, that's all.'

'You may be right,' Commander White said. 'Although there's been a lot of talk about whether the Japs take prisoners.' He handed her the bandage and she began to unroll it in front of the fire to dry it out. 'I suspect they don't,' he added darkly.

'We can't think that way,' Minnie murmured. 'These people need hope. We all do.'

'Hope is for fools,' he told her. 'Our best bet was getting out on the damn ships. Now that's gone, it's anyone's guess.'

'Don't share your theories with the civilians, please,' Minnie said. 'They've got enough on their minds. We don't need people giving into panic.'

'I'll keep mum. But you're army, so I think you should know.'

'I'm just trying to do my job, if you don't mind,' Minnie said. 'It's the only way I can get through the night – keeping busy, looking after these people. I can't think about tomorrow. I have to keep everyone comfortable *now*.'

'Well,' Commander White said, 'I wish you luck.' He gave her a brief, sad salute and moved off into the shadows.

Minnie shrugged, decided the bandage would just have to do, and went back to her patient.

As morning light spread out across the water and crept up the beach, Minnie woke to the sound of voices. She ran her fingers through her hair to push it back into place and went to join Matron Drummond, sitting stiffly against the trunk of a small tree with Commander Sedgeman.

'Good morning, Sister Hodgson,' Matron Drummond said. 'We're just making a plan for today, now that we can see what's about us.'

'Yes,' the commander said. 'We've had plenty of arrivals overnight, but we need to work out how to keep everyone safe.'

'We'll need to prioritise water and mobility for the patients,' Matron Drummond observed. 'They obviously can't stay here without proper medical care. I'll get a group of the girls together to fashion some stretchers so we can transport them to a local village. There must be help somewhere.'

'I rather think there will be *Japs* everywhere.'

'Surrender, then?'

'We'll see if we can get the lie of the land, and discuss it later.' Commander Sedgeman poked the fire.

Matron Drummond cast an assessing glance across her ward, arranged up the beach in a row. 'Many of my nurses are fine to form groups. If the fit men can join them, we could send each group out.'

'Yes, I was thinking we'd send two groups up and down the beach, resupplying water and finding suitable timber – both for the fire and for stretcher poles. Then a third group would head inland along that track.' He glanced briefly over his shoulder. 'It presumably heads towards a village. We may find help of some sort there.'

'I think that sounds very satisfactory,' Matron Drummond agreed. 'Minnie, would you be happy to take a group a mile or so to the south?'

'Of course, I'll take Dot and Agnes, if that's all right.'

'Yes, and good luck.' Matron Drummond turned back to her patients.

Minnie and the girls walked for some distance before they found fresh water and filled the canteens they'd brought. They were feeling very pleased with themselves as they returned to camp. A captain from another group was already making his report.

'We found a fishing village not too far from here, there's a small population living there,' he told Commander Sedgeman and Matron Drummond.

'Were they any help?' the commander asked.

'Not really. The women were kind – they gave us some fresh water – but the men got angry with them and sent us away. We tried to get some information before we went and it's not good news, I'm afraid.'

'What is it? The Japanese are coming?'

'They took over the island a day or so ago. The men don't want to help us in case they're punished. They told us we have to go to Muntok to surrender.'

'Matron, how are your patients?' Commander Sedgeman asked.

'Some of them need more medical attention than we are likely to receive on this island. We've been building stretchers to transport them, I've sent the most seriously injured to the little fisherman's hut there on the edge of the jungle, and we've set up an intensive care ward in the shade at the foot of the jungle as well. There's not much else we can do.'

'I'll get most of my men on making stretchers, and those not able to help there will be beachcombing for firewood, and anything else we may find useful,' the commander told her.

'Let's meet again later this afternoon to discuss our options.'

Minnie took some water to a soldier who was just waking.

'Have we surrendered yet?' he asked.

'Not yet, but I think we will,' she told him.

'Never!'

'What are we going to do? All these mothers and their children? All these elderly people? Wounded soldiers?'

'Those bastards don't take prisoners – everyone knows that.'

'We may have no choice.'

The soldier fell back onto the sand and closed his eyes.

The sun was low in the sky by the time another meeting was called. Matron Drummond, Commander Sedgeman, Minnie, Dot and a small selection of sailors and soldiers gathered in the shade of the trees along the edge of the beach.

'Now, I'm sorry to say, not much has changed since our last meeting, except that our patients are in a worse state, and no one has eaten,' Matron Drummond said.

'As I see it, we have three options,' the commander began. 'The first is, we could repair the boats, find some provisions, then attempt to leave Bangka Island and find a friendly port. The second option would be to get off the beach, where, I'm sure you're all aware, we are very exposed, and try to survive in the jungle, perhaps with the help of local natives.'

'That doesn't seem likely,' a sailor said gloomily.

'The final option would be to venture down the path to Muntok and surrender to the Japanese for the duration of the war.'

There was silence.

'Is there another option?' Dot asked quietly. Minnie elbowed her in the ribs.

'Thoughts?' The commander looked around the group. Silence. He continued.

'We can't seriously entertain the thought of moving this many injured people, along with young families, onto boats which have been under attack and almost destroyed, any more than we can imagine that we can find enough food and shelter to safely live out the war.'

'There must be food in the jungle if you know where to look . . .' Minnie suggested.

'Yes, but we *don't*, and the locals are too frightened to help us – and I can't say I blame them – I'm scared too,' Dot said.

'I don't think we'd find enough food to feed this many mouths, anyway,' the commander said. 'It's just not feasible.'

'I agree,' Matron Drummond said. More silence. 'Which leaves us with only one option.'

'We must surrender at Muntok.'

'They'll kill us all,' a voice from the group of soldiers countered.

'Perhaps not. We need to consider the safety of the civilians, the nurses and the wounded. The safest option for them all is to surrender.' The commander's face was grey. He was almost a jolly sort of man, Minnie thought, as she stood beside him, but his face had lost its life, as if his heart had given out.

She felt a chill slowly crawl up her spine. Their lives had been thrown off the ship, scattered on the beach and their freedom was almost gone. Everyone had heard the stories. She wanted to run away, or to wake up somewhere far from here, with a tale to tell Margot, but she pressed the impulse down. Minnie looked up and down the beach at the wounded soldiers, the elderly and the young families scattered along the shore of an island no one even knew existed.

Dot spoke up. 'I don't trust the Japs.'

'No one does, but there it is,' Commander Sedgeman told her.

'Then we must surrender,' one of the army captains added.

'All agreed?' Matron Drummond asked.

There was a slow show of hands.

'All agreed.' The commander stood and brushed down his trousers. 'I think we should spend one last night here, get some rest, then head into Muntok in the morning. I'll take a group of men with me to surrender, and we'll bring the Japs back to collect the rest of you.'

'One more night of freedom,' Matron Drummond said.

'We'll have food in our stomachs this time tomorrow.'

'I do hope so.'

While daylight remained, the nurses worked on their patients, and that night they watched silently as a distant searchlight flashed over the water, again and again. They gazed on in horror as the Japanese ships found their prey and fired upon it. The gunners on the ship fired back, but it was too little, a splatter into the black sky, a brief battle, and another Allied ship was sunk.

'There they go,' murmured Agnes. 'Poor bastards.'

Just over a hundred people were now on the beach, seeking safety. Just before dawn another group of evacuees joined them by the fire, arriving out of the darkness, like ghosts.

In the morning a final meeting was held.

'It's agreed,' Matron Drummond said. 'I've been speaking to the nurses and we all feel that we can't escape the Japanese, and we refuse to leave our patients. We were forced to leave patients in Singapore and we won't do it again. We will remain here with the wounded.'

'Very well,' Commander Sedgeman nodded. 'I'll take a couple of sailors from the *Prince of Wales* and head into Muntok. I'm not sure how long it will take, but I believe you can expect us back by late morning.' With a final nod, the commander and the crew members departed.

'Right, nurses. Let's work quickly to build more stretchers before the Japanese come to collect us. Bully and Agnes, I have some fabric here, do you think you could make a large Red Cross symbol on the beach before they arrive? I'd like to remind them we're a nursing ship.'

'Yes, Matron.'

A tall willowy woman in a navy skirt and white blouse approached Matron Drummond. It was Greta Howard, a diplomat's wife Minnie had briefly met while aboard the *Vyner Brooke*. 'Excuse me,' she said. 'Do you have a moment?'

'Certainly,' Matron Drummond replied.

Greta looked apologetic. 'I've been talking to the other British and Dutch women here. We all have children, you see, well, some of us don't, some of us are rather elderly. The thing is, do you think it would be appropriate if we all went as a group to surrender in

Muntok without waiting for the Japs to come here? I'm sure you can hear the children. They're hungry and tired. We have nothing to feed them, and we're of no use to you here.' She glanced back at the other mothers and old men and women who looked anxiously on. 'If we walk to Muntok, we can rest and feed the old and the children far sooner – and we'll be one less thing for you to worry about.'

Matron Drummond glanced up and down the beach. 'I must say, that does sound reasonable,' she said. 'Does anyone else want to join these ladies?'

A bedraggled cluster of women scrambled to their feet. One elderly lady didn't. She settled back on the sand, pulling her scarf around her shoulders to protect herself from the sun.

'Mrs Soames?'

'No, thank you. My Henry is here and unable to move. I'll stay. We've been together for over fifty years and I shan't be leaving him now. You young ones take the babies. Be safe.'

'Well, I can't disagree,' Matron Drummond said. 'You'll save the children a long wait since we're headed that way anyway.' She reached out and shook Greta's hand. 'Good luck, Mrs Howard. I hope you find Muntok with no trouble. I'm sure we'll see you there later this afternoon.'

Greta smiled and held on to Matron Drummond's hand for a long moment. 'Thank you. And thank you for the care you have taken with us all. We'll see you soon.'

Minnie watched them walking away, the weary children stumbling on the sandy path, pulling at their mothers. She smiled as a small boy clutching a teddy bear held on to his mother tightly, tugging on her hand. It was Henry and Winston. She watched as his frightened mother, already exhausted, swept him into her arms, pretending his little warm body weighed nothing at all. He snuggled forward and kissed her cheek before his eyes closed. Winston regarded Minnie sadly, dangling almost forgotten from the little boy's hand as they passed through the first line of trees and vanished into the shadows.

'Come now, girls. I want that cross to be so large the Japanese can't pretend they haven't seen it. I want it visible from the air. Stretch it out and weight it carefully.'

'Yes, Matron.' Agnes pulled again on the fabric.

'Now, we know the Japanese are unlikely to help with these stretchers, so can we please make certain we have built them correctly? We'll need around twenty, possibly twenty-five. Do a good job, we'll be dragging them a long way.'

The nurses worked quietly, very aware they were waiting for the Japanese Army to arrive. Minnie tended her patients, her mind rolling like the ocean. How would they cope in the camps? What would they find? How long would they be prisoners of war? Would she find Margot?

A couple of soldiers propped themselves up on their elbows.

'This place isn't so bad,' one of them said. 'Perhaps we could come back to visit one day, have a holiday by the sea.' He glanced at Minnie and Hazel. 'What do you say, girls? Fancy a beach vacation?'

'Don't talk nonsense,' Minnie told them. 'Once I get home, I'm never leaving again.'

'You sure you won't be bored by that after this?'

Minnie glanced around at the collection of people on the beach, waiting to be saved. 'No, I'll be quite content. You know the saying: there's no place like home.'

The soldier looked out to sea for a long time.

*

By mid-morning, Commander Sedgeman and his companions were back, marching with a troop of some twenty Japanese soldiers clad in khaki shirts, trousers and hats with neck flaps to protect them from the sun. They crossed the small beach to the dishevelled group. Minnie stood up as straight as she dared, and saw Matron Drummond pull herself up to her full height and adjust her wire-rimmed glasses. The Japanese soldiers were heavily armed.

'Here are the survivors of the *Vyner Brooke*,' Commander Sedgeman was explaining. 'Captain Masaru, these are the nurses of the 8th Division AIF and the wounded from the Australian and British Armed Forces.' He indicated the group with a formal sweep of his hand, then saluted. 'We offer our surrender to the Japanese Army, and wish to be taken into custody.'

Minnie held her breath. There was something about Captain Masaru. He was looking through them all, as if they weren't even there. He stared at the ocean, perhaps weighing their fate, the commander barely a distraction. The patients lying on the beach twisted their heads so they could see what was going on, and the nurses stood to attention at the end of the rows.

Finally, Captain Orita Masaru spoke, giving brief orders to his sergeant major, who barked at the troops.

They loaded and cocked their rifles.

'We are members of the Australian Army, and we surrender to you, General Orita Masaru!' Commander Sedgeman repeated, his voice rising. 'We demand fair treatment under the Geneva Convention.'

Captain Masaru ignored him and gave more orders to his Japanese troops. The sergeant major seemed irritable. He shouted at his men, who stepped forward, bayonets aloft.

'*Ugoku! Ugoku!*'

The bayonets were jabbed into the soldiers standing, waiting to be taken. '*Ugoku!*'

'What's going on?' one soldier muttered.

'You know what's going on,' another said quietly.

The Japanese prodded the soldiers into two groups. '*Anata!*' The men did as they were told. '*Anata!* Up!' More Japanese soldiers marched up and down the rows, jabbing the wounded, demanding they stand and join their comrades. 'Up! *Koshin! Koshin!*'

'You only need to give your name, rank and serial number!' Agnes called out.

There was a rocky outcrop at the end of the beach and the men disappeared behind it. Twenty men with twelve captors. Silence descended. Minnie looked around at the remaining Japanese soldiers. They were shorter than the Australians. They glared at her, as if they were angry at her for daring to look at them at all. But she did dare, because something had replaced her fear. Sitting quietly on the beach with the other nurses, she wasn't certain what it was.

She thought about her parents, still watching the door, waiting for her to come home. There were so many stories she could never tell them, stories she'd saved up in her mind, sorting through the details of the people she'd met, the monsoons of Singapore, Lola's sweet voice, Beth's friendly drawl and Margot's kind heart. She wished herself home again, and for a moment, like a ghost, she was there, a breeze across the paddocks. Her father was taking the ute up the race. And she felt the wheatbelt wind in her face and her hair, she was flying, and her father's leathered elbow was resting on the open window, his hair dusty, and although Minnie couldn't see his face, she could tell he was smiling.

*

On the other side of the outcrop the men were called to a halt. One of the Japanese soldiers pulled strips of fabric from his rucksack. He handed them out to the captives. Blindfolds. 'You!' the Japanese soldier shouted. 'On!'

Even before the last of them had tied the blindfolds, the killing began.

One by one, their bodies slumped to the ground.

It took less than two minutes for them to die, and a few minutes more to drag them all into the jungle, remove their blindfolds and dump them there.

The Japanese soldiers returned to the main group, still cleaning their bayonets.

'Here they come,' Agnes whispered.

'Hush now,' Minnie said.

'We're all dead.'

'*Hush*.'

The Japanese soldiers marched towards them. 'Up! Up!' Captain Masaru was indicating the remaining men.

'He can't stand,' Matron Drummond said. 'Don't poke him, he *can't stand*.'

A soldier approached, drew his bayonet and stabbed the man in the heart. The Japanese soldier then scowled. '*Anata!* You!'

The remaining men struggled to their feet, glancing uneasily at each other.

'March!'

They stumbled towards the headland, some limping and hold-ing their friends. They were followed by more troops this time. Once they were around the headland the Japanese took out the blindfolds.

'This! This!' They handed them around. There weren't enough. Captain Masaru went over to one of the soldiers and tore a strip from the bottom of his shirt and handed it to him, indicating that those without blindfolds should do the same. 'You! You!'

'I say! You can't do this!' an Englishman shouted. 'This is barbaric! This is illegal!'

The sergeant major took out his sword and slashed the Englishman's face from forehead to chin. He slumped to the sand, groaning, then fell silent.

The machine gun was being set up behind them.

'Hey, mate, we can make a break for it,' one of the soldiers muttered. 'We might be quick enough to get away. Maybe we can get out of range.'

Three men dashed into the ocean and dove under the waves, striking out and away from the beach. A shower of bullets rang out, pelting the water like handfuls of gravel. The men floated back up to the surface.

The rest waited to be blindfolded, to be bayoneted or shot, piled on the beach, and left to rot.

The nurses sat waiting, watched by their guards. They were silent. They heard the shots.

'Bully, they've murdered them all,' Minnie murmured.

'It's true, then,' Vivian said. 'They don't take prisoners.'

Minnie glanced around at their Japanese captors. 'Matron,' she whispered, 'do you think we could make a run for it? Some of us are good swimmers, or good runners. If we took off into the jungle or the sea, perhaps a couple of us might make it?'

'No. We shall remain with our patients. Our soldiers rely on us. How could we allow the last thing they see to be us running away from them to save ourselves? Nurses, we took an oath and today is the day we will live that oath.' She smiled gently at them all. 'Besides, where there's life, there's hope.'

But there was no hope, really. There were moments, there might even be minutes, but there was no hope left on Radji Beach.

This was the fate worse than death.

Minnie would die with the shame of it in her heart. She fixed her eyes on the sky and forbade herself tears. The filth of it was now in her, would remain when she died. She turned her face away from the soldier above her and looked up the beach to where the water was washing the sand clean. There was rubbish lying along the pure white sand, no, there were *people*, soldiers bayoneted where they lay, nurses with their uniforms torn from their bodies, their skirts dragged up past their waists. *They* were the flotsam and jetsam of the ships, preyed upon by warplanes and devoured like carrion.

Minnie clamped her eyes shut. She placed her hand on her wildly beating heart, and told herself it was still hers.

As the soldier sat up and secured his belt buckle once more, Minnie glimpsed the sky again. The heavens were endless and free. Her face was wet with tears and she closed her eyes. When she opened them, the sky above her was bright blue. And she realised that when they closed, it was still above her, as beautiful as it had ever been, it was just that she couldn't see it anymore.

On Radji Beach the day was ending. There would be no sunset over the ocean. There would be no sunrise to follow the moon.

The Japanese soldiers squatted to clean their rifles and prepare to reload. One soldier was setting up his machine gun. It was positioned low on the sand, pointing towards the ocean. The nurses pulled their uniforms back into shape and sat with their arms around each other in silence.

'Don't you dare feel ashamed,' Agnes whispered. 'Don't you dare. It's *their* shame, not ours!'

Minnie nodded, her heart thundering in her chest. She stood slowly, waiting to disappear into the winds of war. She thought of Oliver. *I'm still brave*, she told him. *I'm going home, Oliver. I can be brave until I make it home.*

Vivian clasped Minnie's hand and squeezed. It was a strong hand, full of warmth and care. Minnie wondered how many other dying hands it had held. She squeezed back. The ocean crawled to shore and then ebbed away, the slow eternal heartbeat of a planet. This outrage was nothing, this fear, this pain, this flicker of ending life, was nothing.

Captain Masaru gave an order in a quick staccato before the men pushed forward with their bayonets, forcing the girls into a rough line, facing the sea.

'Which direction is Australia?' Minnie whispered. 'Is it this way?'

'Yes, yes. It's just over the edge of the ocean.'

'Our Lord, who art in heaven, hallowed be thy name . . .'

Minnie didn't pray. No one was listening, and no one would ever know what had happened to the nurses on Bangka. They were lost on an island, they were a secret. They were forgotten girls on a beach.

CHAPTER 15

MARGOT
Muntok, Bangka Island
15 February 1942

As night fell at the cinema, the Japanese soldiers delivered meagre supplies to their captives; a little rice, some water, a few pieces of fruit. It had been a long day, with no resolution. The nurses slept on the floor or on the ground, heavy with exhaustion and dread. Margot lay next to Gull, still afraid, still hearing the sea at the edge of her dreams.

'*Okiro! Okiro!*' came the call early the next morning.

'Gull, are you awake?' Margot murmured, stroking his hair.

'I . . . I where?' He struggled to sit up.

'We're on Muntok,' Margot told him. 'You're quite safe, although the Japanese are our companions now.'

Gull appeared to wake fully, his face flushed. Margot pressed her palm across his forehead. It was warm, certainly, but she wondered if it was too warm, if he had a fever.

'Yes, of course,' he said eventually. 'I wonder where they're taking us today.'

Margot glanced around at the crowd slowly getting to their feet. Dr Goldberg was hovering near the guards at the gate, Beth was

talking to some Dutch nuns who were sitting on their small knapsacks, nodding at the few words of English they could understand.
She could see Joy fetching some water for a soldier with a bandaged
leg, and a group of children lying on an old blanket, unwilling to
face a new day. The birds were starting to rustle and call in the jungle and the breeze from the ocean still held some coolness.

'*Tachiagaru!*' The guards gestured for them to stand and lined
them up in pairs.

'*Koshin! Koshin!*'

The crowd looked at them blankly. A guard approached an
elderly man and pushed him in the back. He staggered forward.
'*Koshin!*'

'I don't know why they get to yell at us,' Beth said. 'The way
I see it, we took Bangka Island *first*!'

'Yes,' Margot agreed. 'Only with fewer troops and guns!'

The prisoners were marched slowly through Muntok, closely
guarded by soldiers bearing rifles and machine guns. The local fishermen watched on silently until they reached the end of a road.
Gates swung open.

Beth peered around. 'What is this place?' she said. 'Do they have
a prison here already?'

'I think this is a coolie camp,' Joy said quietly.

'What's that?'

'It's cheap housing for Malay workers in the tin mines. I'd say
they've moved on because of the war.'

Margot looked around at the huge yard enclosed with barbed
wire, the basic open buildings around the perimeter and the long
ditch running through the middle. It held a trough, or a *tong*,
they had seen before that was used for washing. The ditch was to
carry the effluent from the drop toilets located further up the hill.

The small brick buildings had few walls, to allow the breeze through, and were thatched with palm fronds.

'Looks pretty basic,' Beth said.

'It'll do. I don't think we'll be here too long,' Margot said.

'I bloody hope not.'

'When you say we won't be here long, do you mean because we'll be dead?' Lola asked.

'Where're Matron Drummond and the other girls we saw by the bonfire on the beach?' Hatty wondered. 'Do you think we'll see them soon?'

'Do you think there's another camp?' Margot added. 'Perhaps Minnie and the others are there.'

'You! Here!' The soldiers began pointing to the men in the group. They shuffled forward. 'No! You! *Koho!* Back!' A soldier began to drag at an old lady still carrying her life vest, her only possession. She went white in fright and fell back behind Margot and Hatty.

'Where are you taking us?' a middle-aged man asked in alarm.

'Yes, where are you taking them?' another middle-aged woman demanded.

'You go back! *Iku!*' The soldier pointed the bayonet at the woman's chest and she fell back beside the other women, who put their arms around her in fright.

'I believe they're taking them to another camp, that's all,' a slightly stout British woman said calmly. She pushed her glasses higher up on her nose and glanced among the soldiers. 'That's right, isn't it, gentlemen? Another camp? Men's camp?'

'*Dansei!*' the soldier said. 'Men! All men!'

The men shuffled forward.

'Not you!' A young mother grabbed her son, a tall boy of possibly nine or ten. 'You stay with me!' She clutched him to her chest and turned to the stout British woman. 'You tell them, Margaret, they can't take Thomas!'

Margaret Dryburgh was short, with glasses and fading hair, and a quiet confidence in her pale blue eyes. She glanced back at the soldiers. 'I've been in China for years, I'm afraid I don't really know any Japanese.' She turned to them anyway. 'No boys?' She held her hand low. 'Too small?'

The guard glared as if she'd misunderstood. 'No children. *Dansei*. Men.'

'Father! I want to go with you!' The boy dashed forward and held on to his father, who leaned down and briefly cradled his small head against his lips.

'Not today, Thomas. We'll meet up soon, eh? We'll have a marvellous trip home and be safely back in Oxford before you know it.' He ruffled the boy's hair. 'You be brave for Mummy now, all right?'

The child sniffed and stumbled back to his mother, who clung to him as her husband was slowly joined by the other men.

Margot was horrified. She was going to lose Gull. This was the moment she was going to lose Gull forever.

'Gull,' she said and crouched next to his stretcher. She took his hand in hers. 'You're going to the men's camp, but I don't think it's too far away. It's probably another coolie camp. Make sure you get as much rest as you can. If we have access to medication, tell whoever is in charge you need medicine for your infection. Tell them I can nurse you. Tell them there are nurses in the women's camp.'

Gull smiled weakly up at her. 'Will do. Good luck, Margot. I'll see you in a couple of weeks when this is all over.' He held out his hand and she took it. 'You're strong. Try not to forget.'

Margot reached into her pocket and pulled out a penny. 'Here's your lucky penny. You'll need it.' She looked away and wiped her tears on her arm.

'No, I won't. You keep it for me,' he whispered, folding it into her fingers again. She kissed him until three Australian soldiers came and picked up his stretcher.

'We'll look after him, Sister,' one of the Australians told her.

Margot nodded and stood silently as they carried Gull up the hill into the jungle. He was to join the other patients being transported on stretchers or makeshift constructions. British, Dutch and Australian civilians marched away. Once, Margot might have imagined that they would be their saviours – strong men who could take charge and keep everybody safe. But they had been stripped of their weapons, their wealth, their assumed kingdoms, and now they were just men, imprisoned, injured, dislocated. The women went to the wire fence to watch them leave, disappearing into the deep green of the jungle. Before long they were out of sight.

The coolie houses began to fill with the different groups; Dutch planters' wives, Dutch nuns, English expats, nurses from England, Singapore, Holland and China.

'Piss off!' Beth was holding high-level negotiations with the wives of some Dutch plantation owners who were trying to put down their bags. 'This is an Australian Army building. I've claimed it in the name of Prime Minister John Curtin. And the King. And Errol Bloody Flynn! You heard me! Get lost! You're on Australian territory!'

'This is *Dutch* territory!'

'Not anymore!'

'Beth, that's enough, we mustn't be rude,' Margot said.

Beth gave her a sideways grin. 'Nah, you've got to start out tough or these buggers will take the lot. That bloody Dutch woman thinks she owns the joint. I've seen it before. We'll be friends – later. Today it's a bloody land grab.'

'Looks like a small hospital across the way,' Hatty said. 'If you think you have things under control here, Beth, I might go see if there's any supplies in there we can use.'

Beth tossed a leather overnight bag out of the hut window, to shouts of annoyance from a pair of Dutch ladies in floral dresses. 'We're all right here, Hatty!' she called out. 'You go and see what you can find!'

Margot sat on the edge of the verandah. She could hear Lola and Beth settling into their quarters like ruffled chooks, relieved to have found somewhere to stop. The *tong* ditch hadn't been used for a while, but the smell remained and a queue was already forming to use the one tap available for drinking water. Ladles, jugs and cups were filled one by one, as the tap slowly drizzled out. The *tong* water would be just as meagre. It would be faces and armpits until it rained. She watched the groups finding their places in the little open huts, some mute with shock, some shrill and desperate to find a home, however meagre. She yearned for a cup of tea. She yearned to wake in her own bed, far away from here.

As night fell squadrons of mosquitoes took to the warm air and fell in clouds upon the internees.

'Ouch!'

'Bloody Jap *mosquitoes*!'

They lay uncomfortably in the humidity, resting on concrete slabs, waiting for morning. Margot, wishing for Gull on every breath and waiting for Minnie to walk through the gates, didn't think she'd ever sleep, but the memory of the ocean, even as she lay there in the coolie camp, weighed her down, and she drifted into a grey nightmare of endless rolling waves, of mosquitoes and bayonets. And dreamed of Matron Paschke, bravely holding a tiny child on her lap, drifting out to sea.

In the morning they held a meeting.

'Everyone here?' Margot asked.

'All here,' Lola confirmed.

Of the sixty-five nurses on the *Vyner Brooke*, only thirty-two had made it to the camp, and they had no way of knowing if anyone else had survived. Margot glanced down at her hands and took a long breath, pushing away the heavy thought that her friends were gone forever. The stretch of water at the bottom of the South China Sea was so small, really, you'd never even notice it on a map. It flowed between the islands of the Dutch East Indies and into the Java Sea, providing prey for fishermen, and an alleyway for trade. Thousands of people had disappeared in those waters never to be heard of again, as if the sea had pulled out a handkerchief and performed a terrible magic trick.

'Let's think about accommodation and our routines while in camp,' Margot said. 'A few of us have been discussing the areas we'll need to focus on – obviously health and diet – but we'll also need to keep morale high, and hygiene will become vital. These camps are filthy, mosquitoes are rife and, as we know, a huge problem for our troops. We'll have to find barriers against the blighters as it seems unlikely we'll be able to get rid of all the still water in the jungle around the camp, and it rains constantly. Covering up at night may be all we can do.'

'What about our uniforms,' Beth said. 'Are we to wear them in camp?'

'Mine's terribly stained,' Joy added. 'I'll be scrubbing marine oil out of it for months.'

'I don't think we should wear them around the camp,' Hatty said.

'Why? Isn't it good for morale?'

'It's important to keep our uniform as pristine as possible,' Hatty explained. 'I think we only wear them in certain circumstances, such as when we're acting in our official capacity as nurses of the Australian Army.'

'I agree,' Margot said.

'We must wear uniform anytime we're on the move, for instance, if we're moved to another camp. We must be seen to be Australian prisoners of war.'

'Good point. That's the first. When else do we wear them?'

'Ceremonial occasions,' Beth said, looking apologetic. 'Funerals, most likely. I'm sorry to say that some of us may well die here. We wear our uniforms to bury our dead. Military funerals.'

'Agreed.'

'In the same vein, if one of us dies, we should be buried in our uniform.'

'Agreed.'

'Anything else? Any other time we can wear it? Or have we covered them all?'

'One more,' Lola said. 'We must wear our uniform at the end of the war – when the Allies win – and we all walk to freedom.'

'Yes, yes, when we all walk to freedom!'

There was a light in the window of their little hut, the sun shining through the dirty glass. As they thought of that day, which surely must come, the day they walked to freedom, Margot glanced again at her upturned palms. The light of the sun was warm; it filled her hands as they lay open, it turned them pink, despite the scabs and oil which had been ground into her palms. These hands were all she had to recommend her for what lay ahead. These hands, and this tiny, timid heart.

*

The Muntok camp was basic. The hospital had no medical supplies, except for a towel. There was no soap. Margot, Lola and Beth did the rounds every day, never quite getting through all the women who were in need of help. There were six hundred in the camp, including some orphaned children and elderly nuns, and they soon organised themselves into small groups of nationality and class, looking after their own. Information was eagerly sought, groups mixing in together to listen to gossip, to hear who was newly arrived, who was working in the camp hospital. They were provided with enough rice for two small meals a day, and just enough wood to keep the fires going.

One little boy Margot had noticed earlier was standing patiently with his mother.

'Mischa?' Margot asked. The boy grinned, his blue eyes alight.

'Yes! Mischa! It is my Russian father's name for me, it means bear!'

'And are you fierce like a bear, Mischa?' Margot asked.

'Yes! I'm Mother's best helper!' He gazed proudly up at his mother, a thin woman with flushed cheeks. 'When we fled Poland to escape the Nazis, I carried my own suitcase,' he assured her. 'And I kept carrying it, all by myself, through Shanghai, and on to Singapore so that we could be safe.'

'That is a long way to travel, Mischa. Your family are very brave.'

'Yes. We have escaped the Nazis now. I'm very pleased.' Mischa declared.

'And your father? Is he in the men's camp?'

'No,' Mischa said, solemnly. 'He drowned. He jumped from the ship as we were bombed. He was afraid, but he began to drown.' Mischa took his mother's hand. 'Another man, a British soldier, jumped into the sea to save him, but Father panicked and dragged the soldier with him, beneath the waves. We were most distressed.' Mischa's mother stared at the floor, ashamed of her tears.

'I'm very sorry and upset to hear that, Mischa,' Margot said. 'Do you think I could have a quick check with your mother, to see that she is well?'

'Yes please. I think that Mother must be very tired.'

'And what is your mother's name, Mischa?'

'Her name is Evelien. She's very beautiful.'

'I agree. Now, you run along, little bear, and I'll make sure your mother is getting some rest.'

Mischa relinquished Evelien's hand and wandered off to introduce himself to another nurse.

'Evelien,' Margot began. 'I'm so sorry for your loss.' Evelien remained silent. 'But you must be very proud of Mischa. He's a force to be reckoned with!'

Evelien allowed herself a small smile.

'May I quickly take your temperature? You seem flushed . . .'

'I know I have a fever. I believe I have a heavy cold, that is all. I find it difficult to breathe. Perhaps we will all rest soon, and I will be well again.'

Margot placed her hand on Evelien's forehead. She did indeed have a high fever. Evelien coughed heavily.

'It sounds like you may have a lung infection,' Margot said. 'I'm afraid we don't have any medicine to give you, although perhaps some will be provided soon.'

Evelien's smile didn't reach her eyes. 'Perhaps,' she said.

'At least we can find you a spot in the shade to rest. Don't worry about Mischa, we'll look after him.'

'Thank you, nurse. He is a bear, but only a *little* bear . . .'

Evelien died of pneumonia the following week.

*

'I've taken a list,' Hazel said. 'It looks like we've all come from a total of seventy different boats. The Japanese had quite a time blowing us all out of the water.' She looked down into her rice. 'And now they have to feed us all – should have let us leave, I reckon.'

'Let that be a lesson to them,' Lola agreed.

'Yes. I'm not very interested in rice,' Hazel said. 'Two tiny bowls a day is a bit grim. It's got weevils in it.'

'I'll have it!' Beth held out her hand.

'Hopefully we'll all be too constipated to use the toilet.'

'*That's* not a toilet – it's a public drain.'

'Well, I promise you, I'll close my eyes if I so much as suspect anyone is about to squat,' Lola declared.

'Well, thank you, I'm sure,' Margot said and swatted another mosquito.

'I'm exhausted, and we haven't really been doing anything,' Hazel said.

'I can't sleep while I'm being eaten alive,' Margot grumbled.

'Last night I'd *just* fallen asleep when a bloody guard came through and shone a torch directly in my face. I woke up with such a fright!'

'That's nothing. I was asleep a couple of nights ago and one jabbed me in the foot to wake me up,' Beth said.

'Perhaps he thought you were dead?' Hazel said.

'He wishes!'

'Bully!' Margot and Hazel whirled around as Beth called out. Vivian Bullwinkel was limping through the gates. 'Bully! You're alive!' Beth shouted. 'What took you so long?'

The girls leaped to their feet and rushed to welcome her. Vivian was a tall woman, with a prominent nose and wide, kind mouth. She smiled as she saw her friends, limping and holding her side tenderly as she made her way towards them. Her dark hair was pushed back, as uncared for as the rest of her, her torn uniform stained with blood.

'Oh, I am glad to see you all,' she breathed.

'Oh dear, Bully, how are you?' Margot asked. 'Do you need to sit down? Where have you been?'

Vivian gazed around at them all, overwhelmed. Her voice failed her for a few long moments and the nurses pressed her again, trying to convince themselves that she had survived.

'I really do need to . . .'

'Sit down? Of course you do!'

'Come over here in the shade,' Lola said. 'We'll be very patient, won't we, girls, and we won't talk over you so much . . .'

They waited in breathless silence for her to speak. Other nurses rushed over at the news and the gathering grew. Margot took her hand and Beth warmly patted her back.

'Girls, oh dear me,' Vivian breathed. 'Is everyone here?' She glanced around.

'Well, no,' Margot said. 'We have a number of us missing, but we're not sure if there isn't another camp.'

'How did you get here, Bully?' Lola asked.

'I hid in the jungle with a soldier. His name is Pat. He was injured, but we managed to survive in the jungle for almost twelve days.'

'That's very brave of you,' Beth exclaimed.

'It seemed like our best option,' Vivian said. 'But it was hard to find food, and the locals wouldn't help us – they were too afraid.' She glanced around again, uneasily. 'Pat wanted to spend his last birthday as a free man, and then we risked it, and surrendered.'

'Where is he now?'

'In one of the men's camps. But he won't survive long. His injury will kill him without medical attention.'

'But the others,' Lola whispered. 'Where are they?'

'Have you seen Minnie?' Margot said.

Vivian looked over their shoulders briefly before speaking again. 'I made it ashore after the *Vyner Brooke* went under and joined a larger group of nurses.' She glanced about. 'What I say now must never be repeated. Do you swear?'

'I swear,' the girls whispered back.

'There were around a hundred survivors – including twenty-two nurses.'

'Was Minnie there?' Margot pressed. Vivian nodded and Margot's heart fell.

'We made camp, looked after the wounded. But we had to surrender, or we would have starved.' There was silence. 'A small group walked to Muntok to surrender, and a Japanese party came back with them.'

Margot glanced at Lola, who made the sign of the cross.

'We surrendered,' Vivian said. 'But then the Japanese soldier in charge ordered the men be taken around the headland.' The nurses leaned in, glancing around to make certain the coast was clear. 'They killed them all,' she whispered.

Margot gasped. She wanted to stand up and walk away. There was a story approaching she couldn't bear to hear.

'What happened after that?' Beth murmured softly, her eyes fixed on Vivian.

Vivian took a deep breath. 'When the Japanese came back, we knew we were going to die,' she said. 'A soldier set up a machine gun and we were told to wade into the sea. They lined us up and shot us all in the back.'

A muffled cry went up from the gathering.

'Everyone died?' Margot breathed. She slumped back as darkness gathered around her, but Beth pulled her to her side and gripped her so tightly it hurt.

'*Everyone?*' Beth asked. Vivian nodded.

'The bullet hit me lower,' she said. 'I fell into the water and just lay there. They came around to check us – bayoneting girls who were still alive.' She shuddered. 'They missed me. I was lucky.'

'But there's more,' she whispered, and the girls, awash with tears, leaned in again. Vivian took a deep, ragged breath. 'They raped us first.'

The nurses slowly settled Vivian into camp life, watching her anxiously, tending the wound in her side. They were outraged by what had happened to their sisters. Lola spent hours praying for their souls, Beth spat on the ground, cursing and clenching her fists. *Low dogs – that's what they are. Low dogs – and there's no hell bad enough to take 'em.* Margot kept herself busy around the camp, helping mothers with medical advice for their children, washing clothes in precious water from the well, tearing rags into bandages, and allowing herself the privilege of weeping silently at night, after another day was done.

Vivian often sat quietly in the coolie camp, watching the constant movement around her. The British and the Dutch women, the nuns, the Chinese women and the children, all swept up by the same hand of fate.

Joy, who had appointed herself chief scrounger, insisted on finding an outfit for Bully. Her mother had worked in church jumble sales in Ballarat for years, and she'd developed an eye for a bargain. She often disappeared for short periods, and would return, almost always with something useful, like mosquito netting or a soup spoon.

'Would this do you, Bully?' she asked on her return one day. 'The mozzies are bad at night . . .'

Vivian glanced at the net, distractedly. 'I'm sorry, what was that?'

'I found you a mosquito net,' Joy said. 'I thought you might be able to sleep a bit better if you weren't being eaten alive.'

Vivian smiled. 'Joy, did the army know they should have recruited you as a supply officer? This will be so useful.'

'It has a few holes,' Joy admitted.

'I'm sure we can pull some thread from something and stich them up a bit,' Vivian assured her.

Joy grinned. 'And while we're sewing, I found trousers in the hut in the corner, under a trough. We can use these for clothes. I'd say each pair is a set of shorts and a top, easily. We'll be quite the thing!'

'Well, I don't know that I'll fit into anything made from a pair of trousers, but I think they could be very serviceable for some of the smaller girls,' Vivian said. 'Rita is tiny and Lola is so slim, she'll only need one trouser leg.'

'Lucky we've got a set of nail scissors,' Lola agreed. 'We'll be the height of jungle fashion.'

CHAPTER 16

MARGOT
Sumatra
March 1942

Nights at Muntok were long and uncomfortable. Sleep skittered around the nurses where they lay, refusing to allow them to settle. Margot tossed and turned for hours in the sticky air and when the floodlights flashed on, she sat up, startled.

'Up! Up!' The guards were marching up and down the rows of sleeping women, poking them with bayonets, slapping their feet and shouting. One stood in the doorway of their hut and was shouting something about 'Palembang' in the pre-dawn light. The nurses rolled off their mattresses and stood, blinking, confused.

'*Mono o sumero!*'

'What's he saying?' Beth grumbled.

'Well, he obviously wants us to get up. Ouch!' Lola was kicked in the knee as she struggled to stand.

'You! You! Pack camp! We leave! *Ichi jikan!* One hour!'

'Oh, great, and this place is just so nice,' Lola said. 'I'll be sorry to leave.'

Margot stepped into her uniform and started gathering her things. The few possessions they had were precious and she didn't think the Japanese soldiers would allow them much time. She grabbed her kerosene cooking tin with a wire handle and a couple of old blouses she'd found in an abandoned hut and stuffed them into the base. Then she dropped her spoon on top, a broken comb she'd found near the *tongs* one morning, and an abandoned set of sandals Joy had found on a rubbish pile just outside the camp. She shoved a straw hat on her head which had been mended by Lola but was already starting to unravel, and took the few medical supplies she'd pinned into her uniform before the bombing.

'Where do you think we're going?' Kath asked, tossing a small bag of rice and a ladle into a huge cast iron pot Joy had found and named Matilda.

'Home?' someone called out from the verandah, and there was a low chortle among the nurses sitting on the concrete slab.

'Sounds like Palembang – it's in Sumatra.'

'I hope wherever it is, it has a toilet.'

'More than one!'

'And something other than bloody rice!'

'I wonder if we'll meet some other nurses there?' Margot said. 'I mean, there are a few of us unaccounted for, we can't be the only camp. Or perhaps we'll be moved closer to the men's camp and the children might see their fathers. Perhaps Gull is there with them.'

'Well, it is possible,' Beth allowed. 'Everyone, grab everything you can and we'll hope for the best, eh?'

A few battered rucksacks and suitcases had made it to shore, and they were now crammed with meagre belongings, clothes found in abandoned houses, cutlery, tin cups, a small mirror, a tiny sewing kit, a tiny vase shaped like a cat. The women gathered their treasures together and within an hour were marching down to the Muntok jetty.

'Outrageous!' Mrs Brown was up in arms. 'Middle of the cursed night! I may well die of a heart attack if this keeps up!'

'We can only hope!' Margot muttered.

The jungle track was wide and a riverboat was waiting for them at the end of the jetty. They were loaded on board and quickly departed, crossing the mild seas of the Bangka Strait and heading up the Musi River. The jungle hung over the water on both sides of the river, with small clearings where they could see villages. Children were fishing in some spots, and as they rounded one bend, they saw women washing clothes.

'Palembang. Why have I heard of it?' Beth asked.

'Dutch tin mines, I think,' Margot said. 'The Dutch detainees will be able to tell us more, but I'm pretty sure it's a base for mining.'

The riverboat wasn't built for so many people and as the day grew hotter and steamier, the women wilted on the top deck. After a while warm rains came and they hid under tarps. Then the sun came out and steamed them like puddings as they sat, impatiently waiting for their next destination.

The facilities consisted of a long drop toilet suspended over the side of the boat, encased in a narrow square box, no more than shoulder width.

'Good Lord!' Beth said as she came back from a trip. 'Don't look down while you're in there. I could barely fit.'

'I wonder how Mrs Brown will cope?'

'The same way she copes with most things – loudly!'

Mrs Brown was preoccupied with the same concerns. She hovered outside the toilet for half an hour before giving up and declaring, 'I need to use the facilities! I shall require some assistance!'

Beth rolled her eyes. 'Jesus Christ, here we go.'

Mrs Brown put her head inside and found that her expansive girth wouldn't follow. She huffed in exasperation and backed out, turning to the women gathered to help.

'Looks like you'll have to back in,' Beth told her.

'Ridiculous! I've never had to use such shoddy facilities in my life!'

'Well, you've never been taken prisoner by the Japanese before, have you?'

'I shall move backwards, you can all help me find my way.'

Find my way was a discreet way of saying, *help to push me inside, then wait until I've finished and you can pull me out again.* The girls nodded.

'You'd better lift your skirts now,' Beth said.

Mrs Brown huffed again and glanced about, but she knew it was true. 'Very well,' she muttered, and dropped her bloomers to her ankles.

'All right, girls, let's help Mrs Brown relieve herself,' Mavis announced.

'I do believe this is way beyond the bounds of the Geneva Convention,' Margot muttered.

They pushed gently, then more firmly, then with increased determination, until Mrs Brown was in position.

'Disgraceful,' she complained. 'I have never been so insulted!'

'Yes, well, things are different now, Mrs Brown,' Lola told her. 'But don't worry, I'm sure we'll all be in Palembang shortly.'

Margot looked up ahead as the riverboat motored through the thick vegetation.

'What do you think the new camp will be?' Joy asked.

'Hard to say,' Beth said.

'Probably won't be there long, anyway,' Lola added.

'Perhaps the war will be over soon,' Joy said.

Margot considered this as she observed a stork, with its long yellow beak, watching them from a tree overhanging the water, perhaps hoping their riverboat would stir up breakfast. She didn't think so. It seemed the war had plenty of fire left to burn. The battle against Germany raged on in Europe, and now it had found its way to her in the Pacific. The Dutch had declared war on Japan with the bombing of Pearl Harbor, and Japan was sick of white men dominating Asian countries. It needed fuel after years of fighting with China. Pearl Harbor had been attacked to prevent the US interfering in Japan's plan to plunder Malaya for oil after the US cut their supply. And so the Japanese Army had arrived on bicycles, and had taken Singapore with their slogan 'Asia for the Asians!'. They had collected south-east Asia like a hand of cards in a bridge game, except that the cards were thousands upon thousands of people.

And now, under the gaze of the stork, the prisoners were disappearing up the river of an island far from home. Perhaps no one would ever find them. Perhaps they'd be buried in the jungle and forgotten altogether. Margot reached into her pocket for her lucky penny and thought of Gull.

'Look, we're slowing. This must be it.' Lola leaned from the side of the riverboat and observed the sagging timber jetty ahead of them. 'Grab your things,' she said, as the Japanese guards rose to their feet. 'We're about to dock.'

After disembarking, they were loaded into the back of trucks, clutching their belongings to their chests.

'My God, it's hot, but I'm too thirsty to sweat.' Beth leaned back, trying to catch a breath of air.

'We must be there soon,' Lola said. 'I think I'm about to pass out.'

As the trucks rounded a corner, the town of Palembang came into view. It had been an important oil refinery base for the Allies, until the Japanese had taken the island for themselves. The women were driven down the streets of the town, past the colonial churches, government buildings and modest timber homes. A crowd formed as they passed, local workers and townsfolk jeering at the exhausted women as they rolled through, clutching on to their precious children and few shabby possessions.

'Out of Sumatra!'

'You English are not in charge!'

'Sumatra! Japan!'

The nurses were unimpressed. Beth spat on the ground from her spot on the truck. 'We'd love to get out of Sumatra! Just put us on a boat that bloody floats!' she shouted back.

'Go to hell!' Joy yelled. 'We don't want your damn country!'

'We were trying to *leave*! It's not *our* fault we got bombed!' Lola added, poking out her tongue for effect.

The crowd jeered their discourtesy and the trucks rattled further up the hill to a new camp, and a new prison. The gates opened and revealed what had once been a school. Now the jungle was threatening to creep in through the loose windows and shutters and drag it all back to the warm damp earth again.

'What's that smell?' asked Joy. 'Is that *food*?'

Margot breathed in. Stew. 'I do believe it is!' she marvelled. 'Who's been cooking?'

The trucks rolled to a stop and the girls lurched forward.

'Out! Out!' They climbed down, ignoring the shouts of the Japanese soldiers, following the scent of the stew. One of the soldiers began to point. 'Food!'

Inside the makeshift canteen were a small group of Australians.

'G'day, ladies!' a tall skinny man with a bandage around his shoulder said. 'I'm Ernie, and these are my cooks. We've made you dinner to welcome you to Palembang.'

'Oh, thank goodness, actual food!'

'We haven't eaten all day, this is wonderful!'

The little boy Mischa the Bear, who'd lost both his father and mother, took Margot's hand. 'Food!' he declared with relish. 'Food after a journey is *always* the best!'

'We'll make sure you have the largest bowl, Mischa,' Margot said.

'You won't be staying here, but we think they've found housing for you nearby,' Ernie said. 'Palembang is a Dutch colonial town, really, so chances are you'll be reasonably comfortable. The Dutch wouldn't live just anywhere.'

'I was wondering if you knew of a friend of mine,' Margot asked him. 'A soldier with a head injury and a damaged hand – by the name of Gull?'

'Gull? Yeah, I know him. He's all right. His wounds are infected – probably didn't like the dip in the sea – but he's in sick bay at the men's camp.'

'Do you have a doctor? Is he being looked after?'

'As much as we can,' he assured her. He must have noticed her tense, because he leaned forward and gave her shoulder a squeeze. 'He'll be fine. I promise.'

Margot's heart leaped with excitement and relief. She was nearer to Gull again. Perhaps she'd see him, and make sure he was okay, or perhaps the war would end soon, and they would make their way back to Australia together. She tried to visualise his smile in her mind, but it wasn't there.

'My name's Margot. Can you tell him I'm here? That I'm all

right too? That . . .' She didn't quite know what to say; part of her wanted to say everything, just in case. 'Tell him I've got his penny.'

The man grinned. 'I'll tell him,' he said. It would have to be enough.

The women were herded into the kitchen and formed long queues for the welcome meal. The children were sent to the front, and then their tired mothers, before the rest of the camp sat down to some warm stew and a mug of sweet tea. Immensely grateful, Margot collapsed onto a bench and ravenously scooped the gravy into her mouth.

As they finished eating, they were joined by an air commodore from the men's camp. He held out his hand to shake theirs. 'Don Richards. Now. I think it's important we sort something out right away,' he said. 'You nurses are here as prisoners of war. You are serving officers of the Australian Army and we have to try to get the Japs to recognise that.'

'I don't think they will,' Beth said. 'They seem very disparaging of any attempts we make to point out that we're officers.'

'Well, they would be. Nonetheless, if we can get you recognised as POWs instead of internees, it will mean that you will have more rights – for example, the right to a small but useful payment for the duration of your captivity.' He glanced across at the Japanese guard, sitting in the shade watching them closely. 'I'll have a go, give it my best shot. I don't think they're as keen on women as we Australians are . . .' Beth harrumphed quietly. 'But it's worth a shot. Even if it just lets the bastards know someone's watching.'

'I suspect that if they feel someone's watching, they'll probably just shoot them in the face,' Margot said.

The commodore grinned. 'Any more words of confidence before I go over and plead your case?'

Margot smiled. 'Sorry, no. Say we like Japanese food – the more the better!'

The commodore winked at her. 'Will do,' he said, and stood up to cross the yard.

They watched as he bowed low to the guards and asked to speak to the captain in charge. There was some discussion, some offence taken, some apology given, and finally the commodore was led into the small office near the gate. He wasn't inside for very long. Discussion, shouting, and he was swiftly ejected. He came back to the group apologetically.

'Sorry, girls. No chance. You're internees for the remainder of the war, not POWs. That means no special privileges and no payments.' He shrugged. 'Frankly, I don't think the Japs are too keen on the Geneva Convention in general, so try not to feel too badly about it.'

'Tell him we're getting sick of bloody rice!'

'Ladies, I think you'd better learn to love it. Now.' He glanced around. 'I believe Vivian Bullwinkel wanted to speak to me?' He lowered his voice. 'Some news?'

'Yes, she has a story so shocking you won't want to believe it.' Margot stood. 'But it's true.'

'And it's to be kept a secret,' Lola added. 'There'll be more deaths in this camp if the Japanese find out what she knows.'

'Our fear is that the truth will die with us if we don't make it back,' Margot went on. 'But we're determined to survive, to make sure Australians know what happened to those girls on the beach. We'll carry them home, any way we can.' A tear slipped down her cheek and she brushed it away.

'Fetch her now,' the commodore murmured, his face dark. 'If we couldn't protect them, we can at least one day seek justice.'

*

The girls slept on the floor in the classrooms, exhausted. As Margot lay in the warm night air, the jungle rustled and moved all around her. The sound was nothing like home, there was nothing to comfort her; no familiar scent, or bird call. No distant sound of the Fremantle-bound train pulling into Subiaco, or the rumble of the milk truck pausing on its rounds, or the familiar voices of the ABC news filling the kitchen as the kettle boiled. What did her parents think had happened to her? Did they imagine she was dead? And Neville? How was he? Still making the finest pork sausages west of Kalgoorlie? How she missed her family in Perth, now that it had been taken from her.

Joy rolled over and muttered something in her sleep. In the light of the moon, Margot could see her smile. She looked as if she too, however briefly, was home again.

Margot tried to settle and thought about Sumatra. She had no way of knowing where their captors would take them, or what they would find. She lay very still and imagined them all climbing into the back of a truck at the end of the war.

Then she wondered which one of them would die first.

CHAPTER 17

MARGOT
Irenelaan, Sumatra
March 1942

'So, girls, looks like this is home,' Margot said as the truck drove through the gates on the jungle path.

Irenelaan had been a pleasant Dutch suburb in the hills of Palembang before the war. The houses were of brick and tile, with wide verandahs at the front and space underneath for the air to circulate. There were fourteen houses allotted to the women's camp.

'We'll need two, I think,' Margot said. 'We're the biggest *kongsi*. Together would be good, but nearby might have to do.'

Beth took off at a trot and quickly secured a home. She threw her things onto the verandah. 'Australian nurses here,' she declared. 'Australian General Hospital and Casualty Clearing Station 2/4th, 2/10th and 2/13th. Hatty, grab next door!'

Hatty set off towards the next house but found a large group of Dutch women already there.

'*Nee!*'

She dashed to the next house along.

'*Nee!*'

Finally she made it to yet another house and threw her belongings on the verandah. 'Aussie nurses welcome here!' she declared. 'Joy, go rustle up some decent beds and a lounge chair.'

'Girls! There's an electric stove in here! And it *works*!' Margot called out from the first house. The three bedrooms and living areas needed a good clean, but some modest furniture which hadn't been removed by locals would allow the nurses to create a couple of basic homes. 'All right everyone! Organise your possessions, we have a meeting in an hour,' Margot said.

Margot glanced out into the street. It really wasn't too bad. But they wouldn't be here long, she told herself, the war would wrest them away again, to coolie lines or to grass huts. But for the moment they were safe. She could hear Lola and Beth dragging furniture about on the timber floors, calling out to Joy to scrounge another bed if she could. 'Or even just a mattress!' Lola shouted.

'Now,' Margot told her colleagues once they'd settled in, 'we may be here for some time, and therefore we need to make some arrangements. Hazel is working out a sanitation roster. We'll have nurses checking the facilities, trying to keep our camp as clean and disease-free as possible. We'll hold daily clinics for the prisoners and anything we can't handle here may be allowed to be treated in a local Dutch hospital.'

'Good. I hope they have plenty of quinine.'

'We'll see,' Margot said, 'but I suspect that, even if they do, we won't be given any. We are the enemy after all, and they won't be wasting their supplies on us.' She glanced around. 'What we *do* have some control over is morale. We must stay positive so that we can support each other through these very trying times.'

'That's an understatement,' Joy murmured.

'I know we have a collection of clever and interesting women here. Let's all find a way to contribute to camp life. Mavis has suggested a conversation afternoon on Wednesdays and it sounds like an excellent idea to me. Everyone agree?' There was a murmur of assent. 'Good.'

'I can talk about what it's like to have a ship blown out from under you,' Hatty announced.

'And I can talk at length about all the big picture stars from Hollywood,' Lola said. 'I can even quote *The Prince and the Pauper* with Errol Flynn – I saw it at the pictures every week for months.'

'We'll look forward to your re-enactment,' Margot said.

'How about some music?' someone asked.

'Lola, we'd love to hear you sing again!' Hatty said.

'And a fashion parade? We could make up outfits from things we find.'

'Utterly ridiculous!' Beth scoffed.

'I'll be Paula of Palembang!' Hazel announced and held a large leaf to her head like a jaunty hat.

'And I'll be Mavis of Malaya!' Mavis added.

'Well, I can see we have some plans to make,' Margot said. 'Let's collect some wood for the fire and get started.'

The black market at camp quickly began to thrive. Local traders would gather at the wire fence and trade goods, fruit, vegetables, books, scissors and bottles. Anything in short supply was valuable, and the Dutch guilder was the currency. Margot often wandered over to watch the exchanges, glancing back at the guards in case of trouble, but fascinated to see the bartering carry on. The traders were usually Chinese or Malay. They were quick on their feet, assessing the mood of the guards as Margot did, then disappearing into the forest again when necessary.

One morning the girls were excited to be visited by two members of the men's camp. Margot was just heading back from the well with water for the *kongsi* when she heard Lola calling her name.

'Margot! Margot McNee!'

She put down her bucket and glanced about, alarmed. 'Yes?'

'Come to the gate! Visitors!'

She put down her bucket and began to run.

Gull was standing there, thinner, but smiling, accompanied by another soldier in a straw hat.

'Davis,' the other soldier said and held out his hand. Margot reached through the wire to shake it.

'Gull! It's you!' She took his face in her hands through the wire, smoothing his hair and looking deeply into his eyes. His skin was badly sunburned, but also developing a deep tan. His eyes stayed on hers as she took him in, amused. His arms were also deeply tanned, while his hand, heavily scarred, had healed, although the scar looked angry and raised, suggesting the infection had gone, but had taken a while, and had done further damage along the way. He'd cut his trousers into shorts at some point, and his legs were covered in insect bites. She looked at his hair and gently felt for the scar. It was there, settling into a knot over his skull that he'd always carry. She felt her body finally exhale. He was safe. It was every wish she'd dared to dream since he'd been taken away.

'Satisfied it's me?' he asked.

'I'm a butcher's daughter,' she said, grinning. 'Just checking the delivery. It's slightly damaged, but I'll keep it.'

He smiled back at her bashfully, and she was surprised to see mist in his eyes. The weeks had been so very long.

Gull held up the hessian bag in his hand. 'Chooks,' he said as he handed them to her. 'We won them in a bet and we thought you girls might like them.'

'Oh, we *will*!' Lola promised from behind Margot.

'Well – chooks! Thank you so very much! I imagine we'll have eaten one before we even get back to the house!'

'How is everything here? Are you all safe?'

'Yes, we're well enough, so far. Food is scarce, of course, and so is medication for the ill, but we have a couple of houses, and we're managing to keep our morale up. A few games of cards, a bit of a singalong, that sort of thing.'

'The men will be relieved to hear it.'

'And you?' Margot asked. 'Your head must be better? Any headaches?'

'Yes, it's improving all the time, and yes, a few headaches. But I'm so pleased to still have a head, I don't like to complain.'

Margot laughed. 'And how's the men's camp?'

'Similar to yours. We do a lot of manual work, we mix in together, but largely the different nationalities keep to themselves.' He reached into his pocket for some letters. 'A couple of the blokes wanted me to give you these – see if you can find their families. They wanted to let their wives and kids know they're all right.'

'Of course, I'll do that right away.' She reached out and took his hand. 'It's so good to see you, Gull.' The guards were approaching.

'Oh, there's a Pommy chap called Harry who wants to know if Minnie is all right. Apparently he helped her and Beth out one night? I said I knew her in Singapore.' Gull glanced back at the guards. 'Any sign of her yet?'

'No,' Margot lied. 'I think she's with a group in another camp. No idea where.'

Gull nodded. 'You must be so worried about her. I'll let Harry know, he'll be pleased to hear it.'

'You go!' one of the Japanese guards shouted. Their rifles weren't drawn, but visiting time was clearly over.

'I've been so worried, it's made me so happy to see you alive and well!'

Davis smirked, and Gull blushed again. 'I'm relieved to find you looking so well too, Margot. We think of you girls over here and we worry. Be brave. We'll be out of here soon.'

'Yes.' She squeezed his hand. 'We'll be out of here very soon.'

'Go now! Go!' The guards had had enough. The taller of the two hit the wire fence in warning and it shook.

'Goodbye!' Margot said and stepped back. 'Thanks for the chickens!'

'Goodbye!' Gull and Davis turned and walked back down the jungle path. Margot stood and watched them until they disappeared.

Lola took the bag and peered inside. 'Three chickens. Let's eat them all tonight.'

'Hang on, what if they're layers? We might have an egg supply. We'd be silly to kill them if they can lay eggs for us.'

Lola stuck her head further into the bag, and the chooks squawked and ruffled their feathers. 'They don't look like girls,' she said, doubtfully.

'Well, they're Sumatran chickens, who knows *what* they look like.' Margot peered into the bag as well. 'Let's give them a stay of execution, just in case.'

Back at the house, they found Beth sweeping.

Margot held up the bag. 'We bring chickens!'

'Excellent, we need some eggs.' Beth took a look inside the bag. 'You sure they're girls?'

'Not really.'

Beth banged the broom against the stairs. 'Let's give them a chance, then. Matilda awaits should they fail to produce.'

The next morning as dawn broke, the girls were startled awake by the sound of their new roommates crowing.

'That's settled, then,' Beth grumbled. 'Rooster for lunch.'

Later that day, Margot answered a knock at the door.

'Good morning. I was wondering if any of the nurses might like to join me at a small service we're holding? I thought it might be a good idea to have a weekly Sunday church service.' A small woman with her hair pulled into a severe bun smiled back at her. Her eyes twinkled from behind her round spectacles. It was Margaret, who had spoken to the soldiers about the men's camp.

'Hello, Margaret,' Margot said. 'We met a few months ago. I'm Margot McNee.'

Margaret shook her hand. 'Yes yes, of course. Margaret Dryburgh. I'm a missionary by trade. So many of us will find comfort in prayer and worship.'

Margot turned to her fellow nurses. 'Girls, which of you would like to go to church?'

There were groans from Hatty and Beth.

Lola and Hazel arrived at the front door, pulling their hair into shape.

'I would!'

'And me!'

'Oh, marvellous,' Margaret said. 'Just head down to the meeting place – you'll find a group already there. I shan't be long.' With a nod, she moved on to the next house.

'Shall I brush my teeth?' Lola wondered. 'I mean, it's not every day we get an outing.'

'Just *go!*' Beth called.

Sunday church became a way to mark the weeks as they passed in Irenelaan. A large group of women and children attended regularly, enjoying the usual prayers, hymns and Sunday school while getting to know the British and Dutch prisoners. Margot liked to do her morning chores listening to old hymns floating across the prison yard, familiar and safe.

Beth felt otherwise. 'They're at it again,' she said. 'Another bloody hymn.'

'I don't recognise this one,' Margot said.

'It's new. I think Margaret wrote it herself.'

'She *wrote* it?'

'Yeah, she's a woman of many talents. I believe she trained as a teacher, then a nurse. She teaches, writes poetry, speaks Chinese – and writes music. And you've read her camp magazine.'

'I don't know how we were supposed to finish her crossword,' Margot said. 'Two of the words were in Latin, for goodness' sake!' She stopped to listen again. 'I must say, I like this hymn, though, very much,' she decided. 'Do we know what it's called?'

'I think it's called "The Captive's Hymn".'

Father in captivity,
We would lift our prayers to Thee,
Keep us daily in Thy love,
Grant that daily we may prove,
Those who place their trust in Thee,
More than conquerors may be.

The patient rhythm wove its way into the house, the warmth of the voices settling Margot's heart. It was as if the simple rhyming couplets were an assurance that somewhere in the world, the rules still applied.

Over the following months, the nurses did their best to build a makeshift community at Irenelaan. The English and the Dutch were mostly from the upper classes and formed their own house-holds, usually keeping to themselves. Some of them had servants, also escaping Singapore at the time of capture. Some Chinese and Singaporean women were also imprisoned, working as hairdressers or cooks, finding a way to survive in their new home.

The young Dutch girl, Henny, who'd lost her father, often helped Margot and the nurses collect their rations in buckets as guards tossed bags of old vegetables and rice stinking of lime sulphur off the back of a truck and onto the road. Occasionally a piece of meat would be tossed onto the ground, and they'd chase the starving dogs away with sticks. Each afternoon on delivery day they would wash the rice and carefully remove gravel to save their teeth.

'What are you up to, Hazel?' Beth and Margot sat down heavily on the top step of their house as children ran up and down the street.

'Not much.' Hazel glanced at the Dutch nuns, hanging huge bloomers on the line strung along the front of their house. '*Goedemorgen!*' she called, and the nuns waved. 'Look at the size of those things,' she said. 'Perhaps they don't put all their faith in the Lord after all!'

'Oh, here he comes – Mr Hollywood.'

The commanding officer of the camp at Palembang was Captain Miachi, a short man with a thin moustache and a side part, of which he appeared to be particularly proud. He was known for his vanity around camp, and was the source of some amusement among the Australians. He was sometimes joined by Captain Seki, known as Seki the Sadist, a thin cruel man the nurses despised. Like all the guards, they'd been awarded nicknames by the nurses. They bowed low to their captors, but privately they referred to them in unflattering terms: Seki the Sadist, Rasputin, Mr Hollywood, the Dance Master and the Snake.

'I reckon he thinks he's got a chance with Lola,' Beth muttered. 'Look at him, preening away in the reflection.'

Margot giggled. 'Stop it, Beth, he'll catch us laughing.'

'Well, he's better than the Snake,' Beth said. 'He beat that poor trader and tied him up in the sun.'

'Don't talk about it, Beth,' Margot pleaded. 'One of them will hear you.'

'And then, when the poor man is mad with thirst and a kind soul takes him some water, what happens? The sainted bloody woman is forced to lie face down in the dirt and gets beaten!' Beth's face was alight with fury. 'I hope someone can find me a gun. I'd shoot that bastard first.' She spat soundly on the ground.

'Beth, I'd shoot him myself,' Margot assured her. 'Now. What are we up to this afternoon?'

'It's conversation afternoon. I think Mona is giving a talk about logging towns in Tasmania,' Hazel told her.

'It probably won't be as colourful as Beth's talk about droving in far west Queensland,' Margot said, and Beth nodded with satisfaction.

'I think Mavis is looking for some more palm leaves,' Hazel said. 'She's teaching hat making next week and she's worried we'll run out.'

Margot glanced around at the burgeoning jungle. 'I think she'll be all right.'

From inside the house came the sound of their old out of tune piano. The girls had found it in one of the houses and had dragged it up the street and into their home. It was a welcome distraction, and they often had singalongs in the evenings. The windows were flung open and once the little lounge room was filled to standing room only, the guests would gather on the verandah and down the steps to listen to the music.

'Play "Minnie the Moocher"!' Beth called out from the verandah.

'I will if you sing!' Lola called back from her place at the piano.

'Don't be silly, I might call out *hi de hi*, but that's it.'

'Near enough!' Lola launched into 'Minnie the Moocher', then 'My Baby Just Cares for Me' and 'These Foolish Things'.

As night fell, the singalong crowd grew. Margot sat on the steps with a pair of Dutch nuns. Vivian and Mona paused for a moment, having arrived from the other nurses' house two doors up. Margot glanced into the darkness, where she could see a couple of Japanese guards smoking in the shadows, taking in the evening's entertainment.

'Do you think they'll come onto the verandah?'

'I hope not, it casts a bit of a pall over a party and we're all singing "Happy Birthday" to Kath later. We've even made her a cricket ball of sorts, so she can teach us all a bit of cricket.'

'They'll move on soon enough.'

'Oh God, here she goes, Rita is doing "The Quartermaster's Store".'

Through the window it came, the words of one of their favourite campfire songs, adapted faithfully by Rita.

There is rice! Rice!
Mouldy rotten rice,
Nothing more, nothing more
There are eggs, eggs . . .

Margot and the girls joined in from the verandah. They'd performed 'Waltzing Matilda' last week in makeshift costumes, complete with a feisty jolly jumbuck. Lola had delivered an inspiring performance as 'His Ghost who may be heard as you pass by that billabong', adding such beautiful harmonies that the song became a prophesy in Margot's mind and her eyes had filled with foolish tears. She had wept every day for weeks after Vivian had told them about the girls on the beach. The outrage and the horror of it stayed with them all.

They had been imprisoned for months by now, with no way of knowing what was going on in the world outside, with no word from their families. Sometimes new prisoners would arrive with snippets of news of the war. In early July, the women learned that the Japanese had lost a battle at Midway Island, located halfway between Hawaii and Japan. They had sustained huge losses of ships because the US had discovered their plan of attack. The gossip spread through the camp like wildfire, and Margot had looked up to the sky and prayed Gull would hear the news also, and he would know that he was going to be all right.

One afternoon, after Hazel's talk about the suffragettes of the UK and Australia, Margot and Kath were approached by Captain Miachi. He stood before them awkwardly for a moment, sweat beading along the edges of his moustache.

'You, come to my office,' he said. 'Now!'

'All right,' Margot said softly, looking at the ground. It didn't do to rile them up. She'd had her face slapped for not bowing low enough to a guard. The impact had almost knocked her off her feet and left her with a black eye.

She marched across to the office with Kath, wondering what the problem could possibly be. Had they been too loud? Had another *kongsi* complained about them? All the prisoners got along well enough. Certainly, there were occasional tensions between them over the bathing *tongs*, or the food rations, but it passed quickly.

Captain Miachi went into his office, sat down behind his desk, drew his sword and placed it before him. The girls waited. Kath entertained herself by gazing about the room with undisguised fascination. She managed to appear relaxed as they stood to attention, tilting her head a little in apparent appreciation, and smiling at Margot serenely, as if they visited their hosts every day.

'Close the door!'

They complied and stood silently with their hands behind their backs.

'We have a good camp,' Captain Miachi told them.

Margot wasn't sure how she should respond, so she nodded.

'We have many prisoners. Japanese officers work hard.'

Again, Margot nodded. *Of course,* she thought, *you could let us all go home, then you wouldn't have to work so hard.*

'Japanese officers will have an officers' club.'

'How nice for you,' Margot murmured.

'We will have drinks and conversation.'

'Yes, you can do as you please—'

'Australian nurses will be hostesses at officers' club.'

'I beg your pardon?'

'Australian nurses. Give drinks. Talk. Laughing.'

'At your club?'

'Yes, yes, at officers' club.'

'I should think *not*,' Kath said.

Captain Miachi's face fell. 'Not? You think *not*?'

'We are *nurses* and *officers* in the Australian Army, Commander, whether you choose to acknowledge that or not, and the rest of the ladies here are *respectable* women. We will not be *comfort women* to your officers,' Margot told him.

Captain Miachi's face flushed as he stood. 'You *will* serve drinks at social club. My men are making the clubhouse now.' He held up a piece of paper. 'Here is a list of nurses who will be at club. Tell them they must do as ordered by the commanding officer.'

'Oh well,' Kath said. 'I suppose if you'd like someone to serve drinks, *I'd* be willing. I mean, I'm forty-one and the years have *not* been kind, but—'

'No.' Captain Miachi shook his head vigorously. '*Not* suitable. *These!*' He thrust the page at Margot.

Margot's hand shook as she took the piece of paper. On it were six names. She glanced back up at Captain Miachi who was watching her closely. Kath touched her elbow in warning. She bowed her head.

'I will talk to the nurses. But you mustn't expect us to provide entertainment to Japanese officers. We are not *prostitutes*. We are *prisoners of war*.'

'You are internees! *Internees!* You do as ordered.' He sat back down. 'Now go.'

Kath took the list from her as they made their way back to their house. 'All the small dark girls, look: Joy, Rita, Hazel, and you, Margot. I don't think you've been chosen for your ability to pour a drink.'

'We will *not* become prostitutes for these bastards! We *won't*!' Margot took the steps two at a time. 'Call the girls, we need to have a meeting.'

She glanced at the Dutch houses next to theirs, and saw that the women were packing up. One woman was carrying an old sheet filled with children's clothes and some pans from the kitchen.

'What's going on?' Margot asked her.

'We've been told to move out. These are to be clubrooms. For the Jap officers.'

Margot swore under her breath.

Before long the nurses were gathered in the lounge of Margot's house.

'All right. What are we going to do?' she said.

'We are *not* sending nurses over there,' Beth declared.

'What will they do if we refuse?' Lola asked.

'Will we be beaten? Shot?' Joy asked.

'We don't know,' Margot said. 'We can refuse them – we *have* refused them. But who knows what might happen.'

'Well,' Beth declared. 'We know what happened to the nurses in Hong Kong. Raped and murdered. And there are plenty of stories about comfort women. The Dutch women have been targeted at other camps. They won't be taking *any* nurses.'

'I'd rather be murdered first,' Lola said.

Kath had been watching the empty houses through the window, and suddenly she stood. 'Look,' she said. 'They've got a team to turn those houses into clubhouses.'

'What?' The girls rushed to the window.

'There are beds being taken inside. Beds! And a piano . . . a lounge . . .' Lola reported.

'Oh, they want their officer's club all right,' Beth said.

*

It wasn't long before Margot was again pulled aside by Captain Miachi.

'Australian nurses ready to be hostesses?' he asked.

'The girls you chose,' she answered. 'Why those girls, exactly?'

He glanced over her shoulder, in case any of the other nurses were nearby. Perhaps he didn't want to hurt their feelings. 'Those nurses look medically clean and free of disease,' he said.

'They need to be clean to serve a drink?'

'They come?'

'No. They do *not* come.'

'They will come! They *will* come!'

'And if they don't?'

'They *will*!' Captain Miachi slammed his fist onto the desk and glared. 'They *will come*!'

That night, as the warm breeze made its way up the hills of Irenelaan, the nurses slept lightly, waiting to see if a drunk Japanese officer would stumble inside their homes and drag them out. Hazel slept with a frying pan in her hand and Lola clutched her rosary beads.

'I believe in God the Father Almighty, Maker of heaven and earth, and in Jesus Christ, his only begotten son, who was conceived by the Holy Ghost, born of the Virgin Mary—'

'Lola! Shut up! You'll remind the bloody Japs we're here!' Beth growled.

'Perhaps God will protect us,' Lola murmured.

'Of course he will, he's done a bang-up job so far.'

Margot rolled over as best she could in the crush of bodies and stared at the black ceiling. 'Girls, go to sleep. I don't think they're coming. We're safe for now.'

*

The next morning Captain Miachi and another guard were outside the door as the nurses woke and began starting the fire for the day's cooking duties.

'No food for you! *No* food!' the guards shouted.

Margot went to the edge of the verandah. 'Why? We need *some* food for goodness' sake, we're your prisoners and you *must* provide it.'

'*No food* until Australian nurses attend officers' club.' Captain Miachi and the guard marched away. 'Tonight!'

'The Geneva Convention requires you to provide prisoners with food, shelter and access to medicines—'

'We do not make this law! Not Nippon! No food!'

Margot sagged against the doorway. 'All right, girls. It looks like we'll have to go to the club tonight.' She turned to look back at the group sitting around the little table in the kitchen, brewing tea. 'I don't see that we have any other choice.'

Beth spoke up. 'I agree. We can't risk everyone's safety by refusing. But I wonder if a few of us older girls might consider going.'

'What do you mean?'

'Well, I'm an old trout. I'm married to my job. I'll never find a husband and have children, and that's all there is to it.' There was silence. 'It wouldn't be so bad for me. I've been around, I've seen some life. If it helps the rest of the girls, I'd be willing to go.' she said.

'No one will marry me, either,' Hazel added. 'I'm happy to remain a nurse all my life. I'll go to these little bastards if it helps some of you younger girls.'

'But you can't. You *can't*. It makes me sick! I hate them!' Lola cried.

'Listen. You're not even thirty yet, you have time. We'll go,' Beth told her.

'Yes. If such a sacrifice is to be made, we will swear to never speak of it,' Hatty said.

'We must all swear not to tell anyone, ever,' Rita said.

'Yes, swear on the Bible,' Lola declared. She paused for a moment. 'How about if we *all* go?' she suggested. 'I mean, there's safety in numbers . . .'

The girls looked at each other. They needed food, they were already weak, and the rice provided almost no nutrition. They wouldn't last long before illness took them if they lost much more condition. They couldn't risk a beating. There was little medicine to help with injuries and infection in the heat of the jungle. Perhaps there *would* be safety in numbers.

'All right,' Beth said. 'But we'll make sure we look our best.'

That night, the members of the officers' club were treated to not six nurses, as requested, but twenty.

'Are you ready, girls?' Hatty asked, admiring herself in the glass next to the front door. Her face was filthy, smeared with mud, her hair was matted and dusty and her feet were almost black. Beth stood beside her with her hair greasy and parted at a strange angle, smelling of something unpleasant, although where on her person it was located, Margot really didn't want to know.

'Final inspection!' she announced, and the girls all stood up straight in all of their glory. Unkempt, smelly, dusty, grimy, with messy hair, or bizarre hairstyles which made them appear twice their ages. Their clothes were unflattering, loose, hanging from their thin bodies, stinking of sweat.

'You all look terrible!'

'Thanks very much!'

As the Japanese officers opened the door of their makeshift club, their faces betrayed an expression of utter confusion. The nurses nodded at them sullenly and entered, standing together on one side of the room, awaiting orders. There was a long moment of silence between the two groups, as they regarded each other with thinly veiled hostility and bewilderment. One of the braver Japanese soldiers spoke up.

'What do Australian nurses drink?'

'Milk,' Beth answered sweetly. 'We only ever drink milk.'

The soldiers glanced at each other in consternation.

'Do you have any milk?' Lola asked, hopefully.

'No milk. Whiskey.'

'No, thank you.'

'Beer?'

'No, thank you.'

'Dance?' Captain Miachi turned on the gramophone and Duke Ellington began to play. 'You like to dance?'

'Most certainly *not*.'

One of the officers made his way across the room and took Kath's arm.

'No!' she shrieked and slapped his hand away. He looked stunned.

The nurses moved to the other side of the room and gazed balefully back at the officers, who stared at them in confusion. Beth produced a hacking cough, shuffled forward and stuffed some rather delicious looking buns down her front for later. Kath and Hazel followed suit, until they had a small stash of food and a couple of forks for their *kongsi*. Margot scooped up some bread rolls while the men looked on in silence.

'Well, we came,' she declared. '*We came.*' There were enthusiastic nods from the assembled nurses. 'Now, we shall *go.*' They formed a neat line in front of the door. 'And we shall expect *food* in the morning.' The last of the nurses departed. 'Good *evening.*'

The room was silent as Margot made her departure, apart from Duke Ellington on the gramophone, swinging it like he had no better place to be than the jungles of Sumatra.

After an underwhelming beginning, the officers' club managed to recruit some Eurasian women who became known as the 'girlfriends'. Mee Ling was a pretty girl who, along with others, had been hairdressers and cooks in the British and Dutch households, but had been forced into sexual slavery to survive. There were rumours of similar arrangements being made in other camps in Sumatra and Java, that any attractive young prisoner could be targeted, that Chinese, Malay and Dutch girls were all routinely being raped in service.

Margot saw Mee Ling inspecting her feet with great care one day and slowly approached her. 'Mee Ling, isn't it?' Margot asked, and the girl turned to her, with a small nod. 'Are you all right?' Margot was closer now and could see her feet properly; they were bleeding. 'What happened to you?' she asked, sitting beside her.

'Japanese,' Mee Ling hissed. Her face was wet with tears.

'Why?' Margot asked. 'Was this a punishment?'

Mee Ling closed her eyes and nodded. 'Pregnant.'

'Oh, dear girl,' Margot whispered.

'My friend pregnant before. Comfort woman too. The Japanese force her to marry. They did this to her feet.'

'This beating?'

'Bastinado. She couldn't walk for long time. Me too, I think.' Mee Ling's shoulders began to shake. She was sobbing, silently.

Margot put her arm out and Mee Ling slowly descended to her shoulder and then her lap, still weeping, with her bleeding feet and her baby, nestled in her womb as evidence of her shame.

'I can find something for your poor feet,' Margot murmured. 'But I'm afraid you're right, you won't be able to walk either, by tomorrow.'

'What become of me, Miss Margot?'

'I'm sorry, dear, I really don't know. But we'll do our best to look after you, and the baby, if it comes to that.'

'My baby die,' Mee Ling whispered. 'She die.'

Tears sprang to Margot's eyes. 'How old are you, Mee Ling?'

'Seventeen.'

Margot sighed to herself. The time the 'girlfriends' spent with the Japanese officers benefited the camp, as goods and medicines filtered through them, but the girls were often shunned for consorting with the enemy. She couldn't imagine what would happen to Mee Ling; if she would be removed from camp and married off, or if she would lose her baby through malnutrition and beatings, and stay on in camp, a pariah. There was room for cruelty on both sides.

CHAPTER 18

MARGOT
Irenelaan, Sumatra
1942

The months dragged on for the nurses, their daily doses of rice, the blankets of mosquitoes at night, the howling of wild dogs in the jungle, the endless rollcalls – known as *tenko* in Japanese – every morning and evening. The prisoners were ordered to bow to the guards, to show their respect for the emperor. If the bow wasn't considered low enough, the woman in question would receive a slap across the face. Kath became Beth's heroine when she halted a guard before he slapped her, to give herself time to remove her glasses. 'The look of astonishment on his face!' She laughed. 'I think even that little bully felt shame for a second!'

Occasionally the women would be lucky enough to see the imprisoned men nearby on their way to work. Beth and Hatty would call out a cheerful *cooee* if they heard male voices, just in case, and Margot's heart would lift as the wives and children rushed to the wire, ever hopeful.

One morning, just before *tenko*, a *cooee* rang out, and everyone dashed out of their houses.

'Look, Bronte! It's Daddy!' Mrs Thatcher cried. Among the gaggle of children a girl called out, waving excitedly through the barbed wire.

'Daddy! Daddy! Look at me!'

Margot and Beth grinned, listening to the men whistling through their fingers, keen to make a cheerful noise.

'Bronte! Is that you? Are you that great big girl I see?' one man said.

Bronte, painfully thin, but dressed brightly in a converted sarong her mother had faithfully remodelled, jumped up and down. 'Yes! It's *me*! ' she called. 'And is that *you*?'

Margot saw Mrs Thatcher freeze. Her husband was emaciated. His skin was hanging from his cheekbones as loosely as his shirt hung from his frail shoulders. He was a wraith in the jungle.

'Yes, it's me!' he called out bravely, as Bronte stopped jumping and stood absolutely still.

'Are you *sure*, Daddy? Is it really?'

'I'll prove it to you,' he told her. 'I know your dog is called Puddles the Puppy.'

'Oh, Daddy, it *is* you,' Bronte said. 'I think you are very tired.'

'Yes, I am rather, but I'm to have a nice sit down this week and I'll be up and about before you know it, Bronte. You be brave for Mummy now, won't you?'

'Oh, yes, Daddy. Mummy says I'm the best at being brave. She cries all the time, and I just play with my pick-up sticks.'

'Very wise and brave, Bronte,' he told her, his voice weaker and further away. 'I'm proud of you both. You give Mummy a big hug – that will help her to be brave too.' Then he was gone, and the Japanese guards were shouting again and calling to them on their way to gather and chop wood. Margot craned her neck to see if there were any other men, but there was no sign, and the bell was ringing for *tenko* again.

A second group did come past later, while Margot and the rest of the nurses were standing patiently on the parade ground. She heard a whistle and a *cooee* and her heart leaped. She quickly scanned the group of men to see if Gull was among them. The men were all looking thinner, but seemed well enough. They smiled as they turned towards the women, nodding and touching their hats in greeting.

'They look all right for a bunch of prisoners,' Lola muttered. 'Anyone we know?'

'Not yet . . .' Margot was still searching the crowd. 'Gull Flannery?' she called out hopefully.

'*Shizukana!*' The guard yelled at her. She glanced to see it was Seki the Sadist.

'Flannery?' she called again.

Seki marched across and slapped her across the face. 'Silence!'

Margot bowed deeply, her face stinging. She allowed herself a small smile as she looked at the muddy earth. If Gull were alive, he'd soon know she was nearby. The pain in her cheek was nothing at all.

Finally, their captors were content. 'Dismiss!' Seki the Sadist barked and marched back to his hut.

The women fell out of their lines. Beth and Lola turned to Margot and put an arm around each shoulder.

'Are you all right, Margot?' Lola asked. 'He's a nasty piece of work, that little bastard.'

'I'm fine, I just thought I might see if Gull is all right. Make sure he's survived.'

'He'll be fine,' Lola assured her. 'I pray for him every day.'

'I bloody hope you're praying for us as well, Lola,' Beth said. 'We could use some divine intervention around here as well, you know.'

'Oh, of course, you're all in my prayers, every night. And a couple of times on Sundays. *And* when it's my turn to make jam.'

'Well, I hope you're not praying for whoever took my grass hat,' Beth said. 'Let them rot in hell.'

'Hazel will make you another one.'

'It won't be the same. I'd just got the last one the way I like it.'

'Look, I'll mention it, but I think God has enough on his plate, quite frankly.'

'Then perhaps if he could just turn the sun down a bit during *tenko*, so it's not quite so hot?'

They made their way back to the shade of their verandah where the cooking fire was in need of stoking. Margot flopped onto the top step, pressing her hand into her cheek.

Beth plonked herself beside her. 'I wonder what's happening at home,' she said. 'Probably bringing in the steers for sale. Hope there's been some rain. Dad'll have been busy branding the last month or so.'

'My dad's probably working on tax returns in Sydney,' Lola responded. 'And being nagged by Mum for not going to church often enough.'

'Your mum sounds very religious.'

'Oh, yes, she's solid Catholic, all the way down. I grew up on Hail Marys.'

'But your father's not religious?'

'He's lapsed. Still shows up for christenings, Christmas, that sort of thing. Mum says his prayers for him.'

'My lot are Methodists,' Beth said. 'We disapprove of all that confessing and getting off scot-free. Seems like cheating to us.'

'Oh, we do have to *repent*, you know—'

'Well, yes, but there's repenting, and there's *repenting*, isn't there? And I can't imagine you'd have much to repent for, anyway, Lola.'

Margot judged the fire was ready, and swung a huge black cauldron into position beside it. 'Now, who's got something special for Matilda?'

'I do,' Hatty said. 'I bartered some sun hats for a few potatoes from the nice Dutch ladies on the hill. Should be enough for an Irish stew, without any onion or lamb – but with rice and *kang kong*.'

Lola began to fossick in her cooking supplies for some spices bartered with local traders and found some chilli. 'How about this to perk things up a bit?'

Hazel held out her hand. 'I've a little salt left, too.'

When Matilda was in position, Hazel kept watch, stirring the mixture, adding water, and chopping the potatoes into small pieces so they'd go further.

'I've just spoken to Anika,' she said.

'What about?'

'Well, I know the Dutch Red Cross is having far more luck helping out their people. The Dutch have access to money, but we don't because we're internees, not POWs. I thought I'd organise a chat about the officers' club. Put in a complaint.'

'How'd you go?' Beth asked.

'Hard to tell. Anika said she'd pass it on – whether or not it will have any effect, I couldn't say.'

'Well, if I had to be any nationality in this camp, it'd be Dutch,' Beth said. 'They've got a bit of money and some of them have local connections so they can get a few things on the black market.'

'We'll just have to work harder,' Margot said.

'It's not fair, we're POWs and we should have reasonable treatment. It's ridiculous.'

'Lucky for us most of the Dutch don't like to do menial work. Too good for it, apparently,' Lola said.

'Oh, yes, I was talking to Mrs van Boxtel the other day about chopping some firewood, and she was happy to pay *me* to do it. She said, "It's all right for you *Australians* – you're used to it!"'

'Well, it's lucky for us they're *not*.'

'Yeah, we'll always have work with the Dutch.'

'Hatty's been making a few guilders looking after their children for them. And I'm cleaning three Dutch houses next week.'

Lola glanced at the sky. 'What do you think the time is?' she asked.

Beth pulled a face. 'About nine o'clock? Where's Kath? She'll know.'

'Poor Kath, I think she sometimes wishes she didn't have the only watch in camp.'

'Really – what do we need to know the time for, anyway?'

'I just like the occasional bit of proof time is *actually* passing, that's all,' Margot said. She grinned as if the thought alone pleased her. Then she stirred Matilda, the thin brown soup slowly coming to the boil. There was nothing Matilda couldn't do. She boiled water, made soup, stew, jam and cooked banana skins and yams until they were broken down enough to eat. A few of the nurses shared recipes with the British and Dutch, and the women found they were able to eke food from almost anything they could scrounge. If they were to move camps again, Matilda would hold belongings and be taken along with everything they valued. The days and months at Irenelaan were measured in meals from within Matilda's warm iron heart.

'Eggs. I never thought I'd give so much attention to the procurement of an egg.' Mrs Edgar was observing her egg with the keen interest of both a scientist and a chef. A scientist, because she was trying to ascertain the species of bird inside the egg she had been peeling, and a chef, because she'd just cooked it.

Margot and Beth added some more banana peel to Matilda.

'Is it a duck?' Beth asked. 'Seems a bit yellow . . .'

'I think it's a chicken.'

'Just eat it,' Beth advised. 'Nice and quick, don't think about it too much.'

'I would, although I'm not sure if it's worth it coming back up, and it did cost me my broken watch,' she said.

'I ate a rotten egg last week and I managed to keep *that* down. I'd regard this as a step up,' Beth told her. 'Good protein.'

Mrs Edgar observed the occupant for another long moment, gripped its tiny head and tossed it into her mouth, chewing as if it were about to explode.

'Think of roast beef,' Margot said.

'No, something crunchier, perhaps a good roast potato.'

'Oh, you know what's good with roast potato?'

'Yes, roast beef!'

'And gravy!'

'I think it's gone,' Mrs Edgar said cautiously.

'Even the beak?'

'I think so. I might just sit here a while if that's all right. Make sure the little chap stays down.'

'You're very welcome. We're just boiling up some jam.'

'Banana peel jam?'

'The very same. And as soon as we're finished we're boiling soy beans. They take ages.'

'You know, I'd love a fresh ham and salad sandwich. With a cup of tea and a plate of sun-warmed peaches to follow,' Mrs Edgar said.

'Oh, that sounds nice,' Beth said. 'I'd really like a bunch of grapes from the vines at home. There's never been a grape like them, I'm not sure if it's the species, or what . . .'

'Joy makes a very acceptable bread from rice, you know,' Margot said.

Beth picked up the mortar and pestle and began to grind some rice into a fine flour.

'Are you making bread as well, Beth?' Mrs Edgar asked.

'No, it's Hazel's birthday, we're having a birthday cake for her this afternoon.'

'How on earth are you managing to make a cake out of rice?'

'We're not,' Margot said. 'We grind up some rice and sprinkle it over an old jam tin like icing sugar, then we sing "Happy Birthday". It's a bit festive.'

'I'm *not* having a birthday while I'm here,' Beth declared. 'I refuse to get *one* year older while I'm rotting in bloody Sumatra!'

Mrs Edgar winced and held her hand to her mouth. She burped loudly. 'Please excuse me,' she murmured, her expression pained. 'I hope the bird felt the same way.'

Tenko began as usual early one warm morning as the jungle came to life with birdsong and the yard came to life with the shouts of the Japanese guards.

Margot let her attention wander and thought about Gull. She wondered how he was coping in the men's prison. It had been months now since she'd seen or heard from him. She'd learned that a number of men had died from their injuries. Infection had set in, and without adequate medicines, there was little the doctors interned with them could do. Men who were injured as they worked suffered ulceration of their wounds; often fever and death followed, and malaria stalked them all. She reached into her pocket for his lucky penny, even though she knew it wasn't there. It was too precious. She'd hidden it in the pocket of her uniform and locked it away as safely as she was able. She stared at Captain Hollywood and Rasputin as they went through the list.

'Where's Kath?' Beth whispered.

Margot glanced around. There was no sign of Kath Jenkins. 'Have you seen her?' she muttered to Lola.

'No, she was a bit off last night, but I was up early this morning and I didn't notice if she was up or not . . . I think Rita has recorded the sickbay numbers.'

After *tenko*, they went straight back to their house and found Kath unconscious on the floor, her face beaded with sweat, her breathing shallow.

'Call for Goldberg,' Margot said as she loosened Kath's blouse.

'She won't come,' Lola said.

'Call her anyway. Dr Scott is at the hospital this week, she won't be back before dark.'

Lola dashed away while Mona and Margot wiped Kath's face with a damp cloth.

'Just let me . . . just let me . . . I can do it for the . . . in the end . . .'

'She's got a fever. Must be almost a hundred and four.'

Kath pushed the cloth away and groaned again. Lola came back, her face dark.

'Where's the damn doctor?' Margot snapped.

'She *might* be on her way, but she's not happy.' Lola sat down on the floor beside them. 'She says she's not coming if she doesn't get paid.'

'We can't afford to pay her,' Beth said.

'Yes, well, I thought it best not to mention that part, or she wouldn't come at all,' Lola explained.

'What happens when she gets here?'

'I thought we might appeal to her better nature,' Lola said hopefully.

'She doesn't have one,' Margot said. 'I bet she's selling quinine tablets, and God knows we need more of them. We only have a few bottles, but I doubt we'll get any from her.'

Dr Goldberg eventually arrived. 'Where is the patient?' she asked at the door.

'In here,' Lola called out. There was a brief hesitation and Dr Goldberg entered.

'This is her?'

'Yes.'

'Now. I prefer to be paid *first* for my ministrations.'

'Oh. We were thinking you would help her first, since her condition is—'

'Typhoid. Everyone has it. She has a fever? Diarrhoea? Stomach pains? Sweating? It's typhoid.'

'Do you have something for her?'

'Are you able to *pay*?'

'We'll do our best to settle our bill, Dr Goldberg, but we cannot pay immediately.'

'My *Dutch* clients pay. My *British* clients pay. I sometimes admit them to the local hospital because they know the *value* of my care.'

'We *know* the value of your care, but we don't have *any money*,' Margot said. 'Unless we work for the other prisoners. Which we *do*, and we'll earn your fee as soon as possible.'

Dr Goldberg had been crouching near Kath's exhausted form. She stood. 'Well. I think not. She may die. Then you will forget. It's happened before. A waste of time and medication.' She paused in the doorway. 'Supplies are limited. If she worsens, bring her to the hospital. But it will cost.' She marched out.

'I hate that woman!' Margot declared. 'She only helps those with money. And the milk she's given for the children? She feeds to her cats.'

They gently lifted Kath up off the floor and helped her gingerly onto a mattress.

'She is despicable.'

'Be careful of her, she was asking Bully all sorts of questions a few weeks ago. Bully was too clever for her, but I've no doubt she gains some of her special privileges by giving information to the Japs.'

Kath moaned again. 'Water, please?'

'Just rest, Kath. I'll fetch you some water and you have a good lie down.'

Margot lifted Kath's wrist and checked her pulse. It was fast, and her face was pale, bathed in sweat. Margot perched on the edge of the mattress and fanned her with an old copy of *Nippon Go!*, a Japanese newspaper the guards had allowed. It didn't contain much news, judging from the pictures, just propaganda about how the Japanese would win the war, and how the emperor was going to rule all of Asia.

The previous week, one of the guards had taken great pleasure in explaining some of the more interesting stories to Lola. One was about a Japanese soldier who threw rice at the US fighters, who fled in fear of his terrifying new form of ammunition. But her favourite was a story in which a fighter plane was flying into battle against Australian and English pilots where both sides took heavy fire. As the battle continued in the skies above Singapore, the European pilots couldn't believe the superior Japanese pilot was still battling them, still shooting at them from the sky. Finally, the battle was won and the Japanese plane headed home to base. When he landed, the engineers ran to the plane to help the pilot out, only to discover that he had been dead for some time; the ghosts of his ancestors were flying the plane and fighting the enemy to free Japan from the white man's rule.

The paper rustled in the damp air over Kath's pale face. 'You'll feel better tomorrow, once you've had a rest,' Margot said.

Kath didn't feel better the next day, but nor did she worsen. The girls kept her as cool as they could, feeding her a rice gruel with soft pieces of potato. Eventually her temperature began to drop and Margot allowed herself to briefly feel relieved. The afternoon sun was still at the window when Kath finally spoke.

'It's getting late. Who's going to cook? Matilda's waiting to get on with dinner.'

'Lola? She's a pretty good cook,' Margot said.

'She's working for the Dutch today, cleaning houses,' Beth said. 'And I'm teaching maths to the plantation kids.'

Kath glanced at Margot. 'Despite your culinary reputation, you'll have to do.'

'*Me?* You want me to cook?'

'As long as you promise not to poison anyone.' Kath closed her eyes.

Margot leaned down. 'Kath, you *know* I can't promise that.'

'Just go find what supplies you can and come tell me what they are. I'll direct you for dinner. But first we've got to get the soya beans cooked. Have they been soaking? They'll need to boil for a couple of hours.'

'Are you *sure* you're too sick?' Margot said.

Kath ignored her. 'You'll need to form them into little cakes and fry them. We make five cents a cake, you know, they're a good earner. Look, Mischa is on his way, he'll help you.'

'Hello, Sister Margot,' Mischa said. The little boy's hair had grown longer, but he was still too thin. He had been taken in by a kind Dutch woman who put him to bed safely every night, but he liked to wander the buildings of the camp as if he was on a tour of inspection. Sometimes the nurses would save the little bear a small treat when they could, to pay him for his work stirring Matilda when they were making porridge.

'What are we cooking today?' he asked.

With a dramatic sigh, mainly for Kath's entertainment, Margot stood. 'Your guess is as good as mine, Mischa. Come and help me find some kindling.'

The pair began to collect whatever kindling they could but it was getting more difficult. The Japanese allowed few wood deliveries, so they were forced to scavenge what they could, burning unused furniture from their houses, fanning out into the jungle for sticks when they were allowed outside. The Japanese shouted at them as they collected fuel, but mostly seemed content to leave them to it.

'Oh, look, Mischa, can you bring me that chair?' Margot said, spying an old timber chair.

Mischa dashed away and came back victorious with part of a broken chair the Dutch ladies next door had thrown out. Margot was pleased to see a smashed wooden pallet, which had held supplies from the Dutch Red Cross, down the side of the house. The supplies had been inspected by the Japanese, who had removed all the tins of food and medicines, before passing on what remained. The smashed pallet would see them through the day's cooking, if Margot managed it correctly.

'Mischa, would you mind bringing me pieces of this old pallet once we get the fire going?'

'Of course, Sister Margot. You already know that Mischa the Bear is a very strong boy.'

Margot grinned. 'Mischa the Bear, it's well known among the nursing fraternity that you are the strongest bear we shall ever meet.'

'Mischa has the heart of a bear!'

'Lucky Mischa, I have the heart of a sparrow!'

'Why would you want the heart of a sparrow?' Mischa said. 'Too small, too light. My heart is heavy and strong!'

Margot laughed. 'What a huge weight for a little boy.'

The child grinned and held his skinny arms aloft, before disappearing down the side of the house.

Margot pulled Matilda into position, added the soaked beans and water from a kerosene tin, and began to nudge the fire into life.

'Margot.' It was Beth, walking towards her with her grass hat at a jaunty angle. She had finished teaching for the day. 'I hear you're on cooking detail.'

'Yep,' Margot said. 'And I'm doing my best.' She flicked a couple of weevils into the fire. 'But the rice is almost half weevils. Perhaps we should just give up and eat them? They're protein – and *not rat*.'

'Sounds all right to me, just don't mention it to the others. They might be fussy.' Beth knelt beside her and glanced about to check for guards. 'Here,' she murmured, 'in case you need some extra supplies.' She took her hat in her hands, and Margot could see it held a small mango, some papaya and a couple of sweet biscuits.

'Where on earth did you get these?'

'The cemetery. One of the girls mentioned a Buddhist funeral was held there yesterday, so I snuck under the fence for a quick look. The guards were busy with the traders along the front fence.'

'Oh, my. Mango! Beth! Well done. The sweet biscuits will be crumble – we'll have fruit crumble – then Lola might forgive my terrible cooking . . .'

'Well, you'll end the meal on a high.' Beth settled in next to her, not too close to the heat of the flame on the muggy day. 'I'm sorry a Chinese worker died – but they'll be placing food on his grave for a while.'

'It seems wrong.'

'Not as wrong as watching our friends starve. If the Chinese chap was alive I'm sure he'd want to put the food to some use rather than let it go to waste.'

Lola arrived with a bundle in her arms, and an expression of undisguised hope.

'What have you got there?' Beth demanded.

Lola opened her arms a little to reveal a small black dog. 'He tells me his name is Toby,' she explained. 'We've become friends and now he's living with us here at the camp.'

'We don't have enough food to feed ourselves, and you're bringing in a dog?' Beth said.

'He's tiny and he won't eat much. Just scraps.'

'*We're* eating scraps,' Margot said.

'I thought he might be nice company for Mischa and the children,' Lola replied.

Margot sighed. 'I suppose he can stay, although if I catch you going without to feed him, I'll let Beth sell him for meat.'

'You wouldn't!'

'Well, *I* would,' Beth assured her, 'he's bigger than a rat . . .'

'Hazel sold a pair of rats this morning for two dollars fifty,' Margot said. 'The Dutch bought them. Filthy bloody animals but at least they're meat.'

'I hope it was the little sod who's been pooing in our sugar rations,' Beth grumbled. 'I resent having to pick out rat droppings, knowing full well they're eating our food.'

'Makes them all the sweeter for the Dutch market,' Margot told her.

Beth laughed. And Matilda finally came to the boil.

CHAPTER 19

MARGOT
Irenelaan, Sumatra
December 1942

'Silent Night! Holy Night! All is calm, all is bright!' Lola was ready to celebrate Christmas Day regardless of the wire fence surrounding them, and irrespective of Beth's disappointment at dawn Christmas carols.

'Bloody hell, Lola,' she grumbled. 'At least don't sing a bloody *German* carol!'

'Merry Christmas, Beth!' Lola leaned down and kissed her cheek. 'May you have a wonderful Christmas and freedom in the new year – and "Silent Night" is *Austrian*!'

Beth sat up, with her dark hair sticking up like tinsel. 'Well, it's still a bit early,' she grumbled.

Margot rolled off the edge of the mattress and ran her fingers through her hair. 'Merry Christmas, Lola,' she said. 'Beth, you're just going to have to put up with it. What would you both be doing now if you were home?'

'It's the one week of the year my dad takes time off from his office and joins the rest of us down at Kiama,' Lola said. 'We swim and play cards, and quite often we manage to catch fish for dinner.'

Lola smiled. 'Sometimes I think those weeks on the coast make me feel closer to my family than the rest of the year combined. It's like everyone is completely *themselves*.'

'We have a nice Christmas at Sandy Creek,' Beth said. 'Roast beef, of course, and too many paper decorations all around the dining room. We have a little singalong with some of the drovers, if they don't head off home, and we open our presents early under a huge eucalypt by the creek over a mug of tea if we wake up before the day heats up. Dad orders presents from Brisbane, and it's always a Christmas miracle if they arrive in time.'

'Everyone come into the kitchen!' Rita and Hazel were wearing paper hats made from old copies of *Nippon Go!*, and their smiles were triumphant.

'What?'

'We have a Christmas surprise for you all and we've managed to keep it a secret.'

'What?' Margot said. 'Is the war over?'

'Sorry, no. Just come into the kitchen and you'll see.'

The girls headed into the tiny kitchen in their *kongsi*, to be greeted by the other nurses from two houses away.

'Merry Christmas!'

Rita and Hazel stepped aside to reveal a Christmas feast of fruit, vegetables and a large, plump chicken. The nurses stood blinking in astonishment.

'How on earth?'

'Well. We have our very own Christmas miracle. The boys at the Palembang camp left us a message in some firewood they sent over. They were holding a Melbourne Cup last month.'

'Oh, what a good idea. I hope no one got squashed.'

'Well, no, because a group of jockeys from Singapore are

interned at their camp. So they picked various men to give piggy backs, and they held a race.'

'Sounds like fun . . .'

'Yes, and a money maker, as it happened. The Aussies and Kiwis made *thirty* guilders, which they smuggled to us to make sure we had a merry Christmas!'

'They didn't!'

Rita gestured to the food. 'Yes they *did*. We've been dying to tell you, but we didn't want to spoil the surprise.'

'Although we *did* save a few guilders for absolute emergencies . . .'

'Very wise,' Lola said. 'Now, surely everyone is ready for a singalong?'

Margot was smiling as she glanced around the small house and the rows of nurses waking to Christmas in Sumatra. These women were her family now. She wondered what was happening in Leederville. She thought of her father waking her mother for another Christmas without her. Did they even know she was alive, she wondered. Perhaps they had told themselves she was gone. Perhaps they were right, and she'd never go home again. She sighed, and added the freshly purchased tea leaves to the pot while Lola stood on a chair and started to sing once more.

'Kath, what's the time?'

Kath checked her wrist. 'Nine o'clock. They'll be by any minute.' The girls patted their hair straight and smoothed down their dresses and shirts. They stood, waiting, staring out at the jungle path. The male prisoners were building their new prison and twice a day they passed by, staring into the camp, trying to spot someone they loved, or even just someone they knew, a comrade.

Away in a manger, no crib for a bed,
The little Lord Jesus laid down his sweet head . . .

Lola's sweet voice lifted high over the damp Sumatran jungle, and then Margot, Beth, Rita, Hazel and all the girls joined in.

The stars in the bright sky, looked down where he lay,
The little Lord Jesus, asleep on the hay . . .

The men paused as the carol found them, slowing to feel its warmth, and Margot could see them smiling broadly.

'*Ugoku! Ugoku!*' A Japanese guard prodded a few of the slower men with a stick, but they also slowed, glancing back at the women quickly, and looking away.

Margot stood on her tiptoes in case she could see him. Her Christmas present to herself would be to see Gull alive, smiling at her. To wave at him and let him know they were going to meet again. She craned her neck and scanned the faces. She couldn't find him anywhere. The men paused, and soon the carol fell silent. The women stared at them. More women and their children came outside to see what was going on and, realising their fathers might be there, dashed to the highest spot they could find in case they could see them. Margot glanced at the roof of the house next to theirs to see a couple of women waving tea towels.

Silent night, Holy night – all is calm, all is bright,
Round yon virgin, mother and child,
Holy infant so tender and mild . . .

The men's voices were low. How Margot had yearned to hear a kind male voice. She hadn't even known she'd missed it so much.

She'd been raised to rely on men, on her father, on her grandfather, even perhaps on Neville for a while. She'd respected her male teachers at school, and the doctors she worked with. She'd dreamed about Gull's voice more than once. But now that was gone, and nothing could keep them safe. They were on their own. Except for today, with their Christmas lunch already cooking, delivered by the kindness of the men from home. She couldn't see Gull, so she imagined him there instead while blinking back desperate tears.

'Well, Beth, I don't hear you complaining about "Silent Night" now . . .' Lola murmured.

'Oh, this is *completely* different. *Men* singing about *shepherds* takes me back to the bush,' Beth assured her. 'I could listen all day!' Beth gave Lola a nudge and she grinned.

And Margot allowed herself to imagine once again the feeling of being safe, the comfort of a good meal and the freedom of home.

That afternoon they opened their presents.

'Oh Beth, how marvellous. How did you manage it?'

Beth grinned self-consciously. 'Well, I'm not too bad with a whittling knife,' she said. 'I've been making them for a while.'

Kath turned the chess pieces over in her hands. 'Simply marvellous,' she breathed. 'We'll play tonight!'

'Then we can have a round of Mah-jong with my beautiful tiles,' Margot added. 'Look at all of these designs. You'd never guess they were made from furniture.'

'And I've made you all some new jewellery for Christmas, as well,' Joy said, placing pumpkin seed necklaces and dried chilli earrings onto everyone's dish. 'Merry Christmas.'

Rita had embroidered handkerchiefs out of old curtain fabric she'd earned from a Dutch family for cleaning their house, and Kath had made small dolls for some of the children, adding in kangaroos and koalas when she was feeling particularly ambitious.

The girls had Christmas hats made from pandang leaves, a Christmas tree carefully decorated with handmade ornaments, a baby Jesus made from coconut hair, an angel from dried leaves and petals, and fairies from broken pegs and bright cotton.

'Now. For the brave. My contribution to Christmas.' Hazel entered the room with a large steel bucket and placed it on the table.

'What on earth do you have there?' Margot asked.

'I hope I have the makings of a Merry Christmas,' Hazel announced. 'My attempt at . . . chilli wine!'

'Are you sure it's safe?' asked Lola.

'I'll have hers!' Beth said. 'I want to toast to Christmas with our families. Next year.' She took a sip and winced. 'Spicy, but refreshing. And a toast to the Japs, who recently bombed the Sydney Harbour Bridge.'

Lola was shocked. 'Oh, Beth. They didn't. Are you joking?'

Beth rolled her eyes. 'Really Lola, you are gullible. I was assured they'd bombed the bridge only last week in a submarine, while I was bowing and scraping. The guard seemed to think he knew all about it.' She took another sip of wine. '"Oh dear," I said. "How distressing!" And he said, "Yes – your bridge collapsed when we bombed the central pylon!" Ha! The central pylon! I shook my head in despair!'

Hazel raised her glass. 'To the central pylon – that marvellous feat of engineering!'

'To the Harbour Bridge!'

'And to the Melbourne Cup!'

It was just after dark when Mischa found Margot. He had taken to looking after Toby, who'd become a welcome part of the nurses' *kongsi*.

'Sister Margot!'

'Mischa, what is it?'

'Toby needs a walk. Will you come with me?'

'Oh, perhaps in a minute. How about you take him today, it's getting dark, so I don't suppose the guards will notice him.'

'I'm worried I'll get in trouble, Sister Margot . . .'

'Oh, very well, then, although it's the first I've heard of you being worried about anything . . .'

Mischa grinned. 'I would like company on Christmas night. That's all!'

The evening was warm and still. Sometimes the winds came in and rattled the tin roofs of the huts around the camp, but tonight it was pleasant wandering along in the shadows with Mischa and Toby, who carefully sniffed every tree, verandah post and blade of grass. Margot hardly noticed they had strayed towards the wire fence at the back of the compound.

'We should probably head back, Mischa, the guards will be angry if they catch us back here . . .'

'Margot!'

She stopped.

'Margot!'

It was Gull.

'Gull! How did you get here?' She crept to the fence and crouched in the shadows.

'I called in a gambling debt.'

'So your luck hasn't run out, then?'

'Not yet, it hasn't.'

Margot dropped to her knees. He was thinner, his hair was cropped short and he winced as he dropped to the ground as well, but his smile was the same, and the warmth in his face was just as she remembered it. She put her fingers against the wire and he placed his hand in hers.

'I know why you're here,' she whispered.

'Do you?'

'Yes, things are getting tough and you want your lucky penny back.'

'Do I?'

'Yes, and you're in luck, because I've kept it in my pocket all day.'

'Why on earth would you need luck today?'

'Well, it worked, didn't it?' She smiled.

'How are you, Margot? Really?'

Margot glanced around. 'Oh, you know, pretty good. We've got some great girls here, and the women from England and the Netherlands have been wonderful.'

'Are they feeding you?'

'Not much, but we work for the richer internees to earn money for food, we trade what we can, and occasionally we're not above stealing vegetables from the camp vegetable garden.'

'I'm pleased to hear it. Do whatever you can. The war can't last forever. The one thing we hate to think of over there is that you lot are suffering.'

'We're pretty tough, you know. You look after yourselves.'

'Margot. Can I say something ridiculous?'

'Probably, it's happened before.'

Gull rolled his eyes. 'Hush. You might want to pay attention, I'll have to go in a bit, so you don't get in trouble.'

'What? What am I paying attention to?'

'Me asking you to marry me.'

'Pardon?'

'Will you marry me, Margot McNee?'

'*Now?*'

'After the war – when we go home.'

'Ask me then! Not *now*, for goodness' sake!'

'Margot, I love you and the thought of knowing we have a real future together will give me something to work towards.' He squeezed her fingers. 'I know this is a terrible time, but we'll make it home again. I want to marry you and grow old beside you.'

'Gull. This is nonsense!'

'No, it's not. Say yes, and let's make plans. It doesn't matter what happens to us here, we'll know that we have each other.' He kissed her fingers. 'I'll never let anything bad happen to you again.'

Margot looked into Gull's eyes. She wasn't surprised to see that he meant it – she was surprised she believed him. She would grow old with Gull, and if they were lucky they would raise beautiful children together. They would rise early each morning and drink tea, read the newspaper and talk about their day. At night he would come home from work, and she would be there, waiting, this horrible captivity behind them. She suddenly felt closer to freedom. She reached into her pocket and pressed the lucky penny into his fingers.

'Yes,' she said. 'I will marry you, as soon as this is over.'

And they kissed between the wires of her prison.

'You *what?*' Beth and Lola were still wearing their Christmas hats, their chilli earrings bobbing jauntily as they gaped.

'I just got engaged.'

'To who? Mischa?'

Mischa beamed. He knew he was quite a catch.

'No, to Gull,' Margot explained.

'Gull? He was here?'

'He snuck over from the men's camp. I think he may have bribed one of the guards. He wanted to see me for Christmas Day – and he proposed.'

'And you said yes? I must say that seems a little impetuous.'

'Well, yes. But why not? I love him, and if we get out of here, then nothing would make me happier than to be married to Gull.'

'Congratulations.' Lola hugged her close. 'Gull is a sweet man, and I know you'll be very happy together. Oh, it gives me hope just to think of it.'

Beth dabbed her eyes. 'Well, you'll probably live to regret it, but I'm very happy for you both. You'll have to give up nursing, you know.'

'I won't even care, I'll have Gull, and a thousand babies, and a house with a front yard.'

'And I'll come babysit for you,' Lola said.

'You'll have children of your own . . .' Margot assured her. She sat down on her mattress, thinking about Gull. The exact blue of his eyes, the warmth of his fingertips. Suddenly she had a future.

The next few weeks flew by. Gull's promise was the doorway to the life she was going to live. She finished her nursing rounds of the children in the camp and made her way to sit on the verandah, where she found Lola's mind had also turned to romance.

'What's that you're reading, Lola?' Beth was at work, grinding eggshells and bones to powder with a mortar and pestle. They would be added to their rice as a meagre form of nutrition.

'*The Lady's Lover*. It's rather good. It's about a young lady on the run from her terrible husband who's only after her money and she meets a scoundrel on the road—'

'Oh, for goodness' sake! It was your turn at the library and you took *that* out?' Beth said. 'What garbage! I was hoping you'd take out the Marie Curie biography.'

'It's in *Dutch*,' Lola protested.

'It has pictures . . .'

Lola flicked through the novel to a dog-eared page. 'Here you are. "When Persephone turned, she found she was in the arms of Captain Bartholomew. His dark eyes upon hers, his fine mouth a breath away from her full lips. His gaze pierced her heart. 'My dear, you have undone me entirely. I would give all my lands for a kiss of those sweet petals.' 'But, Sir, I am yet a maid!' He would hear no more, crushing her ruby lips to his own, plundering her mouth until she opened like a flower beneath his ministrations of love." Let's see Marie Curie do that!'

'Marie Curie would be too busy discovering polonium. Really, Lola, you're such a romantic. I don't know why you even joined the library if this is what we've got to read.'

'Well, you used to have to bring a book to join the library,' Lola said. 'But they've had to review that rule now.'

'What's the rule now?'

'I think the only rule is – don't eat the books!'

Beth hooted with laughter. 'Go on then, make me blush!'

The next morning, the girls woke to the sound of lonely howling.

'Missed one,' Beth sighed, pulling her knapsack over her head.

The wild dogs around the camp had been starving. Their owners had fled, and they had been surviving on whatever they could find in the jungle or rubbish bins in the towns of Sumatra. They had haunted the camps, snapping and growling, fighting over scraps in desperation. It had become such a problem that the guards had eventually herded them together and shot and bayoneted them en masse, much to the horror of the nurses. Some they had drowned, tossing them into the river and poking them under the water with long poles as they struggled and whined in fear. Joy and Lola were horrified, but the Japanese guards were mystified by their emotions. *You Australians*, they had said. *We tell you of the Australian soldiers we have killed, and you smile. We kill some dogs and you cry . . .*

'Stay indoors while the guards are around,' Beth warned Toby, 'and you'll stop barking at them if you know what's good for you.'

'They're bound to hear him. Do you think we could shut him out the back somehow?'

'I think he'd just run under the house and give them a good telling off anyway.' Beth scratched Toby's ears, while he panted in appreciation.

'He's lucky he's got Mischa to look after him,' Margot said. 'Perhaps he could teach him some manners – or at least take him to the Dutch houses if we're having a visit from the guards.'

CHAPTER 20

MARGOT
Men's Camp, Palembang, Sumatra
September 1943

In September the nurses reached for their uniforms again as the women's camp was packed up and moved to the deserted men's camp at Palembang. By now the women had become used to the patterns of life at Irenelaan, the supplies dumped onto the road, the black-market traders sneaking goods to the camp, the endless counting at *tenko* twice a day, the guards, the warm winds and afternoon rains.

When they arrived at the new camp, it had been destroyed. They surveyed the broken huts and muddy wells.

'I suppose they did their best,' Lola said sadly. 'They didn't know it was *us* coming to take up residence, after all. I wonder where they moved them.'

'Somewhere better, I hope,' Beth said.

'If they'd known we were taking their camp, they'd have been good enough to leave us some firewood,' Margot said.

Joy picked up a huge tromper and held the homemade sandal to her own small foot. 'I think we can burn these, unless anyone thinks they might fit?'

'Keep them for now, we'll need them for the fire soon enough.'

The nurses slowly took in the scene.

The men's camp was in a low-lying area and consisted of a collection of square huts surrounded by barbed wire. The light poles had been kicked over and a pile of broken bed frames sat in the central *padang*, a large yard which held a couple of wells for water and a community building, with a big roof but no walls. There were rows of huts along the fences, set aside for the hospital and for the guards, then a storeroom, and accommodation for Dr Goldberg and the nuns. Many of the roofs were in disrepair and some of the benches in the community area had been broken. Margot's heart sank. It would take them weeks to fix the broken furniture and make themselves at home in the camp. She surveyed the bed frames, the benches, the broken chairs, the damaged lights. At least they'd have some wood for their fire.

The second year of captivity had become increasingly difficult for the nurses. Their ongoing struggle to find enough food to maintain their health was exhausting, and the stress of it began to take its toll. They ate anything they could find, boiled weeds, crushed bones, and the weevils they cooked into their rice. Occasionally they would be supplied with a chicken or a pig, which was shared carefully among the camp, cut down into thimbles of protein. Once, they were given a monkey and they reluctantly consumed that as well.

The Japanese guards began to weigh the prisoners every week, monitoring the women as they withered away.

'Smaller prisoner, no need for so much food,' Rasputin would say, and the rations were cut again.

'It's a crime, that's what it is.' Hazel was outraged. 'We're wasting away out here in the jungle with no one watching. What do they think will happen? No food. Most of us have stopped menstruating . . .'

'And you know what happened last week?' Lola added. 'They gave us some personal hygiene products because "ladies require them". Not *anymore*, we don't. We're *too thin*. I feel sorry for the young ones – how will their young bodies develop, being starved like this?'

'Now,' Beth said, 'while it's true we're all bloody starving, complaining about it won't help. I think we need to discuss a plan to survive.'

'You have the floor, Beth,' Margot said, settling in the camp kitchen beside Lola and Hatty.

'We have no money, and rations are being cut all the time. We won't last very long if this keeps up. And we can expect the war to keep going for a while.'

'How long?'

'None of your business, Rita! Now. We must work if we are to eat. It's that simple. And I don't just mean working around the camp – we must find employment or we'll starve.'

'Agreed,' Lola and Rita said in unison.

'Right. We need a show of hands for jobs we know we can do, and we need suggestions for other forms of income.'

'Well, there are already a few opportunities,' Margot said. 'Joy and Rita are baking with scraps and rice flour, which is earning five cents apiece. And Mona is making handkerchiefs from pieces of material and exchanging those for food with the Dutch.'

'Yes, all good enterprises. We're also having some luck with cleaning houses for the Dutch, so let's keep that up. There's child minding, of course, but another task has arisen we should consider.' Beth paused. 'We have formed a sanitation committee with the English and Dutch as you know, and a small amount of money has been put aside to pay us to empty the latrines.'

Rita and Lola visibly slumped.

'As you know, this is an ongoing issue, and if anyone is going to get paid, it should be us. We need the money.'

'Did I mention I was taking in laundry for the Dutch ladies as well?' Joy said. 'That earns us a bit . . .'

'Can I ask, what *tools* would be provided for emptying the toilets?' Hatty asked.

'Are you volunteering?'

'Not yet, I'm just delaying the inevitable.'

'Well, we have kerosene tins to transport the – waste – and coconut shells to ladle it out.'

'Do we have to carry it far?'

'Not too far. It can be dumped in the jungle just outside the camp.' Beth held her hands up. 'Obviously, *I'm* keen to have a go at carrying other people's sewage – it'll remind me of happier times as a student nurse. Who'll join me?'

There was a pause and a collective sigh before half a dozen loyal hands were slowly raised. Hitam, a black cat who had adopted the nurses, made his way slowly through their legs as they sat considering their future. His tail held high, his small paws silent, he visited Margot and Joy, before jumping up and settling on Rita's lap.

'Hitam is finding all this business a little dull,' she said. 'He was hoping this was the meeting to discuss rat numbers.'

'He caught a family of baby rats in my rucksack yesterday,' Joy said. 'He had quite the feast. They still managed to eat part of my hat . . .'

Later that week, as Hatty tended the fire and prepared dinner, Margot and Rita sat in the shade sewing sets of shorts from some nuns' habits. While they were sewing, Beth chopped wood, much to the fascination of a battalion of children, who had gathered to watch the swearing, smoking Queenslander make short work of the pile. There were nudges and giggles, and Beth worked steadily on, occasionally holding out her hand for a Bible. When it was provided, she would tear out another page, roll it, and smoke it like a cigarette gripped between her teeth as she attacked the logs.

'Looks like Beth has some fans there,' Rita said.

'Yes, although it makes my blood run cold to see them standing so close,' Margot said. 'The damn axe head keeps flying off and poor Joy had a black eye for a week when she copped it.' She snipped the cotton. 'She should have let the doctor stitch the cut but she was worried about infection, so she'll live with the scar instead.'

'Probably wise.'

'Why does she smoke while she chops wood, do you think?'

'I imagine it's because of her father. I think she likes to keep him close.'

One afternoon, some Dutch children were playing with sticks and large leaves rolled carefully into balls in the street. Margot recognised Henny with her long blonde plaits as she whacked the ball and it flew high into the air. Margaret Dryburgh was heading their way with Lola and caught it in her reliable hands.

'Great catch!' Margot called and Margaret smiled, tossing the ball back.

'Thanks very much, I like to think I've become quite handy with a bat and a ball. I was a missionary for years, you know, and learned a few tricks.' She sat down beside them. 'Hatty, Lola here tells me you have a rather fine voice. I was wondering if I can recruit you for our choral orchestra. We call it the Women's Vocal Orchestra of Sumatra.'

'I like to think it sounds rather grand,' Lola added.

Hatty looked surprised. 'Me? I'm no singer. I can hold a tune, but really, I'm not a performer.'

'You'd be marvellous, Hatty,' Lola said. 'I've heard you at our singalongs.'

'Lola has a wonderful voice,' Margaret said, 'and if she recommends you, I trust her. We're rehearsing for our first concert.'

'Oh, I couldn't sing in public.'

'You won't have to. It's just us prisoners, not the Albert Hall.'

'I don't know . . .' Hatty said.

'We already have a couple of Australian girls in our group. You'd fit right in and the music is so beautiful. You'll feel like you're flying away.'

Margaret's face remained serene. 'I must say, I agree with Lola – please do consider joining us.'

'Mmm, I don't think so,' Hatty said. 'Thanks for asking me, Margaret. Very kind of you, but I'm not risking a beating from the Japs for singing *dom dom dom* in a jungle.' She reached down to collect the leaf ball again and tossed it back. 'Why on earth would they want to hear *dom dom dom* anyway?' she asked.

'You know why, Hatty. Because it's music – one of the deepest expressions of our souls. Because it can take us away from all this, from the fear and the pain, and raise us up. We don't *need* words. Music is its *own* language.'

'I think you're mad – and very brave.' Hatty reached forward and stirred the banana peel she'd been boiling in Matilda. 'I will come to watch a rehearsal, though.'

Lola and Margaret grinned.

'Please do,' Margaret said. 'We hold them in the Dutch kitchen. And in the meantime, I shall come to watch your Saturday night concert. Who are you playing this week?'

'This week you'll enjoy an encore performance from Shirley Temple – and perhaps a little Greta Garbo thrown in for good measure. I also believe we have a skit regarding a lost hat.'

'Well, I say. I've never seen a more varied playbill in any theatre in the West End,' Margaret said and smiled. 'Which one are you?'

'You need to ask? Shirley Temple, of course.'

'Splendid. The last time I came for a singalong it was so crowded I was out on the verandah listening in through the open window.'

'Our theatre is very small and intimate. I think the Japs even camped outside for a while. Couldn't tell if they enjoyed the show, but they didn't shut us down.'

'Perhaps they'll be lenient towards the choir?'

'Perhaps,' Hatty said.

'So you'll think about it?' Lola pressed.

'All right, I'll think about it.' Hatty shrugged.

'I'm so pleased. I like to think bringing music to the camp is our way of doing the Lord's work,' Margaret said.

'Can he sing? Maybe you should ask *him*,' Hatty said.

'Ask who?' Beth sat down on the damp ground with a thump.

'God,' Margot said.

'He's not here.'

'He's everywhere.'

'Then I hope for his sake he's learned how to bow to the emperor,' Beth said. 'Hello Margaret – are you coming to see my skit about who stole my hat?'

Margot and Lola perched on a thin mattress on the concrete floor of their hut, watching Hatty's fingers, shaking slightly, as she stitched a small patch onto the blouse she'd been wearing for well over a year. After years of use and careful washing it was almost see-through.

'I used to be a pretty good seamstress,' Hatty said, 'but now my eyes have gone and I can't seem to keep my hands steady. My mum would be disgusted.'

Hitam miaowed and came to settle on Hatty's lap, purring contentedly.

'You'll improve once we're home again,' Margot assured her. 'Have you thought about fixing up this mattress? It's exactly as if I'm sitting on the floor – I don't know how you put up with it.'

'Used to it, I suppose. I have an arrangement with Joy. Whoever dies first will leave their mattress to the survivor. If we stitch them together we'd almost have enough for one very thin and uncomfortable bed.'

Lola laughed. 'I doubt it'll be any better,' she assured her. 'You know they've stopped weighing us?'

'I hadn't noticed,' Margot said. 'I wonder why.'

'I imagine they didn't want it on the record that they're starving us all to death. For a while they could weigh us all and then pretend they were giving us adequate rations as we got thinner – but there's no one left over seven stone now. A couple of the girls are just over *five*. I think even the Japs are thinking better of recording our mistreatment.'

'I ate a rotten egg yesterday – Beth assured me it was a good idea.'

'How did it taste?'

'Rotten.'

'Did it come back up?'

'Not yet, but you know Mrs Edgar ate one with a dead baby chicken still inside a while ago. She's made of strong stuff.'

'You! You!'

The girls looked up startled to find Rasputin pointing at them with his bayonet.

'Us?'

'You!' he pointed roughly at Hatty. 'You do this!'

'What?' Hatty glanced around, confused. 'What did I do?'

He grabbed the blouse she was working on and threw it on the floor. 'This damage – to Nippon property!'

The girls looked around to see a hole in the timber behind Hatty's bed.

'I didn't! There's always been a hole there.' Hatty's voice was raised in alarm.

Rasputin reached down and snatched at her arm, dragging her slight frame to her feet. 'You come with me!'

Lola leaped from the sleeping mat. 'No, sir, I'm sorry, I can see the hole, but I promise you it has always been there. *Always.*'

The guard glared at her. 'Silence!'

'But she *didn't* damage the wall!'

He swung his hand across Hatty's face in a loud slap which echoed around the room, then he dragged her out the door even as she was struggling to find her feet. Lola and Margot ran to the verandah to see her being dragged across the yard to a spot they all knew well, directly outside of the guards' hut. Rasputin stood her in front of a post.

'You stand there!' he yelled and marched back into the shade.

Hatty stood stunned against the pole, staring out at the *padang*, the full heat of the sun beating down on her bare head.

'What's going on?' Beth said as she got to the verandah. 'Is Hatty in trouble?'

'Yes, for nothing. Rasputin says she damaged Nippon property. She didn't. The whole place is falling apart.'

'That little bastard, he's always victimising nurses,' Beth growled. 'I don't see him picking on the Dutch. Maybe they can afford to pay him to bugger off.'

They sat in silence for a while, Margot's heartbeat a sparrow, fluttering out towards Hatty and fluttering back again, sick with fear. 'She's already weak, Beth,' she muttered. 'She won't last long in that heat.'

'Be strong, Hatty!' Beth shouted. The sound carried, and everyone turned to see who'd spoken.

'They can't keep you there forever, it'll be *tenko* soon,' Rita said, and Margot thought she saw Hatty smile.

An hour crawled by. Two. Three. Hatty was wilting in the heat. She'd once told Margot about her fear of travel before she arrived in Singapore, and her mother's aversion to the same. *She doesn't trust foreigners*, Hatty had told her. *Of course I said to her, but we're foreigners to most people, but Mum doesn't see it that way. And now I want to go everywhere! I want to meet all the people in Singapore, then London, then Paris, and then I want to sail down the Nile!*

Margot kept her eyes fixed on Hatty. Her mother had been right. What would she think if she knew how her daughter was suffering? She could stand it no longer. She picked up one of the hats Kath and Joy had been making from palm fronds and gripped it tightly in her hands. The square was empty as she made her way across to Hatty. The sun had burned her skin so much that she was starting to blister. Her body was shaking.

'Hatty,' she whispered. Hatty turned slightly at the sound of her voice. There was movement from inside the guards' hut. Margot ignored it. 'Here, take this hat. I'll bring you some water too. They'll stop this soon. I know they will.'

Hatty didn't respond, but slowly held out her hand to take the hat. Rasputin was suddenly there, his face dark with fury. He slapped Hatty's burned face again and as she dropped to the ground, he whirled on Margot and struck her as well. She fell back at the force of it. 'No!' she screamed. 'Get away! She's sick! Can't you see?' Rasputin pushed her away roughly, slamming into her shoulder, forcing her back. 'Stop it! Please! Stop!'

He screamed something at her she couldn't understand and pulled out his revolver. Before she realised it, Margot was being dragged back to the safety of the verandah by Beth and Lola.

'Those bastards. They'll go to hell! Straight to hell!' Lola said.

'I'll set fire to them myself,' Beth promised.

They watched while Hatty stooped further in the heat. Bending lower and lower, despite the screams from the guard, incensed that she'd show such little respect. Lower. Her legs were shaking. Finally she collapsed.

Beth and Margot exploded from the house, rushing to pull her to her feet and gently carry her home.

'Hatty, Hatty, it's over. You're coming with us.'

'Home?' Hatty mumbled.

'Not *that* home, dear, your home with *us*, your sisters. We'll look after you.'

'I'm sorry . . .' Hatty was barely conscious. 'I think I might . . .' She flopped in their arms and her legs buckled beneath her.

'Water! Get some water, and let's strip her,' Margot said.

'Grab a sarong, make it soaking wet.'

'Hazel and Lola, you fan, we'll take it in turns.' Beth was pale, but Margot could feel her fury.

Hatty took to her bed for a long time. She hovered in and out of consciousness, burning with heatstroke and the terrible blistering on her skin.

The injustice dealt to Hatty was the beginning of the end. As the months dragged on, Margot, Beth and Lola watched in vain as the women and children around them suffered. Malnutrition and disease became commonplace. They woke, they struggled to find food and medicine, they failed to help those who needed help, they slept fitfully, and they awoke again to the same cruel nightmare. The nurses suffered along with the other internees; the British, the Dutch, the Chinese. The children struggled to grow, their mothers struggled to feed them. The men were occasionally sighted, but the camps were ever-changing and Margot couldn't tell if Gull was near, or if he was gone forever. The months stretched out before them all, with no respite. The women were together in the jungle as comrades, but very aware they were alone.

One morning, their Dutch friend, Henny, arrived at the nurses' quarters immediately after *tenko*. She was a little taller now, but thin, her few imagined curves whittled away by months of deprivation. She liked to sit and listen to the nurses chat, often bringing a small piece of embroidery to keep herself busy while she kept vigil, observing them cooking in Matilda, or weaving hats from grass which they'd sell to buy more food. Sometimes she giggled at their jokes, then blushed and sewed even more carefully, staring into her tiny stitches until she was sure they had forgotten her again.

'How's everything with the Dutch this week, Henny?' Lola asked. 'We saw a large group go into your mother's hut. Is everything all right?'

'No,' Henny said. 'We are very sad this week. Mrs Van Turnten has been desperate to see her husband – so very desperate. She begged the guards.'

'What happened to him?' Rita asked.

'Well, Mrs Van Turnten begged and begged. She has two small children. "Please – please!" she would say. "I can survive anything,

but I must know my Ewout is all right." They refused to allow her to
see him.'

Beth ground the rice in her mortar and pestle fiercely. 'Of course
they did.'

'Then eventually they *did* allow – after many weeks of begging.
They took her there a few days ago.'

'And?'

'He was dead. She was allowed to see him laid out in his coffin. He
had been tortured. His face and body were terribly injured.' There was
silence as the thought of it settled. 'She had been so excited, so *relieved*.
She came home and lay down on the floor. Then it was as if she started
to have a fit. She shook and shook, her eyes looked beyond us all.
She went mad with grief.' Henny looked embarrassed. 'I had to leave.'

'The poor bloody woman,' Margot said. 'Where is she now?'

'They are transporting her to the mental asylum. It's a long
way from here. Mother says we won't see Mrs Van Turnten again.
And . . .' Henny paused.

'Yes?'

'Mrs Orifici. She used to run an asylum before the war. The
Japanese sent her to help Mrs Van Turnten. Mrs Orifici begged and
begged to stay.' Henny focused on her embroidery. 'I was sad for
her, and I wished her well. Mrs Orifici just stared at me – it was as if
she had already died. She knows about the asylum.'

There was silence around the fire.

'Lola!' Margot whispered again. 'Lola!'

Lola shifted uncomfortably in the night air on her thin hessian
mattress. 'What?'

'Poor Hatty's terribly ill. I've been nursing her all day, but she's
getting weaker. We have to find her some food.'

Lola propped herself up onto her elbows, then winced in pain and sat forward. 'What do you mean?'

'We're going bandicooting,' Margot whispered.

'We'll get caught. You saw the beating poor Mrs Davis took.'

'It's still worth the risk. If we play by the rules, we'll die. I've been watching the guards' hut, and I think they're asleep. No movement for ages.' She gripped Lola's hand. 'You coming?'

Lola glanced around. Rita slapped a mosquito on her cheek in her sleep, and Beth gave a low grumble. 'All right,' Lola whispered. 'Just let me find something dark to wear.' She pulled on a grey tunic they'd bartered from the local tailor when he'd visited the prison. It hung loosely around her shoulders. She glanced about nervously. 'You're *sure* no one's awake?'

'Yes. But we must go quickly.'

Margot and Lola went to the side of the hospital building, skirting the side of the *padang* so they could stay in the shadows. The vegetable garden was behind a wire fence, overlooked by the guards' hut and Dr Goldberg's house. The girls looked around briefly, then dropped to the ground.

'You're thinner than me,' Lola whispered. 'I'll hold the wire up, you roll under. Take what you can, but be careful. We don't want anyone to notice.'

'I'll keep my thieving to the essentials,' Margot whispered. Lola was already hooking her fingers under the wire, lifting it off the ground a few inches, then a few inches more, so Margot could crawl underneath.

'Too low! I can't fit!'

'Of course you can. Scoot under! That's as high as I can make it go.'

Margot placed her cheek on the dirt and dragged herself

sideways. She made a scraping noise which sounded, to her ear on the ground, deafening. She paused.

'Keep going,' Lola whispered. 'You're halfway under now – you'll have to keep going. Quickly!'

Margot held her breath and did just that, pulling herself under the wire and glancing warily about. She could see sweet potato vines and carrots, and a few chilli bushes. There were *kang kong* leaves and plantains growing along the far edge of the garden. She decided they were not for her and slowly raised herself onto her hands and knees and started to crawl among the vegetables.

'Hurry!' Lola whispered again, just as a door opened to the guards' hut. Both women dropped to the ground, Margot pressing her face into the dirt. The Snake came outside and glanced about, then went to the corner of the hut, overlooking the garden. Margot held her breath, her heart pounding as he undid his trousers and urinated on the power pole the girls had paused behind a few minutes before. Margot couldn't see Lola, but she hoped she'd managed to curl up out of sight. The Snake, much relieved, began to hum a little tune, then turned and went back inside. Margot lay still, waiting for her heartrate to steady, then slowly pulled three carrots out of the ground at random, snapping them off a few inches beneath their leafy tops and replanting them so the theft wouldn't be immediately noticed. Then she stuck them down the front of her tunic and crawled out in reverse, feeling the wire again with her feet, and Lola's hands lifting it up again, and pulling her through.

They crept back to their accommodation in silence.

'Not bad.' Lola smiled. 'Hatty'll have a good breakfast at least!'

'I thought we were caught for a minute there.'

'Me too,' Lola giggled. 'What would Matron say?' She squeezed Margot's hand again. 'Well done, Margot, I know you're not a rule-breaker, in general.'

Margot held Lola's hand for a moment in the darkness. 'I don't even know myself anymore,' she said. 'I'm even getting good at spitting in the Japs' water delivery every day. Beth's not satisfied if she can't see at least a bit of foam on top, and I must say, I'm finding it quite satisfying!'

When they woke Hatty early the next morning, Margot and Lola had a tin cup filled with chopped, cooked carrots. Hatty's face was white, her lips parched and pale.

'Hatty,' Margot whispered. 'Wake up, we've got some food for you.'

Hatty groaned and turned away. Lola stroked her arm. 'Hatty. Food!'

'What?'

'But you must eat it quickly before anyone sees – we stole it from the gardens.'

'You *stole* it?' Hatty breathed. 'Oh dear. There'll be trouble.'

'Not if you eat it quickly, before anyone sees,' Margot said.

'Carrots,' Hatty breathed. 'You bandicoots!'

'Shh,' Lola whispered. 'Just eat as fast as you can!'

Hatty smiled, and did her very best.

CHAPTER 21

MARGOT
Palembang, Sumatra
December 1943

As yet another Christmas approached, the nurses remained trapped in their jungle prison. They'd grown used to camp life, its rhythms and random injustices. They missed the men passing by, although there were still some at a nearby camp who managed to sneak the occasional message into firewood for their loved ones. Rumours ran through the camp daily, stories of bitterness and cruelty. There had been outrage and heartbreak when Hitam, their cat, was kicked to death by a guard. But still they dreamed of freedom and luscious meals, conversations with families at home they missed. Occasionally, there were tantalising tales from the war, bringing hope that one day soon, it would all be over. But other than the guards, the traders and occasional movement between camps, the girls had little contact with the outside world. They rarely received mail or care packages. On the odd occasion they were able to get messages out, they rarely received a reply, and the world outside fell away.

Lola dedicated her time to the choir – the Women's Vocal Orchestra of Sumatra. Norah Chambers, a British internee who'd attended the Royal Academy of Music in London, spent hours writing classical music into vocals for the women. Lola could be found rehearsing smaller choral groups while they cooked bread in Matilda, or while she sewed shirts for growing children. She sang every moment, savouring the sweetness of music once again, shaping and perfecting each note before setting it free.

Eventually, December loomed ahead.

'Well, it's nearly Christmas again,' Beth said. 'So much for wishes and prayers. No bloody good for any of us.'

'What do you think's happening?' Lola asked, humming as she turned rice cakes on the fire. 'Do you think they've forgotten about us? Sometimes I wonder if the war is over and they don't know we're even here.' She placed a tiny rice cake onto a tin plate. She would sell them to the Dutch ladies later.

'I'm sure they know we're here,' Margot said. 'We'll be saved soon, I'm sure of it.'

'I don't want to lose hope,' Lola said. 'But I can see how one might.'

Margot tried to smile at her, then, but found she couldn't. She was too tired. Hatty had been resting in their hut, but at the sound of their voices, she crept out and lay beside Margot on the mat, placing her head in her lap. Margot stroked her sparce hair; her beautiful curls were long gone.

The weight of another Christmas in captivity sat heavily on Margot. It spelled another year away from home; another year of not knowing what their futures held; of not knowing if Gull and the other men were surviving in the camps elsewhere on Sumatra and Bangka Island. Life was passing them by, and the meagre satisfaction of surviving another twelve months was little consolation.

'Remember our first Christmas here?' Rita asked. 'It was such a pleasant day. I don't suppose we imagined we'd still be in Sumatra all this time later.'

'No, but at least we're still alive,' Margot said. 'We can still make it home.'

'Where there's life, there's hope,' Beth agreed. 'We'll stay alive, and we'll go home one day soon and tell them all about what happened to us – and the girls on the beach. I'm bloody well going to survive – just for *that*.'

'I do rather feel as if we've been forgotten,' Rita murmured.

'Forgotten or not, I hope we can at least make things a bit jolly for the children.' A British woman was carefully cutting out pieces of paper and drawing images onto her playing cards. She'd finished a few packs of Happy Families and Snap.

'Oh, they're marvellous.'

She looked pleased. 'I hope it cheers them up, that's all,' she said. 'I've finished some rather nice embroidery projects for some of the ladies – I used cottons I unravelled from old clothes.' She gave a final snip to the card she was working on. 'It's nice to make an effort.'

'Stop!'

The girls all looked up in surprise to see an elderly Chinese man running past the prison gates pushing a dressed pig in a wheelbarrow. He was heading in the direction of the camp kitchens.

'Oh! A pig!'

'Looks like the guards want their piece.'

The old man kept running until he was caught and beaten, the leg and hind quarter of the animal removed and the remainder allowed to proceed to the kitchens to be shared between the five hundred prisoners.

*

The months passed slowly, the long days passed the same way. After the men's camp moved it became almost impossible for the married women to find out what had happened to their husbands. On one occasion, just before Christmas, the guards organised a visit for some of the children to see their fathers.

'Henri van Boxtel, Finley Ziebell and Louis Blitvitch – you stay here.'

The boys sat down, bewildered, as the other children filed through the gates. Their mothers, their faces ashen, pulled them close. And as the boys watched the gates close again, they knew their fathers were dead.

Mrs Brown called to see Lola on occasion, enjoying her descriptions of Sydney and the Blue Mountains. Margot joined them one day as Mrs Brown sat in the shade with her fan, her figure diminished by captivity and chronic deprivation. Her hands were busy making grass-stuffed mattresses for sale. 'I'm the breadwinner of the family, now!' she said. 'Who'd have thought?' She worked quickly, slapping at mosquitoes absent-mindedly with her handfuls of long grass, her mind sharp and ever hungry for camp gossip. 'I see those girlfriends are about again,' she said. 'Umbrellas now, I'll bet they got them from their Japanese owners.'

Lola looked uncomfortable. 'You mustn't judge too harshly, Mrs Brown,' she said. 'They manage to get some valuable supplies into camp through their contacts. And it might be said that their sacrifice has saved others from the same fate.'

'Oh, I'd *die*. I'd just *lie down and die*,' Mrs Brown declared, fanning herself in shock.

'I was referring to *Shelagh*,' Lola said, gently. 'Imagine if she was forced to – well – to become a *comfort woman*.'

'My Shelagh would never do such a disgusting thing. A common prostitute? Never!' She leaned in a little closer. 'Of course, I imagine it's *easier* for some of us with looser morals to allow ourselves to be used in such a fashion.'

'I imagine *not*, Mrs Brown, but some of the girls have children, and I imagine there is *nothing* they wouldn't do to keep them safe.'

'Yes, well. We women can bear anything, it seems.' She rose slowly and wandered off, frailer, older and far from home.

Lola was still watching her make her way across the *padang* when Margot spoke. 'You're a kind soul, Lola.'

'I can have sympathy for fallen women, Margot,' Lola said quietly. 'I'm quietly living in shame too.'

'You? What on earth do you mean?' Margot moved closer.

Lola began teasing red threads out of an old curtain she'd been given by Mrs van Boxtel to use for Christmas decorations. 'I was . . . caught out. You know, with a young man – my fiancé at the time. We were careful, but . . .'

'You fell *pregnant*? I didn't know.'

'Of course not. It's a secret I'd rather take to the grave.' She smiled. 'Maybe sooner rather than later, that's why I suppose I can speak of it now.'

'Did he stand by you? Your fiancé?'

'Of course not. He gave me ten pounds for a backyard abortion, as long as I kept his name out of it.'

'Oh, Lola.'

'And I'm a nurse, so I know how dangerous that is.' She picked at a long thread. 'But the shame of it, Margot. You don't know what you'll be willing to do until the shame of it sits on your chest at night like it really might kill you. We're Catholic. My mother would have died. She literally would have died. I couldn't tell her.'

'Surely she'd have understood.'

'I know she wouldn't. I still think of it, all the time. I was told to stand on the side of the road, to wait to be picked up. I was to be taken somewhere wearing a blindfold, so I wouldn't be able to identify the place or the people.'

'I thought doctors performed abortions sometimes.'

'They do. But I couldn't afford it. And I didn't want to meet any-one I worked with.'

'So you went through with it? With the blindfold and the stran-gers using who knows what?'

Lola lowered her head. 'No, I didn't.'

'Thank God.'

'But only because they didn't come to collect me.' She was wind-ing the thread around her finger. 'So, I went home to the garden shed, and used a syringe I'd taken from the hospital.'

Margot sat wide-eyed with shock.

'And I flushed myself out with Lysol.'

'Oh, Lola.'

'I was in bed for days, bleeding, cramping. It burnt my insides. I was lucky – I could have died. Plenty do.'

'Oh dear, you poor woman. I am so sorry,' Margot said. 'I would never have imagined.'

'No,' Lola replied. 'Neither would I. My mother realised what had happened, of course. She nursed me. But she never really spoke to me again. I joined the army to get away from the silence.'

'Does she know where you are?'

'I don't know. I'm not sure she cares.' Lola shifted uncomforta-bly on the hard bench. 'I know you all think I'm a romantic, but I'm not. I'm a fallen woman. And the Lord shall be my judge.'

'Lola, don't speak that way, the Lord *must* love us all, or what's he even for?'

'I think he's punishing me,' Lola whispered, her eyes shining. 'I'm afraid that I'll die here. Or that, even if I survive, he won't send me anyone to love me again. I know you all think I'm silly. But singing, to me, feels like love, and who are we without it?'

'I'm so sorry,' Margot said, 'for everything you've been through – you were so let down.' Margot wanted to spit but restrained herself. 'I wish that you'd been safe, with a doctor or a nurse to care for you. And I wish that you hadn't been so abandoned.' She reached out and put her arm around Lola's shoulders. 'There will be love for you, Lola, great love.' She kissed her cheek. 'I'm sure of it.'

On Christmas night the Women's Vocal Orchestra of Sumatra held a gala concert.

'Are you nervous, Hatty?' Lola asked, combing Hatty's thin hair, and adorning it with a bright floral scarf.

'Oh, yes, terrified,' Hatty said. 'I've never sung in front of a crowd before.' She looked frail as she checked her appearance in a small mirror. 'I feel weak at the knees at the thought of all those ladies watching.'

'Nonsense,' Beth told her. 'You'll be fine. If you get weak at the knees I'll put a chair on stage for you to sit on!'

'She'll be wonderful,' Lola said. 'You won't believe your ears, Beth, you'll think you've died and gone to heaven.'

Beth rolled her eyes. 'That's what I get when I die, is it?' she grumbled happily. 'More of your singing!'

'I imagine you're pretty safe from facing the gates of heaven,' Margot laughed.

'Now,' Lola said, 'a few of the girls have found some attractive flowers and leaves for decorations, so I'll just dash over and make sure they're properly arranged. Beth, can you get the audience to move closer to the stage? I don't want anyone missing out because they're worried they're not supposed to sit in the front benches.'

'Yes, I'll drag them all up the front, although I suspect you'll have standing room only at the back,' Beth told her. 'Don't worry, it'll be a good show.'

'I've heard the rehearsals, I think you'll be wonderful,' Margot told her. She ran her fingers through her hair. She had her best dress on, and a scarf to add a bit of glamour. The rest of the girls were also looking their best, dressed neatly with their hair adorned with flowers, or a threadbare blouse brightened up with a cheerful cotton scarf.

The British and Dutch women had also dressed in their finery. Mrs Wentworth was a vision in blue silk. Her wardrobe was rumoured to have once adorned the Duchess of Monaco. (*Never heard of her*, Beth had sniffed.) Her dresses were works of art, and wealth had allowed her to pay for the rather astounding wardrobe to accompany her into the jungles of Sumatra. Beside her sat Mrs Roberts, once a model for Norman Hartnell, designer to the British royal family, and the beautiful but frail Charlotte Tunbridge-Beckersley, both dressed immaculately in dresses from Mrs Wentworth's marvellous suitcases.

Mrs Brown sat proudly beside the ladies in a respectable cotton blouse and long skirt, brightened with a scarf of local design around her shoulders. The Dutch ladies looked wonderful in their vibrant lipstick, curled hair and smart frocks, the children neatly turned out in shorts and skirts.

The Japanese guards watched on from the verandah of their hut. There had been concern that the concert might not be allowed to proceed, after Lola had refused the Japanese guards' request that a Japanese song be included in the repertoire. Norah and Margaret had transcribed thirty classical pieces into four-part harmonies entirely from memory. The choir had practised under fear of punishment in the kitchen after dark. They were extraordinary and brave, and when Lola was forced to stand in the sun for her refusal to include the Japanese song, it was a price she had been willing to pay.

At last, the Women's Vocal Orchestra of Sumatra took their positions, and a hush descended on the crowd. The choir stood proudly, their backs straight, their gazes ahead. Margot smiled broadly at Lola's face, alight with excitement. She had placed flowers in her hair, and had borrowed a bright pink blouse from one of the British ladies. She stood in the second row, gazing out at the assembled crowd. She caught Margot's eye, and gave her a wink.

Norah strode to the front of the choir, acknowledged the rapt audience and turned to her musicians. She raised her baton. And the women's voices flowed softly out like sunlight. A hush, a hum, a sweet song low in their hearts, then gathering and joined by another note, higher, the soft call of women singing across the sky like birds on the wing.

Bach, Beethoven, Brahms, Chopin, Mendelssohn and Mozart. The music, like hoof beats, took them home, following the white crests of the waves at Bondi and the long flat plains of the wheatbelt. They flew across the Sydney Harbour Bridge, floated up the spires of the cathedrals in Adelaide, swept up the Swan River, dipped low over the Grampians and the mallee, then soared across the cane fields of Queensland to the shining ocean. And every last note entered their hearts as they found their homes again, opening the gates, walking up the front paths, seeing the doors held open in welcome. And their mothers baking in the kitchen, their fathers pulling them close to their hearts.

The music was a spell, soothing their fears and reminding them of who they were. It was a hymn to their freedom. The songs rose over the jungle and the assembled ladies might have sighed as they sat in the warm night air, their souls fluttering within their exhausted bodies for a moment to fly away. Capturing hope in the soft wings of memory.

As the melodies faded away into the jungle, and the prison gathered around them once more, the crowd, wet with tears and warmed by the fires of their own hearts, applauded with a joy that would have lifted the roof from the Albert Hall.

When the concert ended, the crowd moved away, hand in hand, humming the tunes they could still catch hanging in the air around them, forever changed.

'Well, I never,' Hazel declared as they made their way back to their quarters. 'I never imagined I'd hear such music in my life. And, as if by magic, here it was, right here among us – in the middle of the bloody jungle.' She walked slowly, exhausted but thrilled. 'I'll never forget it, if I live to be a hundred!'

Beth had been silent on the way back across the prison yard, her arm supporting Hatty.

'And what did you think, Beth?' Lola asked.

Beth gazed up at the night sky. 'I felt as if a mob of cattle had broken through the old gates of the yard and stampeded down to the creek, right to where it swells out by the river gums. And I could see the silly creatures, bellowing in joy, stamping about in the mud and slurping up the cold water. And the cockatoos shrieking down at them all, and the sunshine, pure gold across the countryside.' She sniffed. 'I didn't know those old German men wrote songs about *that*.'

Lola put her arm around her and hugged her as they walked. 'Neither did I,' she said. 'But I'm glad they did.'

*

Following the concert, the choir became a source of comfort to Margot. She often found her way to the Dutch kitchen, listening to the melodies as they rose and fell like waves. The Japanese guards would sit quietly in the dark, smoking cigarettes and listening in the shadows, but their presence made the choir anxious; the guards were convinced any gathering was a cover for spying or plans to escape. 'I don't know how they think we've all got the energy to escape,' Lola had complained, 'we're all half-dead with hunger!'

Disease continued to stalk the camp, dysentery, typhoid and malaria settling into the *kongsis*, chewing away at the edges of every gathering. But the choral orchestra kept singing, week after week, their voices still rising out of the gates and over the jungle, until Margot wasn't sure they could go on much longer. A handful of British ladies went down with malaria in a single week, and three died on the same day. Margaret Dryburgh was determined that they would carry on. 'It is one of the only things we have that will sustain us,' she often said. 'We must hold on to our music as long as we are able.'

The Dutch ladies then lost members to malaria, and a few to dysentery. They buried their friends in the afternoons. They held each other's hands tightly and kept singing.

Eventually, disease and starvation took its toll, and the choir fell silent, its few surviving members too frail to sing anymore.

'Well, I never!' Beth declared. 'We've got some mail.'

Matilda was boiling some bones for broth, tended by Margot and Lola. They were skin and bone themselves, barely able to stir the pot.

'How? Why?' Margot asked.

'I think the Japs are thanking Australia for their treatment of the bones of some Jap sailors.'

'What did they do?'

'They cremated them and sent their bones home, I think,' Beth said.

'I wish they'd send *our* bones home,' Margot responded. 'With us still around them!'

'Is there anything for me?' Lola asked.

'No, afraid not,' Beth told her. 'But I've got a letter you can share. And there's one for Hatty.'

'I'd like that,' Lola said. 'Hatty's still sleeping – I'll leave her letter beside her bed as a surprise for when she wakes.'

'There's also one for Minnie,' Beth said, lowering herself to the kerosene tin she usually claimed. Silence fell.

'I suppose we should read it?' Lola asked.

'Should we?' Margot asked. 'It may be personal.'

Beth barked a laugh. 'Well – we've been living together with not so much as a curtain between us for years now; I'd say we're way past personal already.'

'I think you should read it,' Margot said. 'Perhaps we'll visit them one day.'

'All right,' Beth said. She slowly pulled out the envelope and, giving a quick glance skyward, proceeded to read.

Dear Minnie,

 I have written to you many times, I know you won't have received my previous letters, because I've never sent them. The government has contacted us to tell us you are missing, and we are very low. Dad says you are most certainly in a camp in Java or Sumatra, and I'm praying to God every day that he is right. Dad says he's always right, so I suppose it must be so.

*I hope that this letter finds you safe and sound with your
nursing friends, and that you are looking after each other.
I can't bear to think of anything else, and it is only fear which
has prevented my writing to you before.*

*The farm is as you left it. We had a good season, and Dad
says the Sunshine harvester is really saving time. I passed on
your regards to Stan, he looked a bit shamefaced, but I'm
certain, with time, we will all get along well. Dad was upset for
you, he knows how much Stan meant to you.*

*Mrs Lamont has been taken by lung cancer. We buried her
next to her father, who always waylaid Dad at the hotel on
Friday nights, do you remember? We laughed about it – that
now he would have his daughter to make him behave in
God's house. I took some flowers to Oliver's grave this
morning and told him to send you all the luck in the world.
He's your guardian angel now – at least I hope so – Dad says
I'm being foolish.*

*I don't have any other news. I pat the dog for you every
day and I pray for you every night. Looking forward to the day
I see you again, dear.*

Your loving Mum and Dad xx

CHAPTER 22

MARGOT
Muntok, Bangka Island
October 1944

Beth was scrubbing the kitchen floor with a handful of coconut fibre when Lola came running into the room. 'Pack up! Pack up!'

'What's that? What's going on?'

'Mr Hollywood says we're leaving. We've got an hour to pack up and go.'

'Go *where*?' Margot asked.

'I wish I knew. We're moving camps, following the group that left last week,' Lola told them. 'At least we'll be back with our friends again.'

'I bet it's because they're losing the war,' Beth said.

'I think we're going back to Muntok.'

'Oh, for goodness' sake,' Margot sighed, 'half the people here are too weak to travel. They're starving to death and now they have to move? It's inhumane.' She could already hear Seki the Sadist knocking on the walls of the houses.

'*Ugoku!*'

'All right!' she snapped. 'Hold your horses, it's going to take a while to pack.'

They scooped up their measly possessions into rucksacks and bags, loaded Matilda with cutlery and some soy beans they had planned on soaking, put on their uniforms, and stood waiting to be counted again. It was a warm morning. The temperature was often cooler at night because of the altitude, and the breezes could find their way in from the ocean, but daylight always brought stillness and a sticky hot sun.

'*Tenko! Tenko! Ugoku!*'

The women and children dragged hessian bags and kerosene tins filled with their precious belongings and struggled down to the little jetty.

'It's no good, I just can't walk . . .' One of the British ladies had been bedridden for weeks. Her body was emaciated and now eaten away by malaria and beriberi. 'Leave me here . . .'

'We won't leave you here,' Margot told her.

'They'll shoot you,' Lola said.

'Let them.' The woman sagged onto the damp path.

Another woman hoisted her up, with her arm under her shoulder, and they teetered there for a moment until Mavis got on the other side. 'We'll just get you onto the boat, and it'll be better, you'll see,' she told her.

It wasn't. They left for Muntok in two groups and by the time Margot, Lola and Beth were squashed onto the decrepit river boat, the heat was oppressive.

'I need the toilet!'

Margot turned to see who had spoken. It was a young girl who'd tied her Christmas doll to her waist to make sure she wasn't lost.

'Hang on,' Beth called out. 'No room to move, use the helmet.'

A tin helmet was passed from hand to hand until it reached the child, who glanced about, embarrassed, then squatted in position as best she could. Her mother smiled encouragingly at her. When she was done, her mother handed it back so that it could be tipped over the edge.

'Anyone else?'

Another small hand shot up in the air, and the helmet was passed again, while the boat chugged and spluttered down the river.

As they were approaching Muntok hours later, the rolling waves caught her, and Margot could feel her stomach heave. She hadn't eaten much and her stomach was mostly filled with well-boiled banana skins and *kang kong* leaves. She glanced to the side of the boat, longing for the simple pleasure of throwing up. 'Send me the hat!' she called and it was rapidly passed along to her. She promptly threw up.

Seconds later she felt an elbow nudging her.

'My turn.' Hazel was green. She grabbed the helmet and added a few more inches. Lola leaned away. 'Sorry,' Hazel muttered.

In time, the long jetty of Muntok finally came into view.

'I never thought I'd be pleased to see this place again,' Margot said. 'But if it means I can get off this bloody boat, I'm happy.'

'Looks like it's back to the coolie lines for us.'

'Maybe.'

'Oh look, there's Joy!'

The girls craned their necks to see Joy, who had left Palembang with the earlier group, standing next to a bucket. She was in her faded dress and homemade trompers. 'Welcome to Muntok!' she called.

'Hello, Joy,' Lola said. 'Have you come a long way from camp?'

'It's a decent walk. I thought you'd need some help.'

'What's in your bucket?' Margot called.

'Water. In case you'd like a drink.'

'Surely she didn't carry it herself,' Margot said to Beth. 'She was down with dysentery all last week. It looks like she could snap like a twig.'

'Well, the Japs didn't carry it for her. Good old Joy,' Beth said.

As the group walked slowly from the jetty and up the bank of the river, Joy came over to Margot. 'I have a note from the men's camp. I assume it's from Gull.' She slipped a piece of paper folded many times and tied in a small snatch of string into Margot's palm.

'Did you see him?' Margot whispered.

'No, another Australian gave it to me, no one I knew. But he said it was for you.'

Margot held her breath. She hadn't heard from Gull for so long. She was always eager for news, but the camps were constantly changing and moving, and it was almost impossible to keep track. She glanced around and slipped the note into her pocket.

The new camp at Muntok stood ready, with a hospital and huts arranged for the internees. The women and children straggled through the gates, gazing around at the clear space, the buildings, the trench latrines. Margot's head pounded with dehydration and heat exhaustion. She longed to lie down, but there was too much to do.

'Oh, look, a hospital,' she said. 'Do you think it's equipped to deal with all of us?'

'Don't talk nonsense,' Beth told her as she pulled herself up the stairs. 'They won't have given us any damn medicine, much less quinine or vitamin B supplements. More than half of us are already down with malaria or beriberi – or both.'

They looked hopefully around the makeshift hospital ward. The basic beds were there, and a couple of old towels, but little else. Certainly no medicine, medical equipment, running water or toilet facilities that might have helped a patient. There was a small cupboard in the corner, which Joy knelt down to inspect. It was empty. The nurses fell silent.

Margot had been constantly touching the note in her pocket, and as soon as she could, she moved away from the other girls and opened the letter.

The lucky penny fell into her palm.

Gull wanted you to have this back. He said you can keep all his luck.

There was nothing more. Margot squeezed the coin in her fingers, feeling the hope in her heart unwind like a spinning wheel. 'Just a moment,' she said quietly. 'I think I'd better sit down.' She fell to the floor with a thump.

'Margot, let me help you.' Beth gently pulled her up and put her arm around her waist. 'Get her into bed, she can be the first patient.'

Margot wasn't even sure she was still in there. She was home again, in darkness, then light, hearing voices, feeling pain. She was trapped in her body, she was wet with sweat and dry and rasping for water. She gave up. She doubled down and tossed the kip high in the air, gazing up after its arc to see the coins tumble to the floorboards of the hospital in Singapore. She shook so hard with chills and fever she fell from the bed to the concrete floor and had to be lifted back up. She dreamed of her mother, washing sheets in summer, sweating from the heat from the copper. She was pushing a folded sheet through the wringer. *Don't worry about helping me, Margot*, she said, *I'm quite capable of washing a couple of sheets.*

When she woke she was drenched in sweat and vomit.

'Don't fuss, Margot,' Hatty was telling her, 'we'll have this mess cleaned up in a minute.'

She stared at Hatty, recognising her voice, but not her face. She was skeletal, and whiter than a sheet.

'Hatty, he's gone.'

'Who?'

'Gull. He's gone.'

'Oh dear, we can't know for sure. Perhaps he just got ill and sent you the lucky penny in case—'

'He's gone,' Margot whispered. 'I shouldn't have thought we could get out. It was silly. I was just . . .' Tears crept down her cheeks.

'Don't cry, Margot.' Hatty held her hand, her skin like paper.

'I have to, Hatty. I *have* to.'

'I'll fetch Beth,' Hatty said. 'She's been here night and day waiting for you to wake up. She'll want to see you for herself.'

Beth sat by Margot's bed for the rest of the night. In the morning she was still there. As Margot woke, she held up a cup of water.

'Your fever's broken, at least,' she said.

'Yes.' Margot closed her eyes.

'Now, I've sent word out to as many as I can, to find out about your Gull. He may be all right yet, we'll see. But you mustn't give up. Where there's life, there's hope.'

'He's gone, Beth. I can't go on. I'm just going to lie here. Perhaps I'll finally be lucky enough to die.'

'You *will not die*,' Beth growled.

'Because you say so? *Everyone* is dying, look around. It's just a matter of what order it happens.' She took a sip of water and coughed. 'I'd rather go first, than suffer through everyone else's bloody deaths.'

'Don't be irritating. *I* need your help. As soon as you're well enough, you'll get out of that bed and get on with it.' Beth leaned forward. 'I think *Hatty's* about to drop.' Margot turned her head away. 'What would Matron Drummond say? *You're* going to *leave* your post? I don't believe it for a second.' She sniffed in disgust.

'No. I can't go on any longer. There's nothing left,' Margot said.

'There's *you*,' Beth said. '*You're* left. And you *can* go on. Because I'll walk beside you.'

Margot slowly turned back to face her friend. Under her kind eyes, Beth's face was hollow. She was exhausted. Margot reached out for her hand, which shook under her touch. 'I'll help you out today,' she said. 'Beyond that, I can't promise anything.' Beth gave her a wink as Hatty made her way slowly through the small ward of beds, holding on to the wall where she could.

'Poor bloody Hatty,' Beth muttered to Margot. 'I think it's beri-beri and malaria. She's pretty crook.'

'Hatty, I'm coming good,' Margot said. 'You're ill, dear. It's your turn in the bed—'

'No, you just stay there and recover,' Hatty replied. 'You've been out for a couple of days and you need to recover properly, you'll probably have another turn . . .' She gripped the doorway for a moment.

'Get in the bed,' Margot said, swinging her legs out. 'Here. I'm getting up, I need the bedpan anyway.' She held up an old helmet. 'You jump into bed as soon as we . . .' Her head swam and she held the thin mattress so she didn't pass out, '. . . change the sheets.'

'We don't have sheets,' Beth reminded her. 'We're boiling some old curtains, but if Hatty can lie down, we'll have her as comfortable as possible.'

Hatty lowered herself onto the bed reluctantly. Margot wondered if she suspected she wouldn't get up again.

'Have I ever told you the story about the woman who used to always complain about Dad's sausages?' Margot asked her.

Hatty barely smiled. 'Tell me again . . .' she murmured, closing her eyes.

She didn't leave the hospital for weeks.

Margot lay awake at night knowing that her life was over too. If she could just help a few of the girls make it home, then she could die in peace. She wept silent tears of frustration for the life she'd never have with Gull, and woke each day as if it were her last, going through the motions of caring for the ill. The rules she had learned at nursing school no longer applied. There was no medicine and the few doctors were stretched beyond limits, only able to diagnose the relentless illness and despair – but not treat it. It wasn't long before Hatty was joined by others – young mothers, old women, Dutch nuns – everyone was touched by malaria, beriberi or Bangka fever.

'Well, it's a sad day for the medical profession when a nurse is in bed next to an old lady with a heart condition!' Mrs Brown, painfully thin and pale grey, was placed next to Hatty.

Margot passed her an enamel mug. 'Have some water, Mrs Brown. We're going to make you both better. You'll be out of here in no time at all.'

'Oh, I shouldn't think so,' Mrs Brown said. 'The old pump is clapped out now.' She tapped her chest, a thin cage for her heart. 'Too many miles. Most of them sad. I've only stayed around this long for my Shelagh.'

'Then you should hold the course,' Margot told her. 'The war will end, and you, Shelagh and Captain Brown will sail home, drinking champagne.'

Mrs Brown barked a weak laugh. 'Well,' she said, accommo-dating the thought. 'Wouldn't that be nice. I did used to enjoy the odd glass of champagne. Now I'm a businesswoman. Who'd have thought? Me and my mattresses? Shelagh says I'm the breadwinner of the family now, and I suppose the thought of it makes me a tiny bit proud.' She sank back into her pillow, her eyes fading in the dim light. 'How silly I am,' she whispered.

'I don't think you're silly at all,' Margot told her. 'I think you're wonderful.'

Mrs Brown died within a week. She was given a simple cere-mony and buried on Bangka Island.

'You do realise,' Lola said one morning as she tossed banana peel into Matilda to make jam, 'that I'm the *only* nurse here who hasn't had a bout of malaria?'

Margot slumped on the bottom step, her head swimming. She had thought she'd beaten the illness, but it had crept up on her again. 'Has Hazel gone down with it too?' she asked.

'Last night,' Lola said.

'Damn it, poor woman. She's already so weak. Thirty-one nurses sick – and still no medicine. They really don't care if we die.'

'Oh, I think they'd absolutely prefer it,' Lola said. 'I think they regard us as rather rude for continuing to survive.'

'I'm worried about Hatty. She's been raving,' Margot mur-mured. 'It might be time to get our uniforms out.'

Lola glanced around at the other nurses cleaning rice. Her eyes were shining when she turned back to Margot. 'Yes,' she whispered.

Their uniforms had been carefully stowed away in a couple of rucksacks that had survived the *Vyner Brooke*. They were faded and stained, but they were precious. They had been worn while they moved camp, then reverently packed away, waiting hopefully for the day they walked to freedom.

Margot prodded the fire. When she'd worn her uniform in Singapore she had felt pride, of course, but she hadn't felt the weight of it; not really. It had been her work uniform, but now it was so much more than that. It hung from her shoulders, and it spoke of her commitment to her sisters and her patients. It was a symbol of service to her country, a pledge to stay true, and a vow to keep going, no matter what.

She slowly stirred the banana peel jam, wondering how many more friends she would lose in Sumatra.

Hatty had been growing weaker for months, but the final weeks were painful for her sisters to watch. The beating she had received the day she'd stood out in the sun had broken her, and she hadn't been the same again. The beriberi and malaria had taken their toll and even though the girls nursed her night and day, there was nothing they could do. After days of rambling and fever, she'd fallen silent, and the stillness of her gaze was even more frightening.

'Girls, come now, it's Hatty,' Hazel said. The nurses slowly rose to their feet and looked to the doorway, where Hazel stood, white-faced and emaciated. 'She's dying, I thought we could be with her when she goes.'

'Of course,' Margot murmured.

They all stood and passed across the yard to the hospital. Margot could feel her knees clicking with every step, as if her bones were playing a march.

Hatty was unconscious by the time they arrived. They gathered, fanning her in the humid air, talking quietly. The room was still, voices from the *tongs* drifting back to them across the prison yard, sunlight puncturing the attap-palm wall the girls had built alongside the hospital beds to keep out the afternoon sun. Hatty's breathing was shallow, her gaze fixed. Lola reached out and held her hand. Margot willed her to keep breathing. Just another breath. Just one more.

'We'll all be home again soon, Hatty,' Lola said. 'I just know it.'

'Don't lie to her, just because she's dying,' Beth muttered.

'We can't help her now,' Lola said. 'What harm is there in giving her some comfort?'

'Shall I say the Lord's Prayer?'

'She's not religious.'

'But still . . .'

Though poor and in trouble I wander alone,
With a rebel cockade in my hat;
Though friends may desert me and kindred disown,
My country will never do that!

Margot recognised the poem. She'd learned it at school. And as Mavis started the next verses, she began to speak as well.

Australia! Australia! So fair to behold –
While the blue sky is arching above;
The stranger should never need to be told,
That the Wattle-bloom means that her heart is of gold,
And the Waratah red blood of love.

More soft voices joined in the poem learned years before in classrooms across the country and the nurses recited the final stanza together, their hands touching.

At last Margot felt Hatty go home.

Australia! Australia! Most beautiful name,
Most kindly and bountiful land;
I would die every death that might save her from shame,
If a black cloud should rise on the strand;
But whatever the quarrel, whoever her foes,
Let them come! Let them come when they will!
Though the struggle be grim, 'tis Australia that knows,
That her children shall fight while the Waratah grows,
And the Wattle blooms out on the hill.

That night, Margot kept vigil over Hatty's body in an attap hut on the side of the prison yard. The candles on the table beside where she lay flickered in the still night air, and the noises from the jungle drifted across the yard; the soft rustling of leaves, the croaking of frogs and the distant shriek of an owl.

'Shoo!' She stamped her foot. A rat had been making its way towards the scent of death, scurrying along the perimeter of the hut, climbing the rough posts to the roof, edging closer to its prey. A couple of dogs had come sniffing around earlier and she'd growled at them to scare them away. Mosquitoes found her in the darkness, buzzing into her ears, tickling her nose. She slapped her face.

'Trying to stay awake?' Beth had arrived for her shift.

'Mosquitoes.'

'Hello, Hatty.' Beth crossed to where Hatty's body lay beneath a sheet. She placed her hand on her forehead. 'You go get some sleep, Margot.'

'I'll stay a while longer, if I may,' Margot said. 'I won't sleep tonight, anyway.' She rubbed her arms, not to keep out the chill, but to ward off the feeling of mosquitoes settling on her skin.

'She won't be the last,' Beth said.

'I know. Sometimes I think I envy the girls on the beach.'

'Poor bloody Hatty,' Beth said quietly. 'If I make it home, I'll visit your parents and let them know how brave you were. How you could make a meal out of nothing at all. I'll tell them what a wonderful nurse you were.'

'Will you go home after the war, Beth?' Margot asked.

'Yeah, I'll head up to north Queensland again, back to the bush. It's where I belong.'

'Will you keep on nursing?'

'I don't know. I might be like Clancy of the Overflow – I'll go a-droving and you won't know where I are!'

Margot smiled. 'I'll know,' she said. 'I hope I'll always know.'

Beth barked a laugh.

The rat was back. Margot stamped her foot again, and it scampered away into the shadows. She picked up a candle and moved around the shed. She sighed. 'We won't forget you, Hatty. We'll tell the world what happened here, and they'll never forget.' A grey moth fluttered down onto Hatty's face, and Margot brushed it away. 'You were so brave. You took all of this and you stayed game, right to the end.'

As soon as the sun rose the next morning, a small group of nurses dressed Hatty for her funeral.

'I had hoped none of us would need to wear our uniform for the third reason,' Lola said as she smoothed Hatty's skirt. It was still stained with oil, as if the *Vyner Brooke* had bled onto her as she died. Hatty's thin face was white and still, her cheeks and eyes sunken. Her mouth had fallen in and the teeth she'd lost through malnutrition made her look terribly old. Her uniform swam on her tiny skeleton and the girls had to tuck it in around her like a blanket.

The grave-digging crew had arrived back at camp an hour earlier, exhausted and drenched in sweat. 'We found a nice spot in a clearing,' Mavis said, flopping down on the verandah. 'The digging wasn't too bad, but it took us a long time – none of us can dig for long – too weak. I used to be able to dig like nobody's business.'

'Are the girls ready with the coffin?' Margot asked.

'Yes, they're just bringing it over now.'

Margot watched as six nurses strained under the weight of the roughly hewn timber. She went outside to help them lift it, observing the large gaps between the slats of wood. There was never enough. 'Did we get enough flowers?'

'Yes, some of the Pommy girls are fetching some more for us, so Hatty isn't visible anymore.'

'Good,' Margot said. 'I think that'll be more dignified. All right, girls, we're all here, and I must say, I'm proud to see you all in uniform. It breaks my heart that we're burying one of our dear comrades today, but we'll give her the best military funeral we can, in the circumstances.'

Beth was struggling into her uniform. It hung from her shoulders. 'Four reasons to wear our uniform, we said. I hope we don't put it on too many more times before we walk to freedom.'

'I must say – it's a sad day. I didn't see all of this when we sailed from Australia,' Margot said. 'I mean, I wasn't expecting a picnic. But you just never know, do you? We might not have been sent to Singapore, we might have been on a ship that made it through the strait to Australia, we might have died in the bombing. We might have been with the girls on the beach.'

'Flowers, we need more flowers.' Mavis tucked more blossoms through the gaps in Hatty's timber coffin.

Finally, Margot stood and solemnly regarded her friends. 'It's time,' she said.

They buried Hatty in a clearing outside the camp, among the trees. The coffin rested across three long poles and they carefully lifted it to shoulder height, nine nurses at the poles on each side, one at the end to keep it from rolling, and one at the front to direct the cortege. They were so weak that even with twenty nurses carrying the coffin it was slow going. When they got to the gates, the Japanese guards opened them and saluted as they passed.

They shuffled in step, carrying Hatty McArthur to her grave.

'Our reading today is from Revelations, Verse 16,' Mavis said. They bowed their heads. 'They shall hunger no more, neither thirst anymore; neither shall the sun light on them, nor any heat. For the lamb which is in the midst of the throne shall feed them, and shall lead them unto living fountains of waters, and God shall wipe away all tears from their eyes . . .'

The nurses sang 'Jerusalem the Golden' in the jungle, their voices thin and exhausted at first, but growing stronger with every line.

Oh sweet and blessed country,
The home of God's elect,
Oh sweet and blessed country,
That eager hearts expect.
Jesus in mercy bring us,
To that dear land of rest,
Who are, with God the Father,
And Spirit, ever blessed.

Hatty's headstone was a wooden cross nestled in the creeping jungle. 'Is it too small?' Margot wondered aloud as they hammered it into the damp earth. 'Will people even know we were ever here? That Hatty is here, alone?'

'We'll know,' Beth had whispered, 'and she's not alone.'

Silently, they marched back to the prison camp together, as the warm wet winds flooded through the jungle like heavy tears. When they reached camp, Joy reverently stitched Hatty's old mattress to hers.

Mona died next, from beriberi. 'Of course she'd been dying for ages,' Beth said later. 'But when she passed away, she just said, "More breakfast, please," and she was gone. Poor darling Mona, so kind and so full of fun and life. "More breakfast, please," and she faded away.'

More women died, and more children. British, Dutch, Chinese; death came for them all without favour. Margot held a woman who fitted so badly she thought she'd bite off her tongue. She died from cerebral malaria the next day.

Mavis followed her soon after. Her cough wouldn't stop, perhaps it was cancer, they thought. They sat by her bedside for days, until Mavis, aware they needed to dig the graves in the morning, to bury her before the rains arrived in the afternoon, repeatedly apologised for wasting time.

'I'm sorry I'm taking so long to die,' she whispered. 'I do wish I'd just get on with it . . .'

'You take your time, dear, we're with you.' Margot reached out and took her hand, already cool to the touch.

There was the briefest of smiles and Mavis lost consciousness.

She died thirty minutes later.

Kath died of starvation and dysentery two weeks after that. Her body was so emaciated she went into her coffin already a skeleton.

'I'm so cold,' she said. 'How can I be so cold in the tropics?'

Joy had sat with her for days. 'Here, take my mattress. Hatty gave me hers so it's extra thick.' And they'd smiled, because it absolutely wasn't.

They'd called Dr Goldberg, who'd slapped Kath's face and refused to admit her to hospital, declaring her to be hysterical. Joy reported Kath was saved this final indignity, having already lost consciousness. They collected extra flowers for her because she'd taken such pleasure from them in life. Soft, sad blooms, flowers from the jungle and some leaves from the vegetable patch. As they sang 'Jerusalem', the afternoon storm blew through the trees and soaked them to the skin.

Illness gripped the camp. Dysentery, beriberi and malaria slowly took hold, killing women and children alike. The nurses treated them as best they could, horrified that they were mostly only able to watch them die, only able to offer kindness instead of medicine.

Bangka fever carried more away. As they died, they sighed, having finally given up. The sound seemed to come from the very depths of their soul, as if their fate had been too cruel, had stolen their hope, crushing the air from their lungs. It echoed softly through the hospital, night and day, and became known by the nurses as the song of death.

Goodbye, goodbye, goodbye.

CHAPTER 23

MARGOT
Belalau, Sumatra
May 1945

'It's time to make out our wills,' Beth announced one day at the end of her shift. Her hands were raw from scrubbing and smeared with blood as she absent-mindedly scratched at the sores on her legs.

'We already have – only way to stop the Japs stealing our things if we die,' Rita said.

'No, I mean *really* make our wills.' Beth sat down by the fire where Matilda was boiling drinking water. 'We've lost four girls already. I don't think we're all going to make it.'

'Don't talk like that,' Lola said. 'You don't know. The war could end tomorrow and we could all be going home.'

'Except the bloody war *won't* end tomorrow – and we'll probably all be staying here.' Beth gestured to the gate and to the graves which lay beyond, hidden in the jungle. 'One way or another.'

'We've got to have hope, Beth.'

'We can still bloody hope,' Beth said. 'But we need to face facts and write wills – and letters home. Whoever survives can deliver them.'

'I haven't heard from my mum since I left for Singapore,' Rita murmured. 'I'm not sure I have anyone to leave a letter *for*.'

'Write one, anyway. If those of us who survive can't find some-one to give it to, we'll publish it in the bloody paper.'

They gathered closer to the fire, so thin now that the tropical nights felt colder, and so hungry those nights were impossibly long.

'How's the English girl? Is she going to survive?' Rita asked.

'No. No one who falls into the latrines ever survives. Too thin and weak to sit on the toilet. The poor girl fell into raw sewage. She'll be dead tomorrow.'

The English girl died punctually the next day.

The weeks at Muntok were filled with starvation, building coffins, digging graves and sewing bags for the island's tin mines.

'*Tenko! Tenko!*' the guards called each morning.

'Bloody *tenko*! Why the hell do they have to keep counting us? Just where do they think we're going to go?' Lola moaned.

'I think we keep dying so they're trying to keep up,' Margot murmured.

The nurses straggled out to the prison grounds with the rest of the bedraggled women and children, and stood in the sun, waiting to be counted so they could collapse in the shade again.

Captain Seki adjusted his small wire-rimmed spectacles, took a stool and stood on it to address the prisoners. 'We are leaving camp!' he announced.

There was a rumble among the prisoners. 'Leaving?'

'What does he mean?' The women glanced at each other uneasily.

'Tomorrow we take boat to Sumatra. New camp better for health!'

The assembly was dismissed and the Japanese guards began to make their way back to their huts.

'Oh, so they've finally noticed we're all dying here?' It was just a whisper from Margot.

'What a relief. And I thought they didn't care,' Lola whispered back.

'They don't,' Rita breathed.

'Oh God – we've got to get back on that damn boat,' said Beth.

'I hate to point out the obvious, but we're not all going to make it. These women can't even stand – they're not going to survive,' Margot sighed.

'Well, they're going to have to try,' Joy said.

'We'd better build some more coffins.' Beth stood slowly and began to head for the woodpile.

Two English women died before they left camp the next morning and more died before they'd stepped off the pier at Muntok. When Polly Edgar died during the morning *tenko*, Margot fell to her knees beside her stretcher.

'Polly, don't go,' she whispered. 'It's nearly over! I'm sure of it!'

'Stand! Stand!' the guard commanded, prodding her with his bayonet.

'A woman just *died*,' Margot snapped. 'Does it mean nothing to you?'

The guard brought his bayonet down with a thud, just inches from her hand. 'Stand!' He moved on with his inspection, and the rollcall continued, amid the humidity, the buzzing insects, the sweet scent of rotting fruit, and the sound of the ocean slapping against the pier. Margot stared back at the guards and wondered if she would ever forgive them.

They were headed further inland from their old camp at Palembang, to a place called Belalau, an old plantation high in the hills. The distance was bound to take its toll.

'Belalau. That's the destination? Is Belalau going to fix us all?' Lola grumbled. 'Wouldn't a decent meal and a dose of quinine do a better job?'

Margot put her arm around her. They both weighed less than six stone now. It hardly seemed to make any difference anymore.

'Connie? Connie?' A short woman with a Scottish accent was shaking Connie with increasing alarm. The journey had taken hours. They departed the jetty at Muntok in a rickety wooden boat, slowly moving towards the next camp. Illness accompanied them and they sagged together in the heat, defeated by the very thought of the journey.

'Help her, please, my sister Connie's really sick,' the Scottish woman said.

Margot shuffled up the bench to where Connie lay slumped. She reached out and touched her cheek. It was hot. Margot paused, then held her wrist, waiting, while the ocean rolled beneath them. The sister looked to her for the answer, when the answer was plain. She shook her head. Connie was to be buried at sea.

She wasn't the only death on the journey, she was merely the first of the handful who wouldn't make it to the new camp and who were buried at sea along the way. Starving, sunburned, parched and wretched. As they died, they were rolled overboard.

'Someone should say something,' Lola said. 'Something nice.'

'We're on a boat, dying like flies, Lola,' Beth said. 'And I'm holding a helmet filled with vomit.'

'How about a prayer, then?'

'You can pray to your bloody self. I don't want to hear it.' Beth passed the helmet to her left and Hazel tipped it overboard. One of the older nuns sank to the deck, moaning quietly. 'You can pray for *her* – she'd appreciate it.'

'I can recite "My Country" for Connie.'

'She was a Pom. She wouldn't care.'

'Then let's just do the Lord's Prayer.'

'Our father, who art in heaven . . .'

The women, thrashed by disease and starvation, continued to drop, until no fewer than eight were buried at sea, like sheep who'd died in the back of the truck already on the way to the abattoir. Margaret Dryburgh fainted and couldn't be revived for over an hour. When Margot touched her forehead, she was ripe with fever.

'We're nearly there, Margaret, I'm sure we're nearly there,' Margot told her.

Margaret briefly gripped her hand, her gaze focused on some invisible destination ahead. Beth came to perch on her other side.

'Beth, can you tell me, are we going to survive?' Margot whispered.

'Not all of us.'

'I don't think I can take it anymore.'

Beth gave her a sideways glance. 'Bull. You can take it. I know who can tough it out and who can't. It'll hurt. But it won't kill you.' She gave a bitter laugh. 'You won't be that lucky.'

'I don't think it'll kill you either, Beth.'

'Nah, couldn't kill me with an axe. You know what keeps me going?'

'What?'

'You do. All you girls.'

They travelled for hours up the Musi River, to the town of Palembang, where the nurses had lived in the first year of their incarceration. When the boat finally pulled into the little harbour, the women and children on board were almost beyond caring where they were. Conversations had ceased, even idle talk had petered out as they struggled onto the timber pier.

'Line up!'

'Oh, for the love of God, another count,' Lola sobbed, falling to the weathered timber in the heat. 'Can't they just shoot us all and finish this damn counting?'

'Line up! Line up!'

The women obeyed and waited to be counted. It took some time, and during the count two more women died where they lay, in their stretchers, past caring what number they were, or if anyone would notice they'd gone.

When the train arrived to carry them through the jungle to Loebok Linggau, they were herded slowly aboard, breathing heavily in the crush, the stink and the humidity, already numb to the deaths along the way. The train pulled out of the station to begin the journey to the new camp, stopping only to discard the accumulating corpses at the next station. Margot gazed out of the window as the women's sunken bodies were laid on the wooden platform and the train pulled away again, continuing up the hill to the plantation where they would all surely die.

The next day, they slowed at a station, and a Japanese doctor and his wife boarded. The guards shooed the prisoners from the bench seat opposite Lola and Margot, although a few women drifted back in to be near the fresh air from the window and to lie on whatever floor space they could find.

'Where do you go?' the doctor asked Margot in hesitant English.

'I don't know. A camp,' she told him. 'Our old camp is overrun with typhoid and malaria.'

The doctor nodded. 'It is bad for all.' They regarded each another silently as the train shook and rattled its way up the hill through the Sumatran jungle.

He glanced at the women lying unconscious on the floor. 'Is there anything I can do for you?'

'Quinine,' Margot blurted. 'We hardly have any, and we can't do anything about the mosquitoes.'

The doctor reached into his medical bag while Margot and Lola watched on, withdrawing a small bottle they recognised well: quinine tablets. He passed it to her and she took one, and gave one to Lola. The doctor held out his hand expectantly. She paused, and a long moment passed. Her hand gripped the bottle, unwilling to let it go. Lola stared hungrily at the medicine, and at the doctor. His hand remained suspended, waiting. Margot felt a hot wave of anxiety wash from her feet to the roots of her hair. She blinked and forced herself to meet his gaze. She would *not* be returning the bottle of quinine. If he wanted it back, he would have to either fight her for it or call the guards and have her beaten.

The doctor glanced at his wife, who was also suitably embarrassed. What could they do? Margot watched the indecision pass across the man's face. She tightened her grip around the bottle. He bowed briefly and chose to look out of the window.

The next day, the train finally stopped.

'Out! Everyone out!' The guards were banging the sides of the carriage to wake the prisoners.

'What's happening?' Joy had been dozing. 'Are we there?'

'I think so, but I can't see the camp.'

'Out!'

'All right, all right, hold your horses. We'll get out when we can manage it, you little toad,' Beth muttered.

'Now we march to Belalau,' the guard announced.

'Where is Belalau?' Hazel asked. 'How far must we march? We need water. We need rest. Everyone is sick.'

'Nine miles. *Then* you rest,' he told her.

The village of Belalau had once serviced a Dutch rubber plantation, but as the Japanese had approached the island, the owners had destroyed as much of their home as they could, smashing the wells and dragging the smaller structures to the ground. The jungle had been pushed back, but it was already encroaching upon the plantation on the hill. The prisoners halted, and stood staring dumbly about, unable to walk anymore, but with nowhere else to go. Margot and Beth had been walking with their arms around Margaret Dryburgh. Spying a rickety wooden bench, they lowered her gently down. Her head slumped forward.

'British. Dutch. These are your quarters.' The captain gestured to some timber houses higher up the slope. They were huts, really, no doubt with leaky roofs and dirt floors. The women marched slowly towards them, not in the quick dash they'd made years earlier to secure a house in Palembang. The years of starvation and illness in prison had made them lighter and heavier at the same time.

'Nurses, nuns – you live there.'

The girls turned, unsurprised, to see they'd been allocated the old coolie houses near the hospital, two timber buildings attached by a verandah. Their new homes were sheds, with roofs made of thatch and walls open to the weather.

'At least we don't have to walk up that hill.'

'And we'll be close to work.'

Margot eyed the stinking *tong*. 'And the facilities are first-rate. Let's get Margaret into a bed immediately. If anyone has some water, bring it now; we'll collect some more as soon as possible.' She put her arm around Margaret and lifted her gently to her feet.

'I'll just lie down briefly,' Margaret assured them. 'I'll be up and about before you know it.'

They managed to find a bed and make her comfortable, taking her small wire-framed glasses from her face. It was the first time Margot had seen her without them. It was a difficult thing, she thought, as she slid Margaret's few things under the bed, to see such a capable woman brought so low. She was so intelligent and full of life and adventure. It was her bravery and love of music, combined with Norah Chambers' talent, that had seen the Women's Vocal Orchestra of Sumatra perform the concert of a lifetime. It was Margaret who spoke languages, who taught children, who had left her home for adventure as a young woman and who had lived the sort of remarkable life of which Margot could scarcely conceive. She stroked her hair and bathed her face with a little water. Margaret Dryburgh looked ancient, as if her colourful years were squeezing and collapsing inwards as her spirit finally left her.

A small stream ran through the camp, following the slope down through the rubber trees. Some of the stronger children helped to collect water in kerosene tins and metal bowls, bringing it to the nurses at the campfire.

'More water, please!' Henny called out. 'Come along now, we need more and you are so slow!'

The boys grumbled at her rudeness. 'How can you say that we are slow? We carry faster than you, Henny, you spill every drop!'

'What nonsense. You'll have to do many more trips to fill the pot.'

'All right. Get Matilda out and we'll start boiling water,' Margot said. 'Beth, can you gather some firewood? And Rita, can you see if there are any supplies at all in the hospital?'

'We shan't hold our breath.'

The hospital contained no medical equipment or supplies. Rita and Lola inspected it slowly, exhausted.

'I'd be angry if I had any energy,' Lola said.

'I'd *cry* if I had any energy, but then I'd be even more dehydrated and we'd have to boil Matilda for another hour,' Rita said.

'Have you heard about the water supply in the stream?' Beth asked, dumping a pile of kindling on the ground.

'No, what about it?'

'The Jap guards live in houses upstream and they have their latrines sitting over it. We'll be drinking their crap.' Beth glared up the hill.

'One day we'll laugh about this,' Lola said.

'One day we'll probably all die of dysentery or cholera,' Beth told her. 'And we'll run out of nurses to bury us.'

Two days later, Margaret Dryburgh died at the age of fifty-four from dysentery. She was buried among the trees of the rubber plantation. The clearing was a peaceful, shady place where the nurses and other prisoners could gather around her grave. They sang the song she had written for them all, 'The Captive's Hymn'.

Give us patience to endure,
Keep our hearts serene and pure,
Grant us courage, charity,
Greater faith, humility . . .

'I wonder how many more of us will make this journey along Paradise Road,' Joy said as they walked along the track through the jungle.

Margot glanced around at the shadows and the trees and breathed in the damp scent. The light was dappled, and here and there small blooms burst forth from the dark leaves. At one end of the track lay their prison, filled with hopelessness and disease, and at the other, eternal rest in the jungle floor, their spirits free at last.

'Is that what we call it?' she asked. 'Paradise Road?'

Joy smiled. 'Well, that's what *I* call it,' she said.

The hospital quickly filled with women suffering disease, starved and exhausted after day after day of scratching out a living, earning what few guilders they could, making deals for rationed quinine tablets, sometimes storing a tablet in their cheeks to later trade for food. Their hair was falling out, their teeth were loosening through malnutrition. Their hands shook, their eyesight was failing. Their stomachs cramped constantly, expelling every last morsel of food and every sip of water into the latrines, squeezed dry by typhoid, malaria and dysentery. Their bodies were wasting away, and the nurses watched on as one by one, their patients died before their eyes. The Japanese guards stopped coming to guard them at night for fear of getting ill, ordering the nurses instead to take the nightshift.

'I'm so cold,' Hazel complained, lying on her concrete bench. 'I can't sleep.'

'We're too thin to stay warm anymore,' Rita murmured, and lay behind her, her bony arms gently pulling her close. 'Just pretend I'm Cary Grant.'

'If you were Cary Grant, I'd expect you to at least provide me with a damn blanket.'

'And a lamb chop!' a small voice added from the gloom.

Margot walked the hospital beds at night, on her rounds, shuffling on painful feet, lightheaded with hunger. She braced herself against the beds and the walls of the hut in order to stay upright. In the cool night air, the women slept fitfully; they muttered, shivered and sweated. Sometimes they cried in the darkness. Margot crept between them. 'I'm an Australian nurse,' she would repeat gently. It was a whisper, really, a shadow in the night. But her voice was still there, and her loving care was still there too, reaching out to touch a blazing forehead, or to hold a hand. There was no medicine; it was all she had to offer. And she was moved to see that the simple knowledge an Australian nurse was watching over them was enough. And that each of her patients settled in that moment, and drifted back to sleep, knowing that somebody cared.

CHAPTER 24

MARGOT
Belalau, Sumatra
July 1945

Death continued to stalk them. Women and children were dying, so many the nurses could barely remember who had gone. Familiar faces disappeared, bodies aged and withered before their eyes, and children were orphaned, or died in their mothers' arms.

Barely a week after they arrived at the new camp, Joy wandered over to the hospital late one night while Margot and Hazel were doing the rounds.

'I think I might need a spare bed if you have one, dear,' she murmured.

'Joy? You too? What do you think it is?'

'Malaria. Probably dysentery too.' Joy pulled herself up the final step and slowly approached, her bony hands running along the wall of the shed. 'I really do need to lie down,' she said apologetically.

Margot rushed to her side. 'Of course, here, take this bed, it just became vacant.'

'I know,' Joy said as she lowered herself onto the thin blanket. 'I helped dig the grave.'

Margot helped her settle. 'Can I get you some water?'

'Yes, please, I'll probably throw it up shortly, so don't waste your good stuff. Save that for the children, eh?'

'I'll do my best to find you some clean water; I think we have enough on hand,' Margot told her.

'You'll see Rita in here tomorrow. I could hear her when I left the hut. She's not well.'

'I can't see why the Japs thought moving us here would change anything when they've refused to supply us with basic medication.' Margot wiped Joy's hot face. 'We managed to get a few quinine tablets from the Dutch prisoners last week, but we have to ration them so much they're almost useless. If there's one left, I'll give it to you.'

'Give it to Rita. I'm worried about her.'

Margot took Joy's hands and gazed into her face. Her eyes were dimming, her skin forming a mask as her skull pressed through like it was trying to escape. Margot had seen it before. She nodded. 'Of course,' she said, as if it was the best course of action. 'We'll give it to Rita.'

Joy died late that night. The next day, Margot dressed Joy once again in her uniform and marched with her sisters to her tiny grave along Paradise Road.

Rita was too ill to go to the funeral. 'Sing her "Bringing in the Sheaves" for me – she always loved that one,' she said, and she was dead by the time they returned, their hands full of firewood collected from the jungle, and the warm wet winds blowing at their backs.

'I'll watch over her tonight,' Lola said. 'It'll probably be me soon, so I'll take my turn now.'

'Don't be dramatic,' Beth grumbled. 'You've got another season in you yet.'

'I think our season's over, Beth,' Lola told her. 'It's just a matter of time.'

Margot lowered herself painfully to the concrete floor, where she sat with her eyes closed, refusing to faint. 'I agree with Beth,' she murmured. 'We've got to believe we'll see our homes again – it's all we have.' She leaned back against the doorway for a moment. 'I'll come with you on rounds, Lola. I won't sleep anyway.'

'And I'll take over the shift at midnight,' Beth sighed. 'Those bloody dogs are getting hungry. They'll cop it from me if they come round.' She headed out into the late afternoon, her face hollow, her thin shoulders sagging beneath the weight of grief.

Margot and Lola watched as the wind blew again; the warm rain rushing down the walls of the attap hut, a few prisoners outside putting pots out to catch the fresh water, the eerie sound of slapping on the fat green leaves of the jungle and on the muddy prison yard. Rita's body lay silently on her mattress, waiting for her uniform. Some weak and wretched coughing broke out in the hut, followed by the sound of weeping.

'You know,' Lola said, 'I never thought I'd envy the girls on the beach. But I do.'

'Do you have my will in the box?' Lola asked the next morning as she and Henny prepared some rice.

'Yes, it's in there with Beth's,' Margot said. 'She keeps going back to change it whenever she finds something new she wants to keep from the Japs. For a while there she had a few choice words she wanted us to read out for their benefit, until I pointed out that we'd no doubt be beaten or made to stand in the sun. So she changed it again so that Dr Goldberg has to read it to them.'

'She'll survive this. I know she will.'

'Lola, I promise you, we're nearly there. I can feel it. You know it's always darkest before the dawn. This is *so* terrible, we must be near the end.'

'Margot, I'll do my best, I can promise you that, but I think that God has abandoned me. I think he's sent me here to die.'

'What nonsense. God wants you to live. He's got too many souls arriving as it is with this bloody war. He wants you to damn well stay down here until you're ninety-five. Don't you disappoint him. Beth would be furious!'

'I must admit, Beth is even more frightening than a dose of dysentery.'

'I saw a huge rat under the verandah an hour or so ago; what's say we get Beth to help us trap it? It's the size of a dachshund and we could either eat it or sell it to the Dutch for a couple of guilders. A rat that size is worth at least two dollars in banana money.'

'Good idea.'

'I have some food – eggs and potatoes for the sick.' It was Hazel.

'Hazel, where on earth did you get these?'

'Dear old Margaret Dryburgh left me her cardigan when she died and I traded it in for food for our girls.'

'Not Miss Dryburgh's? She left that cardigan for *you*, because you were so cold at night.'

'Yes, but she was a good Christian woman, so she'll forgive me for trying to help a fellow prisoner.'

'Good Lord, you're a saint,' Margot told her.

'I'm so sad she didn't live to see our freedom once again – and our victory over the Japanese,' Henny said.

'You think we'll see freedom, Henny?' Margot asked.

'I'm certain,' Henny said. 'And then what pleasure we shall take in our lives. And we shall watch as the Japanese are held to account.' She stirred the rice. 'As father used to say, *Berouw komt na de zonde.*'

'What does that mean?'

'Repentance comes after sin.'

As the sun rose the next morning, the girls slowly crept from their beds to face a new day. One nurse, Val, remained still.

'Val? Are you getting up? It's nearly time for *tenko* . . .'

Val's hand twitched. Lola came and leaned over her. 'Val, are you all right?'

Val's face was ashen and her skin was blazing. Malaria. 'I'm going to school to school to see headmaster . . . first but I must get . . .' She lapsed into whispers, her eyes staring into the distance.

'Quick, help me get her to sickbay,' Lola said. 'Do we have any more quinine tablets?'

'No, all gone, I'm afraid.'

'Oh, Val.'

'Get my uniform . . .' Val gasped.

'You won't need your uniform, Val—'

'Oh, yes I bloody will – help me put it on . . .' She lapsed back into silence.

Margot gave her a drink of water and her lips moved silently. 'We can't put her in the damn uniform – she's not dead yet.'

'Where's my uniform?' Val said again. 'Where's my uniform, Margot?'

'Val, you're sick, that's all. Your uniform is folded and stored carefully, waiting for the day we walk out of here.'

'Bull, put it on me now.'

'Val, you are *not* going to die.'

'I am. I'm dying – I can feel it. Now . . .' She breathed heavily and her eyes closed. Margot wiped her face and smoothed her hair from her forehead. 'It's *my* uniform, and I wish to . . . wear it. I've earned that uniform fair and square.' A long pause. 'And if I want to bloody die in it, I *bloody well shall*!'

'I'll go get it, Val,' Beth said. 'You stay here.'

Val managed a tiny smile. 'I'll be here,' she said.

Val died in her uniform the next morning of malaria, beriberi and dysentery. Her body was so thin she looked like a child as she was carried on the nurses' shoulders through the gates of the prison and down Paradise Road.

Charlotte Tunbridge-Beckersley appeared one morning like a wraith, suspended in sunlight at the hospital door. When Margot glanced up, she could imagine she had already followed her baby girl from the jetty on Bangka Island. Margot smiled at her sadly.

I never named her, you know, she'd said to Margot once. *My child. I gave birth to her, and I took her in my arms – but then they came for us and she was taken away – and I never saw her again.*

Margot had squeezed her hand. *It doesn't matter*, she'd murmured. *You'll see her again one day.*

I'd like to name her now, I think, Charlotte had then said. *I want to call her Margaret. After Miss Dryburgh, you understand. She's been such a comfort to me – to us all. With her beautiful music, and her service to God. It's hard to be afraid when Margaret is near . . .*

Charlotte was now painfully thin, and trembled with cold and exhaustion.

Margot held out her hand. 'Charlotte . . .'

'Sister McNee,' she said. 'Do you have room for one more?'

'Of course. Come and lie down.' She reached out to help Charlotte as she teetered towards the mattress. The skin on her arm was like tissue paper. 'I'll fetch you some water, I think you're very dehydrated.'

'I expect I may die soon,' Charlotte said. 'If I do, my will is in my rucksack. There's not much to leave, really, although there's a letter I'd like delivered to my family.'

'Of course, although I think you'll surprise yourself. I think you'll sail back to England and be walking in the hills around Cambridge before you know it.'

'Don't tell lies,' Charlotte said. 'You're already perilously close to hell.' She propped herself up against the wall. 'I've got a gift for you,' she said, quietly.

'A gift?'

'From an old friend of yours.' Charlotte leaned forward a little, concentration on her face, and winked. Then she smiled. 'Did you see?' she asked. 'A wink!'

Margot's eyes filled with tears. She winked back.

'I met Minnie on the boat, that first night out of Singapore,' Charlotte said. 'We had a nice chat, and I thought, "What a nice Australian woman. I wonder if they're all like that."' She nodded to herself. 'And, as it turned out, you're not too bad, on the whole.'

Margot smiled.

'But she gave me a cheeky wink that night, and whenever I passed her, or she found me a lavatory because I was so pregnant at the time, she'd give me that same wink. It was so kind. I found it very comforting.'

'Me too,' Margot smiled. 'Thank you so much. I've missed that wink more than I can say.'

Margot placed her arm around Charlotte's back, shocked by the heat under her hand. She put an old tin cup to her lips and Charlotte sipped half-heartedly.

'I was thinking about Margaret this morning – I was with her only a couple of weeks ago,' Margot said. 'She was washing the rice. I found it quite restful watching her, sluicing water so the dirt came away. I believe she found a way to turn a menial task into a meditation.'

'Wouldn't surprise me,' Charlotte smiled. 'Although I'm still bloody sick of rice!'

Margot smiled and stroked her hair. 'Well – I must say I agree, but I do wish we had *more*!'

'You know what I wish, Sister McNee?' Charlotte asked, as she carefully lay her frail shoulders on the bed and closed her eyes.

'To go home to Cambridge? And to see your husband again?'

Charlotte released a long, exhausted sigh. 'To die in my sleep.'

Malaria continued to tear through the camp after the rains came. The Dutch women and half of the British women were hospitalised, and the nurses were exhausted. The burials became an almost daily ritual: civilians, Dutch, British, Chinese, children. As the storms swept through every afternoon, Margot prayed for an end to it all.

When Lola didn't get up in time for *tenko* one morning, Margot's heart sank. She had been watching her fade for weeks. The pattern was horribly familiar; starvation and weakness, then disease crawling through what was left of a friend's body and taking hold. Pale grey faces, or faces flushed from fever, brittle bodies crumbling to dust before her eyes. Margot and Beth began to put aside an extra spoonful of food from their plates to give Lola strength.

'Just eat this little bit, dear, it'll give you some energy.'

Lola would half-heartedly open her mouth like a baby bird. 'Please try, Lola.'

'I think I'm being punished. I think the Lord has decided it's my time. Because of what I did.'

'Nonsense, if that's true, we're all being punished,' Beth told her.

'I don't think my mother ever forgave me.'

'Well, we forgive you, Lola.'

Lola drifted off to sleep, her breathing shallow.

'She's burning up,' Margot whispered. 'Did you find any quinine?'

'I made a trade with one of the hei-ho's – my gold bridge for three tablets,' Hazel said.

'You traded your *teeth*?'

'Probably won't need them much longer anyway – and we need the medicine.'

'It'll be for nothing if we don't find her some more food as well. She's just too weak,' Margot said.

'Don't sell your teeth, just let me die . . .' Lola mumbled.

Beth snorted. 'I'm not going to hang about while you talk non-sense, you know.'

'Well, I am about to die . . .' she paused for a long moment, 'so . . . seems rude to wander off.'

'You are *not* going to die.'

'You've been good to me—'

'No, I bloody well haven't.'

'Yes. You. Have.'

Beth clutched Lola's bony hand.

'Beth?'

'Yes, dear?'

'Could you sing for me?'

'You *know* I don't sing,' Beth said.

'I would love to hear you sing. It would cheer me up.'

'What nonsense!' Beth told her.

'Somewhere . . . over the . . . rainbow.' Lola's breath was laboured. Her eyes closed and the lids were bright red. But there was the hint of a smile on her face.

Beth glared at her. 'Don't be silly,' she grumbled. 'Sentimental bloody song!'

Lola held Beth's hand to her lips.

'Someday I'll something something trees . . .' Beth was only able to hit every third note at best, and the lyrics were a mystery to her. She blushed furiously as she continued gamely on. 'Somewhere, something about chimneys . . .'

'Thank you, Beth,' Lola whispered, and Beth clutched both her hands tightly and kept on singing as if she were on a Broadway stage. 'Somewhere, something, can't remember – good friends are irritating, but they are also worth their weight in gold! . . .'

'Beautiful,' Lola sighed, and fell asleep.

Beth collected Lola's uniform from her rucksack, scrubbing small specks of mud from the lapels as the rain fell heavily on the *padang*. 'It won't be long,' she whispered to Margot, her eyes filling with tears.

Late that night, Beth shook Margot awake.

'What is it?'

'I know why I came. I thought it was for Blue but it wasn't.'

'What do you mean?'

'I came here for Lola.'

'But you didn't even *know* Lola.'

'Exactly. I came here for people I'd never met.' She crouched beside Margot. 'Because I don't have a lucky penny – I don't need one. We have *each other*. We're here to look after each other. Lola isn't strong like me – she can't take anymore. But *I* can. I can pick her up and carry her. That's my duty, as her countryman, as her *friend*.' Beth seized Margot's hand. 'Lola is *bloody well going to live* through this, if it's the last thing I do. We're going bandicooting.'

'All right, but Rasputin smokes late at night, and he sits on that side of the guard hut in bad weather—'

'We can't wait until tomorrow,' Beth said. 'We've got to get her some food.'

'You know they fertilise the vegetables with our sewage?' Margot said.

'Hardly even matters at this stage. She's *dying*, Margot.'

They crept out of the sleeping hut and hovered in the shadows, watching the camp vegetable garden, staring at the guards' hut for any sign of movement.

'Follow me,' Beth whispered, and trotted to the barbed-wire fence. Margot lifted the wire as high as she could, only a few inches from the muddy ground, and Beth rolled underneath. She crawled on her stomach through the mud, working her way towards the sweet potatoes. A light flicked on and they both froze. Rasputin wandered out onto the verandah for a cigarette. The girls lay like statues in the rain, waiting. Margot could see Beth's thin form inching closer to the vine. Her hand reached slowly out, she pulled a sweet potato from the mud and curled around slightly to see where Margot was, then quickly lobbed the sweet potato in Margot's direction. Margot rolled over, grabbed it and stuffed it into her pocket.

Rasputin stood and stared out into the yard, watching the rain, or the garden or the *padang*, Margot couldn't be sure. She curled up and hoped the mud would hide them. He then stepped down from the verandah and into the rain, and began slowly walking towards them. Margot began to crawl towards the fence, but Beth shooed her away.

'Go! Go!' She struggled to stand in the mud and Rasputin, peering into the darkness, saw her.

'You! Stop!' Beth froze, staring back at him with her hands held high. Margot knew what she wanted her to do – what she *must* do – so she dropped low, covered in mud, as Rasputin advanced on Beth. He pulled a cane from his waistband.

'Stealing!' he screamed. '*Dorobo!*'

Margot felt her blood freeze as she dashed for the sleeping quarters. She tossed the potato into Matilda and raced back to the garden. 'Stop!' she screamed. 'Stop it! Stop!'

Rasputin was leaning over Beth, thrashing her with his cane in the rain, splashing mud over her as she lay screaming. She held her arm over her head to ward off the blows, but Rasputin brought the cane down again and again. Other prisoners came out of their huts to see what was going on.

Eventually the guard dragged Beth out of the garden and towards the guards' hut. Beth's face was already swelling and her arms were red with welts from the cane.

'Let her go!' Margot shouted. 'Let her go! She hasn't even *stolen* anything! Look!' She gestured helplessly at Beth's broken form. 'Look at her and her clothes – there's nothing there! You're beating her for *nothing*!'

Rasputin slapped Margot hard across the face and she slipped over in the mud. Hazel dashed over and pulled her to her feet, and the women struggled back to their mats. As they lay down and wiped their faces, Margot felt Beth's hand, slick with rain and blood, grasp her own.

The next morning, bruised and swollen from her beating, Beth couldn't get out of bed. 'Have you cooked it?' she whispered to Margot.

'Yes, I got up early. It's mashed so she can get it down. I'm taking it to her now. You rest. Anything she can't eat is yours.'

'You make her eat it all,' Beth said. 'I'll be all right.'

Margot made her way across to the hospital with her enamel mug half-filled with sweet potato. When she saw Lola her heart sank; she was very still pale.

'Lola,' she murmured. Lola slowly opened her eyes, with little interest. 'Sit up a bit, we've got some food for you.' She spooned small morsels of warm potato into Lola's mouth. It took over an hour to eat, but Lola kept it down.

'Where's Beth?' she asked eventually. 'Is she all right?'

'Yes, she's having a sleep-in.'

'I thought she might be in rehearsal to sing another song.' She leaned back and closed her eyes, as if even the effort of being awake was too much.

'She'll be cross about that for years,' Margot assured her. 'How are you feeling?'

'I don't know. Perhaps a little better. How did you afford so much food?'

'Don't you worry about that, you just recover. We have a long way to go before we can go home.'

'You still think we're going home?' Lola asked.

'I'm sure of it,' Margot replied.

When Beth couldn't get out of bed for *tenko* the following morning, Margot felt the fear that dogged her descend again.

'Beth?' There was no response. 'Beth?' she repeated, louder. 'It's me, Margot.' She crouched beside her friend's mattress. 'Beth, are you awake?'

There was a mumble. 'Yeah,' Beth said. 'Although I think I need a few days' sleep, if you don't mind.'

Margot sighed with relief, and held a tin cup to her lips. 'I have some water for you, and a little rice.'

'I'll be right in a bit,' Beth told her, but her lips quivered at the lie, and as Margot lifted her swollen face to the cup, Beth's broken body began to shake.

'You're ill, Beth.'

'Yeah, probably infection. Check my leg.'

Margot lifted Beth's skirt and gasped. Her leg was red and swollen. The dirt from the gardens had been beaten into her wound, and she had nothing left with which to fight the infection. Margot gripped Beth's hand. Finally, when she felt brave enough, she turned to look into her eyes to see there what she knew she'd see. Acceptance.

'Don't you tell her,' Beth whispered. 'She won't cope while she's ill. You let her recover as long as you can.' She squeezed Margot's hand. 'Promise me.'

'I promise,' Margot whispered.

Less than a week later Beth died from infection, malnutrition and dysentery. Margot had slept beside her for days, her hand on Beth's stout heart, feeling each breath enter and leave her body. One morning, she'd woken in surprise to the rasping sound of Beth's tired voice, and she lay still, listening, wishing that her friend's fierce spirit would go on forever.

'The old grey mare, she ain't what she used to be . . .'

They dressed her in her uniform and filled her coffin with flowers. And surrounded by a guard of honour, diminished, but still so very proud, the nurses carried Beth Scanlon, Lola's gift from God, high on their shoulders down Paradise Road, singing all the way.

CHAPTER 25

MARGOT
Belalau, Sumatra
19 August 1945

The next day Captain Seki summonsed the camp to the parade ground. He had some guards bring a bench to the front of the assembled prisoners, and one of them held out his hand to help the captain climb up on it. He held his hand on the hilt of his sword.

'The war is over,' he said. 'It ended 15 August.'

A stunned silence greeted his announcement. The war had ended four days earlier. Before Beth had died.

'If we have made any mistakes in the past, we hope you will forgive us and now we can all be friends.' Silence. 'As a gesture of friendship, we Japanese will open the storage room.' He stood down.

Silence. The group stood there, mute, as Captain Seki jumped down from the bench, marched away to his office and disappeared.

Margot stood staring. Was it really true? Having dreamed of this day for so long, had it really happened? She thought of Beth, singing her heart out for Lola and chopping wood while she smoked pages from the Bible. And Mrs Edgar eating a dead chicken, and Henny watching the men in cages. She thought of Minnie, tossing a coin so that Gladys would travel on a ship to freedom; of Gull, giving her his lucky penny and his heart; of Margaret Dryburgh's wonderful choir and of Mrs Brown, holding on to Evelyn, no matter what.

Lola, still weak, leaned against Margot and spoke quietly. 'I *do* suppose we won?' she said.

Tears fell silently. This was joy and tragedy, sorrow, gratitude and love. The voices of the camp, so familiar for so long, were a song of hope and disbelief. There were hundreds buried across Sumatra and Muntok, and hundreds gone to the sea. There were letters never received, and reunions that would never be. There were thousands of lives rewritten forever.

They had survived.

As they stood in the yard, singing broke out from the Dutch prisoners, low voices filling with pride and joy. It was their national anthem.

'*Wilhelmus van Nassouwe, ben ik van Duitsen bloed, Den vaderland getrouwe blijf ik tot in den dood!*'

The British and Australians followed with their own, sung louder now, with voices suddenly released again.

'God save our gracious King, long live our noble King, God Save the King!'

Margot breathed in the warm air. She looked down to her feet, bitten by insects and covered in infections, her bony legs, sagging skin, her sharp ribs, sunken chest and emaciated arms. She was still there.

'Henny! Henny!' Mischa the Bear called out. 'We are free! I will go to my aunt in Amsterdam and live like a Dutch boy!'

Henny smiled, and Margot saw her for the first time as the young woman she had become, still so very frail, but with the seeds of life planted deep within her, waiting for kindness and freedom to rain upon those seeds so that she could bloom for the first time.

Charlotte, whose baby girl would forever remain in the earth on Bangka Island, had taken off her hat and was gazing around at the squalid camp as if she had woken and was finally seeing that it had been real, and that the nightmare was over.

Margot heard shouting and turned to see that the storage shed attached to the guards' hut had been opened in Captain Seki's gesture of friendship. She heard the joy and outrage as the prisoners found the supplies they had long been denied. The shed was filled with food and medicine. She watched in silence as the Red Cross boxes were carried out. It could have saved them. Ninety-six men and fifty-nine women had died at Belalau alone in the last couple of months, and it could have saved them all.

Then the gates to the camp were opened.

Margot walked to a nearby tree and slowly lowered herself to the ground. Then she wept with sorrow and joy so heavy she was unable to carry it anymore.

Major Gideon Jacobs, a South African Royal Marine, found the nurses at the camp a few days later.

'Are there any Australian nurses here?' Major Jacobs asked.

'Yes!' Margot stood to attention. 'There are twenty-four of us left – there were more. We lost twelve nurses to the sea when our ship, the *Vyner Brooke*, was bombed. Twenty-one of us were raped and murdered on Bangka Island, four of us died of disease and cruel deprivation on Muntok, and a further four here in Sumatra from the same disgraceful cause. We have been bombed, shot, beaten, starved and denied the most basic supplies. *But we are still bloody here!*'

'Well! The *Vyner Brooke*!' the major exclaimed. 'We'd heard a rumour you were in the jungle somewhere. We've been looking for you.' He held out his hand and shook Margot's firmly, moving on to shake the hands of Lola and all of the girls who had gathered around. 'I can't tell you how glad I am to find you've survived,' he told them.

'Not as glad as us!' Lola assured him.

He grinned. 'I'm taking you all to hospital, we'll do some medical checks, fatten you up a bit, then we'll put you on board a ship and send you home.'

I'm not sure I'd want to get on another bloody ship, Margot heard Beth say, *but I'd be happy to risk it!*

'We'll bring you home in style, don't you worry,' the captain was saying. 'Now, we need to get you to hospital, then we need to send word to your families.'

Margot and Lola embraced with every ounce of strength they had left. As Margot felt Lola's fragile ribs press against her heart, she realised it wasn't her heart anymore, that her heart had been worn down and broken, but that it had grown back, heavy and strong – the heart of a bear.

The doors to the world were open once more. It was finally time to put their uniforms on again. It was time to walk to freedom.

CHAPTER 26

MINNIE
Radji Beach, Bangka Island
16 February 1942 – Three years earlier

The girls on the beach shuffled forward. It was a bright morning and the light was glinting off the ocean. Minnie held Vivian's hand and kept her other arm firmly around Dot.

'There's two things I've always hated in my life,' Dot said. 'The Japs and the sea – and today I got both.'

'Take it, girls, don't squeal!' Agnes called out.

We give them nothing. We give them no sign of fear, or pain. We shall not flinch. We are Australian nurses, and our spirits are our own.

They heard a voice from behind them and they continued their slow march forward. Minnie breathed in the ocean, savouring the warm sea air, the comfort of her friends beside her. A gull wheeled overhead, curious. A breeze bustled around her skirt. She glanced up the line to see all the nurses at her side, looking out to sea.

She remembered her first brave steps away from boarding school, when she had set out on her first adventure alone. She thought of the friendships she'd made, the fears she passed by on the side of the road, invincible. She thought of every decision taken which had brought her here; her decision to be a nurse, to leave home. The terrible loss of her brother, the broken heart that saw her join the army, the friends she found in Singapore. The toss of the coin, the roll of the deck, the wave that had caught her and delivered her here, right now. It was luck, it was chance, it was fate. She thought of her mother and father watching the door, of Oliver, swimming in the lake, and his letter, still sitting close to her heart. And she knew that when she saw him again, she would have a story to tell. She stepped forward, still brave.

When she heard a voice, her heart, rushing towards the sea, calmed. And it was as if she was already home.

'Chin up, girls,' Matron Drummond called out. 'I'm proud of you and I love you all.'

EPILOGUE

17 October 1945

Maisie pulled into the car park next to Hollywood Repatriation Hospital and looked about. A couple of women were walking past her ute carrying huge bright bunches of roses in large tins. The heavy yellow flowers glowed in the sunlight, and the sprigs of jasmine sparkled like fireworks.

'Good afternoon,' she called out and the ladies paused. 'Is this where we're to bring flowers for the nurses?'

'Yes, this is the place, come along with us. I believe we can leave them at reception.'

Maisie glanced into the back of the ute, where her roses were like a sunrise. 'I may have to make a couple of trips,' she said.

'Oh, well done!' the older of the ladies said. 'Let's take these first and then we'll all come back together to collect the rest.'

'Do you have any left in your garden?' the other lady asked.

'None at all,' Maisie said. 'Not one.' She reached into the ute and pulled out the first bucket. 'And it will give me great pleasure when I get home tonight – to think of them here, with our girls.'

They turned the corner to see them all, the local women carrying flowers from their gardens in Nedlands, Applecross, Belmont, Mount Hawthorn and all over the city to give to the nurses from the *Vyner Brooke*. The flowers spilled out of the reception area, and the staff were moving great waves of blossoms to the nurses' rooms and the waiting areas. There were huge soft blooms in vases on the floors, and coffee tables drowning in cascades of pink roses. The garden benches at the front of the hospital had been filled with makeshift vases of flowers, like beautiful wooden rafts, glowing brightly, while more vases of daffodils and irises sprayed from the pavement below like fountains.

They had cut every last flower from their gardens and had brought them to Hollywood in baskets, buckets and wheelbarrows. It was an ocean, filled with tides and currents.

And the flowers said everything they always say. They said, *Welcome Home. Well Done. Congratulations*. They said, *Deepest Sympathy*. They said, *I Love You*. They were funeral flowers and welcome blooms. They said, *Get Well Soon*, and *Best Wishes*, and, *Always In Our Thoughts*. They said, *In Loving Memory*.

And they said, *Thank You*.

Maisie gently put the last of her blooms down and smiled.

Then she climbed back into the ute and headed for home.

AUTHOR NOTE

Around three years ago, I stuck photos of some World War II nurses up on a filing cabinet next to my desk. Minnie Hodgson, Blanche Hempsted, Vivian Bullwinkel, Dorothy 'Buddy' Elmes, Shirley Gardam, Mary Cuthbertson, Irene Drummond and Betty Jeffrey. They have watched over me ever since.

If you've read *The War Nurses*, I promise you, nearly every little story you think I've made up is true. Some of my favourite parts of the novel are the small anecdotes I've squeezed inside. A family paddles a canoe through Singapore Harbour, begging to be taken aboard any ship that will take them. A man sings 'Rule, Britannia!' as he dies on the deck of the *Vyner Brooke*, a woman suffers a still-birth on the end of a jetty on Muntok, nurses go bandicooting to steal food, a woman halts a Japanese guard for a moment so that she can remove her glasses before he slaps her face. The nurses systematically spit into the Japanese guards' water, a nurse gives away her precious yellow cardigan to buy food for her dying friend, a nurse asks a Japanese doctor for quinine, and silently refuses to return the bottle. A Dutch girl sees soldiers in cages. Women die of malnutrition and disease while being moved between camps, a British woman sends a Japanese soldier into the water for her handbag, filled with money, and loses the lot, a man insists on keeping his watch and instead digs his own grave. The hymns they sing, the poetry and Bible verses they recite, Hitam the cat, Toby the dog, Agatha the houseplant, Mrs Brown, Margaret Dryburgh, Vivian Bullwinkel, Mischa the Bear, Mr Hollywood, Seki the Sadist. All of it is real.

While I have fictionalised the love story between Margot and Gull, and the surrounding hijinks, the small stories are real, many of the conversations are real, and the details you think I've invented – are real.

I wrote *The War Nurses* a lot, and I *rewrote* it even more. The research took a long time, and there are conflicting stories and factual inaccuracies I'm certain to have repeated. I read biographies, World War II histories, recollections written by the nurses, endless online articles, explored Trove, and spent time in the amazing collection at the Australian War Memorial.

As I read, I noted hundreds of facts that interested me, or that I thought would be important to the story. Then I rewrote the history from my notebooks as fiction, substituting any name that came to mind, tracing the events. How many on the *Queen Mary*? Where did the nurses stay in Singapore? How were they evacuated? How did the *Vyner Brooke* make it through the mines of Singapore Harbour? How many bombs fell in the attack?

As I wrote, I added in each small detail that brought the history to life and left out anything that didn't serve the story. Those moments were painful to lose. Eventually, more than twenty thousand words were edited out, and it felt like a betrayal every time. I wanted you to hear about the Dutch lady who wore bright lipstick and evaded the furious attacks of a Japanese guard, and the Dutch mother who lost all but one of her children to starvation and disease. There was story after story I loved, but *The War Nurses* had to keep moving, even through the long years of internment. I owed it to the reader to keep the story engaging, and I hope that if you are interested in reading more, you'll look up some of the books I've used for research.

Once I had recorded this remarkable true story from beginning to end, I added my characters. There were sixty-five nurses on the *Vyner Brooke*, so it would have been impossible to represent them all individually, but it would work to represent them more collectively. I wanted to show their courage and humour, their loyalty and grit. I chose to tell the story with four main characters, Minnie, Margot, Beth and Lola. These girls are fictional characters, with details borrowed from the lives of the real women who trod through history, although two of them are inspired by actual nurses. Minnie is obviously based on my great aunt, Minnie Hodgson. Beth is based on a rather wonderful nurse from Queensland, Blanche Hempsted. In real life, it was Beth who, shorter than I describe, and not from station country, really did put a German doctor in a headlock and roll her off a raft and into the ocean, and she really did insist to the Japanese guards that Australian girls only drank milk. She was such fun to write!

In the end, Beth's death was different from Blanche's, for a couple of reasons. Blanche died in the camp, but the nurses suspected it may have been due to lung cancer. As she lay on her deathbed, knowing that the nurses had a small window each day in which to dig the graves, she apologised for taking so long to die. Eight nurses died in captivity, as well as Mrs Brown and Margaret Dryburgh, and while I have recorded their deaths faithfully, I admit to using artistic licence to fit in Beth's more dramatic and purposeful death.

I grew up with Minnie's story – my great aunt who had died in the war – and the stories of the nurses who survived the bombing of the *Vyner Brooke* and went on to suffer through captivity as prisoners, and of the incredible bravery of Lieutenant Colonel Vivian Bullwinkel, who survived the massacre on Radji Beach and the camps of Sumatra, and who finally testified at the Tokyo War Tribunal. When ANZAC Day came around each year we told ourselves we didn't really have anyone to commemorate. Minnie had only been a nurse, we said, so it wasn't as if she'd seen active duty, like the men. Her name is on the gates to our lake at Yealering, but we never really talked about her while my grandfather was alive. For his part, he never really spoke of Minnie, and their lives, before the war, or later.

We knew she'd been taken with a farmer from neighbouring Kulin and a broken heart had led her to enlist. We knew of the loss of two of her baby brothers as toddlers and of the tragic loss of her brother Oliver in the Swan River in the 1920s. It more recently emerged that Minnie had run away from school, having received a report which read in part 'Unsatisfactory', and had found her own way home, greatly surprising her family when she walked up the front drive of the farm. And we learned that Minnie eventually returned to another school, finally finished her nursing studies in Perth, then headed to the bush to work as matron at the Kondinin Hospital.

I used Minnie's name as a tribute to her, and altered part of her story because I wanted my novel to be historical fiction, and even though it's peppered with real characters, the nurses' stories had to be an amalgamation of sixty-five women, not a biography.

The story of the Bangka Island Massacre is one of tragedy, loyalty and bravery. But most people won't read a history book and

The War Nurses isn't just for history fans; it's for everyone. This means it isn't enough to just tell you the story; my job is to make you care.

I have fictionalised the four main characters for a couple of reasons. The first is that, in condensing the experiences of so many nurses, I had to give more experiences to each of these four main characters so that I could fit such an extraordinary story into a novel. The second is that all of the nurses still have loving families, who know at least a little about their aunts. I didn't want to disrespect the nurses, by using the name of a loved aunt and then employing the artistic licence I've needed to tell this story. It became necessary to add to the cast because so many of the nurses had specific fates, portrayed at the end of the novel, and I felt that the reader needed to meet them along the way.

History is already storytelling, but fiction brings shape, colour and meaning. At its most basic level, history is just stuff happening in order. Some of it is funny, inspirational or heartbreaking, but, even though the significance of an event can give it gravity, and the events can be reinterpreted a number of ways, at its core, history is a narrative about *what happened*.

To engage the reader I needed to write characters with a satisfying character arc. My nurses couldn't break free from the Japanese soldiers, or steal a ship and sail home. They couldn't end the war in the Pacific. *The War Nurses* isn't just inspired by events, it's a fictionalisation of real events, so Beth, Margot, Lola and Minnie had to continue their heartbreaking and incredibly inspiring march towards death or freedom.

Beth had to die, not only because I loved her, but because she was willing to sacrifice herself for others. She was willing to die if it helped Lola to live. Lola, who thought she wasn't worthy of love, had to discover she had been truly loved by her unlikely friend Beth; perhaps not the love she'd imagined, but a great love, indeed. Margot had to survive, as a witness to it all, to discover that her heart was strong, that her journey was to grow from a timid girl into a fierce woman. A survivor.

The girls on the beach had to die. But their Matron was with them, and their journey was to die with dignity, carrying the brave and loving words of Irene Drummond in their hearts. Minnie had to die on the beach, because history is *what happened*, and I couldn't save her.

My nurses are still on my filing cabinet, watching me. I cannot bear to take them down. They have waited for me to tell their tale, to thread it all together, to move through time as if it was nothing, to bring them back. And I have sat with them for countless hours, crying, singing, railing against their fate. Creating a fiction of truths. Trying to tell the stories of the nurses and those who suffered as Singapore fell around them.

This book is many things. It is a history of what happened, listed faithfully in order; times, numbers, names, dates. It's also a work of fiction about four friends caught up in a war, and the grit, determination, love and loyalty that helped them survive. But sprinkled throughout its pages like little flowers pressed into a diary are small recollections of the nurses, bright moments in time; tragic, frightening, funny and sweet. This book holds within it a love letter to my great aunt, Minnie Ivy Hodgson, who died on Radji Beach, never imagining that anyone would ever know of her fate. And, of course, this book is a thank you to all the brave girls, who lived so much, so little and so long ago. And, finally, it is my plea to you, that you will carry them, high on your shoulders – singing all the way.

ACKNOWLEDGEMENTS

Writing *The War Nurses* took years of my life. It was literally a labour of love, in the long hours of writing and research – and in the love I have for these remarkable women and this story. I had to write this novel, because I couldn't write anything else. Now it's done, and while I dare hope that it's worthy of the nurses of the *Vyner Brooke*, I still feel a sting of regret that there are so many more stories I couldn't fit into these pages, when I really wanted you to know it all.

Thank you for reading *The War Nurses*! I hope you've enjoyed your time with Margot, Minnie, Lola and Beth; although so much of the story is difficult and at times tragic, I think it is the most important story I will ever write, and I feel very privileged to have done so. This book would not have happened without wonderful readers like you.

It's late now, and as I sit in my office at the front of my house and look to my right, the photos of the girls from *The War Nurses*, who have watched over me for so long, are still there, and I don't want to take them down. I think they'll stay with me another year.

In all the time I was planning, researching, writing, mucking up, starting again, I had a team of wonderful people cheering me on and I'm very pleased to have the chance to thank them.

When I met my friends Sarah, Lara and Tricia at boarding school, I was twelve years old, and, it was universally acknowledged, a bit weird. I'm happy to say I'm still a bit weird and I'm lucky that these three wonderful women are still my friends, who supported me every day I was working on this novel, cheering me on at every turn. Thanks, girls!

Huge thanks to my writing crew; Rachael Johns, Fiona Palmer and Tess Woods. Writing a novel is hard; it's a balance of inspiration, hard slog and lashings of stress. Other writers get this, and I'm lucky they are willing to share their wisdom with me. Fiona, Rachael and Tess never fail to inspire me, lift my spirits and give me great advice. They've been waiting for this novel for a long time!

A special thanks to Marty, Finley and Audrey, who are totally wonderful in every way. They make me laugh, make me coffee and always have a story to tell. They have been with me all the way on this novel, and I can't thank them enough. Even more appreciation goes to Marty for his proofreading skills. Thanks, Z!

As a deeply professional author, some time ago it became necessary to employ a professional writing partner and labrador, Possum. She has been a wonderful support and joke writer through all the years we've been together. Her relaxed attitude, ability to close her eyes and 'go deep' for extended periods of time and her willingness to take me for walkies means that her upcoming contract negotiations are likely to go well. Thanks, Possum.

During the process of writing and editing *The War Nurses*, I was lucky enough to visit the Australian War Memorial, the WA Medical Museum and the archives at Presbyterian Ladies' College, where the very knowledgeable archivist, Shannon Lovelady, was able to show me documents and photos of Minnie I'd never seen.

It was fascinating to see another side of my great aunt, and I was very grateful for the opportunity.

I was lucky to have the advice and recollections of Cuno van der Feltz, whose family was interned in the camps in Sumatra during the war. Now a very old man, his emails were a delight, and although, I'm sorry to say, most of the stories of the Dutch internees didn't survive the edits for *The War Nurses*, the Dutch story was fascinating, and has been largely cut only to keep pace and focus on my central characters, the nurses themselves.

Thanks also to all those people who have shown support for *The War Nurses* over the time I was writing, rewriting and editing. Your interest in this history – and, at times, your expertise – has been appreciated! There have been so many conversations, but in particular, thanks to Steven Kruger, Ric and Sonja van der Feltz, Alisdair Putt (and Madi!), and Toni Bishop from the WA Medical Museum.

A big thanks to Margaret Hodgson and Libby Heffernan for being so passionate about this story, too, for taking such an interest in the creation of this novel, and for being far better family historians than I will ever be.

I am extremely lucky to be published by the team at Penguin Random House. I know there are many talented people who have had a hand in bringing my novel to life, but I'd like to especially mention Melissa Lane, Bronwyn Sweeney, Lily Crozier, Veronica Eze, Rod Morrison, Joyce Carter and cover designer Laura Thomas. Thanks so much for all your attention to detail and enthusiasm for *The War Nurses*; you've made this novel shine! And special thanks to the hugely talented and kind Kelly Rimmer, for her interest in this story, and her wonderful cover quote.

Finally, I must thank my extraordinary publisher, Ali Watts. I love her so much it's creepy. I sent her the rough manuscript of this novel because I trusted her to tell me the truth about the project I'd been working on for years. She loved the manuscript, as ill-formed and uneven as it was, and I am deeply grateful that she had faith we could bring this story to life. Ali's gentle guidance and clear vision for story has made *The War Nurses* a novel of which I will always be proud. Thank you, Ali.

(And yet another silent thank you to the nurses still watching me silently from their position beside my desk. They won't stay with me for another year. They'll stay with me forever.)

Minnie Hodgson

READING GROUP NOTES

1. *The War Nurses* is a novel based on true events experienced by Australian nurses in World War II. How much of this remarkable story was new to you?

2. Why do you think Minnie, Margot, Beth and Lola became such good friends?

3. Did you have a favourite character among them, and why?

4. The nurses aimed to be every bit as brave as their male counterparts in the war. In what specific ways did you see evidence of this?

5. Can you find examples of instances where the women exceeded their duty as nurses?

6. On the way to Singapore, one of the Australian soldiers says, 'Good luck, girls, I hope you have a good war.' What do you think they might have imagined 'a good war' would entail?

7. In what ways do the characters in the story use music to cope with the extreme pressures they face? What other techniques do they employ to help keep themselves positive and support each other through trying times?

8. Margot's fear of abandoning her patients and her friends is greater than her fear of being harmed herself. Can you understand this?

9. The novel contains some intense and harrowing moments. Which was the most unforgettable for you? Which did you find the most moving?

10. Lola fears that she will never be loved, but one could argue that in Beth she finds the greatest love of all. Discuss.

11. *The War Nurses* is a different genre to the author's previous rural romances, but what similarities did you find in the writing style and the themes?

12. 'We'll tell the world what happened here, and they'll never forget.' Through the writing of this book, author Anthea Hodgson aimed to pay tribute to the Australian nurses in war. Do you think she has done them justice?